MW01135026

The Dark Lord's Handbook

Paul Dale

Copyright © 2008 by Paul Dale

Second Edition

Paul Dale has asserted his moral right to be identified as the author of this work in accordance with the Copyright, Designs and Patents Act 1988.

All characters and events in this publication, other than those clearly in the public domain, are fictitious and any resemblance to real persons, living or dead, is purely coincidental.

All rights reserved.
No part of this publication may be reproduced, stored in a retrieval system, or transmitted, in any form, or by any means, without prior permission in writing of the author, not to be otherwise circulated in any form of binding or cover other than that in which it is published and without a similar condition, including this condition, being impressed upon the subsequent purchaser.

ISBN: 978-1-5008-1994-1

Cover art by Jaka Prawira http://about.me/ellinsworth

Edited by Incandescent Phoenix Books

For my mother,
who told me to do what I enjoyed most.

Acknowledgements

I would like to thank the following people for their help and support along the way: Bodhiketu, Jon Spence, Jim Grimmett, Louise Dower, Andrew Dale, my parents, Kate Frost, Judith van Dijkhuizen, Tamsin Reeves, Lucy English and the Bath Spa University Creative writing staff, Chris Bagnall, Adam Reynolds, Jaq D Hawkins, Brenda, and Kath Middleton.

Chapter 1   Good and Evil

RTFM
The Dark Lord's Handbook

In the eternal war between Good and Evil, things were not going so well for Team Evil. While Death walked unseen by mortal eyes among the dead that lay on the sunburned field of battle, Evil mooched around as Death went about his work gathering souls. Death waited patiently for some to die as men and orcs bled out slowly, voicing their pains and thirst. If they were lucky, the scavengers would help them on their way as they looted the dead and dying.

Evil made his way to where it had all ended. A neat ring of corpses lay around the blasted ground where the Dark Lord had fallen. Evil sighed. He'd had high hopes for this one. The early signs had been good, with notable successes, but then this? How had the Dark Lord managed to get it so wrong? It wasn't that hard. All he had to do was read the fucking—

"Loser," said a voice from behind him, interrupting his thoughts.

He didn't have to turn to know who had come to gloat. "I wondered when you'd turn up."

"Looooooooooser," repeated Good.

Evil turned to face his old adversary. "Is that necessary?"

Good shrugged. "You had me worried there. For a while. Attacking from the east at dawn. That's my trick."

"Nothing in the rules says I can't," said Evil. It was one of a number of small things that had all come together to give him real hope he would win this time. "The burnished shields were a nice touch."

"Thanks," said Good. "I had them up all night polishing. It was close."

"Not close enough. And I honestly thought this one was different. He seemed to be doing so well."

"They always make a mistake."

Evil sighed. "I even wrote it all down, in easy-to-read chapters."

"Pictures?"

"Of course."

They had come to stand where the Dark Lord had met his end, stabbed in the back by the Hero he had mistakenly thought defeated. Evil scoured the ground. It had to be around here somewhere, he could feel it.

"Looking for something?" asked Good.

"Nothing." Now where was it? It was close.

There it was, half hidden under a corpse, the edge sticking out. He had to work quickly now. He could see Good trying to nonchalantly kick dirt over it, but Evil wasn't going to let his opus get buried and lost. *Over here*, he called to a weasel of an orc trying to hack a finger off a nearby dead knight. *OVER HERE*. The orc looked up and sniffed. *HERE, YOU STUPID CREATURE*. The orc scrambled over the dead, arrowing in on where the book lay.

"What have we here?" said the orc to no one in particular as it tugged at the book. With a final tug, the book came loose and the orc fell backwards. When the creature saw what he had, he squealed and let it drop. A skeletal hand still clutched the book; a hand that had been severed at the wrist.

Take it and go, instructed Evil. *Quickly*.

The orc looked up. A troop of knights was riding across the battlefield, scattering the scavengers, and adding to the dead as their lances caught those who would dishonour the fallen. The orc grabbed his prize and fled.

"No matter," said Good. "You could wait a millennium before another one is born, still longer before one who can read as well."

"I'm very patient."

"Until next time?"

"You can be certain of it," said Evil. There would always be a next time.

Chapter 2   The Fat Lamb

Even a Dark Lord has a mother.
The Dark Lord's Handbook

The snowstorm had passed and left a clear sky, a bitter wind, and a blood moon. The Fat Lamb, with its blazing fire and warm beer, was enjoying a busy night. The storm and the blood moon—its red light reflecting disturbingly off the fresh snow—were all the talk among those who sat huddled over their mugs.

"It's not natural, I tell you," said Jurgen. There was a murmur of agreement. Whenever Jurgen fell into this mood, his voice solemn and brow knitted, everyone paid note. He was a big man with a moustache that hung low on either side of his mouth, framing a smoothly shaven chin. "I've seen many things, as you all know, and I'm not one to keep quiet when something is not right. Mark me. It's not natural."

"Right you are," said Tibault. "Not natural."

"What isn't?"

Heads turned to Kristoff as he planted his mug on the table and eased himself into a gap on the bench. There were grumbles as he squeezed himself in. Unlike Jurgen, Kristoff was a slight man, and he'd been educated away in some fancy college. Many were surprised he'd come back to the village of his birth at all. Kristoff had waved Tibault away when questioned about his reasons, his wounded expression the only clue to a mysterious past. A broken heart or a run-in with the law were the favourites being wagered on.

"What do you mean?" said Jurgen, pulling his shoulders back. He was not used to his pronouncements being challenged, least of all by a lad like Kristoff.

"What isn't natural?" continued Kristoff. "This isn't the first time we've had such a storm, or a harsh wind from the north."

There was silence at the table as these facts were digested.

"But what about the moon?" said Jurgen, somewhat triumphantly.

"The blood moon!"

There was a collective sigh of relief.

"Aye, the moon!" dared Tibault. "Jurgen's right as ever. It's the moon."

"Ah, dear moon," sighed Kristoff, gazing off into space. "What sadness have you seen?"

"See, I told you," whispered Tibault. "He's had his heart broken and no mistaking. Let's just hope he doesn't start with his poetry."

Jurgen sat back, his chin jutted out, and folded his arms. "It isn't natural."

Heads nodded all around. Kristoff seemed lost in melancholy and made no reply. Just then there was a scream and heads looked to the ceiling.

"She still at it?"

"Aye. Sounds like."

"How long has it been now?"

"A good few hours, I dare say."

"First one's always the longest. Least that's what the wife says."

"Harold seems happy enough."

"Wouldn't you be? Look at the place! With this many customers he's too busy to be worrying about a first born."

"My round?"

"Aye, it is at that."

"Harold! Five. No, six more ales over here when you have a minute, would you?"

There was another scream and Harold looked with the others heavenward. For a heartbeat there was silence.

"For the LOVE of the gods will this never end?" came a woman's cry, quite clear through the thick beamed ceiling. Sympathetic glances shot in Harold's direction, who ran one hand through tight brown curls, a worried look on his face.

"Could be a while yet."

"Aye."

"Did you get that, Harold? Six ales if you would."

"Right you are," said Harold, tearing himself away from the worry and setting out mugs in a line on the bar. The chatter in the bar resumed and Harold set about pulling the pints.

Harold was young to be a landlord. He had inherited the inn that spring as a result of his father's sudden death. Heart failure was the general consensus, as pronounced by Jurgen. He'd been found by the first of the lunchtime customers, eyes wide, standing perfectly upright, hands rested on the bar, his apron tied around his massive girth as though ready to serve. Quite how he'd managed to stay upright when he died was a mystery, until they'd tried to move him and found his hands and feet solidly stuck in place; the soles of his boots had burned clear through and on closer inspection his hands had melted into the bar top. Still, heart attack was what Jurgen had reckoned and who was to doubt his keen insights? So Harold and his new bride, Jesobel, had inherited the business sooner than expected. Harold had put a beer cloth over the burn marks his father's hands had left until his wife had insisted he didn't, as people came a good distance to see them.

Jesobel had taken a keen interest in the business. Right from the start, she made everyone welcome and takings soared. Harold often said how lucky he was that the most popular girl in the village, if not the county, had married him, and almost immediately announced she was with child. Harold was the happiest man alive, the recent tragedy forgotten. The only worry now was the birth of his first child.

Kristoff got up and offered Harold a comforting word, something about being lucky in love, and began to carry the ales over to the table when the main door clattered open and a sharp blast of air blew in.

"Shut that door!"

"Bloody freezing!"

Annoyed patrons looked over to see who had upset the warmth. A tight group of four brown robed men shuffled in, the last turning to close the door. They stood, heads bowed, hands clasped in front of long, hanging sleeves. One took a step forward from the rest and threw back his hood to set his gaze upon the patrons. He had rime on his goatee, a red flush to his cheeks, and a pudding-bowl haircut that immediately placed the men as being of an Order of brewing monks.

"I am Francis of the Seekers. We seek a child born this evening."

There was a momentary pause and the patrons returned to their drinks.

"Has a child been born here this night or not?" asked Francis somewhat angrily, his voice rising above the commotion.

One of the other monks nudged Francis and whispered something.

"Ah yes. A child born of a maiden?"

The monk's question silenced the room.

"A virgin birth," continued the monk.

Heads turned to Jurgen.

"What do you mean, exactly?" asked Jurgen.

"Good grief," sighed the monk. "A maiden's birth. A child born of a woman who has not known the intimacies of a man. Her maidenhood intact."

Jurgen pulled at his moustache. "You mean a girl who's not yet married, and whose father would be upset with her condition, so she says she was visited by, I don't know, a swan, or an eagle, or a bull?"

"That would be it," agreed Tibault. "A bull. We have them kind of maiden births all the time round here."

The monk stood shaking his head when, from upstairs, Jesobel shrieked once more. To any who had heard the sound before they knew the time was soon. As one the monks looked up and a triumphant expression lit their faces.

"It seems we are just in time," said Francis and he pushed further into the room, his fellows close behind.

"Hang on there," said Harold from behind the bar. The monks stopped. There was iron in Harold's voice. "You're not going up there. That's my Jesobel."

"And?" said Francis.

Harold, and for that matter everyone else in the room, looked at the monk in disbelief. Everyone knew the name Jesobel, least all in the shire. These monks must have travelled some distance.

"I am her husband," said Harold. "There's been no swans or eagles around here. Or bulls for that matter. You've got the wrong place. I'll be asking you to leave."

The monks looked more than vexed.

"Harold," piped up Tibault. "Harold?"

"What is it, Tibault? Another ale? I'll be with you shortly."

"No, Harold. Sorry. I mean. That is to say. I heard ..." Tibault faltered as everyone looked at him. "I was only going to say that Diona, over Wellow way; the blacksmith's daughter. She's due about now and swears blind it wasn't Kristoff, like all suppose, that did her up." Tibault licked his lips as his news was digested.

All eyes turned to Kristoff.

"I don't know what you're all looking at," said Kristoff, blushing.

"You're right," said Jurgen. "It's not like limericks can get a woman pregnant, now is it?"

"I'm a poet!" insisted Kristoff above the laughter.

"There you have it then," said Jurgen once the laughter had subsided. "You'll be wanting to head over Wellow way."

The monks huddled in a discussion which grew quite heated.

"We will not be stopping for a beer and that's final," said Francis, his voiced raised above the babble of the room.

There were grumbles as Francis dragged his group from the inn to shouts of "Shut that bloomin' door! Bloody freezing!"

"Strange bunch," remarked Kristoff, and saying so he headed for the privy.

"Aye. Who would want to be out on a night like this?" said Jurgen. "Listen to that wind. They'll be back."

"Sounds like it's picking up again," observed another at the table.

The wind did indeed sound like it had picked up. There was a tremendous buffeting and the entire building shook.

"Did you hear that?" asked Tibault.

Jurgen cocked his head to one side. "Hear what?"

"Thought I heard screams?"

"That'd be Jesobel. I expect we'll be wetting a baby's head soon enough."

"No. Not Jesobel. From outside."

"You're hearing things."

The inn door clattered open and a fresh blast of air blew in.

"See, told you they'd be back," said Jurgen. "I've never known a monk pass up a beer. Shut that bleedin' door, will you please!" He turned to look over his shoulder to see what Tibault was staring at.

In the doorway stood a man, tall and thin, yet powerfully muscled, long black hair falling over leather-clad shoulders. To one as observant as Jurgen, there was something not quite right about him. His skin, for starters. Black, like obsidian, and as smooth. It could have been passed off as a rare skin condition if it wasn't for the blazing red eyes that swept the room with their glare. Jurgen had heard stories, legends really, about all manner of strange creatures, but not for a second did he imagine one would walk through the door of The Fat Lamb, right as day.

The stranger strode over to the bar. He spread his hands on the surface in front of him and smiled. "You must be Harold." Harold's mouth moved but no sound came out. "I knew your father," said the stranger. "He left quite an impression."

Harold's eyes darted down to where the stranger's hands rested and gulped. The stranger's smile widened, making plain a set of razor-sharp teeth.

"I do hope I am not too late," continued the stranger smoothly. "I understand young Jesobel is due." He let his eyes slip from Harold and cast around until he came to the passage at the back of the bar and the flight of stairs that led up. "Ah, yes. Up there, if I remember? I won't keep you. I can see you are busy."

As the stranger made his way up the stair, it creaked as though a great weight was upon it. The conversation in the room returned, if somewhat quieter than before.

Kristoff came out of the privy next to the stair. All heads turned his way. He fumbled at the buttons on the front of his trousers. "Did I miss something?"

Chapter 3   Fatherhood

If you want it done right, do it yourself.
The Dark Lord's Handbook

Lord Deathwing had a weakness for the ladies. It had often got him into trouble with Lady Deathwing, and so he had curtailed his gallivanting in the last decade. But when he had happened across the painfully sweet Jesobel, all resistance had melted away. She had been helping a buffoon of an innkeeper waiting on the tables. She had cascading blonde hair and a body that wriggled in all the right places under the thinnest of cotton dresses. He had felt his blood rise until he could bear it no longer.

The inn was empty but for the three of them and she had been wiping the tables down, leaning over, bodice loose, full milky white breasts struggling to stay confined. When she had brushed past him on her way to empty her pail, and let her hand play down his leg, he knew not only was she sweet but also ripe for the picking. He'd lost control completely. It was unfortunate about the innkeeper. He may have been a buffoon but he had been affable enough.

His dragon seed was a powerful thing, and when planted could be hard to bear. Most mortal women died in a shuddering, pain-filled, ecstatic, thrashing bundle, but not Jesobel. She had brushed her skirt down and pinched his cheek. He was more used to being begged for death by the recipient of his recent attentions, the pain and ecstasy too much to live through.

"Are you feeling well?" he had asked.

She had looked at him, a hint of a smile on her cherry lips. "Much better for a good seeing-to, my lover."

"No pains? Headaches? Spasms?"

Her brow had wrinkled. "No? I don't mean to be rude, but although I've no complaints, I've had better."

After that, he hadn't been able to perform for six months. Not that his wife had noticed. Dragons only mated among themselves every twenty years or so. It had taken a scullery maid to die in legs akimbo bliss for him to regain his confidence.

That any fruit had been born of this tryst with the barmaid was a further surprise—and also problematic. It wasn't as though he could tell the wife he was expecting an heir. He wasn't sure how the child would turn out. What he was certain about was that he had better be there for the birth, if for no better reason than he was insatiably curious. Moreover, if a dragonling of his was going to take its first breath, and doubtless fry the mid-wife, he wanted to be there to see it.

Then there was the small matter of the Naming.

He had only just made it in time. Standing outside the door, Jesobel's panting and screams were all too clear. The birth would be soon. He hadn't brought flowers and a faint flicker of remorse played across his black heart, but there was no surviving a dragon birth, so there seemed little point. The one concession he did make was to alter his appearance; he didn't want to frighten the poor girl.

He pushed the door open and recoiled. The smell was like being mugged by an outhouse. He stepped in and was met by a ghastly tableau. The room was hot, cramped and filthy. Bedding was strewn around with fleas so big he could see them hopping in the tallow light. Two ugly young girls held a woman's legs high and apart, a skirt between them. A hag was kneeling in the gap, rummaging between the legs.

"Nearly there my lovely," crooned the hag. "I can see his head now."

Everyone was too busy with what was going on in Jesobel's nether regions to take notice of him.

"Shut the door behind you, Harold," said the crone without turning around.

Deathwing took a step into the room and closed the door behind him. Let her think what she would. He peered over the hag's shoulder to catch a first glimpse of his son. He expected the hag to recoil in shock and fright as his son's lizard head made its appearance, but it was he who was repulsed. Rather than black scales he could see a patch of black human hair.

In a surprisingly short time, the baby popped out in a mess. The way the hag managed the process with a dexterous hoist, slap, snip, knot, and swaddle was impressive. She had obviously done this before.

Jesobel had, in the meantime, been returned to a more dignified position and was craning over to catch a glimpse of her newborn when she caught sight of him at the door. He managed a weak smile. He was still in shock. Was this child his after all?

"Oh my! It's you!" she exclaimed.

This earned him the attention of the hag and her two helpers.

"Who are you and what you doing here?" demanded the hag.

Jesobel took the wrapped, and strangely quiet, child from a helper. Deathwing had heard enough human runts around his palace to know they were forever crying, but not this one. Jesobel instinctively pulled away her dress top to reveal a full bosom. He stepped closer.

The baby's eyes were tightly closed and its mouth worked hard in search of the proud and waiting teat.

The hag and her women were taken by the sight and ignored Deathwing, once more to assume a fawning ensemble. They muttered all manner of nonsense.

"Oh, how sweet."

"A good head of hair and no mistake."

"He's a big one, isn't he?"

"Like his father."

As the baby took its first urgent sucks there was a collective sigh, though Deathwing's was more of annoyance that he had come all this way to see a human baby born.

Then the baby's eyelids shot open and it let go of the teat and screeched. Jesobel screamed.

Curdled milk oozed from Jesobel's teat and ran from the baby's mouth. The hag and her helpers joined the mother's hysteria, which amplified when they caught sight of the baby's eyes; they were black pits in his skull. Jesobel fainted clean away when her son flicked out a forked tongue.

Disappointment fled Deathwing faster than a peasant caught stealing.

He had a son!

Deathwing reached down and picked up the child. He held him close and whispered in his ear so no one but his son could hear, and gave him his True Name.

He then held up his son to take a better look. Malevolent dark eyes stared back, a keen intelligence in them that even Deathwing found disturbing. There was no question from whose loins this lad had sprung.

Satisfied, he returned the baby to his mother's arms. The hag and her helpers were frozen, eyes wide in fear, staring at him.

"Help her," he commanded. "Feed the child warm blood until he can take solids, and then only meat. Look after him well or face my wrath."

The women didn't move. They were clearly terrified.

"Get to it!"

There was a flurry of activity and Jesobel was brought around. For a moment, she seemed unaware of where she was and what had happened. But then she saw the baby and screamed.

"Enough!" ordered Deathwing. He knelt at her side and spoke to her. "This is your child. He will be like no other. You must look after him."

She stared at him, uncomprehending. "You can't leave me. What am I to do?"

Deathwing reached into a vest pocket and pulled out a purse. He wrapped her hand over it. "This will help. He will have ... special needs."

He kissed her forehead, placed a spell of forgetfulness on her, and stood. She would not remember what had happened and see nothing but a normal baby boy. From another pocket he took a chain with a small, golden dragon pendant and put it around his son's neck.

"He wears that always," he told Jesobel. It would not only protect his son, but make him seem more human. "Now I must go."

"But what shall we call him?"

Deathwing stopped at the door and turned to take a last look at Jesobel and his son. He had given his son his True Name, but that was never to be spoken. He needed a human name.

"His name is Morden."

Chapter 4   A Dark Lord

Your Will is your strength.
The Dark Lord's Handbook

Morden sat on his throne and surveyed his realm. All that he could see was his and it was good—in the sense that it was his. In reality, it was a long forgotten storeroom he had come across while exploring the school. Little used, it had been ideal for a lair from which to direct his empire. He had it in mind that something bigger would be more in keeping for someone whose interests extended beyond the school and spread across a larger part of the Western Reaches. Not much was brewed in these lands without him having a share of the profits. A storeroom, not much bigger than a cupboard, tucked away off an outer yard of the school was not ideal for a criminal genius such as himself, but it was where he had started and it had a special place in his heart.

There were times such as this—when he sat and brooded on his throne—that it didn't seem so long ago that he had been sent to this school. He had known from an early age he was not like other children in the village. He wasn't weak like the others and he had a way about him. Nobody liked an eight-year-old who instilled despair and fear. He was an oddity and reviled by the rest of the village. Takings at the inn had plummeted and his parents had little choice but to send him away. He bore them no ill will for doing what was necessary. His abandonment was understandable; he would have done the same if his business was suffering.

Kristoff had been given the task of delivering him to town, being well-travelled and worldly-wise. The pouch of money Jesobel had been given at his birth contained more than enough for the fees, with a little left over for a new jerkin for Harold and a frock for Jesobel. Morden had been waved off; his parents looked dapper in their new clothes and the gathered villagers were in good spirits as he left. Crows flew overhead and cawed as the cart made its way down the rutted road.

When Kristoff had asked him if he was going to miss his parents it took him by surprise. Was he supposed to miss his parents? It was a notion that had not occurred to him. He remembered frowning as he thought about it. Kristoff had misread him and had said it was all right to cry. Instead Morden had laughed and said he was grateful for the opportunity he was being given. Kristoff had kept quiet for much of the rest of the journey to Bindelburg.

First word from the school was that, although precocious for his age, Morden had settled in well and had established himself among his peers, who seemed to respect him greatly.

And he had indeed settled well. When Morden had dictated the letter home to Master Jeffrey he had wanted his parents to have no cause to call him home. He was more than satisfied with life at the Bindelburg School for Young Masters and Prospective Brewers. The Monks of the Order of Divine Brewing had proven more than pliable. And the beer wasn't bad.

Ten years later, here he was, sitting on his throne, surveying his realm and pondering. Though over the years he had acquired much— power, influence, and a stack of brewing yeast that was mysteriously in short supply throughout the region—he wanted more. Trappings came to mind. What was he if he was short on trappings? To this end he had already commissioned and taken delivery of his throne, but was that enough? He didn't think so.

Not that he wasn't more than pleased with his throne. It was an icon of his power and had taken a good deal of making. He had been lucky to find an able carpenter in a classmate, Pilfew; there wasn't much he couldn't do with a wood chisel and dovetail joint. The boy had been reluctant to offer his services, but once Morden had discovered Pilfew's taste for torturing small animals it was only a matter of convincing the school cat to catch him mice. The rodents had bought his throne. He especially liked the hand rests carved as skulls. They gave the throne a certain style.

He remembered the first time he had sat on his throne and brooded. Brooded deeply. It was all well and good having a throne, but there was something missing. It was a feeling he had always had. When he had left the village for Bindelburg, and waved goodbye to his parents, it was not with sadness but with hope that perhaps this hollow in his being may be filled.

Over time he had become adept at brooding. No one in school could brood like he could. He took it to levels where a single brooding stare could turn away even a schoolmaster. It was all in the eyebrows. But a truly great brood had to be done sitting on his throne, hands clasped over the skulls, staring into a space beyond … well, just beyond.

His rise to power had come when he had been set upon for the first time by Billard and his cronies. Billard was big, stupid and had fists that were calloused from the beatings they had given. Morden had been on his way to class when he had rounded a corner to see Billard coming the other way, Mjecki and Klonker in tow (twins from Krisling on a cultural exchange).

The corridor was narrow and offered no opportunity to pass safely. Morden had snapped into a brood but it was as though Billard was too stupid to understand.

"Look who we have here," said Billard, planting his feet so his enormous bulk blocked Morden's way. "If it isn't Crow Boy."

Morden hated that nickname. Though no one dared to use it now, when he had first come to the Bindelburg School for Young Masters and Prospective Brewers, it was one he had been labelled with almost immediately. His sharp features and straight, jet-black hair may have been reason enough for the name, but it was the crows that followed him everywhere that were the real reason. He had grown accustomed to the crows; they had been there as long as he could remember. Wherever he went there was always at least one crow in attendance, sitting on a fence pecking at a snail, or flying above his head, like a dark angel watching over him. In the country it had taken a while for anyone to notice, as there were always birds around, and even then they had paid no attention to it. It was common for certain animals to take a shine to a person. Milly the cow maid attracted mallards and Old Bill Plenty always had a badger not far off. Morden's escort of crows was not remarkable.

When Billard had stopped him, somewhere outside a crow had cawed.

Then the fists had started to fly. Morden had shielded his head as best he could and took the beating. He had clutched at the medallion around his neck instinctively, as he tended to do in times of stress, the miniature dragon quite distinct in its feel, and calm had settled over him.

Curiously, the beating hadn't hurt much at all and the lack of pain allowed him to take in exactly what was happening. Later he would sit in his lair and brood upon it—and this time dark fruit would come from the brooding. Previously he had brooded in an undirected fashion, but in this instance he had a serious subject to brood upon: the idea of doing violence on a fellow.

It was a matter of will.

Billard inflicted pain to no end, other than to make his peers fear and dislike him. He had no will to inflict real pain. He was a child playing at cruelty; he had no idea what real pain was or what it may achieve.

Morden had gone to Billard in the dead of night. He had taken Billard's finger and bent it over until he could feel it snap at the knuckle. Morden's free hand had stifled the screams and he had whispered what he would do the next time if Billard ever gave him cause.

The next day he had sought Billard out. The bully had held his hand and flinched when Morden stopped to speak.

"Follow me," Morden ordered, and Billard, Mjecki and Kronker did so.

He had taken them to his room, and sat them on the floor and brooded at them for a while. Then he had done something new. He had bent them to His Will and made them His.

He had realised that all Billard wanted was to have attention, feel important, and inflict pain. Mjecki and Kronker were far from home and lived in Billard's shadow to be safe. Morden could offer each of them what they wanted, and in return have their unswerving loyalty.

Until then, Billard had been a hazard to be navigated in school life. With Morden's guidance he became a brief and violent reign of terror. Cuffs around the ear were a forgotten luxury next to bloodied noses, dead legs and vicious nipple twists.

The weak were cowed and the strong found their footwear would mysteriously go missing or their clothes go pink in the wash. Everyone got the message that Morden was in charge, and the faster they recognised the fact the sooner life would get better for all.

And with compliance came reward. He could get things most found nigh impossible. A chocolate for a sweet tooth? No problem. A kiss and fondle with Mercy the scullery girl? A suitable fee and she was yours.

Ten years on, life was indeed good. But the hollow in his being was still there; a hunger, a void that demanded satisfaction.

"I'm going into town," he announced and stood.

Kronker fetched him his coat, an ankle-length black wool affair with a hood that allowed him to pass unrecognised in town; at least as unrecognised as a six-foot, black-cloaked figure could be. Morden had grown quickly, and if he could bulk out he would be happier, but he was still a commanding figure.

Slipping out of the school—unnecessary as the monks wouldn't hinder him for a second, but he enjoyed the slipping part—Morden navigated the quagmire in the alleys with a deft step and headed towards the centre of town.

It was autumn—Morden's favourite time of year, as it heralded the bringing of death by winter while not being too chilly. Today, however, there was the first hint of the coming winter frosts and Morden plunged his hands into his sleeves for warmth.

The centre of town was impressively built. The town's wealth was evident in the two- and three-story stone buildings, and the flourishes in their masonry—a rose here, a gargoyle there. Each addition of detail would have cost that much more. Morden had developed an eye for costs. Nothing was free. This town had money to burn and Morden could smell it. Bindelburg's wealth came from its position. Situated on the river Clud, and at a crossroads, it was the trade hub of the region. Lord Wallee was ruler in name but it was the merchant houses who held the power.

Morden pondered this as he crossed the town square. There was no market today, and the chill kept many indoors, so the square was empty. Morden decided he needed to warm himself and headed for the Swan Inn —or Slap and Tickle as it was often called, for reasons that had begun to interest him.

A lone beggar thrust a rusty can at Morden as he passed under the statue of King Ribald IV, which dominated the centre of the square.

"Spare a penny for a poor orc," coughed a voice from under a mass of rags.

Morden was in mid-stride and almost tripped when he heard the request. *A poor orc?* Morden had heard every line from a thousand beggars and thought he'd heard them all: need a penny for a night in the shelter, a penny for a potato, a penny for the last cart home. Spare a penny for a poor orc was new.

According to their history teacher, Brother Pinchard, orcs had been rendered almost extinct five hundred years ago. In the last great war the world had seen, Prince Theo the Marvellous and his general, Uther the Merciless, had brought ruin to the Dark Lord, Zoon the Reviled. Dragons and the other mythic creatures had disappeared into legend. Trolls no longer lived under bridges but in the imagination. Orcs too had passed largely into myth, only growing in numbers centuries later. To this day they were an underclass living in ghettos.

Morden had never met an orc before. He rummaged for a penny. "Did you say orc?" he asked, reaching to toss the penny into the beggar's tin cup. He didn't want to get too close; he knew how far fleas could leap.

The thing, whatever it was, coughed. It was a phlegm-filled cough, one that sounded like the thing was about to bring its lungs up onto the cobbles.

"Most kind," it wheezed.

"It was not kindness," said Morden. "It was payment for an answer to a question. Did you say orc? Look at me."

The hand that came out of the rags to reach into the cup was green and had nails like talons. It clenched the penny between two fingers and held it up before pulling it back into the ragged mess of cloth. Seemingly satisfied, the beggar lifted his head.

Morden took a step back. The beggar was certainly no man. Though man-sized, the features were bulkier and Morden sensed there was hidden power under the bundle of rags. The orc's face was thick-set, with a broad, heavy nose. The skin had a definite green tinge to what some may have said was a heavy tan. The two tusk-like incisors that protruded over the lower lip were definitely not human either. According to the stories, the orc was a vicious fighter and would rip a fallen enemy's throat out with those teeth.

A shiver of delight passed through Morden.

"Yes, Morden Deathwing, I am an orc," said the beggar, his voice suddenly clear and strong.

"Deathwing? You are mistaken. My parents are Harold and Jesobel of Little Wassop."

"Harold and Jesobel Thrumpty?" asked the orc.

"Aye, that is them. What of it?"

The orc chuckled and goose bumps rose on Morden's arms and the back of his neck. Never had he heard a laugh so deep, so resonant, so implacably dark.

"You are no Thrumpty, young Morden, but a Deathwing. And I have been searching for you for many years. You must come with me."

Morden stared at the orc. "What do you mean, searching? Go where?"

The orc made no reply. He held Morden's gaze steadily.

"It's destiny," said the orc at last.

And with those words, the void in the centre of his being that had been crying out went silent.

"Lead on," commanded Morden.

The orc raised an eyebrow at Morden's tone, and smiled, revealing a set of yellowed teeth that looked like they could rip the throat from a hippo, let alone a man.

"This way, my lord," said the orc, bowing.

Morden's heart skipped a beat at the honorific.

Chapter 5   Conspiracy

The ignorant will oppose you. Educate them.
The Dark Lord's Handbook

They met in secret in a high tower hidden deep in a forest. It was an ornate folly of a long dead lord. The meeting room at the top was circular and had a white marble floor. Arched windows gave a resplendent view over the forest canopy, but the lack of glass made it draughty.

Count Vladovitch fidgeted under his white robe. He was used to the feel of coarse wool and armour rather than the touch of silk, but their leader had insisted they do this right; and that included suitable attire for conspirators. It did have a certain practical side in that none of those present was immediately recognisable, though the sheer bulk of Tulip (the Countess of Umbria) could not be mistaken.

The use of adopted names did seem ridiculous. That he should have to be referred to as Hemlock was not only demeaning, but daft. He had a famously grizzly voice that none who heard could forget. It wasn't as though he didn't know exactly who any one of the nine present was either.

Foxglove, who had suggested the idea of the names, had explained he was missing the point entirely. The robes, the names, the secret meetings were used so what they plotted was plausibly deniable—a term that once explained seemed equally absurd since, in the count's experience, a conspiracy that was plausibly deniable would become eagerly admitted upon the threatened use of a hot poker.

Nevertheless, there they were, shivering in the flimsiest of white silk, waiting for the last of their number to arrive.

Petunia and Marigold were discussing a point of order when there was a strong buffeting and heads turned to the steeple dome. There was a crash and several tiles slid past a window. Curses could be heard and more crashes before Black Orchid made her entrance.

Unlike the rest, Black Orchid's robes were sable. And unlike the rest, the count had no idea who Black Orchid was beyond the fact that she was the leader of this conspiracy and was not to be trifled with in the slightest. They had started out as an even thirteen, but Pansy and Carnation had made the mistake of challenging Black Orchid's leadership—on the basis that she was a woman. Bits of them were still unaccounted for, though there was little doubt that the parts that had been found belonged to the pair.

"I see I'm the last to arrive," said Black Orchid from under her hood. "Let's cut the formalities and get down to it, shall we?"

There was a sibilant hiss to Black Orchid's voice and the count found the accent hard to place.

Feet shuffled but there was no response. The count was happy for the hoods that hid their faces. Though he had lived a life of martial hardship, and was no stranger to danger, he was also no stranger to fear and there was something about Black Orchid that made him deeply afraid. When he addressed his men before battle he could hide his fear, but he was not sure he could have hidden the terror he felt when Black Orchid was addressing them.

"How goes the search?" asked Black Orchid.

This was the first question Black Orchid always asked and the count dreaded it. Years ago, she had given them the prophecy and sent them out to search for the Hero. Since then, they had been meeting every six months to report any news, and at every meeting, there was no news.

The world was a big place. Finding one particular child in all the villages, towns and cities across a dozen lands, was no mean feat. True, there had been candidates, but none had turned out to be the Hero Black Orchid had revealed to them; the Hero who would throw off the yoke of the merchant classes and return the aristocracy to its rightful position. Too long had they lived under the burden of loans and interest rates. Darkness was coming and the Hero would lead them in the final battle against the Dark Lord. The aristocracy would hail them as saviours and they would take back everything they had lost in promissory notes. The only problem was that it had been a long wait so far and none of them was getting any younger.

From the count's left, Hogweed coughed.

"Yes?"

"I ... I think I found him," said Hogweed. In the count's experience Hogweed, the Prince of Greater Wallencia, was not a timid man. But even he seemed to show nerves.

"Oh, really? Pray tell us more."

"I found a monk."

"And?"

"He spoke of a virgin birth."

Black Orchid sighed and fear rippled around the group. This was hardly news. Stories of virgin births were the staple of a good night's storytelling in many an inn across the Western Reaches.

"I brought him here with me," said Hogweed.

The count's fear turned to terror and he took a step to his right. He could see Foxglove, on Hogweed's left, had likewise distanced himself from the visibly trembling Hogweed. *He was either brave, tired of living, or certain he had found the child*, thought the count.

Though it was hard to tell, Black Orchid seemed to be considering Hogweed with some interest. It was a terrible breach of protocol to bring anyone to their meetings.

"I do hope you're right," said Black Orchid at last. "Bring him in."

Hogweed bolted to the stairwell and returned moments later. When he led the monk into the centre of the gathering, the count understood why Hogweed's gamble was perhaps a safe one. The monk was blind, a terrible scar running across the man's face from ear to ear. He looked frail and was mumbling to himself continually. The man was dressed in a torn brown robe and his grey hair and beard were unkempt. He looked more a hermit than a monk.

"A blind man will lead and the Hero will be found," gasped Lilly, quoting the prophecy.

Black Orchid raised a hand to silence the excitable Lilly and addressed the monk. "Tell us your name and story, old man."

The monk stiffened and turned his blind stare toward Black Orchid. "I am Brother Francis of the Seekers," said the monk, his voice as frail as his body. "And I am the last of my Order."

The monk coughed and brought his hand to his mouth. The count could see flecks of blood in the man's spittle. If he had a story to tell, he had better be quick as he did not look like he would make sundown.

"You must excuse me, I am old and not long for this world," said the monk.

Perhaps he's a prophet as well as a storyteller, mused the count.

"I was there when He was born, more than ten years past," continued Brother Francis. The monk paused and scratched at his beard. "Perhaps nearer twenty years. Maybe more. Maybe less. It was such a long time ago."

The monk stopped and started to count on his fingers.

"Let's call it twenty, shall we?" said Black Orchid. "Please, continue."

"It was twenty years ago," said Brother Francis. "Or there about. On the night of a blood moon he was born and I was struck blind."

Brother Francis told his story of how he and his fellows had been Seeking, as was their wont, and had been directed from an inn to Wellow, a small village in the Reaches. On leaving the inn they had been attacked by a great dragon. After the attack he had stumbled blindly, his cries unheard in the wind, for miles. He had at last been drawn to the cries of a woman giving birth.

To the count it sounded implausible at best. Dragons were the stuff of legend and the pure chance of wandering miles to the exact spot he had been trying to find was more than unlikely, it was ridiculous.

Brother Francis continued his tale. He had been there when Diona of Wellow, who claimed she had never known a man, had given birth to a boy. She had died in childbirth but her father, a widower himself, had raised the child.

"Diona's father is a blacksmith," said Brother Francis with a hint of satisfaction.

The count was astonished, and it seemed his fellow conspirators were equally taken aback. There was a stunned silence.

"That makes him an orphan child of virgin birth and raised by a blacksmith," explained Brother Francis, turning his blind eyes as though sweeping the assembly. "If he isn't the Hero then I'm no Seeker!"

The count had never believed in prophecy or suchlike. He had always held the belief that it was expedient nonsense. If prophecies were true, then why were they always so vague and unspecific? He'd never once come across a prophecy where the prophet who delivered it hadn't been so imprecise as to be obtuse. If they could really see the future then surely they could be more accurate?

"Yes. Yes. We do understand, old man," said Black Orchid. "You said you were attacked by a dragon?"

"Terrible it was," said the monk. His hands went to scarred eyes. "If it wasn't for the clear night, and the moon, we would not have seen him, so black was he."

"A black dragon?" said Black Orchid, her head tilting to one side. "Really? How interesting."

The monk coughed as though to continue but a raised hand from Black Orchid silenced him; his lips moved but no sound came.

"Brethren, it seems after these fallow years our search may well be over," said Black Orchid. "Who has the sword?"

There was a general muttering and fidgeting. The count prayed that whoever had the sword had brought it.

"I do," said Tulip at last, heaving her massive bulk a step forward.

Her hand delved into voluminous folds of cloth and emerged with a sword that sang as it left a hidden scabbard. Of good length, it was as bright as burnished steel—mainly because it was burnished steel, but also because of the charm that sat upon it. There was a terrible elegance about the keen edge and simple hilt. You could do someone real harm with that sword.

"Have it placed where He may find it," commanded Black Orchid.

Tulip's hood turned to one side and she whispered something to Lilly. There was an exchange of sorts before Tulip's hood turned back and a quavering voice rang out.

"And ... well ... I mean to say, where would that be, exactly?"

Black Orchid let go a sigh that shrivelled the count's heart and made his breakfast make a bid for freedom.

"I don't *know*! Somewhere near to where he lives. The charm will take care of the rest."

"You mean like in a hedge?"

Black Orchid's head turned heavenward and she roared. "No. Not in a *hedge*. Plunge it into a stone or something. Put it on display for all to see but only the chosen to wield. Am I making myself clear?"

Tulip collapsed into a blubbering wreck on the ground. It was hard to tell whether she was nodding vigorously or merely shaking in terror.

"As ... as you wish."

"Good," said Black Orchid, regaining some composure. "Now, the rest of you, go and prepare. You'll need lots of money, so borrow more. And don't worry, it's not as though you'll be giving any of it back."

"We won't?" said Lilly.

Black Orchid's hood turned in Lilly's direction. "Of course not. How stupid are you? Really? The world is going to be laid to ruin and we are going to save it. Saviours don't give anything back. Now go. Quickly."

The ten left hurriedly by the spiral stair. Black Orchid presumably would leave the same way she had arrived, by *alternative* methods. The count tried to suppress the notion that Black Orchid flew, either under her own power or on some creature, and the associated connotations should that in fact be the case.

There was little small talk as was normal after such meetings. The mood seemed tense. Until now their conspiracy had been mostly talk and complaints about the continual rise in the cost of living and the horrendous overheads in maintaining their stations in life, spiralling ever more into debt with the loathsome middle classes. Now, however, it seemed to the count that perhaps things were going to happen. For a man of action such as himself, the prospect was invigorating. It was all well and good leading a small army of highly trained knights and footmen, but such a waste if they did little more than control brigands and have the odd prearranged border skirmish. War was coming, proper all-out-and-bloody war, and the more the count thought on it the more invigorated he became.

Chapter 6   The Handbook

A strong right hand has many uses.
The Dark Lord's Handbook

Morden followed the orc into the warren of alleys that led off the town square toward the poorer part of town. Morden forgot the lure of warmth, beer, and the maids that purveyed the latter in the Slap and Tickle.

"What should I call you?" he asked of the hefty back in front of him.

The orc stopped to face Morden and grinned. Morden couldn't decide which was worse: the teeth, or the breath that escaped from between them.

"My orcish name is Kzchtk," said the orc in a contortion of vowel-less grunts that sounded like he was about to vomit. "But you can call me Grimtooth."

Morden observed the orc with what he hoped was a dry smile. "Kzchtk, you say?"

The orc's eyebrows rose like two hairy caterpillars heaving themselves off a branch. "Few can speak the orcish tongue. You've had your tonsils removed?"

Morden smiled. "Not at all. Let's just say I have a gift for pronunciation. So what does Kzchtk mean?"

"It means Grimtooth," said the orc, his fierce grin widening.

"Touché," said Morden. "Lead on, Grimtooth."

The alleys narrowed. The filth became ankle deep and the dwellings became hovels. Though there weren't many people outside, Morden noticed that many of those they did pass seemed to share the same physical bulkiness of Grimtooth, and many had a greeting for them as they passed.

"You seem well known and much liked," observed Morden.

"They are my people," said Grimtooth. "Here we are."

Grimtooth had stopped outside a hovel that was larger and better kept than the rest. There were fewer holes in the walls and the roof was complete, bar a smoke hole. There was no door as such, merely a heavy leather flap. Grimtooth was obviously waiting for Morden to enter. Morden considered how wise this was. He was well known, and of some means. This could be the simplest kidnapping ever done if he just walked in and was held, but something about Grimtooth told him this was not the case. The deference with which he addressed Morden seemed sincere.

Morden pushed the leather aside and ducked into the doorway.

His hood caught on the hanging as he entered, so his head was bared when he stood upright. He was greeted by a circle of orcs sitting around a fire pit, its smoke rising out of the hole in the roof. Woven mats covered the floor and the walls were covered in hangings that depicted scenes of battle; orcs mostly, dismembering opponents with wicked axes. One was roaring at the sky, his victim limp in his arms, throat torn out.

Perhaps this wasn't a good idea after all, thought Morden, and he instinctively reached for his dragon pendant. Oddly, it was warm under his touch and seemed to pulse. His skin suddenly felt burning hot and there was a terrible itch between his shoulder blades.

His entry had not gone unnoticed and as one the orcs sprang to their feet, swords and axes appearing like magic in their clawed fists.

"Gr'k-k'h!" they roared.

Morden had no idea what Gr'k-k'h meant but was quite sure it was not, 'Hello, how good of you to drop in.'

Unbidden words came to Morden:

"Kznk d'lak!"

Morden felt like he was two people. He could barely recognise the voice that spoke. There was power and authority in it that surprised even him. The accent had a faint hiss about it, but there was no doubting its strength; it was deafening.

The effect on the orcs was dramatic. Brief astonishment was replaced by a curious mixture of joy and terror. They threw their weapons and themselves onto the matting—in one case causing a nasty gash—and pressed themselves as hard and as flat as they could manage to the ground.

Behind him, Morden was aware that Grimtooth had entered.

"I see no introductions are necessary," said Grimtooth, pushing his bulk past Morden. "Brothers, please. Get up and sit."

Grovelling in the dirt, the orcs seemed torn between what Grimtooth said and fear of Morden. Grimtooth tugged one by the arm and Morden tried a reassuring smile.

It had the opposite effect.

"When an orc shows his teeth it means he is ready to use them," said Grimtooth, observing the effect of Morden's smile.

"But I'm not an orc," protested Morden. "And when we met you smiled at me when I told you to lead on." Morden took a second to think on the realisation. "Oh."

Grimtooth looked at him steadily. "I am not used to allowing anyone to speak to me like that, and no, you're not an orc. You're something a lot worse. Come sit. Set my brothers at peace." Grimtooth snatched a hard leather cushion from the floor and tossed it into a gap in the ring of orcs. "Sit there."

Morden took his place and kept his teeth firmly behind his lips.

Grimtooth spoke sternly to the orcs in their tongue and, with some cajoling, they regained their positions—with a noticeable gap on either side of Morden.

None of them seemed to want to hold Morden's look, finding more interest in the ceiling, wall hangings, and the copious amount of dirt under their fingernails. Grimtooth barked something at a dark space beyond the ring and what Morden presumed was a female orc emerged with a tray of mugs. Another followed with an earthen jug. Morden was given a mug first and it was filled with brown frothy liquid from the jug. Morden hoped it was beer, but from the smell he suspected something else. It smelt less of hops and more of urine. Orcish lore represented a huge gap in his education to date, so he had no idea whether they drank their own fermented piss or not.

Trying hard to be nonchalant, Morden took a drink. It was surprisingly good. Refreshing even.

"It's good," he said with some relief. "I've not had this before. What is it?" He took another large mouthful and let it rest in his mouth.

"Fermented goat piss," said Grimtooth.

Morden almost doused the fire as he spat his mouthful out. Wiping his lips, all he could see was a ring of grinning orcs. Some had teeth like

Grimtooth, though not as large, but some seemed to be filed flat. Regardless, he couldn't see himself getting out alive.

Grimtooth was the first to laugh, the rest joining in and mimicking Morden by spitting mouthfuls of drink at each other.

"I don't see what's so funny," said Morden. "I'm not used to drinking goat piss."

Some of the orcs lost control and rolled over on the mats, clutching at their bellies. Grimtooth got up and came to sit next to Morden, slapping him hard on the back. *There's iron in those arms*, thought Morden, wincing.

"It's not goat piss," said Grimtooth. "It's beer with a few special ingredients. Go ahead. Drink."

Morden stared dubiously at the mug in his hand. Though it did smell like goat piss, it had tasted like a rather good hoppy beer. He took a large swig and the orcs roared their approval.

Though no stranger to beer, Morden found himself edging quickly towards drunkenness. "This is good stuff," he remarked, emptying his mug, "but you didn't bring me here to get me drunk."

Grimtooth drained his mug and set it aside. "Indeed not, Morden."

Grimtooth clapped his hands and said something in orcish and the mood turned sombre. One of the orcs slipped out and returned with a cloth-covered bundle which he handed to Grimtooth before resuming his place. There was a tangible air of expectancy in the gathering now, bordering on excitement. Grimtooth set the bundle down in front of Morden. It was hard to make out what was under the grimy cloth.

"What the hell is that?" he exclaimed, as much to himself as to the assembled, when Grimtooth whipped the cloth away.

Though in some part it was obvious what had been wrapped—it was a leather-covered book—it was what was clasping the book that had Morden confused. "Is that a hand?" Whatever it was, it resembled a skeletal hand that was gripping the book; a hand that had been severed at the wrist.

The orcs sat in a ring transfixed, no hint of teeth, no sound, no movement. They were like statues. With a sideways look at Grimtooth first, Morden reached out and picked up whatever was grasping the book to examine it more closely. Without doubt it was a hand, maybe even human. Up close, Morden could see that there were vestigial fingernails.

The hand looked as though it had been hacked from its arm and horribly burned. If that was the case, then how was the book in such good condition? It didn't look like the book could have been forced into the hand's grasp, it was too tight. The cover resembled hard leather but bore no title. Morden twisted the hand to see if the spine of the book held any mark. It didn't. Nor the reverse.

"Interesting curio," said Morden, holding out the book to Grimtooth.

"Take the book," said Grimtooth.

Morden tried to read something into the way Grimtooth was looking at him, but could not. He shrugged and looked down at the hand again. It was gripping the book tightly—an exploratory tug confirmed that. Morden pulled harder and the book remained firmly in the grip of the white bone fingers.

"Doesn't seem to want to come," he said, and as he did so he could feel the observing orcs tense. Trying hard not to show fear, Morden turned the book over to examine it again. This was obviously a test. Quite a weird test for sure, but one he felt absolutely certain his life depended on.

The book was grasped with fingers on one side, a thumb underneath, and so firm it wasn't going to release the book easily. If it was held by magic then he was doomed to fail, as magic was again, much like orcs, stuff of tales and fiction rather than something taught at a school for prospective brewers.

"I claim this book," he said, and tried to tug the book from the hand's grip.

Nothing.

The orcs seemed to be getting restless.

Then it came to him. If there was one thing he had learnt in the last few years, it was how to break a finger. He flipped the book over, gripped the thumb at its knuckle and used the leverage of the thumb's length against the book to push it sharply. There was a snap as the thumb came free in his hand.

He tossed the hand and its now separate thumb onto the mat and handed the book to Grimtooth.

"There you go. Interesting puzzle. How did you get the book into the hand like that?"

Grimtooth was showing his teeth again, but this time it was because he had gone slack-jawed with seeming amazement. "You broke the hand."

"Wasn't that the point? Like I said, a clever puzzle, as there was the inherent idea of preserving hand and book, but in fact all you wanted was the book."

Morden was still holding out the book and Grimtooth was making no effort to take it from him.

"Open the book," said Grimtooth, his voice a stunned monotone.

Morden shrugged again. "Sure." He held the book in the flat of his left hand and reached for the cover to open it. There was an audible intake of breath. He flipped open the cover onto the first page. There was a whistle as breath escaped between teeth.

"What does it say?" asked Grimtooth.

The paper was unlike anything Morden had seen before; though of a similar texture to normal paper, it was thick, almost skin-like, and light seemed to skate over its surface. It was also blank.

"It doesn't say anything," said Morden, looking up at Grimtooth.

"Nothing?"

"Not a word. It's blank. See?" He held the book up.

Slowly, Grimtooth's face broke into a wide smile. The kind of smile that Morden knew was the one where the teeth were going to get used.

Then a thought occurred to him and he flipped the book over. With some relief he could see spidery writing.

"Oops. Wrong way up."

Grimtooth's smile froze and Morden hurriedly read the title page:

The Dark Lord's Handbook
A Guide

Words appeared on the page, filling it as Morden read.

Know this, young Morden: it is your destiny to rule. You will be the greatest Dark Lord this world has ever seen. You will cast your shadow across all the lands and your name will be whispered in every corner of every city, town and hovel. You will have great wealth and be successful with women (or men if you prefer). Do not doubt this. It will come to pass.

Along the way you will doubtless need help; after all, you are still young in years, so there are two things you must do:

Listen to Grimtooth. He is older than he looks and will be the rock on which you build your empire.

Read this guide whenever you have a problem. By all means seek the advice of others, but ignore it. They are all fools. Instead, take heed of Grimtooth and the words you read herein above all.

As Morden read it was as though everything slipped into place and, when he dragged his eyes from the text to look at the still grinning Grimtooth, he was no longer Morden the boy, entrepreneur and criminal genius but Morden the soon-to-be Dark Lord. It was exciting.

It was also odd.

"It says I am going to rule the world," said Morden.

The smile vanished from Grimtooth's face. "You can read the book?"

Morden read the first line out loud, and as he did the orcs behind Grimtooth flattened themselves on the straw mats and started a throaty chant. Even Grimtooth lowered his gaze.

"Is this some kind of jest?" asked Morden. "Are you trying some kind of scam? It says you will be the rock on which I build my empire. How could this possibly have your name written in it? For that matter, how could my name be in it unless written by someone who knows us both?"

"My name is written?"

"Strange, isn't it? Look." Morden turned the book around so Grimtooth could see the text. Behind Grimtooth, the other orcs were straining to catch a surreptitious glance. A glare from Morden and they resumed their prostrate positions.

Grimtooth's eyes glanced down and then back to Morden. "Only a Dark Lord can read this book. The words mean nothing to me."

"Well, it's right here," said Morden, spinning the book back around. "It says you are older than you look and that I should seek council from you." Morden snapped the book shut. "How old are you, anyway?"

"Five hundred and twenty-three," said Grimtooth.

Behind him there was a cough, and what Morden swore was a giggle. Grimtooth spun round and glared. "Okay, okay. Five hundred and fifty," he mumbled.

Morden was almost dumbstruck. "Wow, that is old."

"Thank you for reminding me," said Grimtooth. He glared over his shoulder at his fellows. "Happy now?"

"You don't look it," said Morden. "Though I have to say I haven't met anyone who claims to be as old as you before. You don't look bad. No, really. You must work out."

Grimtooth seemed to brighten a little. "It shows?"

"Oh, yes. Definitely."

There was an embarrassed silence. "Do you think we could talk more privately?" whispered Morden, suddenly aware that there were twenty pairs of ears hanging on his every word.

"Scram," barked Grimtooth, and the other orcs disappeared in a frenzied scramble.

Morden was relieved to be alone with Grimtooth. He had a thousand questions, but first he needed to get warm. He'd been sitting next to the door-flap for the last ten minutes and there was quite a chill running under the hem of his coat. He edged himself out of the draught and warmed his hands. Grimtooth remained standing, head bowed.

"Come sit," said Morden, realising the orc was waiting for his command. Though the orc could have ripped him limb from limb and used his sinews to floss, somehow Morden knew that Grimtooth would now only ever do Morden's bidding, even if it cost him his life. At this realisation, a surge of energy swept through his body. So *this* is what real power felt like.

"I have so many questions," said Morden when he was comfortable. "Where did you get this book?"

Grimtooth was staring into the flames and began to speak:

"The last Dark Lord was Zoon the Reviled. He had a mighty army and his power covered the land like a bad rash, one that itches and causes extreme discomfort. But he was thrown down, for the salve to his rash bore a righteous weapon and Zoon's hand was hewn from his body and he fell. A young orc bore witness, and unseen this orc took the hand that was hewn and the book that it clutched and kept it."

"And that young orc was you?" Morden was quite incredulous at the idea that Grimtooth had witnessed the stuff of legend.

"No, that was my cousin, Nimblefinger. He was always nicking stuff. I got the hand when we were sorting through his belongings after his *accident*."

Grimtooth shuddered and Morden decided any accident that made a savage orc such as Grimtooth shake at its memory was probably one best left unexplained.

"But how did you know to find me? And how is it that our names are written in it?"

"I am as puzzled as you, young Morden, as to how our names are written, but they are. We are bound to this book somehow. I have dreams, and those of late had me come here to visit my brethren. I know not why, but I knew you would pass by me; I had been given the name Deathwing in the dreams, and when I first set eyes on you I was sure."

"But we've never met."

"It was the robe. I was looking for a Dark Lord and there you were, striding into the square in an ankle-length black robe, hooded, and with your hands plunged into your sleeves."

"You're kidding."

Grimtooth gave Morden a sidelong look. "Well, what else did I have to go on? Anyhow, when you got close I could smell something different about you."

"Ah, well. That could be the lotion that matron gave me. I've been getting this rash, you see."

"A rash?"

"Yes. And no, it's not what you're thinking. My skin sometimes goes a bit ... scaly." Morden couldn't believe he was telling Grimtooth about his rash. When he'd first gone to the matron she'd told him to wear boxing gloves to bed and not to fiddle with himself. When he insisted she take a look at his chest and the rash he had there she was as mystified as he had been. His skin had blackened and become scaled in a small patch over his heart. She'd given him a cream and told him to come back in a week if it didn't go away.

"It was no lotion I smelt," said Grimtooth. "It was the smell of ambition and power, a scent the world has not had waft around it for five hundred years. It was the smell of a Dark Lord."

Again, Morden felt a thrill run through him and deep down he knew there was some truth to the orc's words. He had no idea what it meant to be a Dark Lord, but the very words made his spine tingle and his teeth itch.

"You will set us free, Morden," said Grimtooth. "For five hundred years we have lived as slaves, a forgotten race, our teeth filed flat, bred like animals to be docile and do the most menial jobs. We have passed into legend but we are still here, a few of us unbent in spirit, waiting. And now my burden is passed to you and you shall lead us. We shall throw off our shackles at last."

Morden was quite taken aback by the fire in Grimtooth's words. He was doubtless a proud orc.

"What burden?"

"I have been the bearer of the book all this time. While those around me grow old and die, I remain, destined to forever walk the world, searching for the one who can take the book from the hand and set me free."

Morden looked at the book and weighed it in his hand. It was without question magical. No other book could write itself as he read, nor include the reader in its words. And to have kept Grimtooth alive so long was further testimony.

"What should I do?" said Morden, suddenly aware of the huge burden he had taken on. He was to be a Dark Lord and he didn't have the faintest idea where to start. How could he, a teenage boy, one who had only recently discovered beer, women and a good pipe of weed, be anything in the world, let alone a Dark Lord? Though it thrilled him, it also scared him. His life was more than comfortable. His operation pretty much ran itself. There was no hurry.

"You should go. Return to the monks and read. I shall leave and spread the word. A Dark Lord will be rising. Preparations need to be made. Leave it to me."

"Preparations?"

"We've no time to waste. Go. Read. I will return in the coming months."

"But you haven't even told me who I am—what I am."

"There will be time enough, Morden. Go now."

And with that, Morden found himself being ushered out into the cold and shooed down the street back the way he had come. As he trudged back towards the school, the book clasped firmly under his robe, Morden brooded. Grimtooth was right. He had a lot to learn and he had better be a quick study.

His feet had carried him back to the main square, which was now lit with torches to push back the night. Across the square he could hear music and laughter coming from the Slap and Tickle. The school and his bed were in the other direction, but what harm in a pint and pipe before bed? Pulling his hood down over his head to shield it from the bitter northern wind, he headed to the inn. There he could find a dark corner and brood some more, and maybe steal a kiss from Trudy.

Chapter 7   Food and Beer

There is no limit to your genius.
Be sure this is well known.
The Dark Lord's Handbook

Chancellor Penbury considered the choice of dishes laid out on the table. The first was sirloin of Paguar, a rare cat that lived on only one small jungle island, Pag, in the Great Outer Sea. It was served on a crisp potato patty with a crescent of puréed cauliflower and a sweet red currant and Port gravy. The meat's aroma hinted of musky distant lands.

The platter in the centre sported a rough haunch of mountain yak served with an unceremonious dollop of celeriac mash and gravy thick enough to paint a wall. It was as inelegant as the first dish was sophisticated, but sometimes junk food really hit the spot.

The last dish was a bowl of soup that bubbled and had something swimming in it. An eye stalk occasionally popped out of the pale brown broth and twitched around before plopping back down.

"And this is?" enquired the chancellor, indicating the soup with the most subtle twitch of a digit.

"Erubian Swamp Broth with a live spriggle served with a side of soda bread," said a gangling chef standing behind the dish. He was gripping his hands in front of himself and had beads of sweat running down his prodigiously long nose, threatening to drip into the soup.

The chancellor arched an eyebrow. He'd never had spriggle in a broth; it was normally served in a cage of pork ribs. Spriggle was not only tremendously rare but fantastically dangerous. Only three gastronomes in the last three hundred years had managed to eat one and live to describe its taste. The chancellor was one of those three, and although there was an exquisite piquant flavour to the spriggle, he hadn't taken the requisite pain suppressants nor did he have any of the seven poison antidotes on hand.

"I'll go with the yak," said the chancellor. Though the Pag was tempting, his stomach was feeling a little fragile and he fancied the stodge. "And I'll have the Pimpaho Red to accompany it."

"A wonderful choice, sir," said the wine waiter.

The unwanted dishes were removed and the yak placed in front of the chancellor. The spriggle chef seemed relieved as he took his dish away. Despite the spriggle's well known tendency to kill, it was always the chef who got the blame when someone died.

The yak was good, the gravy every bit as rich and cloying as it had promised, and the celeriac mash was passable. The chancellor settled into a measured pace. It was a big portion and would take some effort to polish off. The Pimpaho helped wash it down, as he knew it would. Each grape that was used to make the wine was squeezed between the thumb and forefinger of a virgin, which imbued the resultant wine with innocence and freshness; it was a wine whose spirit had not yet been crushed. And it brought out the full flavour of the yak.

The chancellor was mopping up when his personal private secretary, Chidwick, slid into the room. He was as thin a man as the chancellor was bulky, and he had a dark viscosity about his looks.

The chancellor could see that Chidwick was somewhat agitated, but whatever was disturbing him was still not strong enough to disturb his master while he was eating.

Not fancying the last of the mash, the chancellor dabbed his lips with his napkin and pushed his chair back. A servant swept in and magicked his plate away.

"Yes, Chidwick?"

"Some disturbing news, Chancellor," said Chidwick.

The chancellor raised an eyebrow. He was the richest man alive by far. He was head of the largest merchant cartel that spanned dozens of fiefdoms and kingdoms. There was a three year waiting list for royalty to be invited to dine at his table. For centuries his family had effectively ruled across two continents; perhaps not in name, but certainly in fact. He found it hard to imagine anything that may have been disturbing, except perhaps the failure of the Roseberry harvest, the rarest and most sweet of all fruits that he alone in the world ate.

"Oh, really?"

Chidwick was the chancellor's aide for many reasons. Aside from his efficiency, ruthlessness, superior intelligence and unswerving loyalty, he was also one of the few men who was not afraid of the chancellor. But now, he didn't seem to be able to look the chancellor in the eye. Rather than be angry, the chancellor felt something jump inside him, and it wasn't wind. Perhaps Chidwick did have something interesting to say.

"Spit it out, man," said the chancellor.

Chidwick's chest heaved and he at last brought his eyes up to meet his master's. "We have a serious beer problem," he blurted.

Now it made sense. Beer was close to Penbury's heart, and indeed he considered himself a foremost authority on all matters pertaining to beer. Beer and its production was also a vital grease to the economy. In a world where beer was safer to drink than water, it was a matter of importance that beer was both plentiful and cheap so the average working man could turn up to work half cut. Better a slightly drunk worker than a dead one.

"Explain," said Penbury as Chidwick hovered.

Chidwick laid out what had come to his attention. There was a new force in brewing, it seemed; one that had managed to corner the vast majority of the Western Reaches' beer production. It was obvious to the chancellor that this person, whoever he was, was both skilful and yet stupid. They obviously did not understand that such activity would not go unnoticed.

"Very good, Chidwick. Excellent work. You were right to bring this to me. I want you to go and pay this brewer a visit. Wrap up his operation and bring him here. Do you know where he is based?"

"Bindelburg, sir."

"The Brothers of Divine Brewing?" asked Penbury. They had been purveyors of the finest beers for centuries, once the time they had spent in prayer had been freed up through drunkenness. "Curious. Nevertheless. Go, Chidwick. Settle this matter quickly. We can't have anyone messing around with beer."

Chapter 8   First Lesson – Preparations

Suffer no fools. Rather make fools suffer.
The Dark Lord's Handbook

With all matters for the day taken care of, Morden settled himself with a mug of tea, a plate of squashed fly biscuits, and the Dark Lord's Handbook. He hadn't had a chance to read any of it so far. When he had got back to the school, he had been snowed under with his empire of organised crime, the majority of which revolved around extortion and selling beer. All thought of being a Dark Lord had gone when faced with the reality of running a business.

But now that he found himself with an hour clear, he thought he at least ought to read the Handbook, seeing as he was in it after all.

He dunked a biscuit and took a swig of tea. Now where did a Dark Lord start on his path to becoming a tyrant? He turned the cover to a blank page. Just as he thought maybe there had been a mistake, and that he was not going to be a Dark Lord at all, spidery writing started to skitter across the page.

A Dark Lord Rising

I hope you are settled, Morden?

There it goes again, thought Morden. How does it know when I am reading?

I just do. Now settle down and listen. You have a lot of natural talent, young Morden, but becoming a Dark Lord is no easy matter. There is a lot to learn, and many things to do before you can call the world your own.

Fair enough, thought Morden. After all, it had taken him several years to put his empire in the school together. Some people seemed to think it was all criminal genius but, in fact, he had worked hard to get to where he was today. He had no problem with that at all. He hated slackers and led by example when it came to putting the hours in.

Good. It's not going to be all rape and pillage, but a lot of hard work. So let's get started at the beginning, shall we?

A Dark Lord does not just appear, He Rises. This is the first and perhaps most crucial step a Dark Lord must take. But beware! Rising is not a simple thing. Many things can go wrong. You are not a Dark Lord quite yet. You have not assumed your full power, and therefore you are fallible (never admit this in company though).

Rise? thought Morden. That makes no sense. He wasn't a yeast based product. What on earth was it going on about?

Patience, Morden. Let me explain.

Think of Rising as a game where you get to choose your position and lay out all your pieces before you engage your opponent in the game itself. To Lay Waste a world and have Dominion over it takes some effort. Power and resources must be gathered. This is what you will be doing while you are Rising.

It is an inescapable fact that a Dark Lord who gathers his powers and forces will not go unnoticed. Traditionally this leads to expressions such as: there is a darkness come to the world; a power is rising in the east; and, there is evil abroad in the land. All of these are roundabout ways of recognising that a Dark Lord is Rising.

Fortunately, those who will oppose you once you have Risen will do nothing while you are actually Rising. Rather than nip the problem in the bud they will dither and dally, rush around in a headless panic, and observe from afar but not actually do anything to stop you. This is good. Use the time well.

While your opponent may not be willing to take the initiative and stop your Rising, he will be making his own preparations. Heroes need to be found, relics discovered, prophecies read, etc. It's all time consuming. You must use this time to be ready first—and this is the real pressure you are under.

I'm not sure I like the idea of Heroes, thought Morden. They sound dangerous.

Indeed they are, but we will come to those in a later lesson. For now, let's stay on track with Rising. Now, where were we?

A good Rising should be followed by a sudden Coming Forth (see next chapter). If you have Risen well and disrupted your opponents' preparations, you should be able to Come Forth and manage some Laying Waste (see chapter after Coming Forth) before the Forces of Good are properly marshalled.

And how might I disrupt these Heroic preparations? thought Morden.

There are many ways in which you may disrupt Heroic preparation. The trickier part is knowing who your opponent will be, but once known there are several acceptable methods. Dark riders of various kinds are a favourite but they tend to be more bark than bite. Monsters abroad, theft of holy relics, and kidnapping are all worth a try.

I understand.

Good. Now, when Rising the first decision to be made is where to Rise. As with any real estate concern, it's location, location, location. Traditionally a Dark Lord will seek to Rise in either the north or the east. For some reason, the so-called Forces of Good prefer the west, so south may well be an option as well. This will be where you have your fortress.

The first thing is to look at the geography and consider important features such as impenetrable mountain ranges, nasty indigenous flora and fauna (poison swamps, dragons, immense spiders and man-eating plants are all favourable) and the weather. If you are coming into the Dark Lord business later in life, perhaps the colder north may not be the best choice as it will play havoc with the rheumatism. But seeing as you are so young, you can worry about that later.

The east is generally a safe bet and has the advantage of having the rising sun behind you for those dawn battles. Nothing seems to upset a Dark Lord's army more than sun in the eyes.

Wherever you choose, you are going to need property, lots of it. There is plenty of land that isn't owned by anyone but with a little work is more than adequate for your purposes. You are looking for an area that preferably inspires dread and fear; mountains that are volcanically active tend to have this effect.

Do research and find out if there is anywhere that a previous Dark Lord has Risen. The Forces of Good tend not to be very efficient in following through and often leave much of a Dark Lord's domain in a salvageable state from which another Dark Lord may Rise. This is an ideal case as it saves on construction.

Mental note to self, thought Morden. Ask Grimtooth about Zoon's fortress.

Once you have your location you are going to have to Marshal your Power. You'll need an army. This may at first seem a daunting prospect but it is easier than it sounds. All you have to do is put out that you are offering a share of the entire world's wealth. Throw in sweeteners, such as the opportunity to Lay Ruin and general Mayhem, and pretty soon the greediest, most black-hearted scum of the world will be at the front door wanting in. The quality may not be all that, but you'll not be lacking in quantity.

So you have your Dark Fortress, it's all decked out and there's a growing army. All that remains for you to do is take on your Mantle of Power and you're set. No matter how tempting it may be to Come Forth before you have your Power, do not do it. Many a promising Dark Lord has Come Forth without first having gathered his full Power. This is a big mistake. Remember, the Forces of Good are almost obliged to do nothing while you are still Rising. After all, what wrong have you done? There's no law against establishing a fortress and gathering an army. But as soon as you Come Forth all bets are off. If whatever you need to assume your full Power is not in your hands at this point, then it's fair game and, in the worst case scenario, the Forces of Good will discover it and destroy it. And then it's Game Over.

The Mantle of Power sounded exciting. Morden wondered what his might be. He hoped it was some kind of staff. Staffs were good. One with a skull on the top that shot death beams would be ideal. He could hardly wait.

Your enthusiasm is good, young Morden, but let me offer a cautionary tale.

There was a promising Dark Lord who had Risen well. Despite all this he made a number of crucial mistakes after good preparation, not least of which was investing all his power in a ring, and then losing it (fool!). Such a shame. He had real promise.

So if you are going to put all your power into a staff with skulls and death beams, make sure it doesn't get stolen, and check the wood for termites.

Chapter 9   A Bad Start

Image is everything.
The Dark Lord's Handbook

Morden set the Dark Lord's Handbook down, rested his hands over the skulls that adorned the armrests of his throne, and pondered the words he had read. It was obvious that if he were to become a Dark Lord there was much work ahead. Though the Handbook had shown him in broad strokes the things he must do to successfully Rise, he instinctively knew the devil would be in the detail. He understood what must be done, but it was not clear to him exactly what the first step should be.

Maybe it was because he was comfortable with life as it was. His throne room in the Bindelburg School for Young Masters and Prospective Brewers was quiet. His minions were abroad in the town, leaving him to mull over these weighty matters. He wished Grimtooth were here so he might question him further. Though the Handbook was a bottomless well of information about Dark Lords, it was still a book. He couldn't talk to it (at least not out loud) and it didn't have the comforting presence that Grimtooth somehow had, despite his terrifying orcish demeanour. Grimtooth had intimated he would be gone for weeks and eventually send word. Was he supposed to stay in Bindelburg, or was he meant to head east towards Zoon the Reviled's ruined empire, which seemed the best bet for his own Rising? He was not sure. Something kept him in Bindelburg. Like those delicious hours on a sweaty late summer's afternoon, when the air was thick and there was the smell of lightning in the air, and the clouds were dark with stormy promise, he could feel that something was going to happen. Something was going to give. He could almost taste it.

The door shattering off its hinges in an explosion of wood and splinters was not quite what he had been imagining, and for a second he froze. He had been so deep in thought he had heard no one approaching. The sentry boards in the floor of the corridor should have warned him.

In the doorway stood a lumpy bulk of a man with a steel hat and a bill hook. He had to squeeze himself through the splintered door frame to get into the room. A knot of smaller men followed quickly behind and formed a ring around Morden.

There seemed little point in doing much more than recomposing himself and giving the assembled soldiers the full benefit of his brooding glare. As he swept them with what he hoped was pure malevolence, some shuffled their feet, others looked away, and only the hulking brute who had busted the door open met his stare ... and winked. The toothy grin that followed made Morden shudder. He was an orc, but his teeth had been filed flat. It explained his hugely muscled frame. Having learnt what a smiling orc meant from Grimtooth, Morden couldn't help but raise a hand to his neck and gulp.

Behind the orc there was movement, and Morden sensed that someone else had come into the room behind the soldiers.

A soldier next to the brute stepped aside and a thin man, with pale skin and dark looks, stepped into the gap. He regarded Morden with what looked like a mixture of bemused interest and contempt. From the body language of all the soldiers, bar the orc, it was clear to Morden that any trepidation they may have felt concerning himself was nothing as compared to this man.

The man had a dagger in his left hand—a thin blade that looked of the highest craftsmanship. After a minute of studying Morden, he examined the nails of his right hand and started to clean them with the tip of the dagger.

"Do you know who I am?" asked the man, keeping his attention on getting the grit out from under his nails.

Morden straightened. It was show time. He slowly pushed himself up out of his throne and stood towering over the assemblage, in part due to his natural height, and in part due to the plinth he'd had made for his throne. "You are the man who will regret he ever laid eyes on me. I am a Dark Lord."

He cast his gaze around the soldiers and exerted his considerable Will. He was a Dark Lord. Who were these scum to come in here?

Some of the soldiers visibly buckled; others took a step back.

The thin man darted his eyes in Morden's direction, a faintly bored expression on his face.

"You don't say." The man stopped his manicure and slid the dagger into its scabbard. He met Morden's glare and arched an eyebrow. "I am Chidwick, personal private secretary to Chancellor Penbury. And you, lad, are in a lot of trouble."

Morden hadn't had cause to fear much in his life. When he was young his parents had given up on gruesome bedtime stories when it became apparent all they did was encourage Morden to ask a slew of questions. How exactly did an ogre get the marrow from a bone, for instance? In recent times, Grimtooth had managed to send a chill down Morden's spine merely by baring his teeth, but then he imagined there were few men who could stand a five-hundred-year-old orc's grimace.

Apart from that, there was only one name he had heard and learnt to fear: Penbury. In itself, an innocuous enough name, but behind it was a man who was rightly feared by every man who ever went into business. And Morden was very much in business. Chancellor Penbury was nominally in charge of the financial matters for King Olaf VIII, but in reality was the head of a business empire that spanned continents. It wasn't the huge empire Penbury had that inspired fear as much as his innovative business practices. Where old-school merchants may have leaned on competitors with well-placed slander or the use of hired muscle, it was Penbury who had pioneered hostile takeovers and asset stripping. His latest coup had been the acquisition and subsequent dismantling of his closest rivals, Clack and Stingbee, international purveyors of snuff and other tobacco products. Seemingly a niche business, it was also rumoured to be the international conduit for God's Dust. Headfucker, as it was known on the street, was the most powerful narcotic known to man and in huge demand.

"Trouble?" said Morden, trying hard to stop his voice breaking. "Surely my business is far too small to concern Chancellor Penbury."

"Indeed," said Chidwick. "But you've been messing with beer. And we can't have that." Chidwick waved a languid arm towards Morden. "Take him and any personal effects you find. Burn the rest."

Morden's hand went instinctively to the pendant that hung around his throat. The orc's grin widened, mistaking the gesture. Morden felt panic rise, tightening his chest. The massive orc spread his arms and advanced on him like he was a rooster about to bolt. But there was nowhere to go. He was trapped.

"I don't suppose we could come to some kind of understanding, could we?" he managed.

Chidwick turned. His eyes narrowed and he stepped back to Morden. His hand went to Morden's pendant. "Let it go," ordered Chidwick, and Morden let the chain hang. Chidwick raised the pendant and examined it. Was that a glint of recognition in Chidwick's eyes? Chidwick let it drop and spun around. "Burn it all. Quickly."

Chidwick's men produced oil cans and sloshed the liquid around liberally. Some surreptitiously pocketed various knick-knacks before they became doused. The air grew thick with fumes and Morden found it increasingly hard to breathe, made harder when the orc wrapped his knotted arms around him and lifted him clean off his feet. The orc slung him over his shoulder to carry him out of the room. There seemed little point in struggling. Morden watched the soldiers efficiently strip and douse his empire.

"Anyone got a light?" asked one soldier.

"Didn't you bring one, Gunther?"

"Not me. I quit two weeks ago. The missus made me."

"I've got one. Just a sec."

The last thing Morden saw of his throne room was a lick of flame that quickly spread and engulfed his throne. It looked like a plaything now, burning fiercely. The soldiers beat a hasty retreat as the flames caught and they were all soon outside. Morden could see Chidwick talking to Brother Limpole, who was shaking his head somewhat dispiritedly. Brother Limpole had been one of Morden's closest friends among the Brothers; a borderline alcoholic, he had always been happy to take back-handers and look the other way. Morden would miss him.

While Chidwick settled whatever business he had with the Brothers —Morden's sharp eye caught sight of a purse, and what he suspected was a bottle of Krinth spirit, pass from Chidwick to Limpole—the soldiers loaded a cart with swag. Then Morden was rather unceremoniously thrown on top. He landed badly, his knee banging against a barrel of yeast. A yelp of pain escaped his lips. They hadn't bound him—he guessed there was little point as there was nowhere to run—so he pushed and tugged the pile of bits and bobs in an attempt to make a comfortable seat.

"Sorry."

Morden looked up to see the orc standing watch over him. The soldiers had formed up behind the cart and were paying him little interest; the scrabble of the town's fire militia and the burning brewery were far more interesting.

"Sorry?" enquired Morden of the orc. "Are you talking to me?"

"I'm sorry if I hurt you when I threw you on the cart," said the orc, "but I've got a job to do."

For an orc built like a terrace of houses, it was an odd comment. "You're an orc, aren't you?" said Morden.

This seemed to startle the orc. He looked back over his shoulder and then leaned forward somewhat conspiratorially.

"Shhh," hissed the orc. "Don't say anything or you might blow my cover."

It was Morden's turn to be startled. An undercover orc?

"You're kidding." Morden hadn't heard something so ridiculous since—well, since he had found out he was a Dark Lord in the making.

"Keep it down," whispered the orc, bringing a fat finger to his overly large mouth.

"But ..."

"But what?"

"Well, look at you."

"What about me?"

"How many men have tree trunk legs and look like they've been hit square in the face with a plank?"

"I tell them I'm a big-boned giant."

"What about the green skin? You think they believe you?"

"I broke the legs of the last man to call me an orc, so yes, I think they believe me."

"So they don't call you an orc any more?"

"No."

"Well, that's a great cover."

The orc's eyes narrowed. "Don't get all sarcastic on me now. I don't like sarcastic. I may be an orc, but don't confuse that with being stupid."

"I wouldn't dream ..."

"Right then. Best be quiet for now."

The orc straightened himself and cuffed Morden round the ear. It was like being swatted by an oak branch.

"Ow!" screamed Morden.

"Trouble, Private Stonearm?" Chidwick had materialised next to the orc.

"Just showing the prisoner who's boss, Boss," said the orc, stiffening to attention.

"Very good. Carry on." Chidwick stalked around the side of the cart and climbed up next to the driver.

"Did you have to hit me so hard?" growled Morden in a low whisper.

Stonearm considered the question for a few seconds. "Yes. I reckon I did."

With a gee-up from the driver, the cart jerked forward and began to judder along the cobbled road. Everything in the back, including Morden, rattled around. Stonearm kept an easy pace a few yards from the back of the cart and the dozen or so men marched in rank behind him. It struck Morden that it must have made an odd procession to any passers-by, but those he saw seemed to studiously ignore Chidwick on his cart.

With his ears still ringing from the slap he'd received, Morden decided there was little he could do right now. He tried to make himself as comfortable as he could and began to sulk.

He'd lost everything. Looking back to the monastery, he could see a thick plume of smoke rising from where his little empire had been centred. In the grand scheme it hadn't been much, but it was his. It had taken years to get to where he had and now it was all gone. He had nothing to his name.

Well, almost nothing. Tucked under his black robe was the comforting bulk of the Handbook. Until now, he'd been happy with the notion of being a Dark Lord, but had been lacking in motivation. He had needed a spark to set his fire and now Chancellor Penbury had both figuratively and literally set that spark. He was a Dark Lord with a purpose. Penbury would pay. And if that meant the world coughed up at the same time, then so be it.

Chapter 10   An Orcish Escape

Your minions willingly give their lives for you.
Don't disappoint them.
The Dark Lord's Handbook

The cart rattled and rumbled its way for what seemed like forever, but in fact was until sundown. Bindelburg had been left well behind and they had travelled south towards the coast. Morden didn't know much about Penbury, but what he did know was Penbury preferred the warmer climates and he spent much of his time in Firena, the second city of the Kingdom of Byzan, that Olaf VIII ruled over. Based on that, he guessed they were heading south to Firena.

When they had left town, Morden had realised that he had not been out of Bindelburg for two years. Rather than go home to visit his parents, they had come to see him and shop. He had, therefore, no reason to leave the city. He liked the variety of sights, smells and people. Countryside was dull. And it played havoc with his sinuses. Although, with winter settled in for the duration, his sinuses were one concern he didn't have to worry about. Instead he was freezing. His robe was wool, but the cold seeped in and took root in his bones. He tried to take his mind off it by concentrating on his surroundings, but all that consisted of was stark tree lines, ragged copses, wonkily ploughed fields, and crows.

Ah, the crows. In Bindelburg he had almost forgotten them. Their cawing had been washed over by the noise of the city. But out here there was no escaping the bloody things. It wasn't long before others noticed and were cursing them as well. Caw. Caw. Caw. They wouldn't shut up. One soldier tried his luck with a crossbow but all that did was turn up the volume, as though they were mocking his effort.

Fortunately, by the time Chidwick had called a halt at a wayside inn, the crows had gone; perhaps they needed a rest from all that racket.

By its looks, The Fat Goose promised both warmth and good food, but Morden's hopes were dashed when he was bound and thrown in a barn with a guard set on the door. An hour later he was untied briefly to eat slops off a plate before being rebound. The ropes chaffed his wrists and ankles, and the straw tickled his nose into fits of sneezing. It had been cold during the day but now that the little warmth the sun had offered was gone, it was freezing.

Morden was confused with what was going on. Chidwick treated him like a sack and showed little interest other than to ensure he was secure and not about to run off. Surely Chidwick hadn't been interested in Morden's business interests. What he said about the beer must have been a diversion. If not, did that mean he knew about Morden's destiny? But the Handbook had said that while Morden was Rising the Forces of Good would be impotent until he was ready. On the other hand, it felt quite a presumption that he was indeed Rising—trussed like a turkey in a barn he didn't feel remotely Dark Lord-like.

The line of flawless logic that followed sent an unfamiliar shiver through Morden. Was that fear? If Chidwick knew he was a Dark Lord in Rising and was *not* with the Forces of Good, that could only mean Morden had a rival. Was there another Dark Lord Rising? Or indeed, a Dark Lord already in place and working his evil from the shadows? It did make some kind of sense. Was Penbury a Dark Lord? The world had not seen a Dark Lord for over five hundred years. That was not to say one had not Risen but perhaps was taking a non-traditional approach to world domination through Laying Waste and Pillaging, etc. It was worth considering and, as such, presented Morden with quite a worry.

Morden needed an ally but the only candidate, Stonearm, was being equally enigmatic. He'd marched all day not ten feet behind Morden and made no attempt to communicate or reassure. Morden had tried to engage the orc in conversation a few times, but had been silenced by a grin. If the orc didn't want to talk then Morden figured he'd best keep quiet. Still, he did wonder what all this fanciful talk of being undercover was about. Undercover for whom, and for what purpose? It was hardly a masterpiece of covert insertion, placing a seven-foot orc built like a buttress into a guard of men on a grab mission.

Morden fell into fitful bouts of sleep; tiredness kept closing his eyes and the cold kept opening them. A noise at the barn door brought him fully awake. Someone was giving orders and it sounded like his guards were grumbling. The barn doors were pushed open but instead of

Chidwick, as Morden had expected, Stonearm tramped into the barn. Two guards were standing at the door holding torches, obviously not stupid enough to come into a barn full of dry hay with fire in their hands.

Stonearm reached him and hauled him to his feet. "The boss wants to see you," he said in what seemed an unnecessarily loud manner; followed quickly by a whispered, "I'm getting us out of here."

If Morden hadn't been so cold and tired, or bound at the ankles and wrists, or had the slightest confidence in a seven-foot orc's ability to muster any kind of plan, he may have been excited.

"Do you think that's a good idea?" hissed Morden under his breath.

Stonearm's answer was to push him forward. Morden teetered like a marionette, the rope biting into his ankles.

"Less of your lip," said Stonearm, again with theatrical loudness.

Great, thought Morden, *an orc who does pantomime.*

Morden almost fell as he passed between the two guards at the door, as much from the shock of the cold air as the second shove in the back from Stonearm. He had thought the barn was cold but, in truth, it had been warm compared to the bitterness outside. The air stung his lungs as he breathed.

From behind him there was a crack which reminded him of a coconut shy at the last summer fair. There followed a thump, like a sack falling off a cart, a strangled exclamation of surprise, another crack, and finally another sack-like thump.

"Will you untie me now?" said Morden, not bothering to turn round. He didn't need to see the two guards in a heap to know that Stonearm had lived up to his moniker.

"That can wait," said Stonearm from behind him.

Morden was about to protest but faltered when he was hauled off his feet and the wind knocked from him as he was slung over the orc's shoulder.

The two torches had fallen clear of the barn and gave Morden a flickering sight of Stonearm's work. One guard was in a pile and dead still. The other looked like he had more life in him; his head moved and he groaned. He set a hand on the hard packed earth and tried to push himself up, groaning once more.

The groan was loud enough for Stonearm to hear. The orc spun round, all the while grasping Morden over his shoulder. Morden couldn't see forward but could see the orc's legs pump into action. Stonearm covered the short distance to the guard in a stride or two; one leg came back slightly higher as the other planted itself, and swung forward in a vicious arc. There was a sickening thud and the groaning stopped.

Good feet for a big orc, thought Morden.

"Here! What's going on down there?"

Morden twisted his neck to look toward the inn. At an upper story window a man was leaning out with a candle held aloft. He was wearing a white night vest that shone in the moonlight, and a bent-over nightcap.

"Nothing to see," said Stonearm gruffly.

"What's up with them two?" enquired the man.

"They was asleep on duty," said Stonearm.

"What's that you got on your shoulder?"

"Nothing."

"That ain't nothing. I'm not blind, you know."

"Nothing to see. Go about your business. There's a good man," said Stonearm, adopting an official tone.

"Don't you think we ought to be leaving?" whispered Morden.

"You stay there. I'm coming down," said the man at the window.

"I think you could be right," said Stonearm.

"You could throw those torches in the barn first, though," said Morden.

"But that would set the barn on fire."

Morden sighed.

"Clever," said Stonearm. "A diversion. I get it."

From his backward-facing vantage point, for the second time that day, Morden watched a building go up in flames as he was hauled away from it. He wasn't sure which was more uncomfortable, the cart and its rickety wheels, or the knotted muscles that arranged themselves over Stonearm's frame.

There was quite a commotion behind them as the orc settled into a surprisingly quick gait. The fire had taken hold and Morden could see people scurrying around. Morden wondered which one was Chidwick and how long he would take to get a pursuit going.

They had made a mile in what seemed a bare few minutes before the orc turned sharply and jumped the low hedge that ran along the roadside. The cow that had been lying on the other side must have been more than surprised by the sudden arrival of a huge orc carrying a not insubstantial Morden on his shoulder. There was a distressed moo and Stonearm went crashing to the ground. Fortunately the orc let go of Morden to break his fall and Morden was thrown free. *Being crushed between Stonearm and a cow would be one of the more inglorious deaths for a Dark Lord,* thought Morden as he landed face-first in what felt like soft mud but was in fact, if the smell was anything to go by, cow slurry. He was dimly aware of Stonearm's huge bulk likewise face down in the cow patties.

Morden would have said something, along the lines of looking before leaping or some such, but didn't want a mouth full of cow crap. Anyway, it could have been worse. At least they had escaped. He wasn't entirely sure what from, but was certain it was worse than being cold and covered in cow shit.

Morden pushed himself out of the muck and stood as best he could with his ankles still tied. With a groan, Stonearm likewise rose from the mud and crap like a leviathan from the deep. The cow had struggled free and began to complain loudly. Stonearm's fist lashed out and the cow's protest was brought to an abrupt end as it toppled over.

Movement from the direction of the inn caught Morden's eye. Torches were bobbing towards them. The chase had started.

Chapter 11   Second Lesson – Heroes

Heroes

As inevitable as death, when a Dark Lord Rises and Comes Forth, Heroes will oppose him. Armies will clash and great battles will be fought, but all this is naught as compared to the actions of the Hero. They are the sideshow to his main event.

You must know your enemy, Morden. Study closely.

The obvious stratagem to deal with these irksome characters is to simply kill them. Problem solved. And many a Dark Lord has tried; tried very hard indeed, but to no avail. These heroes are made of stern stuff and have the most incredible luck. Their ability to escape inescapable death should not be underestimated. From the mysterious and sudden appearance of eagles to unlooked-for armies appearing at dawn, Heroes may seem down but are never out.

That is not to say that a Dark Lord should not throw hindrances in a Hero's way. It behoves you to make every effort to put their life in peril so that, at the very least, they can expend their energy in saving their own skin rather than actively opposing you. Just be sure to send minions who are expendable. It is upsetting to send your hand-reared Cyclops to kill the Hero and later hear of his demise at the hands of the Hero who got lucky with a stray arrow.

A more considered approach is to study the character of the hero who opposes you to find a weakness you can exploit. This may not kill them but rather have them so tied up in dilemma that they are rendered impotent.

Heroes may have many virtuous qualities, but equally they tend to have many less virtuous ones as well. Both can be of use.

The virtuous Hero cannot pass by those in peril. His moral code demands he be a saviour. The Hero is so swelled by the self-centred, self-important notion that he alone can save the world that he will shoulder all the world's ills. This is to your advantage. Load those shoulders with as many worries as you can conjure. Try to make them personal. The Hero attracts lovers like dung attracts beetles. Even if by some miracle the Hero is seemingly chaste, there are always 'close' companions or family members that can be kidnapped and held ransom. The Hero will, of course, never buckle to a ransom but will try to rescue them. History shows they often succeed, but it takes time, and in the pursuit of rescuing the ones they love they will let the rest of the world be consumed.

Then there are Heroes who have the outward appearance of virtuous intent but in fact have egos almost equal to your own. (Yes, you are an egomaniac, Morden, otherwise why would you want to be a Dark Lord?) They are heroic for the rewards that being a Hero brings. They live for the adoration of the masses. Many a maiden has swooned under their blazing charisma, only to be used and cast aside for the next conquest. (There are certain so-called heroic characteristics that are shared with a Dark Lord and should be admired.)

They will humble kings with their righteousness. They will lead armies to calamity through pride and blind faith in themselves or a divine higher agency. In many respects they are no different from yourself, and you should point this out to them as often as you can manage. Catalogue their so-called qualities and liken them to your own. If you are lucky and they see they are, in fact, no better than yourself then they may become so overwhelmed with remorse that they become useless.

What is more likely is that they will get angry and claim that in fact they are nothing like you and will never be like you. An ironic laugh at this juncture is in order. (You should seek to master a range of laughter for different occasions.) Ask them to join you at your side so together you can bring peace to the world; it will infuriate them further. When they say 'Never!' point out all those who have died as a consequence of their selfishness. (If you have any kind of magical talent, or are able to commune with the dead, then shades of these fallen companions are a nice detail to throw in.)

Though Heroes may be likened to putty—to be shaped to your designs and will—there are hazards in dealing with them. Heroes tend to burn brightly but it is not generally incandescent intelligence. It's more likely their perfect set of pearly teeth, burnished armour, and wicked sword that impresses. Being one of superior intelligence there will doubtless arise the temptation to explain, in excruciating detail, exactly how clever your plan for world domination is and how they are powerless to stop you. This is tempting fate, and fate is easily tempted. The result is not pleasant and frequently results in the loss of limbs and the ability to breathe. The art of monologue is one all Dark Lords should master, but don't get carried away.

Likewise, to use a concrete example, should you be known as Morden the Merciless then be without mercy; do not leave a Hero to his fate, which appears to be certain death. Remember, when it comes to Heroes, nothing is certain, least of all death. Kill them. At least try hard to and with them in sight. Don't assume that because they have plummeted to certain death they are dead.

If you entrust a minion with killing a Hero and when they return you ask them, 'Are they dead?', and the minion answers, 'Yes', but on closer examination it turns out he was left in a pool of ravenous piranhas with a large stone tied around their ankles, he without doubt escaped. It's how it is. Kill the minion and make it clear to those present that recognisable body parts are the only acceptable proof.

There is one more approach a Dark Lord can take when it comes to Heroes and that is to try to stop them appearing in the first place. Heroes are generally only needed when there is a Dark Lord, and they are often late in appearing. This means a Dark Lord may well have the world under his dominion before a Hero rises to challenge him. (There is an interesting literary explanation for this included in Appendix B.)

Assuming the Hero will be male, killing all men is not feasible. Likewise, reading the prophecies and deciding to kill all first born sons under a certain age has met with little success. It's not specific enough. If there is a prophecy, though it is likely it is nothing more than hopeful self-fulfilling generalisations, there may be clues. Historical precedent may also be used. A surprising number of Heroes come from humble backgrounds. Often they are orphans whose parentage has been hidden. They are raised as a family's own but sooner or later the six-foot giant with flaming red hair is told by his dwarf parents that he is not their actual offspring. It comes as quite a shock.

Common professions are sheep herder or woodcutter, but the one that outstrips all others is blacksmith. Morden, if you are up against an orphan raised in the heat of a smithy by a grizzled veteran who took pity on the whelp, then trouble is at hand.

Fortunately, the uncertain parentage of an orphan is a crucial emotional scar that must be opened and used to undermine them. When he is standing before you in the final confrontation, if you happen to be his father, this is the time to reveal the fact. Even if you are not, it is worth suggesting you are anyway. It will mess with his head. It could be the start of a beautiful relationship; one that should end in his unfortunate demise.

And before you set this book aside and get some well-earned rest after a hard day fleeing Penbury's men, there is one more thing to remember about Heroes.

Even though they think they have won, they have not. A Dark Lord is never beaten. One day, you will rise again.

So sleep well, young Morden, and dream of conquests to come.

Chapter 12   A Hero in Love

Most Heroes are merely misguided romantics.
Watch out for the ones with hearts as dark as your own.
The Dark Lord's Handbook.

It was a day that belonged in poetry, and Edwin was trying his hardest to make it so. He lay under the dragging limbs of a willow at the edge of the lake, quill in hand, parchment spread and brow furrowed.

The sky was … was … was as blue as, well, it was blue. And the sun reflected off the still water as though it were off a ~~mirror~~. Off something shiny, like a mirror, but not a mirror.

This poetry was hard. Harder than the villagers of Wellow appreciated. But this wasn't for *them*. It was for *her*. Fair Griselda. How could he compare her? Unto a pretty bloom of some kind; a rose perhaps? (Too thorny.) A lily, then? (Too pale.) A petunia?

Whichever, she was flower-like in aspect and filled his nose with her sweet perfume when she passed the smithy. Except those times when she had just cleaned the privy and then she was not so sweet. But nothing could detract from her perfect frame, her silken hair, her ripe ….

Edwin shook himself. Now was not the time to be having those thoughts. He had poetry to write. He only had an hour and he would be expected back at the smithy. It was a busy time of year. The harvest was in and the farmers had soil to turn before the frosts made the ground too hard. He sometimes wished he hadn't invented the plough that was taking the region by storm and had brought custom from far afield.

It had been a fateful shopping trip to Bindelburg that had started it. He had happened across Brandock, a swordsmith. They had struck up professional conversation and Edwin had been invited along the next day to see Brandock at work. Inspired by the lamination technique, he had bought half a dozen ingots and gone home to make swords. From those he made ploughshares and the rest was history, or so he liked to think.

He glanced over to the stick he had stuck in the soft earth. The shadow from it had moved on from the line he had marked when it was placed. He estimated his hour must almost be up. He sighed and set the quill down and looked out over the lake. The muse had abandoned him. Instead, he would drink in the calm serenity of his surroundings and lose himself in the clouds that reflected so perfectly off the lake's mercurial surface.

Autumn was enjoying a reprise before winter took full hold and there were ripples here and there as trout took small insects from the water's surface. It was perhaps because of this Edwin did not notice one such ripple become more wavelike. Once he noticed, however, it made him sit up. There was something big down there, made obvious by the water that was spreading like a bow wave as whatever it was came closer to the shore where he lay.

It was odd. Odd enough for him to get up to see if he could catch sight of what might cause such a disturbance. As he did so the lake's surface was broken by an explosion of water and a brilliant sword thrust itself into the air. It cleared the water sufficiently for Edwin to see the hilt was grasped by a hand, possibly female, covered in weed. The sword was a few yards out, and not within reach unless he fancied wetting his hose. It was all quite surreal and he was left wondering what he should do.

The sword shone, water dripping down its length, bright and terrible in the sunlight. It was a thing of beauty and Edwin reached for his quill and parchment. If only he could capture in words the razor edge and reflected sunlight that spawned a thousand rainbows, he would have something to show Griselda.

The sword began to shake. The hand that held it seemed to waver, as though beckoning. The position of the sun and the fact that the water had been stirred into murky blackness made it hard to see anything beneath the wrist. Could there be someone down there?

Bubbles broke the water's surface and the hand was definitely trembling. More bubbles rose and then the hand arched back before sweeping forward and releasing the blade. The sword rose into the air, the weight of the hilt sending it into an end-over-end spin. Edwin was transfixed as it spun in slow motion towards him. At the last second, he had the good sense to step to one side and the sword buried itself in the earth where he had been standing a split second before.

From the lake there was an eruption and a great bulk rose, covered in weed; a behemoth that surely had been dwelling in the lake's depths for centuries. It spluttered and shook, sending muddy water and weed in every direction. Edwin could see more clearly now that it was no behemoth from the depths, but in fact a woman of not inconsiderable bulk. She stood up to her knees in the water and placed her hands firmly on cliff-like hips.

"Well, don't stand there gawping," she bellowed. "Help me out of here!"

Without hesitation, Edwin sprang into the lake and helped the woman out. A thousand questions rose in his mind, but they could wait until she was on dry land. Once there he took off his shirt and handed it to her so she might dry herself off.

As she did, he could see she was appraising him. He was quite used to this. It was hot in the smithy and he often worked shirtless, even with the hazard of sparks. In the past few years, it had drawn some attention from the village girls. All but Griselda. Perhaps a physique that looked like it was hewn from granite was not her thing. Maybe she didn't like a washboard stomach and a hairless chest (what hair there was tended to be singed off). He was not deterred though. He'd been told he was attractive to women often enough to believe them, though he didn't see it himself. He thought six feet and five inches was far too tall. His jaw was too square for his liking, and the grey paleness of his blue eyes was watery. He cared not for his looks, and if good looks were not Griselda's thing then perhaps his poetry and charm could win her.

Nevertheless, whoever this woman from the lake was, she was definitely giving him the eye.

"Very nice," she said at last, tossing the shirt aside. She regarded him quite openly, like he was a plough horse. Water dripped from the hem of her embroidered gown. Edwin took the quality of the cloth and workmanship as a sign she was a well-moneyed lake dweller. "You'll do," she continued. "I dare say, you're going to break a few hearts along the way, but you've definitely got the … well, you've got it."

Edwin wasn't sure how he should reply, and believing that when there was nothing definite to say then it be best left unsaid, he did just that.

"Bit quiet though. Do you know who I am?"

"A lady from the lake?" With only the facts to go on it was the best he could surmise.

"And so sweet," said the lady, smiling. "No. Well, yes. In a manner of speaking, but not exactly the Lady from the Lake, but a lady from a lake is close enough. I am the Countess of Umbria."

She pushed a hand forward with a ring on it and Edwin dropped to his knee to kiss it.

"At your service," he said, rising to his feet and bowing with a flourish in the manner he had read of in fiction, that unfortunately caught the countess in the stomach and would have put her on her bottom if she had been less substantial.

"Steady there," she said, taking a step back. "No need for all that."

"I beg your pardon."

The countess continued to look at him strangely and Edwin was at a loss. He would be late returning to work, but there were genuine extenuating circumstances, especially if he escorted the countess back to the village. But this was secondary to why she had tried to kill him by tossing the sword at him from a lake. What had he ever done to her?

"You look confused," said the countess.

"I am, yes," answered Edwin.

"Could you fetch me that?" asked the countess, waving a hand at the sword that stood embedded in the lakeside mud.

Edwin turned to do so, as though he had no choice. The aristocratic tone of the countess's voice was hard to resist. And yet, as his hand reached out to take the sword by the hilt something deep down seemed to be shouting: 'Noooo.'

Perhaps it was the voice of a poet who was never to be heard, for when Edwin's hand pulled the sword from its muddy sheath everything changed.

There was a wide plain on a baking hot day, the dust stirred by thousands of horses and feet that wheeled towards a wall of darkness rolling in from the east. Dragons rose above the darkness sweeping toward the gleaming host. A knight rode at the point of the host's vanguard, sword raised, urging his men on.

"To Glory!" Edwin mouthed the words as though he spoke them.

The Hero was at the tip of a lance of steel that thundered toward the wall of dark creatures. There was a collision that shook the ground. He could smell blood. The cries of those being hacked and hewn filled his head, and his own voice sang in ecstasy as the sword cleaved its way through the ranks of orcs and ogres and other foul creatures that writhed around him.

"Are you feeling well?"

The countess's voice seemed distant. He turned to face her, lifting the sword so it stood straight and proud in front of him.

"I am well, madam," said Edwin. "I thank you for returning my sword."

The countess arched an eyebrow. "Your sword?"

"Indeed." Edwin took a few practice swings. He had never been trained in any martial affairs, but the sword felt like it was part of him.

"I can't tell you how relieved I am to hear that," said the countess. "You must be a Hero!"

The sword urged him on. He started to move his feet and twist and turn and lunge as though he were beset by attackers.

"Jolly impressive," said the countess. "Black Orchid will be pleased."

He spun, the sword carving a vicious arc.

The countess's head left its body with a mild look of surprise and plopped into the lake, where it bobbed for a second before sinking. The torso sprayed a fountain of blood before toppling slowly backwards.

Blood ran down the length of the blade and Edwin could feel hot stickiness on his face and chest. And it felt good. It was unfortunate about the countess but it had been an accident, and accidents do happen. He cleaned the blade with his wet shirt and then rolled the countess's body back into the lake from whence it had come. He then washed himself off and, apart from the red stain on the grass, there was no sign that anything had happened.

Edwin picked up his parchment and quill and threw them in the lake. He wouldn't be needing those any more. Poetry? What had he been thinking? He had to take what he wanted—and Griselda would be taken.

Chapter 13   Birth Right

There is no retirement plan for a Dark Lord.
The Dark Lord's Handbook.

Morden woke. It was cold and a rock was sticking into his back where he had rolled over in the night. But that wasn't the only discomfort. There was something else, in his head, like he ought to know something but didn't. It was as if the world had changed. As he tried to catch the thought, his discomfort grew and his pendant started to feel warm against his chest. That only happened when he was in danger, and that was one thing he had become all too familiar with in the last week.

Stonearm was still asleep, his massive bulk a heap across the cave entrance. Morden crawled over to him. He shook the orc gently and then ducked. Stonearm's fist swung instinctively back to where Morden's head had been a moment before. Morden's eye was still tender from the lesson he had learnt the first time he had woken the giant.

Stonearm sat up sharply and cracked his head on the low cave entrance, dislodging a stalactite. Morden winced but Stonearm seemed not to have noticed.

"What? Eh?" asked Stonearm, looking around.

"Quiet," said Morden. "I think they found us."

Stonearm sniffed the air. "You sure?"

Morden had grown to trust the orc's nose. It was an odd trait, but Stonearm seemed to have a nose that would put a wolf to shame.

"Well, something's not right."

The look Stonearm gave Morden showed the orc had as much respect for Morden's instincts as Morden had for the orc's nose.

"I'll take a look," said the orc, and he slid from the cave with surprising stealth for a creature so large.

They had been on the run for what seemed an age but had only been a week. Then they had come across the river Loos and lost their pursuers by riding a tree Stonearm felled with a body charge. Morden was not a good swimmer, never having needed to learn, so he had gripped the trunk like his life had depended on it. The two of them had spent a day riding the torrent—the rain that had kept them soaked for the previous few days being of some use after all—until they had washed up on a gravel spit, hungry and exhausted.

Morden hoped the churning in his gut was more of that hunger, though that was unlikely; Stonearm had killed a deer with a well-aimed stone the night before and a roasted haunch had been their supper. The more Morden focused on the thing that was bothering him, the more it felt different from his normal sense of danger. The skin on his chest itched, which was normal, but there was also a curious sensation between his shoulder blades. The cave was suddenly claustrophobic and Morden scrabbled out after the orc.

For a second, he expected an arrow to come out of the trees, but all was quiet. The river had taken them east into lightly wooded farmlands of the Lower Loos region. This was the food basket of the port city of Bostokov, which was the place they had agreed on getting to next. The city was vast and Stonearm said he had many kinsmen there. Grimtooth may even be there, and that had settled it for Morden.

Morden listened intently but, apart from normal woodland sounds, he heard nothing, not even Stonearm until the orc broke wind loudly from behind him.

"Hush," hissed Morden. "They might hear us."

"There's no one out there," said Stonearm. He broke wind again as though to reinforce the point.

Morden suspected the orc was right.

They cleared up as much as they could and headed east. Now that food was not a problem they could move quickly without having to forage. The undergrowth was sparse under a thick woodland canopy, so the going was easy enough. Even when it thickened Stonearm ploughed his way through and Morden followed in his wake. They were leaving a track a blind man could follow but after an hour Morden was convinced there was no pursuit and speed was more important.

With Stonearm taking the lead, and not being one to chat, Morden had time to reflect on the big orc. His size and outwardly stupid demeanour had turned out not to reflect the orc's true nature. He was brutal, direct, and uncompromising, but also cleverer than he let on and as steadfast a companion as Morden could hope for. And he could cook.

Morden hadn't expected the woods to go on as long as they did. He was wondering if they had gone wrong and in fact were circling when Stonearm stopped suddenly and raised a fist in warning. Fortunately they were in good cover. Morden leaned around the broad shoulders of the orc to see what had stopped them. There was a gentle bank and two mules dragged a covered wagon along the top. A bearded man sat on the wagon paying more attention to the contents of his nose than the road or mules.

This was the first person they had seen for two days. Morden had the urge to come out of hiding to speak to the man but, as if Stonearm could read his mind, the orc held an arm out to one side to block Morden as he shuffled forward.

The wagon was level with them when the trap was sprung. On either side of the road the bushes rose up. An arrow embedded itself between the wagon rider's legs. Someone grabbed the halter of each mule and a commanding voice cried out:

"Ho there. Stand!"

The man on the cart dropped the reigns and put his hands up. "Don't shoot!"

The wagon was quickly surrounded and two figures went to the flaps at the back. From the body language they seemed relaxed, as though the job were done. Maybe if they had paid more attention they would have had a chance to dodge the sword thrusts that came from the flaps and took each of them in the throat. There were shouts and the sound of hoof beats. From out of the back of the wagon came mail-covered soldiers and riders thundered down the bridleway from either direction.

"We've been rumbled!" shouted one of the bandits.

Steel was drawn and a melee ensued.

Morden's dragon necklace gained heat under his shirt. "We'd best be off," said Morden. He was sure they were far enough away not to be heard above the sound of battle, but he didn't want to take any risks.

The two of them turned and walked straight into the points of three swords.

"Going somewhere?" said one of the men.

Morden could see Stonearm tensing.

"Lin'chzk," said Morden. He was fairly sure it meant 'Now is not the time' in orcish but as it had come unbidden to him he couldn't be sure. He hoped it didn't mean 'Attack!'.

Stonearm remained tense for a second and then relaxed.

They let themselves be led up to the road. The fight had been brief and the blood on the rutted track was testimony to the cost to the would-be bandits. Three lay dead, and one guard, and another eight were kneeling, heads bowed before a plated knight.

Now that they were closer, Morden was shocked to see the familiar features of orcs among the dead. Stonearm must have seen as well, since Morden could see the orc's muscles bunch once more. But there was little they could do. They were pushed to their knees next to the bandits and their heads forced to the floor.

"Found these skulking," said the footman who had supervised their capture.

The heavy tread of sabatons passed along the line. Morden could feel steel at his neck keeping his head down. Polished metal and chain boots passed one way before returning along the line. The armoured toes stopped and spun in place to face Morden.

"What have we got here, then?"

A gauntlet tucked under Morden's chin raised his face. The man with the sword in his neck was not quick enough and Morden felt a stab of pain. His amulet burned as hot as it ever had and the itch in his shoulder blades became a searing pain.

He looked up into the face of a man he guessed had seen more than a few skirmishes. He must have been about forty or so—old by any standards—and had a face that looked like it had been through a mangle with razorblades on it. Scars crisscrossed his face like skate tracks on a pond in winter; he looked every inch the grizzled captain. Morden's hand went instinctively to his chest.

The captain looked at him with evident curiosity. "A man with orc bandits? How odd. What's your name, boy?"

Morden was stung by the question. He was a boy no longer, but a Dark Lord. Or so he thought. The entire notion of him being a Dark Lord seemed ludicrous now.

"Morden," he answered as defiantly as he could manage.

"What's that you're grasping at?"

The man's hand dropped from under Morden's chin to the chain around his neck, from which his dragon amulet hung. He tugged it but it held.

"I wouldn't do that," said Morden. He was as surprised with himself as the captain appeared to be.

"Why, you impudent cur," said the captain. His fist swung and Morden's head snapped sideways with the force of it. The taste of blood filled his mouth. The captain took a firmer grip on the chain and pulled hard. The links gave and he held the pendant in front of him. The miniature golden dragon shone in the sunlight.

Off to Morden's left a crow cawed.

Morden felt like he had lost a part of himself and then, slowly at first, but then like a burning torrent, pain spread from his chest and engulfed his body. His skin felt like it was tearing and swelling. There was enormous pressure and he fell forward. His clothes began to smoulder. He writhed in agony and screamed. The guards and captain stepped away from him, and likewise the bandits; even Stonearm tried to inch away from him.

Then something inside him let go and his body was no longer his own. His robe tore as his whole body grew, his limbs lengthened and his hands clenched as his fingers became talons. He looked in wonder as his skin turned black and scaled. From between his shoulders he felt something burst free and he felt like he had grown two extra arms.

Suddenly he exploded in size. His body popped into a new shape, one much bigger than his manly form. New senses filled his head. He could smell fear, hear a dozen terrified heartbeats, see the individual hairs rising on the necks of the men who cowered and then turned and fled. He drew in a breath and exhaled after them. A gush of fire rolled out and caught the fleeing men-at-arms, engulfing them in flame. They became burning, screaming marionettes.

Morden was at once amazed and horrified and pleased.

He towered over those who had remained frozen in place. The captain had his sword drawn and was taking slow steps backwards. The orc bandits grovelled in the dirt. Only Stonearm seemed unafraid. He had got to his feet and looked at Morden with a mixture of delight and pride.

Morden focused his attention back on the captain. "I did warn you," he said. It was strange to hear his own voice in this form, it being so deep and terrifying even to him.

"Take it. Here. Please," said the captain, throwing Morden's pendant on the ground.

Morden's talons were far too large to pick up the pendant. "Would you fetch that for me please, Stonearm?" asked Morden, keeping his stare firmly on the captain.

His inclination was to roast the man, but it occurred to him that if he were to be taken seriously as a Dark Lord then some advertising would come in handy, and a man of standing such as the captain would be better believed than the rank and file.

"I'm going to let you live, Captain, but for one reason only, and that is to spread the word. There is a Dark Lord Rising."

A mixture of relief, confusion and fear played across the man's scarred face. "Let me live? Thank you. Thank you." And then as the full impact of what Morden had said sunk in, "Dark Lord? Rising? But you're a dragon."

Morden sighed inwardly and shifted and became a man. He wasn't sure quite how, it was instinctive, like breathing. Though man-shaped once again, he kept his skin black and armoured. He didn't want to tempt fate if there was a man with a bow hidden somewhere. It also served to disguise his complete state of undress.

"Better?"

The captain could only grunt a reply.

"Shoo, now," said Morden, and he gave the man an encouraging glare.

Clearly astonished that he wasn't being turned into a pot roast, the captain gave a weak smile and fled. Those of his men who remained ran after him. As Morden watched them go he was dimly aware of his giant orc companion coming to his side.

"This is yours, my lord," said Stonearm, holding out the pendant.

Morden turned to look at his friend. His first thought was to tell the big lump there was no need to address him as lord, and was about to do so, when he understood something for the first time. He was going to be a Dark Lord and, no matter what, things would never be the same again.

He took the chain and passed it round his neck. With the strength he now realised he had, he squeezed the broken link closed and let the pendant hang.

Stonearm coughed and his eyes turned to the sky. The surviving orc bandits who had been sneaking a peek at him from their prostrate positions buried their faces back in the dirt.

"What?" said Morden. There was a gust of wind and Morden realised he was stark naked and pinky white once more. He snatched up one of the bigger pieces of the robe he had torn and wrapped it around his midriff. Grabbing the Handbook from where it had fallen, he scurried to the back of the wagon.

"Sort these men ... orcs ... out, Stonearm. I'll be in the wagon."

As he scrambled into the back of the wagon, Morden could hear Stonearm bark out orders and organise the surviving orc bandits. It took a second for his eyes to adjust to the dimness of the wagon. There were no trade goods, just bows, arrows, cooking gear, hard tack and cold meats, a barrel of beer—which by the smell was not up to the Brothers' standards—and not much else.

A huge fist thrust in through the back flap. It held an assortment of clothes, mostly clean but with the odd splash of blood.

"I thought these might be useful," said Stonearm from outside.

The fist released the clothes and the barking commands resumed. Morden got dressed as fast as he could and sat to gather his thoughts. What to do now? So far he'd lost everything, been kidnapped, escaped, been captured, turned into a dragon, escaped again. It was hardly what he'd been expecting. Where was the vast army and towering obsidian spires of his mountain fortress? He felt at a complete loss.

His eyes drifted to where he had put down the Handbook.

Well, it couldn't hurt, he thought, picking the Handbook up and flicking open the cover.

Chapter 14   Third Lesson – Hard Work

On Being a Dark Lord

Being a Dark Lord is no easy thing, Morden. Often people get in to the Dark Lord business because they think it an easy ride with nothing but conquests (of every type), loot, snappy clothes and fortresses. Well, if that's what you think it's all about then do yourself a favour and go do something else, like mugging.

Being a Dark Lord is a hard road to travel down. It's one where you are constantly swimming upstream. There's always another mountain to climb. You'll feel like you're pissing in the wind; struggling to keep your head above water.

No tired metaphor quite manages to convey just how hard it is being a Dark Lord.

You're not appreciated at all. People raise armies against you. They go out of their way to slander you and tell lies about your personal life that involve farmyard animals. They'll try to destroy your armies and bring your fortress crashing down. After all the hard work, it's so inconsiderate.

Even those who work for you are never happy. They always want more. There's not enough blood in the world for some.

So why bother, you may ask?

Indeed, thought Morden. If the book was trying to put him off the idea of being a Dark Lord, it was doing a good job.

Enough of that thinking, Morden. The fact is you don't have a choice. It's like asking a bird why it flies. You are a Dark Lord. It's what you do. Period. There are times it will seem like a poor career choice, but then you'll realise it wasn't a choice in the first place. You were born to rule; born to conquer; born to wear black clothing and terrify all those around you.

So you are a Dark Lord. Get used to it. The only real questions to ask yourself are: How do I be the best Dark Lord this miserable world has ever seen? How can I forge a legacy that will last forever? Shall I go down in history as a death bringer or a privy cleaner?

And once your resolve is set, don't doubt. Don't stop believing. Pull on that black robe and show the world who is The Boss. It's there for the taking.

Have faith, young Morden.

Chapter 15   Bad News

Everything comes from Power.
The Dark Lord's Handbook

One of the distinct advantages of being the wealthiest man alive, or for that matter who had ever lived, was that Chancellor Penbury could live where he pleased, and in choosing Firena he was able to indulge his two greatest loves: food and gardening. Firena was placed on the busiest land and sea route in the known world, and accordingly everything that was of any value eventually passed through. It meant nothing of gastronomic or floral interest escaped him.

Additionally, the weather was good all year round—a fact attested to by the pleasant sunshine that warmed the flowerbeds he was currently weeding. It was an activity he enjoyed for a number of reasons. Foremost, it wasn't often he got his hands dirty—in a literal sense—and the feel of earth on his fingers was a pleasure he found hard to explain. There was also a certain meditative quality to weeding. It was not as though it required his gargantuan intellect to perform, yet it did require attention to the finest detail. A weed could not just be plucked but had to be dug out, its deepest root removed to prevent its return. The chancellor was more than pleased when leading guests through his garden they would remark on how his flower beds were perfectly clear of any weed or blemish. This was compounded when they were genuinely surprised that he attended to the weeding himself.

This attention to detail extended to all areas, and so when Chidwick slid into the garden the chancellor knew what he was going to be told before the unfortunate man said a word. The dirt on Chidwick's boots told him he had not changed but come straight to him. It meant he had important news. The grosser elements of body language were well hidden—Chidwick was a master of many arts—but Penbury was also a master and he noticed the slightest departure from normal behaviour. In this case, Chidwick blinked as the chancellor caught his eye, and

Chidwick never blinked.

It gave the chancellor the head start he needed, so while Chidwick gave his news and filled out the details, he was racing ahead. It had been pure chance that Chidwick had gone to pick up this lad, Morden, to squash his beer enterprise, only to find something potentially more serious. Chidwick was well versed in the danger signs: black robes, skulls, thrones, brooding stares, minions and so on.

Much like messiahs, pyramid schemes and eat-anything diet plans, in the chancellor's experience, a Dark Lord Rising was not something to be too concerned about but deserved attention nevertheless. There hadn't been one for five hundred years, and for good reason. At the merest mention of one making an appearance they had been snuffed out by the chancellor and his predecessors. Amusingly, without fail, the so-called Dark Lords met their fate protesting that it wasn't fair. 'Whatever happened to following the rules?' they asked as they were dragged off. In the archives there was even mention of a school for Dark Lords, where promising defilers and bringers of death had been nurtured. Burningham, the chancellor of the time, had shut them down with a health inspection and locked up the leaders for failure to register an educational establishment. It was all quite pathetic.

From Chidwick's description, and Morden's escape, there was a good chance this lad was indeed a prospective Dark Lord. Chidwick had done well to spot the dragon pendant and recognise its import, and done even better to leave it well alone. It was obvious the boy had no real idea what he was or what was going on. The chancellor approved of the hands-off approach Chidwick had taken. Something as explosive as this Morden had to be handled with care.

Outwardly, though, the chancellor presented a gruffer demeanour. He tutted, furrowed his brow and pursed his lips as Chidwick's report came to an end.

"I am disappointed in you, Chidwick," said the chancellor. "Most disappointed."

The words had their intended effect and for a second Penbury thought he was going to have to leap on the man to stop him killing himself. And that would not do; it was hard to find good help these days.

"If you'd be so good as to give me a second crack at him, I'll not make the same mistake again," said Chidwick.

The chancellor barely acknowledged his secretary's plea; his mind was still racing. There was something else here. Not quite sure how he knew, but increasingly certain, he thought this Morden was maybe the real deal.

A hunch was not enough though. Hunches were for the lucky and the stupid, and Penbury didn't believe in luck. That left the latter, and he was not stupid. He needed more information. His private archives, which held the distilled wisdom of all the Chancellors, would furnish some, but Chidwick was going to have to play his part.

"Chidwick."

"Sir?"

"I think we're going to need some help."

"Sir?"

"Accountants, Chidwick. Accountants. Get me accountants. Lots of accountants."

"Ah, yes. *Accountants*. The Dark Deliverers or The Black Hand?"

"What are you on about, man? I want accountants."

"I'm sorry, sir, I thought you were speaking euphemistically."

"Stenhauer, Berf and Strom should do. They have offices all over."

"Right you are, sir. Anything else?"

Penbury thought for a second. "Yes. One other thing."

"Sir?"

"Some of those *lawyers*. Good ones."

"Bentwhistle and Pearson?" suggested Chidwick.

"Not normal lawyers, Chidwick," said Penbury sternly. "Chancellors don't employ thieves."

Chidwick coughed. "I understand. You want *lawyers*. *Lawyers* that kill people. Got it."

"I see we are on the same page again. Good. Not that I ever said anything about their professional practices."

"Of course not, sir."

The two stood for a second. Chidwick looked a lot happier and expectant.

"That's all, Chidwick." Penbury watched his PPS slide away. He was pretty certain he was chuckling.

There was little else he could do now—the archive research could wait—and so Penbury turned back to weeding. Two small green leaves, like a two-headed clover, caught his eye. His weeding fork stabbed down and lifted. The earth rose and tiny white roots were exposed. With a deft pluck the chancellor pulled the weed and tossed it onto the pile in his barrow.

Chapter 16   Love Lost

Place a barrier around your heart
lest it be ripped from your body.
The Dark Lord's Handbook

A chill woke Edwin. At first he thought it was the same chill that woke
him most mornings, the chill of fear from the dreams—the terrible
dreams that came relentlessly. They had started as the odd nightmare,
but now they came every night, and though the small details changed,
they were all terrifyingly similar. There was always a woman, his
woman. Sometimes she was blonde, other times dark haired, tall, short,
buxom, lithe, but always bewitching. He was a slave to her and he had
lost her. She had been kidnapped. The man in black had taken her. He
had seduced her and now she was his, draped over his arm. The man in
black laughed at Edwin. He stood on a dark stair before his throne with
Edwin at his feet and he gloated. And the woman laughed with him. The
laughter burned Edwin. It ran through him like a fire that made his love
turn to hatred. The laughter grew until he could take it no more.

In his dream, Edwin would rise and his sword would be in his hand,
where a moment before it had been empty. The steel would sing as he
strode up the stair, calling for blood, and he would feed it. When it was
done he would collapse in horror. The sated blade would be quiet and he
would toss it aside, sending it clattering down the stair. Lifting up the
bloodied remains of the woman he loved he would turn and face the host
that was arranged around. As he lifted the corpse they would roar.

He was their lord.

The cold sweat on his back made him shudder. He realised the sheet
had slipped from him and he reached back to pull Griselda close to warm
him. She was always stealing the blankets, but that was all right. He
would give up anything for her.

His hand met empty space. From the corner of the room he thought
he could hear a sound, like a sharpening stone running down a blade.

He jerked around and saw the empty bed. The sheet was tied around the bedstead and hanging out of the open window. The grey light of dawn was creeping in. There was another light as well. As his anger grew, so did the light. In the corner of the room his sword was singing and emitting a baleful glow.

She was gone. She had left him.

No.

She had not left him. He loved her. She loved him.

She had been stolen from him.

The man in black had stolen her.

He looked east as the dawn ushered in the day and he knew where he would find her.

"Griselda!" he bellowed. Sliding from the bed, he sank to his knees. "Griselda!" His arms stretched heavenward. "GRISELDA!"

There was a loud thump and the wooden wall of his bedroom shook. "Edwin! Keep it down in there. I'm trying to sleep."

The sound of his grandfather's voice was like a bucket of cold water on the raging emotions coursing through him. His love was gone and his life was empty without her. She was his destiny and he hers. He would travel to the ends of the earth, face any danger, kill anyone who kept her from him, to hold her in his arms again.

He put on his travel clothes and stuffed a spare pair of breeches in a bag. He took the sword and slung it at his hip in the scabbard he had made. He paused on the way out. He took a last look at the room that had been his and, for the last few weeks, Griselda's. The bed may have been short and lumpy, and he was never one for adornments and decoration, but this had been his world. He looked over to the small dresser he had bought Griselda. Her brush still lay on it, strands of her hair caught in its teeth. He strode over and plucked at the hair. He held it to his nose so he could smell her, then he slipped it into his jacket pocket. It was all he had left of her, but it would keep him going.

There was just one more thing he needed, and that was in the smithy.

He crept downstairs and through the kitchen to the side door. There was enough light now to guide him to his lockbox at the back. From it he took a wrapped bundle. He had been working on it for two weeks. It was to be the first part of a set, but for now the breastplate was the only armour he had. If it was peril he faced then he would need something that would turn a blade. He removed the wrap to look on it before he packed it. Even in the dawn light it was bright. He had used the ingots he used to make ploughs. There had been no design to work from but somehow he knew from the start how to make it. He knew which parts to turn so they may catch or deflect attacks and where to put the fasteners for the chain he would one day wear underneath. It was light, at least to him, but he also knew it was strong. He made ploughs that lasted season upon season; this breastplate would last him a lifetime.

He was putting it back in its cover when he heard movement behind him. He spun and drew in a fluid movement, the sword singing from its scabbard.

"Edwin!" squeaked his grandfather, eyes wide and body stiff, daring not to move.

"Grampa," said Edwin, lowering the blade's tip from his guardian's throat.

His grandfather's eyes moved from his ward to the pack on the ground. "So you're leaving?"

"Griselda has been abducted and I intend to rescue her and make those who took her pay."

"Abducted, you say?" His grandfather scratched at his grey bristles. "You're sure about that?"

Edwin began to wrap the armour back up. What was the old man suggesting? "Of course. They sneaked in and spirited her away before dawn when I was in deepest sleep. It was a cunning plan."

"Sneaked in, you say?" said his grandfather. He made a sucking sound through the gap in his front teeth. "You know how light I sleep, Edwin. A mouse would wake me. I heard nothing on the stair."

Edwin glared at his grandfather and stood, slinging the pack across his shoulder. "She has been abducted."

"Right you are. Abducted," said his grandfather, nodding. "He must have climbed down the sheet with her over his shoulder." His grandfather's eyes drifted over to where the knotted sheets came to the ground at the front of the house. "This abductor, whoever he may be, must be a strong lad."

"Are you trying to suggest otherwise?" asked Edwin, taking a step forward.

"No, no, son. Just saying he must be quite a strapping lad. Let's be fair, Griselda does like her food."

There was some truth in what his grandfather was saying. Griselda was a full figured woman, with generous curves.

Edwin laughed. It was so simple. "The sheet is a mere ruse, to make it look like she ran off so I may not pursue. She is in peril and I will come to her aid."

Edwin dropped his pack, strode to his grandfather and wrapped him in his arms. "I must go, but know this: I will be back. You have been good to me, grandfather, and I will not leave you to die alone in the cold of winter with no one to care."

"Thanks, son," whispered his grandfather.

Edwin squeezed the man who had raised him and taught him everything he knew. Besides Griselda, he was the one person for whom he had any feelings. He could feel a tear come to his eye. He hugged his grandfather as the emotions swelled inside him. Edwin pressed his grandfather's face to his shoulder. The old man patted his back. Part of him didn't want to let go. Even as his grandfather began to struggle in his arms and make an odd squeaking sound, Edwin could only squeeze more love into him. He would rescue Griselda and return to have children, and look after Grampa. And everything would be wonderful.

With one last hug, Edwin let his grandfather go and stepped back to pick up his pack.

His grandfather slumped to the floor.

"Grandfather?"

The old man didn't move. He had become frail in the last few years, much of the muscle from working the smith turned to flaps of skin. Now he resembled a heap of sticks in bedclothes.

"Grandfather?" Edwin bent down to his grandfather to see what the matter could be. There was a blue tinge to the old man's lips. He wetted the back of his hand and placed it at the lips and beneath the nose. He tried to find a pulse at the bony wrist and neck. Nothing.

He was dead.

Anger rose in Edwin. He bellowed so loud the harnesses on the smithy wall shook. How cruel was fate? To take his grandfather with a heart attack? Now he had nothing to return to when he had found Griselda.

Griselda.

Every minute wasted was one her abductor took her further from him. He picked up his grandfather and laid him out on a bench.

"I'm sorry, grandfather. I would see you buried properly but I must be off. The living need me more than those who have passed. I must go to Griselda."

Edwin snatched up his pack and ran from the smithy without a backward glance.

Chapter 17   In Command

Of course you are misunderstood.
You are a Dark Lord.
The Dark Lord's Handbook

Morden tucked the Handbook away and, with newfound resolve, swept back the wagon's rear flaps and leapt down. He took a deep breath and swung round to address the men. He wasn't quite prepared to see eight orc bandits drawn up in two neat rows on either side of the cart facing forward, with one up at the reins and Stonearm two paces in front of the mules at the head. They stood still, chests out and chins up.

They didn't move a muscle as he walked past them, though he did catch the odd flick of eyes in his direction.

"Eyes front!" bellowed Stonearm, all the while remaining face forward himself. Maybe his role as drill sergeant had imbued him with a sixth sense.

Morden reached the head of the procession.

"What are you doing?" asked Morden in a low conversational tone.

"Men ready to move out, sir!" said Stonearm, his chest lifting slightly as he almost deafened Morden with the salutation.

Morden looked back at the line of orcs. Some of them stiffened as his gaze went their way, which was impressive considering the board-like quality of their posture. They had scavenged armour from the soldiers who had died and looked like an impoverished town militia. Looking carefully, there were blackened bits and the odd red stain.

"A word in your shell-like," said Morden, stepping further forward to take Stonearm out of the rank and file's earshot.

"My what?" said Stonearm.

"Come here," hissed Morden and waved the towering orc to him. "You don't think this is a touch conspicuous?" he asked the orc when he got close.

Stonearm looked puzzled. "Is that a problem?"

"Well, we are being hunted by Penbury's man," suggested Morden.

Stonearm seemed to consider the point briefly before resuming his puzzled look. "And that's a problem because? You're a Dark Lord. Every orc here will die for you if it comes to rough stuff. And you can always turn into a dragon again."

"Appreciated," said Morden. "But I'm still not sure how all that fire breathing stuff worked and I'm tired. I'd rather just get to Bostokov without fuss, find Grimtooth, and take it from there. Is that okay?"

"You could have 'em, you know," said Stonearm brightly. "Nothing can stand against you."

"That may well be, but for now bear with me if you would. Get them in the back of the wagon and let's be off."

Morden could see the orc was still struggling with the sense of it.

"Now would be good, Sergeant Stonearm."

"Sergeant?" said Stonearm. The orc's face lit up. He turned to face his men and took a deep breath. "All right, you miserable lot. Into the wagon. Now. Sharpish! Don't just stand there. At the double. Move. Move. Move!"

Within minutes the orcs were hidden safely away and Morden was sitting up front with Stonearm. He had thought about asking the orc to sit in the back, as when it came to inconspicuous Stonearm was the antithesis, but Morden sensed he could push his new sergeant only so far.

They left the woodland a few miles on and merged with a larger trade road that ran alongside the River Loos as it curved its way across rich flatlands towards Bostokov. The road was an ancient artery of commerce and there was other traffic. Apart from the odd looks that Stonearm received, which was to be expected given his size, they seemed to be largely ignored. The friendlier farmers and merchants managed a grunted hello but little more than that.

A few hours passed and the outskirts and smell of Bostokov became apparent. Morden could see a city wall, but it only surrounded an inner part of a greater whole. Housing and other dwellings spread out from the inner wall like a tattered skirt, and a dirty one at that. The onshore breeze brought a hint of the ocean, but mainly the smell of the sewer.

There were no guards on the road as it plunged between the first hovels. There was merely a sign which posted the direction of the city gate, which to Morden seemed more than obvious but proved of some use to Stonearm.

"City gate is straight on," observed the orc on seeing the sign.

"Carry on then," said Morden encouragingly.

"But I don't think that's the way we want to be going," suggested Stonearm.

Traffic on the road was slow at this point, due in part to the volume but also the thick mud the wagons had to be hauled through. Up ahead a team seemed to be having trouble with a particularly large wagon and they were forced to come to a halt.

"Why would that be?" asked Morden.

"Not our people in the city, are they? And you wanted to find Grimtooth, right?"

The orc was right. Looking around, the ramshackle housing was more like the orc dwellings in the seedier parts of Bindelburg, but those had been palaces compared to these. Morden also noticed the people who were loitering and hawking to the traffic. There was a familiar cast about them, and as he looked closer, Morden noticed the attention he and Stonearm were getting. A good number of the people were orcs.

Ahead the merchant who owned the wagon had produced a whip and was applying it to the backs of his mules. A group of orcs pulled at the sides of the wagon.

"Heave, you lazy, good-for-nothing slackers!" shouted the merchant, who ignored the murderous looks he received from the orcs as they pushed.

Morden could feel Stonearm bristle as the merchant's whip strayed and caught an orc across the shoulder. There was strength in the muscle of the orcs, though, and the wagon lurched forward out of its muddy clamp. The merchant tossed a few coins from his purse into the mud on either side and whipped his mules on.

From what Morden could gather, this was a choke point, and any wagon that wanted to get into the city had to make it through the quagmire. The orcs added their muscle for a fee to get each cart through.

"It's a scam," said Stonearm as their turn approached. He nodded to the roadside where there was an orc who was organising the others. "He makes sure the mud is always fresh."

Morden considered what he was being told. It was ingenious. Then he considered that he had no money.

"But don't worry," said Stonearm, as though he could read Morden's mind.

Their wagon faced the muddy quagmire and the orc Stonearm had pointed out came over.

"I'm Murgoh. It's ten flounders to cross the mud," he said, with no preamble.

Morden noticed the orc's teeth were flat like Stonearm's.

"Krch ung klop nigh," said Stonearm.

The orc picked at his nose and then shook his head.

"Nine is the best I can do, orc or not," said Murgoh.

"You realise I don't even have that," hissed Morden to his sergeant.

"I'll get the lads," said Stonearm, and before Morden could say a word, the big orc jumped off the wagon and disappeared around the side.

"Okay, boys, let's be having you!" ordered Stonearm.

There was a clatter of bodies from the rear and Morden's little army made an appearance. It hadn't occurred to them to take off any of the armour, or leave their weapons in the back, and there was instant commotion.

"Who the hell are they?" asked Murgoh.

Stonearm was marshalling his men along either side of the wagon.

"Ready when you are, sir," said Stonearm.

"No, no. You can't do that," said Murgoh, waving his arms. "This is our mud. You can't heave your wagon through yourself."

"Why not?" said Morden.

Murgoh looked perplexed. His brow furrowed. "Demarcation! That's why not."

It was Morden's turn to feel out of sorts. "Huh?"

"An assertion of working rights," said Murgoh smoothly. "It's clear your lads are soldiers and mine are cart handlers. You do your job and let us do ours."

This made no sense at all. What was he on about? "But my soldiers can do your job," said Morden.

Murgoh pursed his lips. "Right you are, indeed they could." The orc smiled. "But you wouldn't want my lads doing your lads' job, now would you?"

Murgoh looked over to where his men were bunched and nodded. It was obvious they were prepared for the odd reluctant payee. Clubs, knives and assorted weapons of the bone breaking type slid into view in the hands of Murgoh's men. It was not lost on Stonearm.

"You don't want to be doing that," said the big orc, squaring up to Murgoh. "We are much better armed than you lot."

Murgoh had to lean back to meet Stonearm's eyes. "Maybe, but there are a lot more of us."

From his seat on the wagon Morden could see other orcs appearing from among the hovels, on either side and behind. Murgoh was right, there were a lot more of them. A street fight was the last thing he needed. He just wanted to find Grimtooth and work out what to do next. He stood on his seat and spread his arms.

"Kznk d'lak!" he roared.

Much like when he'd spoken those words in Grimtooth's tent, they had power that Morden now recognised as his dragon voice. They also had a similar effect on the orcs who froze as one, even Stonearm.

"You," said Morden, pointing at Murgoh. "Get your men and move this wagon through that mud now."

Murgoh seemed incapable of movement.

"NOW!" roared Morden at the unfortunate orc.

Murgoh staggered backwards and then threw himself into the mud facedown. Clearly Murgoh was going to be no use.

"Stonearm."

"Sir, yes, sir," said the orc, snapping to attention.

"Get the men to move us through." He looked over to Murgoh's assembled men. "We're not going to have a problem here, are we?" he enquired of them loudly.

Weapons dropped, heads shook and bodies spirited away among the hovels that lined the road. Where there had been fifty orcs a second ago there were now none.

Stonearm ordered his men along the sides of the cart and then went to the front to lead the mules through. The mud barely made it halfway up the huge orc's calf muscles as he heaved the reluctant beasts across. Morden was sure Stonearm could have lifted wagon, mules and men as one and carried them over balanced on one shoulder. Still, he let his new sergeant have his fun.

It didn't take long for the wagon to get across and they were soon on their way again. There was still plenty of traffic and Morden had to work out exactly where they were going. Entering the city proper probably was not the best idea, as not only would they stand out and there were likely to be guards, but more importantly it was unlikely Grimtooth would be in there.

For now though, they crawled through the outer city. Along the roadside were stalls selling all manner of goods, but trade was hardly brisk. The buildings, or more accurately huts thrown together from odds and ends of wood and canvas, were in a terrible state. Morden shuddered at the thought of what the place was like when it rained.

There was no lack of people though, and Morden couldn't help wonder how they survived or what they did. After a while, he noticed orcs huddled in small groups, sitting in the mud, seemingly oblivious to their surroundings with vacant expressions.

"What's the matter with those orcs?" Morden asked Stonearm when they had passed the fifth or sixth such group.

Stonearm looked over to where Morden had indicated and shook his head. "Bad news, Boss," said Stonearm sadly.

"Bad news?"

"Headfucker," said the big orc, snapping at the reigns and urging the mules on.

Morden had heard of the drug but he'd never seen anyone, or any orc, under the influence.

"They aren't here any more," said Stonearm by way of further explanation. "They are lost."

Morden looked at the stoned orcs and brooded. Such a waste. What they needed was something to live for, or maybe die for; they needed motivation.

The city walls were getting closer now. They came to a crossroads. There was an outer road that circled the city, and ahead Morden could see the gate into the city. The walls were tall and imposing. The gate was well-built and well-guarded. Steel shone in the late afternoon sun. There was less traffic heading into the city, much of it turning left and right. Only the wealthier looking were going straight on.

Decision time.

Morden looked left and the road was much like the one they were on, flanked with hovels and a stinking pile of refuse of every kind;

animal, vegetable and orc.

He looked to the right expecting much the same, and was not surprised bar one small detail that made his heart leap. Standing at the corner, arms folded, looking directly at Morden, was an orc he hadn't seen for a while.

Grimtooth!

When Morden caught Grimtooth's eye, the orc swung round and marched off.

"Turn right," said Morden.

Chapter 18   Weeding the Flowerbed

Your ambition should have no limits.
The Dark Lord's Handbook

The count was wondering if he had the right day. When he had arrived at the tower there was no evidence of the other conspirators. He didn't feel the need for an entourage, but the others normally had personal servants and guards. At the foot of the tower, to one side, was a small but ornate outbuilding that served as servant quarters. He could have expected to see a certain amount of bustle, maybe smoke from a fire, or tied up mounts. But all was strangely quiet.

He left his horse loose to graze the short grass. It was well trained and would not wander. With his ridiculous disguise on, he proceeded into the tower, a legacy of past glories, a folly perhaps, but tall and well-built. The stairs spiralled up the inner side of the tower wall, with rooms off landings filling the centre. The marble of the stair had been worn smooth over millennia of footfalls. For a man less fit than the count, the steps would have been tiring.

Eventually the stairs opened out between two pillars into the circular room that covered the top of the tower. The worst of winter had passed since his last visit and through the arched windows the count could see the forest had a full canopy of green. Across the room was the archway leading to a final small stair that went onto the roof itself, from which Black Orchid normally made her entrance.

The count half expected to see his fellow 'flowers' arranged around —he was late after all—but did not expect to see Black Orchid standing alone, waiting.

"Ah, Count," said Black Orchid in a frighteningly genial manner. "Glad you could make it."

The count was unsure what to do. A bow seemed appropriate.

"I am most sorry for my tardiness, my lady," he said as he dipped his head and flourished his arm in what he thought was a courtly manner.

"How sweet," said Black Orchid. "Less of the formalities, Count."

The count straightened and walked to his prescribed position in what should have been a circle of co-conspirators. This brought a peel of disturbing laughter from Black Orchid. Then it registered. She had called him Count. Twice. Not Hemlock. He tugged the hood from his head.

"Bravo, Count. Bravo. I see you understand," said Black Orchid.

"There has been ..." started the count.

"Some weeding in the flowerbed," finished Black Orchid. "They served their purpose."

Indeed, the count had heard of the unfortunate demise of the Countess of Umbria. It had been covered up, of course. They had circulated the story that Edwin had indeed slain an ancient evil that had risen from the lake, which served a secondary purpose of bolstering his status as a Hero. Unfortunately, Edwin had not followed through and had stayed put in Wellow, in love with some young strumpet. The count had assumed the meeting was to discuss how best to direct him, preferably in a way that would not be fatal.

These thoughts were interrupted by Black Orchid pulling back her own hood.

The count had seen beautiful women of all shapes, colours, sizes, and dress sense. Black Orchid was not one of these women. Those women had been human. Black Orchid was most definitely not human. She was also not beautiful, she was riveting. Her skin was smooth, almost translucent, and black, like polished obsidian. She had a thin face, with high cheeks and eyes that were yellow slits. She had no hair, but what looked like a crest that ran back over the top of her head.

She smiled to reveal a set of teeth that looked like rows of ivory needles.

"Do you know who I am, Count?" asked Black Orchid.

The count felt a lump form in his throat. He had no inkling at all who this woman (for lack of a better description) was at all. No myth, nor legend, suggested itself.

"In truth, my lady, I have no idea," managed the count.

Black Orchid held his eyes for a moment, as though she were trying to read his mind, perhaps for truth? She didn't blink. The count began to wonder whether he was going to be the last flower to be deadheaded in Black Orchid's garden. Again she smiled, and it didn't help matters.

"I am Lady Deathwing," she said. "You may have heard of us? The Deathwings?"

Until this moment, the count had never understood the expression 'paralysed by fear'. At least not in men. Men who were afraid tended to drop everything and run in exactly the opposite direction from what they were afraid of and hide. Now he understood. When there was no possibility of escape, when there was nowhere to run to, or any place to hide, when the fate you faced was as terrible as your highly imaginative mind could conjure—and the count had seen many a bad ending to understand how bad they could be—then indeed being paralysed by fear was very real. The count was sure that if he wanted to he could not even twitch his itching nose, let alone raise a hand to scratch it.

"I see you have," continued Lady Deathwing. "I'm so glad there's no need for any kind of lesson or demonstration."

The Deathwings: the legendary leaders of Zoon the Reviled's Black Dragon Flight. They had so scarred the world that the fear of them was inbred. The count had seen strong men cry and piss themselves with fear and never quite understood. He had been fearful but not as close to losing all control as he was now. With a terrible realisation he knew this conspiracy was not some cunning plan to start a war of convenience, but the beginnings of something that could lay ruin across the world.

Lady Deathwing was standing there, enjoying his terror. But then she would. She was an evil, black-hearted dragon. This womanly guise was merely a convenient form.

"I thought you were ..." started the count.

"All dead?"

The count nodded.

"Guess who thought wrong?" said Lady Deathwing with a smile that, if it was intended to relax the count, failed miserably. "Let's say it has been convenient for us to let the world think we had all fallen, and in truth there aren't many of us left."

Though truth and anything Lady Deathwing said were likely only loosely acquainted, the count hoped this was the case. Then an odd thought occurred, one of those thoughts that ought best be left to rattle around and not be voiced, but he couldn't seem to help himself.

"Forgive me for asking, but ..." The count swallowed. He felt like he was standing on the edge of a cliff and vertigo was whispering in his ear to jump. "… aren't you on the wrong side?"

"The wrong side?"

"What I mean is, my lady, with no disrespect, aren't you meant to be on the Other Side?"

"The Other Side?" asked Lady Deathwing, taking a step towards the count.

It took all of the count's will not to turn and leap from one of the many windows. A short fall and splat, it would be all over.

"The Evil Side?"

Lady Deathwing stopped and let her head fall back, laughing. If there had been glass in the arches, it surely would have shattered. As it was, the count was convinced his ears were bleeding.

"My dear count, what a darling you are. There is no Good Side or Evil Side."

"There isn't?"

"There is the Winning Side and the Losing Side. And I'm on the first."

"The Winning Side?"

"There, you've got it. Now that's settled, I have a job for you. My idiot husband has dipped his wick once too often and we have his mess to clean up."

So there are at least two of them, thought the count. This was not good.

"It seems our Hero … what's his name?"

"Edwin."

"Yes, Edwin. It seems our Hero, Edwin, has his sword—thanks to the countess—and has at last got himself a cause. The love of his life has absconded with a middle-aged poet undergoing a mid-life crisis and Edwin is in hot pursuit." Lady Deathwing sighed. "Men are such fools."

"But if it's the woman he loves?" asked the count. He knew he would have raised mountains if anyone had stolen his beloved wife.

"No, not Edwin, my dear count. The poet. The poet is an idiot. If it's not some young girl it's a fast stallion. Fortunately, Edwin believes her to be abducted by a great evil and not some thirty-something fool trying desperately to be young again. What I need you to do is to go and slow Edwin down. We don't want him getting Griselda back too quickly. He'll need an army, and that will take some arranging."

The count was trying his hardest to keep up, but now he was completely lost. "An army? To defeat a poet?"

"You should hear his poetry," said Lady Deathwing, and she winced theatrically.

The count forced a laugh.

"No, not the poet, Count. The great evil. That's where my idiot husband comes in. Word from Bostokov is that an overzealous commander on a sting operation to catch woodland bandits instead got himself a black dragon. Needless to say, it was not I, nor my husband, so that left only one possible answer."

Lady Deathwing paused. The count was unsure what he was meant to say and just shrugged.

"A bastard, Count. A bastard. And we can't have a bastard Deathwing running around, now can we? But he could be useful. We need a great evil, a Dark Lord, and this bastard fits the bill."

The count shook his head. The thought there were two Deathwings running around was bad enough. Any number above two was incrementally worse.

"We need this other dragon—I think his name is Morden—to do his thing. We can't save the world from the ravages of a Dark Lord unless he does some ravaging first, now can we?"

"I suppose not," agreed the count.

"Good. Good. I see you've got it. Now you'll need to spend a lot of money, so borrow as much as you can. But don't worry, Count. I can see what you're thinking. It's not as though we're going to pay any of it back. If all goes well those filthy money-grubbing middle class merchants and money lenders will all be dead, and if they are not, well, we're called Deathwing for a good reason. And don't worry about the poet and the girl, I'll have my husband take care of them. He needs something useful to do. Now, run along."

Chapter 19   Unpleasant History

Knowledge is power but it is swords that kill people.
The Dark Lord's Handbook

The chancellor's archive was old. It had been gathered by a line of chancellors over the centuries, each one adding his particular field of expertise. It had been moved several times, mainly for reasons of security and size. The current housing was beneath the cellar of the chancellor's Firena residence, and was reached by a hidden stair behind the fake façade of a cask of Firena sherry.

Penbury ran his hand over the smooth wall as he wound his way down the spiral into the musty depths of the archive. After an unfortunate, but entirely predictable, accident with a candle many years ago, no flame was allowed in the archive, naked or covered. Instead he held a staff in his left hand that served the dual purpose of steadying his bulk on the steep stair and lighting his way by means of the Azina gem clasped at the top of the staff.

It was one of the few items some still thought magic. Though he held no doubt magic existed in the world, and all manner of strange creatures to boot, he was not as certain that the gem was magic. More likely it happened to have qualities that made it radiate light. It was probably as magical as a firefly. Nevertheless, its radiance was more than sufficient to guide him and allowed him to read without straining his eyes.

The foot of the stair opened immediately into the reading room, in which there was a large desk covered in writing materials, blank papers and an amusing puzzle ball that once disassembled was a bugger to put back together.

The chancellor set the staff in a floor mounting where, by a cunning arrangement of mirrors and prisms, it illuminated the lines of shelves that stretched away into the rock.

The majority of the early writing was on scrolls, and kept safe from ageing by being secured within sealed earthenware tubes. The scroll's contents were etched on the casings and stacked on shelving carved into the bedrock. There were no wooden shelves, to cut down on potential flammables. The shelves themselves had dates chiselled into them to help searching. It was still hard work to find anything. Penbury thought that had he the time, he should devise a system that would allow faster retrieval of vital information.

The information he sought would be among the oldest scrolls, going back five hundred years to the time of Zoon the Reviled, the last true Dark Lord. Fortunately, some two hundred years ago, the chancellor of the time had re-housed the library and put all the materials in good cases. What concerned Penbury was that the scroll he sought was so old it may well have perished regardless.

The shelves for that time had been subdivided into author and subject, which helped a little. Most of the scrolls were political histories, religious rants, mediocre poetry and satire that had lost its bite. There were no books; those only started appearing a century or so later.

He was surprised there was only one scroll on Zoon, apparently written by Krug Sharptooth. His heart sank. It was an orcish name, which meant whatever the scroll case contained was bound to be written in ancient Blood Rune, a language he had done miserably at in Ancient Studies at college. It was going to be a long day.

Luckily, he had had the foresight to deposit a small cask of sherry next to the reading desk for such occasions. He set the scroll case aside, poured himself a tipple, and recovered a snack pouch from one of his many pockets. One horseradish and beef sandwich later, he was ready for the runes.

The case was in reasonable condition, and its seal was intact. Using a letter opener, the chancellor gently broke the wax seal around the lid before popping it off. A stale smell escaped the case. Using a set of tweezers, he pulled the scroll clear.

He needn't have worried about the condition of it, because it was evidently not paper. The small hairs on the dried, once pink material had him hoping it was pig skin and not from something bipedal. The writing itself had been tattooed onto the skin and was in the familiar, but not instantly translatable, orcish Blood Rune.

There seemed little to do but start at the beginning and so, with a sigh, Penbury placed his finger on the first rune and dredged up long forgotten lessons.

Six hours later he sat back in his chair. A half-eaten sandwich of mature cheese and pickle was long forgotten to one side of the desk. Never being one to waste food, and despite it being well past its best, his hunger was enough for him to finish it off while he went over in his mind what he had just read.

It was an eyewitness account of the Rise and Fall of Zoon the Reviled. It detailed his fortress, his armies, and his plans. It also made several mentions of a book, unusual for a time when books were rare. Zoon had read from it often but when Krug tried to catch a glimpse of what it said over his master's shoulder, the pages were always blank. Zoon had never let the book leave his person and Krug had been observant enough to note that many of Zoon's big decisions had been made after reading it.

The account of the last battle was graphic and the mention of black dragons was disturbing. Could Morden be an ancestor of one of these dragons?

Then there was the way in which Zoon had fallen, and in particular the sword that Uther had used to carve up Zoon. It had howled as Uther went about his work.

A book with no writing and a sword that howled.

Though he preferred natural explanations wherever possible, and even allowing for authorial license, it seemed to Penbury that there was magic here and that was not good. Something told him there were long forgotten forces at work in his world and he didn't like it. He would have to look into it further, but after supper. He had, for all intents and purposes, skipped lunch and it must be well past sundown.

He replaced the scroll in its case, resealed it with wax he heated using the staff head, and climbed slowly back up the stairs.

Chancellor Penbury did not sleep well that night.

The Dark Lord's Handbook   97

Chapter 20   Emancipation Prophecy

Keep healthy. Cream cakes are for the weak.
The Dark Lord's Handbook

They didn't have far to go before Morden could see Grimtooth waiting
for them. After all that had happened, Morden was pleased to see the old
orc. As they got closer, he was shocked to see how Grimtooth had
changed. There was still the imposing physical presence, but age had
crept into his features. His skin was lined and his hair streaked white.

Morden jumped from the cart to greet his friend but Grimtooth
dropped to one knee and bowed his head before Morden could grasp
him.

"My lord," said Grimtooth.

What is this? thought Morden. He looked around for Stonearm only
to find him and the rest of his men similarly bent on one knee. Looking
further, the curious inhabitants of the Bostokov slum were gathering. As
his gaze passed over them and he met their eyes, some remained
standing but those that were orcs sank to a knee in the mud.

"Command me," hissed Grimtooth between his teeth. "My knee is
killing me."

Quite taken aback by what was happening, Morden spread his arms
in what he hoped was a commanding fashion and spoke: "You can all get
up."

There was no movement.

Morden coughed and deepened his voice. "I command you to rise,"
he ordered.

Grimtooth was first up and the others followed his lead.

"If my lord would care to follow his humble servant," said
Grimtooth, indicating a path between the hovels.

There didn't seem to be a choice in the matter, so Morden trudged
off after Grimtooth. Behind him there was a ripple of chatter.

"All right, you lot. Enough of that. Fall in, on the double!" ordered

Stonearm from behind him.

Grimtooth led them deeper into the slum. The conditions were worse than Morden had ever seen. The houses didn't deserve the name, but were more assemblies of sticks and bark. Sanitation was a running, open sewer.

As they passed through, they gathered quite a procession. Morden glanced back and could see upwards of a hundred slum dwellers in tow behind Stonearm and his men. Most were dressed in little more than rags and had a hungry, desperate look to them. And something else. Was it hope?

At last they reached a hovel that was not only bigger than the surrounding ones, but looked like it wouldn't collapse in a stiff breeze or flood in a passing shower. The hovel reminded Morden of the place in Bindelburg where Grimtooth had first taken him. Grimtooth swung a leather flap aside and swept an arm to indicate that Morden should enter, which he was happy to do. Perhaps now he would get some answers.

"No one else enters," said Grimtooth as he ducked into the hut, presumably to Stonearm.

The big orc's orders, organising his men into a cordon, were muffled by the leather doorway as Grimtooth let it fall.

Much like Bindelburg, they were in a circular room with tightly woven straw matting on the floor and painted leathers adorning the walls. The fire pit in the centre of the room held a smouldering and smoky fire that did little to warm the place. The smoke rose to leave by a hole in the middle of the roof.

"Sit," ordered Grimtooth and pointed at a spot on the floor.

"Sit?" asked Morden. "What happened to 'my lord'?"

The orc went to the side of the room where there was tinder and a poker. "You may be a Dark Lord and my master, but don't get too cocky, young man," said the orc. Grimtooth picked up some of the wood and proceeded to bring the fire back to life.

Morden sat and left the orc to it. There was something nagging at his mind. The squalor of the slum had repelled him, but that wasn't it. There was something he was missing. Perhaps the Handbook would tell him. It would have to wait, though, as Grimtooth had finished his chore and sat himself down next to Morden. The fire brought welcome warmth to Morden's tired body and made him feel drowsy.

"No time to sleep now," said Grimtooth. He clapped his hands and an orc entered with a tray carrying two large mugs. Morden wondered if the mugs were full of the beer he had had in Bindelburg. Right now that would send him straight to sleep.

Grimtooth took the mugs and handed one to Morden. To Morden's surprise the mug was warm. The orc who had served them beat a hasty retreat. Whatever was in the mug smelled pretty potent, and beefy.

"What is it?" asked Morden apprehensively.

Grimtooth was already chugging away at his mug. "Hot blood, herbs, vegetable stock, sweet meats, and a drop of beer," said the orc, wiping his mouth and letting out a burp.

Morden gave the brew a second sniff and then took a mouthful. Not only did it taste good, but it reminded him he hadn't eaten properly for a while. He emptied the mug in no time and let rip a satisfying belch to match Grimtooth's.

"Good, now to business," said Grimtooth. He took Morden's mug and set it aside.

Morden was unsure what *business* Grimtooth had in mind. Though in the past weeks and months a lot had happened, for every answer he got a new question had taken its place. He was meant to be a Dark Lord, and be Rising, but apart from a general idea of it involving fortresses and armies, he had no idea how it was all going to happen. He felt more like a fugitive than a terror about to unleash itself upon an unsuspecting world. Morden opened his mouth to tell Grimtooth exactly these things but the orc interrupted:

"I have been travelling far and wide, my lord, spreading the word that a Dark Lord is Rising and that the prophecy will be at last fulfilled."

Morden was taken aback. "The prophecy? And exactly what prophecy would that be, Grimtooth?" In his reading of the Handbook, no mention had been made of any prophecy concerning him.

"Ah yes. The prophecy."

If Morden hadn't thought it impossible, he would have said Grimtooth looked embarrassed.

"Well?" prompted Morden.

Grimtooth took a deep breath. "You know, it's pretty tough to motivate orcs who have been under the heel for so long. And so I took the liberty … well that is to say, I thought it best, so to speak … that perhaps a prophecy might help."

"And where did this prophecy come from?" asked Morden, though a suspicion was dawning.

"I made it up," said the orc.

Morden's suspicion stopped dawning and rose like a blazing sun. "So you told them there was a prophecy, which presumably involves me saving them and setting the world to rights?"

"Something like that," admitted Grimtooth. "There was a fair bit of Pillaging and Laying Waste involved as well."

"Really?"

"Well, wouldn't you want to burn and pillage if you'd been downtrodden for centuries, forced to file your teeth flat, and do all the shitty jobs while being looked down upon? Just look outside. It's the same all over, you know. Many cities have an orcish slum, but they are the forgotten. And they need you."

There was fire in Grimtooth's words and Morden could see it burning in his eyes. This orc was old, and for five hundred years he'd seen his people humbled and domesticated like cattle.

"Well, yes," said Morden, nodding in what he hoped was a sympathetic manner. "I suppose I would. And you've been telling them I'm going to somehow change all that?"

Grimtooth looked Morden dead in the eye and smiled. "Yes. You are."

Grimtooth may have been old, and Morden was fairly sure that if push came to shove he could probably turn into a dragon and deal with it, but there was still something quite terrifying about the orc's four-inch incisors.

"Just one thing," said Morden.

"Yes?"

"How exactly am I going to do this? And without seeming greedy, what's in it for me? You see, I was rather set upon the idea of ruining Chancellor Penbury."

"Spoken like a true Dark Lord," said Grimtooth. "Revenge and greed are good, and in this case, our goals are side by side. It is Chancellor Penbury and his free market economy that is crushing my people. They have become slaves to the merchant classes. And these so-called democratic city-states are a sham. What use is a vote when anyone who ever gets elected only panders to the middle class? The working orc is uncared for and unheard. Even the free dental turned out to be a conspiracy, to remove the one thing that makes an orc an orc, and that's his teeth."

Morden let Grimtooth's words sink in. There was real potential here. A large population of pissed off, downtrodden orcs out for revenge was exactly what he was going to need if he was going to raise an army.

"I'm going to need somewhere to gather this army," said Morden. "And weapons, and supplies, and ..." Morden's mind was suddenly alight with ideas. "There's a lot to do, my friend."

"Indeed there is, my lord," said Grimtooth. "We must leave soon and you must start to gather your forces."

"But where? We can't just have them tag along. We've no money. No food. How can we possibly support an army?"

"We will tell them not to follow us, but to go east, across the sea, beyond the Great Marsh, beyond the Quite High Peaks, beyond even the Dust Bowl."

As the orc spoke, Morden's mind's eye was travelling east across the map he had studied at the Bindelburg school. It moved across the Quite High Peaks, skidded over the great nothing that was the Dust Bowl and arrived at, "The Dreadful Peaks ..."

Grimtooth was nodding. "Yes. The Dreadful Peaks."

"Isn't that where ...?"

"Yes. I have travelled back to the beginning and it is still there. The Dark Fortress may have been broken, its walls thrown down, but the foundations were left, and the depths never fully made clean. There are ... things ... still there." The orc shuddered. "That is where we will send them and where we too will go."

Morden felt a tingle at the back of his neck. A voice that was not his own whispered in his mind. Was it the book? It spoke of destiny. This path was set for him.

"I'm going to need a robe," said Morden. "A black one, with a hood. And some inside pockets would be handy."

"If I may, my lord," said Grimtooth. "I did not come back empty-handed."

Grimtooth got up and disappeared for a minute before returning with an oilskin-wrapped bundle. He set it down before Morden and bowed low.

"This is yours, my lord," said Grimtooth.

Morden looked at the bundle. It didn't look like much but it smelled old, and of death. An aura of evil emanated from it.

Morden peeled the oilskin away and drew a sharp breath.

It was a robe. But not woollen and comfortable-looking like his old one. This robe was quite different. The material was black and seemed to be alive, as though it were breathing. It was a cloth Morden had never seen before, if it was cloth at all. Morden reached a hand out to touch it and sparks leapt from his fingers to the robe. Every hair on his body was standing on end and when his fingers touched the material a shock jerked up his arm.

A vision came, like a far-off picture that swiftly grew and consumed him. He was riding a black horse at the head of a vast horde. Above him a black dragon soared. The horde was arranged across a vast dry plain and a huge cloud rose as they moved. The sun was behind them, and ahead another cloud of dust approached. From within it Morden caught bright glimpses of sun reflected from steel. He could feel the anticipation around him like a living hunger. A word from him and it would be unleashed. But not yet.

A man astride a white stallion emerged from the approaching cloud, and he was resplendent in plate and held a sword aloft. Morden could feel the Righteousness of this Knight as he approached. On either side of him, other knights could now be seen. They formed a wedge Morden knew would break upon him and his army. And for the first time in his life, Morden knew the meaning of real fear.

As quickly as the vision had come, it was gone. A sound like a sigh came from the air around Morden. For a second, Morden thought there was someone else there with them. The fire in the pit flared and whatever had been there was gone.

"That was strange," said Morden. Whatever had happened didn't seem to have bothered Grimtooth.

"You should put the robe on," said the old orc.

The robe looked different now; it was an ordinary-looking black robe, woven tightly from a strange material. Morden stretched his hand out to touch it again, somewhat apprehensively. He didn't want another jolt like the last. He needn't have worried.

The material was thick but light, with a slight sheen. Morden stood to try it on. The fit wasn't bad, and there were indeed inner pockets, one of which was perfectly sized for the Handbook. He was at first disappointed the robe was about eight inches short of a full length and two inches short in the arm, but even as the thought occurred the hemline dropped and the sleeves lengthened.

"Now that's clever," said Morden. "Where did you get this, Grimtooth?"

Morden had no idea what magic was at work, but there was no doubting it was not a normal robe. It felt absolutely perfect, as though it had been made for him.

"This belonged to my previous master," replied the orc.

Morden stopped examining the robe to look at the orc. "Your previous master? You mean this was …"

"Zoon the Reviled wore that robe. Yes. Now try the hood and let's see the full effect."

Morden pulled the hood up over his head and faced the orc, his hands plunged deep into opposite sleeves.

"HOW DOES IT LOOK?" asked Morden, and almost jumped out of his skin at his own voice. The question boomed out with malevolent twists and turns to the syllables as he pronounced them. It sounded like he was uttering a death sentence rather than asking sartorial advice.

The question knocked Grimtooth to his knees. "You look … you look …" Grimtooth sounded like he was in real pain. "You look scary," he gasped. "The hood. Pull the hood back."

Morden snatched the hood back. "Is that better?"

"Much," gasped Grimtooth, getting slowly to his feet.

"How did it do that?" asked Morden, fingering the cloth. "It has to be magic."

"It is," said Grimtooth. "Zoon had problems making himself heard."

"Really? You would have thought a Dark Lord wouldn't have that problem."

"Well, it's all right for you, being half dragon, but Zoon was a Lich King and didn't even have a larynx. Work it out."

"A lich? Wow. I had no idea he was undead."

"Undead?" asked Grimtooth. "No, he was definitely Very Dead. If anything he was More Dead."

"More Dead? How can you be More Dead?"

"Believe me, you can. And it's not something I'd recommend," said Grimtooth. "Why do you think he was Reviled? Not a pleasant smell, I can tell you. Anyway, he put a lot into that robe. The voice thing for one, and it's also warm. He had chronic arthritis."

"That couldn't have been pleasant."

"Being mostly skeletal, no it wasn't. You really didn't want to be around him on a cold damp day, and in his fortress it was often cold and damp."

As Grimtooth spoke, in his mind's eye Morden tried to imagine what Zoon's fortress had been like. Surely it must have had dungeons, deadly traps, and a throne room with the biggest throne in the world. With a throne like that Morden was sure no one could withstand his Will, to say nothing of how good it must have been for sitting and brooding on conquests. Then another thought struck him.

"Grimtooth, were you there when ..."

"When what?"

"You know ... at the end ... when he became ... Dead Dead."

Grimtooth bit his lip and quite possibly a tear came to the orc's eyes. "Aye, I was there."

"Let's sit down and you can tell me about it," suggested Morden.

Grimtooth seemed lost in thought but then snapped out of it. He sat across from Morden and warmed his hands on the fire pit. "We had high hopes that day. Zoon had Risen well, never using too much of his power, so rumour was the most the rest of the world had to go on. All the preparations had been made and we Came Forth. We were going to roll across the world and make it ours. Nothing could stand in our way. Nothing except the knights." Grimtooth sighed and stared into the flickering flame.

Morden was hesitant to interrupt but his curiosity was burning, "Knights? What knights?"

"They called themselves the Righteous Knights. Some of the younger orcs called them the RKs."

"But who were they?"

"Pompous, self-appointed arbiters of what was right and good," said Grimtooth with evident bitterness. "They said they defended the common man, but it was the common man and not them who died in the battles. They had impenetrable armour, and wielded steel that could fell trees, while the common man was lucky if he had much more than a loin cloth and sharpened twigs at his disposal. Sure, they rescued ladies, but only if they were beautiful and slim. If you had a skin problem and a fondness for cake, or had been swept away by a troll, you had no chance. Good luck to the troll, they'd say. They had a leader, Uther the Merciless, who had …"

By now Morden was hanging off every word the orc had to say. "… No mercy?"

Grimtooth looked at Morden in a sideways fashion. "No mercy. Indeed."

"And was it him who …" Morden made a slicing motion with one hand across his throat.

"Yes. It was Uther who cut Zoon down. But it wasn't a fair fight."

Grimtooth fell back into staring at the flames. Inside, Morden was screaming go on, go on! But felt it wise to just wait for his old friend to continue at his own pace.

"They came at us across the plain, a shining steel wedge of knights with a host of plebeians in tow, just as Zoon had anticipated. They broke upon us and the slaughter was terrible. But the knights were few, and we were a horde, the like of which the world had never seen, and we had the Black Dragon Flight. Zoon let his mercenaries take the initial brunt—if they were dead they wouldn't need paying, he used to say—and they had little choice, so great was their fear of the Reviled. When he called the dragons down it was over quickly. They herded the peasants and burned them, so that the air was rich with the smell of their well-done flesh. They roasted the knights in their shells. Only Uther and a handful of knights remained and they were thrown down before Zoon, crying for mercy. Oh, the irony."

Grimtooth turned away from Morden and ran a hand over his face. "If only he'd killed them, shown them none of the mercy they had always denied others. But no, instead he berated them. He pulled that book from his robe and he read from it. He told them exactly where they had gone wrong and then he went on to how he was going to crush the rest of the world and his dominion would hold for a thousand years. What started off as a final word turned into a full-blown monologue for us, his troops. I can hear him now, speaking as though it were yesterday.

We were all going to have our own man-slaves, and a piece of land. 'The world is ours!' he said and he stretched his arms wide. None of us saw Uther pick up his sword. None of us saw him slide on his belly and then rise up and swing that damned sword. But we all saw Zoon cut down. We all saw his hand fly off. And that was that."

"But surely the army was there, and the dragons?" said Morden in disbelief.

Grimtooth nodded. "Yes, they were. But there was no Zoon. This is important, Morden: the Dark Lord is all. No Dark Lord, no army. Everything goes to shit pretty quickly if the Dark Lord bites the big one."

Though Morden wanted to know more about Zoon and the old days, he could see that Grimtooth had sunk into a melancholy contemplation of the flames.

"I'll get Stonearm to organise us some food, and then perhaps we should rest," suggested Morden. Grimtooth nodded without looking up.

After they had eaten, and bedding had been found, Morden and Grimtooth settled down to sleep. Stonearm had hustled and bustled about them and insisted upon there being a guard, promising he would personally see to it that not a flea got close to them.

As Grimtooth snored, Morden fidgeted, still wide awake and excited. His head was full of armies, conquests, terrible fortresses, fantastic wealth, and maybe even a not-so-good girl on his arm.

Chapter 21   Fourth Lesson – Monologue

Take care with what you say;
you never know who might be listening.
The Dark Lord's Handbook

In his dream, and he was certain he was dreaming, Morden was standing on a massive stair that led up to the gargantuan doors of his fortress. Arranged around the bottom of the stair was his army. All the preparations were over and today the terrible host was Going Forth to Conquest.

They were chanting his name. He spread his arms to silence them so he might speak immortal words to send them on their way.

He opened his mouth but nothing came out. It felt like the time in Bindelburg he had dreamt about being in class with no clothes on. He was suddenly naked before a horde that was to ravage the world and he had no idea what to say.

Then he remembered the Handbook. Grabbing it from the pocket where it nestled he flipped it open and began to read.

Though there are various forms of speech making, there is one form that is particular to the Dark Lord and must be mastered. I present to you the art of:

Monologue

There will be times, Morden, when you feel you may as well be talking to yourself. Sometimes you will be. Regardless of the presence or lack of an audience, the fine art of monologue is one that every Dark Lord of any consequence has mastered. It is the great vehicle for your genius and will carry your immortal words to generations, long after you have settled into a nice place by the sea.

Though it may seem like a daunting prospect, monologue is an art that can and should be practised frequently. Being an inherently ironic form of communication, it is well-suited to those of a bitter and twisted, yet inspired, farseeing bent, most markedly Dark Lords; for a Dark Lord engages the full range of emotions. There is the bitter despair of having incompetent minions, and those awkward feelings you have around women. But nothing beats the glorious tirade against all that is wrong in the world and how it will be a better place once certain grand designs have come to pass.

In approaching monologue, as a novice there are certain aspects of the art that need to be made clear. Monologue is fundamentally a melodramatic art. Everything about a great Dark Lord monologue will be big. There should be big ideas, big emotions, and a big performance.

Big ideas should be no problem. If you don't have big ideas you should think about a change in career. A Dark Lord without big ideas is like a poet without a bleeding heart. Common big ideas are world dominion (a little tired but popular with your armies), challenging the gods (may defy instead of challenge), overthrowing oppressors (the irony fits the form well) and naming months of the year after yourself (Mordenuary?).

The associated plans should both be grand and beyond the understanding of the audience. This lack of their understanding will frequently lead to a strong desire to elucidate. Herein lies one of the many pitfalls and traps of monologue.

When playing an audience that is behind you—in the good, non-dagger wielding stab-in-the-back sense—then a Dark Lord is obliged to illuminate the world with his superior intellect and be overly expansive in detailing precisely how the big idea really is BIG.

If, however, there happens to be a Hero within earshot, re-read the section on Heroes. Pay attention to the bit about them escaping certain death and how difficult they are to kill. Gloating is fine, just don't let it run away into a full-blown monologue, and NEVER EVER turn your back on a Hero. EVER.

Emotionally the Dark Lord monologue should leave no doubt that you not only mean business, but that to stand in your way, in any fashion, would at best be fatal and at worst lead to eternal torment. The emotions of a truly great monologue should not only engender terror, which renders well-muscled Heroes to piles of goo, but if done particularly well, a grudging respect, tinged with jealousy.

Practice. And then practice more. Your delivery must be perfect. Dark Lords don't stutter, nor are they ever at a loss for words. This comes from hours in front of the mirror. Try speaking your thoughts out loud, it often helps.

Oft neglected is the physical performance. You may think words alone will be enough, but image is everything. Looking the part is probably the easiest element of the performance. The black robe is clichéd these days, but it's a cliché for a reason. It works. Menacing is good and size does matter. If there are height issues, a suitably long robe and heavy boots with a six-inch sole will work wonders (though that late growth spurt you had seems to have filled you out).

You must be dynamic. Stride around and make the ground shake and tremble as much as those who hear your words. Your gaze should shatter walls as well as will. A throw of your arm should level mountains and have all present ducking for cover. Your laugh should work in variations of derisive, arrogant and maniacal. Pound your fist. Raise your voice from quiet sibilant threats to deafening prophecies of doom for those who oppose you.

Lastly, take pleasure in the monologue. You can't fake it, so put everything you have into every word and gesture. It's your big chance to enter folklore. A good monologue will be repeated the length and breadth of the land and make you legend. Be feared. Be admired. Be remembered. Be Morden.

Chapter 22   Lawyers

You never bluff. Ever.
The Dark Lord's Handbook

As was his custom, Chancellor Penbury took breakfast at seven and went over the pamphlets sent to him daily from every part of the world. The newer printed ones were the best quality, but the wood block pamphlets, though barely literate—one was even produced on bark—were far more entertaining. There was something about barbarian humour that hit a nerve with the chancellor. He particularly liked the series on Bonehead the Barbarian and his adventures, many of which ended with graphic depictions of close encounters with evil seductresses followed by an inevitable beheading. It was coarse, but he couldn't help a chuckle.

The real reason for reading so much was so he could keep up with what was going on in the civilised world, but that was getting more difficult. The printed pamphlets these days spent less time exhorting the populace to overthrow a cruel baron, or worship this idol or that, and more on how Princess Sasha of Brudweldland had been seen going for long rides with her Champion without a suitable chaperone. The cartoons were becoming more graphic, and in some instances there was almost no news to be seen but for the proliferation of phalli and breasts. Setting the results of last week's Pig Ball League aside, the chancellor indulged himself with a sigh.

"Look at this, Chidwick," said Penbury, indicating the pamphlets to his personal private secretary standing attentively to his right.

"Sir?"

"Tits and balls, Chidwick. It's all tits and balls," said Penbury. "What is the world coming to?"

"That's the gutter pamphlets for you, sir."

"Whatever happened to the other ones, Chidwick? You know, the ones you had to fold out and had print on both sides? With a word puzzle?"

"Market forces, sir. Those big old ones were only good for one thing, so they say."

Chidwick had a point and Penbury had to admit he'd been hoisted by his own petard. After all, market forces were his Big Thing. Though controversial at the time, once corporate heads had understood that market forces and free markets were two different things, and that free markets were not so much free as whatever-the-chancellor-wanted markets, they had come around. "So what are they good for, Chidwick? Besides expanding the mind and communicating valuable information across populations?"

Chidwick shuffled his feet. For some reason his PPS had never been comfortable with sarcasm. "They are quite big, and if you're ever caught short, adequately durable."

"So we're left with pamphlets that are little more than privy paper?" said Penbury, indicating once more the pile on the table. "Is that it?"

"It would seem so, yes, sir," said Chidwick.

Penbury pushed his breakfast plate aside and made a mental note to remind his chef that although his physicians advised against too much salt, seasoning was the core of all good food, even if it was only scrambled eggs with a side of bacon.

"Enough of that for now. What have we today, Chidwick?"

His PPS pulled a sheaf from his tunic and examined it. "We have a petitioning group from the wheat guild."

"And what are they petitioning for?" The chancellor raised a finger to stop his PPS speaking. "No, let me guess. They think they have a better understanding of global economics than my good self and believe I should increase the bushel price on the wheat markets with a well-chosen word?"

"Indeed," said Chidwick, nodding his head in recognition of his master's astute insight.

"Well, let's send them packing and save an hour, shall we? What's next?"

"There's the lawyers you asked for, sir," said Chidwick.

"Excellent!" Now this was more like it. Penbury had almost forgotten about his little Dark Lord problem, what with increased piracy in the Southern Sea, the spat in Lower Kris that threatened the spice route, and a blight of black fly in his garden. "Get them in."

"Hrmph."

The polite cough to the chancellor's left almost gave him a heart attack. Even Chidwick seemed startled.

The man who had seemingly appeared out of nowhere and was now standing not two yards from Penbury was of medium height and build, and had brown eyes. Little else could be discerned due to the fact he was entirely wrapped in black leather and cloth. Black hilted swords remained sheathed in black lacquered scabbards. If he was an assassin, then he was confident. The chancellor wondered what had happened to the five or six men that watched him at all times.

As if to answer the latter, his bodyguards came bundling into the room, swords drawn and shouting. One launched himself horizontally at the intruder in an attempt at a tackle but missed as the intruder twisted his body to one side and watched as the guard sailed past. The guard's head met the wall with an unhealthy crack and he slumped to the ground.

In the meantime, the remaining guards had dragged Penbury from his chair and sat on him. Two others had their blades at the assassin's throat.

"Stop!" Chidwick's command held the blades.

"Let go of me," said Penbury, shaking off his bodyguards. He dusted himself off. "Who is this, Chidwick?"

"Allow me," said the assassin. "Josef Snort, of Snort and Snort."

"Never heard of you," said the chancellor. He straightened his robe and tried to regain some of his substantial dignity. "Chidwick, is this the lawyer I asked for?"

"Yes, sir," said Chidwick.

"He said Snort and Snort. Where's the other one, then?"

"That would be me," said a voice to the chancellor's right.

When Penbury turned to see which impudent guard had spoken, he almost died of fright for the second time in a minute. He had to immediately look back to his left to check that the assassin calling himself Josef Snort was still under his men's blades. The two men looked identical.

"And you are?"

"Franz Snort, of Snort and Snort," said the assassin, bowing, and offering a card.

"Get over there with your, your whatever," ordered Penbury,

ensuring a guard remained between himself and the two assassins.

"Of course," said Franz.

Penbury didn't see Franz move. One second he was where he had been, and the next he was standing next to his partner. The chancellor suddenly realised he was holding something. He lifted the card in his right hand to read it.

Snort and Snort
Lawyers and Executors of Estates

"I assure you, Chancellor, we are not here to harm you in any way," said Josef. "If we intended to execute your estate, we would have done so by now."

There was such surety in the words Penbury was in no doubt that Josef Snort was telling him the truth. He still wasn't sure how Franz had both managed to place the card in his hand and move across the room, but if he could do that then giving Penbury a bloody grin from ear to ear would present no problem.

"They had better know what an injunction is, Chidwick, or you are fired."

"I can assure you, Chancellor, we do." It was Franz who spoke this time. Though hard to tell them apart, Franz was maybe an inch taller and had a slight lisp to his speech. "You must forgive us our little demonstration, but it is not often we are called upon for our night jobs. Perhaps if we were disarmed?"

Penbury nodded at his men, who gingerly slid the men's swords from their scabbards. Being a collector of fine arts and merchandise from all over the globe, he immediately recognised finely tempered steel. "Nichi-on blades?"

The two lawyers nodded.

Penbury was impressed. The blades were worth more than several of his larger estates. If they were half as good at law as they were at assassination, judging by their tools, then Chidwick had found him the right men.

"And I take it you can handle unusual cases?"

Snort and Snort nodded. "Whatever you need."

Penbury had the room cleared and his breakfast dishes replaced with sherry glasses. It may have been early but he needed something to fortify himself. The two lawyers sat opposite him patiently. They neither spoke, nor moved, nor scratched a nose or tugged an ear lobe. Being used to picking up on the smallest of mannerisms, this stillness was itself informative. These men were in complete control. They felt no need to speak unless spoken to and had the ability to sit perfectly still. It was hard to do. Penbury had tried when he was convinced he had a physical tell in his monthly Three Card Brag session and failed miserably.

The room was clear, except for Snort, Snort and Chidwick, who had his writing materials out to take minutes.

"I think this best go unrecorded, Chidwick," said Penbury.

"Very well, sir," said Chidwick, and he got up to leave.

"Set the writing materials aside and stay, Chidwick. There are instructions for you as well." Penbury sipped his sherry. Where to start? "Gentlemen. We live in strange times. There are forces at work which threaten the very fabric of our civilisation and we can't have that, now can we? In securing us from this peril I have a couple of estates I need executing, and two items retrieved to ensure this threat never appears again. Here's what I want you to do."

Chapter 23   Love Snatched Away

Love is your strongest weapon,
as long as there is none in your heart.
The Dark Lord's Handbook

It had been raining for three days. In the last two hours it had slackened and was now that annoying kind of rain which barely deserved the name but was heavier than mist. It was the kind of rain that dampened spirits, but Edwin was not downcast. The fact he had eaten sparingly for a week, and he was soaked through and a long way from home—not to mention he missed his grandpa—did nothing to lessen his determination.

He was close now, maybe half a day behind, maybe less. He had tracked Griselda and her wily captor to this road over the high moors. Being so close, it was tempting to push on harder, but he restrained himself from whipping his horse forward; he had already killed one mount. It had died under him mid-gallop and he still nursed the bruised ribs from that fall. No. He would be patient. The nag between his legs was tired and he was alternating between leading it and riding to give it some chance to regain strength.

Judging it about that time again, Edwin dismounted and cast his eye around. He had learnt treachery was often close by and he had to keep his wits about him and sword to hand. There seemed little threat though. The moor was as bleak as the weather. It was covered in lumpy gorse with granite outcroppings along ridge tops. While it might provide cover for grouse, he couldn't imagine bandits lying in wait.

He tugged his mount forward.

There was a desolate and wild beauty about the moor that was deepened by the miserable grey clouds hanging low over it. A cold wind gusted across it. Deep down inside him something stirred and, for the briefest moment, he thought how he might capture this depressing vista in well-chosen lines that would bring tears to the eyes of any who read it. He thought of Griselda reading his stanzas and, overcome with emotion, running wildly across the moor to throw herself from a granite boulder onto rocks below. It would be tragic but beautiful. He could mourn her passing and use the pain for inspiration. He could hear her crying. Her suffering was terrible.

The next big gust of wind brought a cry that was not in his imagination. Surely that was no grouse but a woman in distress? Perhaps even Griselda being tormented by her kidnapper. The wind gusted once more and this time there was no mistaking a scream.

The nag whinnied in protest when Edwin leapt onto the mount and spurred it forward. Despite its protestations, they were soon at a gallop. The path followed a contour along the hillside and then plunged downwards. The sounds of a woman in distress were clear now, along with the sound of men laughing and shouting.

Brigands, thought Edwin. Holding the reins tightly with his left hand, he drew his sword. It sang as it came from the scabbard and Edwin felt the thrill of impending battle. Today was a good day to die, but he had no intention of it being him who died. These brigands would pay.

He rounded the side of the hill. Ahead he could see it ended abruptly in a gorge that was spanned by a decidedly ropey-looking bridge. On this side of the bridge was a ramshackle hut and outside it a group of men, maybe six in all, surrounding two figures on the ground, a woman and a man.

The woman's hair was down and straggled around her head, and her peasant dress was torn. She was clasping her front as the men goaded and pulled at her. The man lay curled on the ground, trying his best to protect his head from the loose kicks that were being thrown his way.

A fire ignited within Edwin, fuelled by righteousness and lit by anger.

The wind meant they didn't hear him coming until it was too late. The first swing of his sword separated a cowardly head from its miserable body. The corpse toppled forward, a fountain of blood pumping from the neck. The head rolled to the feet of the woman. She clutched her face and screamed as she was sprayed with her tormentor's blood.

When the smell of blood reached his horse's nose, it reared and he was thrown backwards off it. He hit the ground hard and the wind was knocked from him. Fortunately his chest armour spread the shock of the landing, though there was a sharp stab of pain in his ribs from where he had hurt himself before.

His being dismounted gave the brigands time to get over the shock of his attack. The woman was forgotten now, shoved to one side, and weapons had been drawn. They weren't the weapons of war but peasantry. Hooks, spikes and scythe blades, designed to grab and slash and puncture. Without knowing how he knew, Edwin recognised the combination of weaponry and hungry looks of anticipation as something many a knight had underestimated. There was real danger here.

The remaining five brigands spread themselves around him. They wouldn't be so stupid as to rush in, but would bait him like they would a bear. They would tire him until he could stand no longer and then finish him. He knew he had one chance.

He got to his feet slowly and assumed a weak guard position, holding his sword one-handed at arm's length, waving it pathetically as though to keep them at bay, while grasping at his side.

"Let's do him slowly, boys," said one. "For Jenk's sake."

"Aye. We'll make him bleed, and feed him his guts," said another.

Edwin arced his sword around. He made weak lunges and they shied away. They weren't brave enough yet to risk him striking. Not only were they cowards, but they were an ugly bunch. Lank hair, rotten teeth, and patchwork clothing showed them for the desperate band they were. The world would be a better place without them and all their kind.

"He's tiring," observed one when Edwin dropped to a knee.

That was good. Let them think he was growing tired.

A bill hook thrust in at him and he parried it away, though he had to spin sharply to avoid a thrust from behind from a pole arm. They were closing in.

On the next attack he parried, but instead of crouching backwards, as he had been doing, he suddenly released all the hate and anger he had been storing and leapt forward.

"Eleonir va rindir!" The words came from him as a battle cry. He had no idea what they meant, but the sword sang in response and a blue fire ran along its length.

His sword swung and cut right through the haft of the weapon that was raised to stop it and into the skull of the brigand. Without a pause, he spun and thrust the sword backwards underneath his left arm to impale the attacker who thought to get him from behind. He didn't have to see to know he had pierced the man's heart.

Blood ran on his blade as he tugged it loose and finished his dance of death. He moved so fast and so surely that surprise was the expression he saw on their faces as he served up justice.

It was over as swiftly as it had begun and six brigands would be troubling the world no longer, at least not after he had hewn the head off the one who was groaning and trying to hold his guts into his stomach. It was a mercy, the temptation being to let him die a slow, excruciating death.

His work done, he turned his attention to the living. The woman was kneeling, her head held in her hands, rocking back and forth. She was covered in blood. The man lay in a foetal position, his hands still protecting his head from blows that would not be coming.

"It's over, you're safe now," said Edwin. He wiped his sword on a corpse and sheathed it. His hopes that the woman was his Griselda were somewhat diminished because, although he had not yet seen her face clearly, this woman was much slimmer than he remembered his love.

Not that it changed matters. She had been in distress and he had rescued her. From what he could see, her comely form was not unattractive, if a little on the skinny side. If she had a favour to give to her Hero then she would not find him ungrateful. It had been a while, after all, and if Griselda were to be kept from him then his manly needs could find other outlets.

The man on the ground raised his head to look around while the woman kept up her weeping. There was fear written all over his face. It passed briefly into what looked like hope as he saw the dead, but returned when his eyes fell on Edwin. There was age in those eyes. They had the look of experience about them.

Realising he must look quite a sight, covered in the gore of battle and dressed in armour, Edwin tried to reassure him: "You are safe; your tormentors have met their just end. Please. Get up and tell me who you are and how you came to find yourselves thus?" Then a dreadful thought occurred: What if Griselda and her captor had come this way and been waylaid as well? What if he had been too late for them? "Quick now. Answer me. Have you seen another couple pass this way?"

"We have not," said the man, getting to his feet and moving over to the woman. "Griselda, it's all right. We are safe now."

Edwin's heart leapt. Had he heard correctly? It couldn't be a coincidence.

The man had reached the woman and knelt before her. He stopped her rocking and gently put a hand under her chin to raise her face.

Now Edwin could see clearly it was indeed the love of his life. Her hair was straggled and dirty, so was not the sunshine blonde he knew, and she had lost some weight. Her face was thinner. Her cheekbones were more pronounced and her face was less rounded. But that did not matter; hearty eating would set her right. The important thing was that he had found her.

And he had found her abductor.

The blade sang once more as he drew it from its scabbard. Its work this day was not yet done after all. At the sound, the man looked over to Edwin and his eyes widened in shock.

"Step away from Griselda," ordered Edwin.

"Wait! What is this?" said the man, stumbling backwards as Edwin advanced on him.

"Edwin!" Griselda's voice stopped him his tracks. Just to hear her voice made his heart sing.

"Edwin! Stop! What are you doing?" said Griselda. She got to her feet and stepped in front of the man.

"Get out of my way, Griselda, and let me dispatch this cur. He deserves to die for your abduction and torture."

Griselda's spread her arms wide. "Abduction? Torture?"

"Aye, it's plain to see he has starved you. Look how that dress hugs your once full frame like damp cloth on a stick. I can see it in your face."

"Edwin? This is Kristoff. He's a poet. And I like being slim."

Edwin was not sure what Griselda was talking about. How could this man be a poet? Then it dawned on him. He had heard of such cases, when someone had been abducted and brainwashed into caring for their abductor.

"It's all right, my love. You are safe now. You don't need to protect him. Step aside and let me send him on his way. You can eat all you want. You need not starve yourself for me." Edwin took another step forward and raised his sword. The two of them shrank before him.

Edwin was stretching an arm out to pull Griselda aside when there was a tremendous beat of wind. It was so strong it made him stagger backwards. A huge shape came out of the cloud above.

It was a dragon.

He had only ever seen engravings of creatures like this. It was entirely black, no hint of colour except for blazing eyes. It had white teeth as long as his hand in a maw that gaped and shrieked. The sound made him drop his sword to put his hands to his ears. Its massive wings continued to beat and he struggled to hold his ground.

"Griselda!" he shouted above the terrible noise. "Griselda!"

The dragon came lower and stretched out massive talons to snatch at Griselda and her abductor. With further powerful strokes of its wings, the dragon rose, clasping the pair beneath it. So he had been right. This man was in league with the foulest creatures in the world and had somehow summoned this beast to his rescue.

Edwin's heart filled with anguish. He had found his love, Griselda, and been so close. So close. Only to have her snatched from him once more. How could one man bear such torment? He could hear the gorge calling at him. *End it all*, it said. *Plunge into me and your pain will be gone*, it whispered in his mind.

No. He would not buckle.

Getting to his feet, he retrieved his sword and held it up. It sang as he cried, "Griselda! Fear not. I will find you, my love. Griselda!"

Chapter 24   Sacrifice

Dead people are of little use,
but they are less annoying.
The Dark Lord's Handbook

Not having slept well, Morden's thoughts were as grim as the breakfast he was being served; it was no more than gritty bread and pasty gruel. He could have murdered bacon, eggs, blood sausage and thick slabs of white bread but instead had been served slops. The fact this was the best all the orcs around him ever had didn't make him feel ungrateful; he was just in a black mood.

Grimtooth seemed happy enough with the fare. He held his bowl close to his mouth and scooped the gruel in with his hand.

"I'm going for a walk," said Morden.

Grimtooth nodded and kept shovelling.

Outside the weather was equally grim. The rain that fell from the low clouds had turned the street into a quagmire. Morden raised his hood and stepped out, expecting to sink knee deep in mud. He was pleasantly surprised. The robe had an aversion to getting dirty; instead of sinking he glided across the surface of the mud. It was also clear the robe was not so much waterproof as water repellent. The rain fell to within an inch or so of the robe and then seemed to decide that getting the robe wet would be a bad idea. The effect of all this was that as he walked Morden skated over the mud with a cloud of mist at his feet and he left no mark.

This did not go unnoticed as he strode off in a random direction. The few orcs who were out and about took a keen interest in him and tagged along behind. Morden did his best to ignore them. He wasn't in the mood to be sociable.

At first Morden walked aimlessly, but after twenty minutes or so of nothing other than hovels and running sewers, and with his stomach grumbling, he decided it was time to see the city proper and find something good to eat. The city's wall rose above the slum and stretched left and right. Even in the gloomy light, it was easy to spot the towers that doubtless flanked the gates into the inner city. Morden headed that way.

Deep in brooding thought about how a Dark Lord could expect a decent breakfast, he vaguely registered the number of orcs had swollen considerably. He also noticed the rain had eased off and was now merely an annoying drizzle. At last, he reached the road that went into the walled part of the city, where presumably he could find the decent food he was after. Traffic was light and mostly heading into the city. Being on foot, Morden felt no need to queue and strode up the side towards the guarded gate. A sergeant and two men were dealing with the foot traffic. An old woman, bent over and carrying a basket of flowers, was ahead of Morden.

"Name, occupation and business?" asked the sergeant.

"I've forgotten my name, and I sell flowers," croaked the crone.

The sergeant shook his head. "All right, go ahead."

Morden was next and he stepped forward.

"What have we got here, then?" asked the sergeant with a hint of amusement. "Name, occupation and business."

"Morden, and I'm looking for breakfast," Morden said, taking care to keep the Voice in check.

"And your occupation? No, wait. Let me guess. You're a student. How many times do I have to tell you people it's not safe outside the walls? Especially if you're going to dress up."

The sergeant's jocular tone was starting to irritate Morden, and the fact he didn't seem to be taking him seriously was more than annoying, but a rumble in his stomach reminded him that causing a scene was not his top priority.

"So what did you go as? Death?" It seemed the sergeant had nothing better to do than continue with his teasing. "No. Silly me. No scythe, so you must be a ... let's see ..."

"A Dark Lord," said Morden. "Yes. Now may I pass?"

The sergeant smiled. "Not so fast, son. Dark Lord, is it? Good one. And I suppose this lot is your army?" The sergeant pointed behind Morden and laughed. He obviously thought he was being funny, but Morden was less than amused. He was hungry.

Looking over his shoulder, Morden was surprised to see several hundred orcs waiting patiently behind him. He had assumed they would have got bored by now and gone home, but they hadn't. They were watching with what looked like curiosity, though some were smiling in a way that suggested the situation might get messy.

"They're with me," said Morden.

The sergeant put his hands on his hips and said in a raised voice, presumably so his men could share his wit, "You invading us, then? You and your army?"

Inwardly Morden sighed. Much as he'd like to teach this buffoon a lesson, farm products cooked in fat were foremost on his mind. "If you like."

"Hey lads, we're being invaded," said the sergeant. A captain, if his armour was anything was to go by, came out of one of the towers to see what the fuss was all about. The smile quickly left the sergeant's face when he saw the officer. "How many times do I have to tell you kids to stop yanking my chain? Be off with you."

Morden's patience was running low. It was time to try this robe out. Overhead a crow cawed.

"STEP ASIDE."

The sergeant's eyes bulged and he staggered backwards. His lips moved but no sound came out. One guard dropped his spear and another wet himself. The officer stopped in his tracks. Morden's orcish entourage roared with laughter and cheered.

"COUNT YOURSELF LUCKY I'M HUNGRY."

Morden strode into the city, dimly aware he still had an orcish entourage in tow. No matter. He was ravenous now and plunged into the narrow streets of the city.

Everything about Bostokov suggested wealth, from the two-story stone buildings to the cobbled road with gutters running with clean water. A city that could afford to keep its streets this clean was a wealthy city.

Morden's long stride carried him quickly into the heart of the city, past shops which were opening up. One street sold nothing but tableware made of beaten copper and painted ceramic. Another street had rows and rows of spice shops with pyramids of primal coloured wares from all over the world.

As the city came alive, he was urged to stop and buy rugs, pots, bananas, a parrot, wicker baskets, silver nose rings, a device for smoking herbs, a giraffe, spices, holy relics, life insurance (he was not sure what this meant but he didn't like the look of the manicured hawker so did not stop to ask) and pomegranates.

None of this, unfortunately, was breakfast.

Eventually Morden broke free of the narrow streets and emerged into a large square dominated by flower stalls. His spirits immediately rose as he saw a number of hostelries on the far side of the square. Urged on by deepening growls from his stomach, he quickened his pace, deciding that following the edge of the square would take him to his goal faster than weaving his way through the stalls and carts. Reaching the corner of the square, he found a clear space dotted with two foot-high pedestals. They were all bare except one, upon which was standing a lanky individual with a placard. His clothes were ragged and his beard was unkempt, bushy and hung to his knees. Morden had never seen such a long beard. The man looked like he was preaching to an audience of one, a short woman with a flower basket over her arm. Even Bindelburg had had its fair share of weird religions and self-proclaimed prophets that evangelised them and so, although it was curious, it was not worth stopping given his imminent demise due to starvation.

As Morden cut the corner he glanced up at the placard the man was carrying.

'The End of the World is Nigh' it proclaimed.

Morden smiled and somewhere close by a crow cawed.

"And the day will come when He will walk among us and it will be the End of Days!" proclaimed the zealot.

Morden eyed the hostelry signs that were close now. The Stuck Pig sounded like a fine bet for the sustenance he craved.

"He shall bring Ruin to the World and Burn it to cinders and all shall be consumed in His fire!"

Morden's mouth was watering so much he was in danger of drooling down his robe. Another forty paces and succulent flesh would be his.

"There! There He is. He has come! He has come! Death walks among us!"

Morden glanced over his shoulder. The zealot was pointing at him, froth coming from his lips as he shouted, "The Dark Lord is Rising! He walks our streets!"

Morden looked around, half expecting to see another Dark Lord but instead he only saw orcs. He'd forgotten they had been following him. Though lessened in number, there were nevertheless a good few straggling behind him and the zealot now had their full attention.

Seeing his audience had increased dramatically, the zealot turned to face the orcs, all the while stabbing his finger in Morden's direction.

"He is Death! He will Ravage the World!"

The orcs looked over to where Morden had stopped and cheered. Something inside Morden stirred, and it wasn't his stomach. One thing Morden had learnt when it came to bending people to his Will was that half the battle was already won because most people wanted to be led. Making choices for themselves was far too much effort for the majority and having someone tell them what to do was just fine by them, so long as some kind of reward was evident. The reward didn't even have to be real; the mere promise of something good often sufficed.

Morden glanced once more in the direction of The Stuck Pig, and though his desire for a fine pork sausage was deep, there were more important things to be done. There was a day to be seized.

Morden turned back towards the zealot and his audience.

"A Darkness shall fall upon the world and He will make us unto chitterlings," continued the zealot. "His power is manifest and it will crumble the mightiest. And his name is ..."

"Morden Deathwing?" The enquiry came from Morden's left and stopped Morden in his tracks.

"Yes?" answered Morden, turning to see who was asking. He was dimly aware that his pendant had grown hot.

At which point everything seemed to slow down.

A man dressed entirely in black—but specifically assassin black rather than Dark Lord black—with a short sword in either hand, lunged forward, one sword aiming to take Morden beneath the ribs, the other slashing at his throat.

Morden froze. He knew there was nothing he could do. The assassin was too quick and he was going to be stuck like the pig he had so craved. He raised an arm instinctively to try to ward the blows but his arm seemed to be moving with painful slowness. He could see the blades cutting towards him.

And then in his peripheral vision he saw someone flying horizontally across his front. The blades struck the body as one, squarely in the chest. Morden staggered backwards and the body thudded to the ground, blood pooling beneath it.

The assassin vanished.

Around him there was chaos. Orcs were stampeding towards him; flower sellers were stampeding away. Women screamed and orcs shouted.

Morden knelt to see who had saved him. It was Grimtooth. Blood dribbled from the old orc's mouth but he was not dead. His eyes were open and when Morden lifted him to cradle his head in his arms relief swept across the orc's face.

"You are unhurt?" gasped the orc.

"Untouched," said Morden. His head was full of inappropriate platitudes; he knew the orc was dying. There was one assurance he could give, though. "I am going to kill whoever did this."

Grimtooth tried to say something but his failing breath was too quiet with all the noise around them. Morden leaned closer to catch what the orc was trying to say.

"Free my people," croaked Grimtooth. The orc clutched Morden's hand in a vice-like grip and a rattle snuffed out the words. With a last hiss of breath, Grimtooth passed from the world.

Morden clenched his jaw. Anger raged deep inside him, but it could wait. He would nurture it and when the time came he would release it on the world. Then woe betide any who stood in his way. He laid Grimtooth down and stood. Someone had tried to kill him, and at the cost of his friend's life. It was not going to go unanswered. Call it paranoia, but he had a suspicion who was behind this. Penbury was going to realise that messing with him was not a smart thing to do. If it was a fight he wanted, then he was going to get one. It was time to get serious about being a Dark Lord.

"Coming through!" Stonearm's familiar bellow cleared a path through the orcs that had surrounded Morden in a cordon.

When Stonearm saw Grimtooth's body he froze. Morden couldn't tell exactly what range of emotions played through his sergeant's mind, but he wouldn't like to be on the receiving end of them.

"Are you hurt, my lord?" asked Stonearm, his concern switching to

Morden.

"I am unhurt," said Morden. He was trying hard not to scratch the itch at the back of his mind, which involved lots of fury and dismemberment. "Lift him and follow me."

Stonearm and three orcs raised Grimtooth's body to their shoulders, no questions asked. The mood among all the orcs present was tangibly grim, and the non-orc population of Bostokov, perhaps sensing this, was making itself scarce as Morden and Stonearm led the orcs from the square.

They moved back through the narrow streets. From the mob of orcs came a dirge and, as if in response, the sky darkened with clouds and rain fell. Pretty soon it was not just spirits that were dampened.

The city did not look so bright now. The cheerful bustle of the early morning was gone. As the procession passed by, shutters were slammed shut, and shoppers scuttled down side alleys rather than face the orcs and their burden.

Soon they were back at the gate. As they approached, Morden could see the captain and his men arrayed in front of it. He hoped they were going to make something of it, but perhaps self-preservation got the better of them as they suddenly disappeared into their guard tower. After all, their duty was to stop undesirables entering the city, not leaving it.

They left the inner city and moved into the slum. Immediately the numbers following the procession grew as more orcs fell in behind. Morden had no idea where they were headed, but Stonearm seemed to know so he let the orc lead them on.

At last they came to a square of sorts—an open muddy area surrounded on each side by hovels and huts. Word must have passed ahead. In the middle of the square there was a funeral bier waiting for Grimtooth's corpse.

His body was laid upon it.

"We'll send him off at sundown," said Morden, partly so the orcs could pay respects and partly because it was still raining and it would have taken an inferno to light anything.

Stonearm organised a guard under Morden's watchful eye.

Once everything was in place, Morden turned to other matters. He was still hungry, but he had no desire to eat. He needed time to prepare himself for what he planned that evening. The time he had spent drifting was at an end. Tonight he would claim his position in the world. He would bend these orcs to his Will and Bostokov would be where he announced himself as the Dark Lord Morden.

Chapter 25   A Hero Gets His Army

Lose the thigh length boots and whips.
You are better than that.
The Dark Lord's Handbook

As instructed, Count Vladovitch had begun to raise an army. It was a complicated affair. First willing recruits had to be found, and if that failed, then not-so-willing recruits. They had to be housed, equipped and trained. Then there was finance, sourcing supplies, marching, then lots more marching, and deciding on a flag. The latter was proving difficult. A good flag had to be something that would be followed, that soldiers would die for and have draped on their coffins. It had to inspire and uplift. A good flag was worth a regiment of men.

The designers had come several times to present their ideas, and each time the count had sent them packing. They had nothing but the same old rampant beasts and crosses. *Perhaps*, thought the count, *I am getting jaded in my old age*. He suspected it was more a case of not being sure exactly what he was fighting for. Though he understood the basic idea, he was to be the general of an army that was to deliver the aristocracy from its penury state, Lady Deathwing worried him. Worried him a lot.

He tried not to think about it. He was a soldier first and foremost; that was what he was concerned about, and in respect of soldiering he thought he was doing a good job. He had five thousand men under his colours (which were being used in lieu of a proper flag) and he had started to put word out that he was looking for knights. The first few had arrived with their squires, sweethearts, and romantic notions. This was all well and good, but what he needed were no nonsense, hard-nosed killers who could do more than pleasure a lady with their lance. He hoped today he would be more successful in finding the hammer for his army that would crush the enemy against the anvil of his pike blocks.

The army was marshalled at his family castle, which had perched for three hundred years on a steep hill. It was surrounded on three sides by sheer cliffs that bordered the River Jon, and commanded a good view of the entire region. As he rode down that morning, he was pleased to see blocks of men parading the grounds in tight formation. Battles came down to manoeuvre and discipline and it was in these aspects the count had his men spend the majority of their time.

The count enjoyed the short ride down to his tent on the grounds as best he could. During his life he had spent more time in the saddle than out but these days the pleasure had been lessened by terrible piles. He was sure the leeches didn't help. (His wife—may the gods protect her—insisted he do what the charlatan physicians said, which meant he had to have leeches suck blood from his backside.) A cushioned saddle would have helped more but he couldn't be seen to be weak. It was a pain he suffered for the greater good.

His aide was waiting for him in his tent.

"Good morning, sir," said Sergei as the count took his station behind his desk.

Given his tent was somewhere his men were unlikely to see him that often, the chair was padded, and inwardly he sighed with pleasure as he sat.

"Morning, Sergei. How's it looking today?"

His aide placed a mug of field coffee to his right.

"Not too good, sir," said his aide, straightening. "Will you be wanting breakfast, sir?"

The count's wife had got it into her head that they would live longer if they ate more fruit and vegetables. That meant eating less meat and so breakfast at the castle these days consisted of a fruit compote (quite what a compote was the count had never been clear on, as it seemed to be a fancy way of saying a bowl of stewed fruit). A field breakfast, on the other hand, consisted of the greater part of a pig, eggs, fresh bread covered in two inches of butter, and coffee blacker than night and as thick as mud. A few years ago he would have tucked away such a breakfast every day with relish, but his appetite was not what it used to be.

"No thank you, Sergei. The coffee will do. So how many knights today?"

"One, sir."

That was, as Sergei had said, not good. "All right, we may as well get him out of the way, then I'll do a snap inspection of the men."

His aide clicked his heels, did a smart about turn, and left the tent. A minute later the flap parted and a man who resembled a peacock followed his aide in. He was not in armour but dress more suited to court, with a puffy sleeved vest and balloon pantaloons. He carried a kerchief that he held to his nose. The count barely noticed the latrine smell of the camp—an inevitable stench when several thousand men crapped in the same hole—and so he was in no doubt that this fop had not spent much time with an army.

"Baron Pierre de Fanfaron," announced Sergei.

The count groaned inside. He needed men who would strip pine trees with their teeth and here was a fop whose only acquaintance with pine would have been its scent in a privy.

The baron performed a complex bow. "At your pleasure, Count."

"I'm sure," said the count.

The baron reached inside his vest and produced a parchment. He laid it on the table in front of the count. "I present you my credentials, sir. You will be finding my certificates of fencing from the King of Pointelle's own tutor and a word of recommendation from the king himself."

The count knew he was only going through the motions, so he picked up the parchment and ran an eye over it. If he had needed a man to duel an army to death then this was his lucky day; the baron had a kill record in matters of honour second to none. Additionally, the handwritten note from the King of Pointelle assured the count that the Baron of Fanfaron was an excellent raconteur and good company. Perfect.

"And what else, besides a useful rapier and a good story, might you offer me?" asked the count, setting the document down.

"Why, my company of chefs," said the baron with a faint smile.

The count though he had misheard. For a second he thought the baron had said chefs. It must have been his accent. "A company, excellent." It wasn't many, but one hundred men were not to be sniffed at.

"You would like to see them, yes?" said the baron.

"Certainly, Baron. Shall we?" said the count, getting to his feet.

Outside the sun has risen high enough to take the chill out of the morning. The count led the way towards his parade ground with his aide fallen in behind. The sound of an army under training filled the air; the clash of sword on sword, sergeants barking orders, drums beating.

"So tell me, Baron, how was your journey?" asked the count, feeling the need to make small talk. It was something he was not generally good at and avoided where possible.

The baron waved his kerchief as if dismissing some trifle. "It was adequate, but I am glad I have brought my men. Your sausage I have been forced to eat is, excuse me for saying, peasant fare. Lucky for you I have come and that will change."

Again, the baron seemed to be talking in riddles, and once again the count dismissed it as cultural misunderstanding.

They arrived at the parade ground where the baron's men were drawn up in four neat rows of twenty-five. It was not quite what the count had been expecting. He had imagined a company of battle-hardened veterans; the kind of veteran that had a hint of grey in his bushy moustache, scars across his face, a tattoo on his arm, and a slight limp from an old wound that he complained about when it was cold.

Unless he was very much mistaken, what was standing rigidly to attention in front of him, spoons snapped upright in a salute, stiff blue-and-white striped aprons catching the breeze, were one hundred kitchen-hardened cooks. Apart from a good number of impressive moustaches, there was little to suggest they had ever been in battle.

"Mon Bataillons des Chefs," said the baron proudly.

The count was at a loss for words. Was the man insane? He didn't need haute cuisine, he needed killers; preferably mounted and covered in half-inch plate.

"They are impressive, non?" said the baron, striding along the row.

The count felt like he was in a bad dream as he trailed behind.

"Indeed," said the count, hoping the despair he felt was hidden in his voice.

The baron stopped at one chef and exchanged words in his native tongue. The man positively bristled with pride.

He's complimenting the man's pastries, thought the count.

"I don't suppose they can fight?" asked the count when they reached the end of the first line.

The baron looked at the count with open bewilderment.

"Forgive me," said the count. Obviously the only thing they could fight was an urge to over-season sauce.

The baron had stopped and was continuing to frown at the count. Then a smile broke on the baron's face and he slapped the count heartily around the shoulder and laughed.

"Very good, my count. Très drôle. Very funny. You have some wit, no?"

The baron continued his inspection down the second line of men. There was a strange air about them that the count decided must be garlic.

"I'm sorry, Baron, it was impolite of me to ask. I'm sure they are most excellent cooks."

The baron came to a sudden halt and spun to face the count, outrage burning in his eyes.

"Cooks? You think these men are cooks?" The baron cast his eye back beyond the count. "That man there, you see? That man has served a regiment of men the freshest hot croissant you have ever tasted before the Battle of Perigourd. You have heard of that battle, monsieur?"

The count had. While there had been few wars in recent history, the civil war for the throne of Pointelle five years ago had been one of the larger and bloodier affairs. The Battle of Perigourd had been the deciding engagement, when the king's forces had crushed a peasant army that sought to install a common man as head of state.

"Cook? Merde. These men here, my count, are the best chefs de bataillon the world has ever seen. Do you know what happened at that battle?"

The count shrugged. One lesson he had learnt in life was that when someone was in mid-tirade, any questions asked were generally of the rhetorical kind.

"Very well, I shall tell you. Our army was small but well fed. The peasants, they were starving. We engaged them and victory looked certain, but we had underestimated these peasants and their hunger. They had caught wind of these men's efforts." The baron waved his arm expansively. "And it drove them crazy. They fought like wild men. There were so many. Some broke through and went straight for our camp. You know what that means, yes?"

Indeed the count did. Many an army had broken with its camp

threatened. Maintaining a line of retreat and supply was all important to an army's morale. Knowledge that your belongings were being had away behind you often resulted in trying to leave whatever battle you were in as swiftly as possible to try to catch the thieving bugger who was about your stuff.

"These men, these few heroes, were all that stood between this ferocious horde and the lunch that was cooking. It was an exquisite casserole de boeuf." The baron wiped a tear from his eye. "Pardon me. Just to remember the gallant deeds of these men fills me with pride. They fought like lions, these *cooks*, as you like to call them."

The count was rapidly sifting through what he knew of the battle. It was in many of the texts as an example of how to be careful with one's supply line. The king had been lucky in that he had not quite committed all his reserves. If he remembered correctly, a small company had held the peasants who broke through long enough for the rear elements to peel back and help. It had been a massacre. Then a name came to mind and with it, a realisation.

"These are the Butchers of Perigourd!"

The baron sniffed. "That name was given, but these men are chefs. They will kill for their entrées and die for their casserole."

"You must forgive me, Baron," said the count, bowing. "I am honoured you have come. I would be indebted if your company of chefs would join this army."

The baron raised his nose. "We may join you, but there are conditions. We are masters in the field kitchen. We must have absolute control. I insist."

"Most assuredly, Baron."

"We shall need dish washers."

"You shall have them."

"And fresh vegetables."

"Of course."

"Very well, then we will cook."

"Sergei, show the baron to his quarters and see that his men are given full control of the field kitchen."

The count's aide snapped a salute. "Sir, yes, sir."

The baron's nose lowered two inches and he smiled. "You like, how you say, coq au vin? Chicken with wine?"

The count had no idea what that was but nodded seriously, "Absolutely, Baron. My favourite."

The baron's smile widened. "Very well, we shall dine on that tonight." The baron turned and addressed one of the men with a volley of words. The man barked a reply and saluted with his spoon. "That is done. Shall we retire?"

The count was about to explain that, much as he would love to spend the rest of the morning in the company the baron, he had his own men to inspect when from the far side of the field a commotion arose. To the count's battle-trained ear it sounded as though they were under attack. But how could that be? The only hostile force in the area was his wife when he came home late from work.

"Some trouble?" enquired the baron.

Among the ranks of chefs, heads turned in the direction of the noise. Fillet knives appeared surreptitiously.

"I'm sure it's nothing. I suggest you stay here and attend your men, Baron, and I shall attend mine and see what the matter is. My horse, Sergei." He turned to see where his aide was but he was not to be seen. "I shall return momentarily, Baron."

The count set off across the parade square. On the far side he could see a growing knot of men. As he approached, men parted and casualties were helped away with what looked like sword wounds. One screaming man was clutching a bloody stump where his hand was missing.

The count broke into a trot and barked orders at the men around him. "You, take the wounded to the rear. Sergeant, take twenty men and form them up here in case the enemy breaks through. You, give me your sword and then find another. You, you and you, form up on me and get me through that." He pointed at the scrum ahead of them.

The detail formed a wedge in front of the count and pressed their way through the men. As they got closer to the front, the count's initial concerns began to dampen. It was obvious that whoever was being fought were few in number. He could see a semicircle of men around a large tree on the edge of the parade ground, next to the wood that stretched off to the south.

His escort finally barged their way through. The scene that greeted Count Vladovitch was not what he had been expecting. Rather than some small group of bandits that perhaps had been caught stealing, he was faced with a single man, dressed in half-plate, his back to the tree, waving a massive two-handed sword like it was a plaything. The blade dripped blood and there was a severed hand on the ground. His armour looked highly functional in a way that hearkened back to the old days when it was intended for battle rather than to impress the peasantry. There was a wild look about the man's eyes as he held the soldiers at bay. He needn't have worried, as the count's men were less than inclined to get within sword reach. To the count's left, a group of archers muscled through and raised their bows.

"Hold!" commanded the count.

The archers held their bows raised, strings half-cocked.

"Someone tell me what is going on here," continued the count. In true military fashion, every set of eyes had somewhere else to look. The count was familiar with the ploy. "You," he said. He knew the command was irresistible and sure enough, a bearded veteran the count knew well turned to look. "Petor, explain."

The man looked embarrassed.

"Speak up, Sergeant."

"Well, Count," began the man. He sniffed and wiped his nose on his sleeve. "We found this man, see, him there, on the edge of the wood, and he was out cold, and we thought he was a knight and been set upon so we tried to lift him and get him back but he woke up and started shouting and screaming and got all violent and he broke free and his sword was out and men got chopped and before you know it there was blood and mess and commotion and that's it really." The sergeant sucked in a breath.

"Griselda!" Whoever the man was, he had started to stagger forward, his sword raised in a guard. "Where is she? What have you done with her? Come on. Cowards! I'll take you all on. She's mine, I tell you. Mine."

As he came forward, men stepped back. An archer glanced over to the count, looking for an order. The count looked at the man, at the sword, and quickly calculated that disarming him would cost blood none present were anxious to spill, and he was buggered if it was going to be his. He tapped a hand on his thigh and nodded at the archer.

An arrow took the man in the leg and he went down.

"Cowards! Face me like men. Scum! Griselda!"

The man was on his knees, blood seeping from the arrow in his leg. His eyes met the count's. The count had seen the look before. In it was madness and blood lust. The count thought he was going to have to kill him and was about to raise his arm to command a volley when the man's eyes widened, his head turned as though listening to something, and then he fell forward flat on his face into the mud.

"Take him," commanded the count. "Take him to the hospital tent."

It took four soldiers to lift the man and haul him off. His sword was left lying on the ground and studiously ignored by the count's men. The count walked over to retrieve it himself. As he got closer, a growing recognition blossomed in his mind, along with a sense of something else, something not quite right, a wrongness. Standing over the sword, he was sure he had indeed seen the weapon before, when the ill-fated Countess of Umbria had brought it forth. This time, however, rather than just being a well-crafted piece of steel honed to perfection for killing, there was something else. If the count didn't know better, he would have said there was whispering at the edge of his hearing. As he grasped to hear what was being said the words would slip away, leaving him with nothing more than the suggestion that the sword wanted blood.

"You, give me your tunic," said the count to a loitering soldier.

The soldier, having looked to his left and right and realising the count was addressing him directly, swiftly de-robed. The count threw the tunic over the sword and only then lifted it. Even so, as he carried it back to his tent, he could hear it clearly now. It spoke of his younger days when he had revelled in battle. It spoke of glory and power and blood. All he had to do was take it and he would be a Hero.

Twenty years ago the count may have succumbed, but he was far too old for that now. He loved soldiering and, despite his growing misgivings as to the rightness of what was unfolding, he would leave the right and wrong of it to others, along with the being a Hero. He would do his job, which was to win battles and make sure his side was more alive than the other. He was good at that and, as he passed through the camp and men greeted him with respectful salutes, he was as determined as ever to keep as many of his men, and himself, as alive as possible.

Without doubt, this sword was not meant for him. If it was a Hero the sword wanted, and Lady Deathwing wanted, then the crazed knight in his hospital tent would be it.

Chapter 26   Fifth Lesson – Pillaging

A little pillaging goes a long way.
The Dark Lord's Handbook

Morden sat in the hut alone. He had sent everyone else away so he could think on what needed to be done. Now that he had made the decision to plunder Bostokov, Morden felt like he had finally accepted what he was, and that was a Dark Lord. At least, what he was professionally. He was still mystified as to what he was physically. After all, he had become a large black dragon and breathed fire. There were so many unanswered questions. Could he fly? Who were his parents? It seemed unlikely that Harold and Jesobel Thrumpty of Little Wassop were his real parents. What did the pendant around his neck have to do with anything?

What he couldn't deny, like it or not, was that he was destined for greatness and power. This was not altogether disagreeable. From the moment he had broken Billard's finger and bent his first lackeys to his Will, he knew he was different. There were things he understood that others did not. They were so consumed with the little things in their lives they completely failed to see the greater opportunities life could afford a smart person with a will to get what he wanted.

Then there was the whole business of who ran everything. Morden knew unswervingly that he was born to rule. He suspected only Chancellor Penbury was of a similar mind. So it would be his Will against that of the chancellor, and the world would be their battleground. Morden knew he couldn't hope to compete with the chancellor financially, economically, or politically, but he did have things the chancellor did not have. He had the orcs and he had himself.

The lessons Morden had learnt when he had broken Billard's finger were that not many understood the real nature of pain, and even fewer understood that true power does not come from indiscriminate acts but calculated demonstrations of Will. Bostokov would be another broken finger and the world would see his Will.

That was the theory, anyway.

The clammy fear lurking at the back of Morden's mind was that he had never pillaged a city before and had no idea how to go about it. With Grimtooth gone, and Stonearm more of a weapon than a confidant, there was only one place to turn to, the Handbook. Morden pulled it out and laid it on his lap. He could feel it, like a living thing. At the back of his mind he could hear it whispering. It wanted to be read. It was another of the great mysteries that had entered his life in recent months. The time would come when he would have to find out what the Handbook really was, but now was not that time. He felt out of his depth and needed advice.

For a Dark Lord there is little more satisfying than his first pillage. There's nothing quite like the smell of a burning city first thing in the morning. To stand upon a battlement and watch cleansing fire burn away the refuse that a city has collected over the years is a moment to be cherished.

Yes, yes, thought Morden, but how does a Dark Lord go about the actual pillaging? Is it the random free-for-all loot and burn it looks like, or is there more to it than that?

The answer is, of course, both. To the citizens of the city, and the world at large, it will look like the Dark Lord has randomly run amok in the city, his horde taking what they please, burning indiscriminately and leaving a trail of corpses in their wake. And all of this may well happen, but a Dark Lord who acts without volition is nothing more than a Warlord.

I sense, Morden, that you have already learnt several of the characteristics of real power. To blindly thrash around for the sheer sake of inflicting suffering is not one of them.

When you pillage a city there are many beneficial things that can result besides the gaining of loot. For a start, it's good for morale. Your troops will love you as they are given license to run amok. The trick is to let them have a good time, but to direct them expertly. A city that is completely burned to the ground is not much use to you. You need to carefully pluck and prune. The slums can go. A cleansing fire that burns away disease will actually be welcomed by the larger populace. Slums are also easy to rebuild.

Don't be fooled by beauty, it is fleeting. Nor be fooled by age, as all decays in time. Do not spare a building because it is beautiful or old. Think of what it can do for you, and if the answer is that it can demonstrate your Will, then it must be pulled down to its foundations.

Be an iconoclast.

You're doing these people a favour. They may realise life is more than stone and sculpture, and the gods don't give a damn.

This was more like it. It was like having a light shone in the dark and seeing properly for the first time. While it was true he had grasped the basic understanding of inflicting pain for purpose, never had he considered it on such a scale. To bend a person to your Will was one thing, but to do the same with an entire city's population was quite another. But then he was going to rule the world, so it shouldn't really be such a surprise.

There have been those who would advocate total destruction of the first few cities you pillage so that future cities will just open their gates on your approach, and this strategy has had success, but it's been done. The smarter city leaders know a city of rubble is no good to anyone.

Most city leaders are also corrupt, thieving tyrants in their own right and will happily see rivals destroyed to better their own end. It will never be difficult to find those who will turn over their fellow citizens for their own gain. Seek them out and make good use of them, and when you're done, dispose of them discreetly; after all, they can't be trusted. But do be discreet. Tell people they've retired into luxury somewhere pleasant. You'll want these people wherever you go and if word got out their life expectancy was poor, they'll be less willing.

It was all fitting into place. Let the orcs have their fun, but point them at targets that served a greater good, like at the houses of unpopular politicians rather than the pubs, which should be looted but not burned. Destroy, burn and steal in such a way as to put fear into people's hearts by the seeming randomness of it all but, in fact, be precise and calculated. Take what was needed. Destroy that which spoke the loudest. Find allies in the cancerous leadership of the city itself.

Morden set the Handbook down and thought a while. He had originally considered standing at the gate, a horde of disgruntled orcs at his back, storming the city and having an epic battle. But he saw now this was his romantic side coming to the fore.

He needed to be a touch more selective. What he needed from Bostokov was a means of transporting his orcish army, supplies, and cash. He also needed to send out a strong message to the chancellor.

All of this could be done at the docks. That is where he would strike. It wasn't yet midday, so he still had time, but there was a lot to do. He had plans to make and orders to give. This was it.

"Stonearm!"

*****

It was early evening and time to set the plan in motion. It had been a busy day. He'd spent most of it poring over maps of the city, identifying targets. Fortunately the city was soft; the only military was a small but decently armed guard whose main duty was to man the gates and look pretty on ceremonial days. Certainly they should bear little challenge to the sheer number of orcs, even less so to orcs set free from their poverty.

Morden racked his mind for anything he had overlooked. It seemed straightforward enough, but he was still nervous.

"Time to go," he said to Stonearm, who had proven to be a more than able right-hand man. His sheer size commanded a deal of respect among the orcs, and this was compounded by Morden's own obvious trust in him.

His sergeant held the leather flap aside and Morden ducked into the gloom of dusk. Straightening, he was momentarily surprised by the sight that greeted him. The square was packed solid with orcs, silently standing. Looking closer he could see some had rudimentary armour, and all had weapons of one kind or another: knives, axes, clubs, hammers, poles with blades strapped on, and forks.

"I thought you'd like to address the men," whispered Stonearm from behind him, and a crate was produced.

Morden set one foot on the crate and hesitated. It was one small step for him onto that crate, but one big step for a Dark Lord. The pendant at his neck grew hot against his skin. If he botched this they'd rip him apart.

He took the second step and gazed over the sea of raised heads from under his cowl. A feeling of power rushed into him like five of those cider spirit shots he'd done back in Bindelburg for a bet.

There was a rumble of impatience from the gathered horde.

Morden spread his arms, but a sudden panic hit him. How should he address them? 'Fellow orcs' was inappropriate. 'Comrades' was too familiar—after all, he was a Dark Lord. 'Men' was inaccurate.

Then it came to him.

"MINIONS! OUR TIME HAS COME!"

The first few rows of orcs staggered back with the force of his words. A few looked puzzled. Morden glanced to his right to see Stonearm's reaction. The big orc was grinning. His teeth, which he had resharpened, showing in two terrible rows. He'd found himself a huge club into which he had hammered a dozen iron nails. He raised the club one handed above his head.

"Gaaarrrrrgggghhhh," shouted the orc.

A host of weapons were raised, teeth were bared, and a cry went up from the assembled horde.

"MORDEN!"

It was like he had been struck by lightning. He felt like he was growing, towering above his minions—for that is what they were; his disciples, his followers, his army to do his bidding because he was their master. As the adoration continued, a primal fury seemed to be let loose in the orcs. It was as if they had rediscovered a voice that had long been lost.

Morden gathered himself and spoke, using his normal voice as he noticed the orcs in the front row had blood streaming from their ears and noses.

"Five hundred years ago orcs were taken into servitude. A proud race, you have had your teeth blunted and your pride taken. I tell you now, you deserve more!"

A roar of approval greeted his words.

"Many of you knew Grimtooth."

There were nods and a grumble rippled through the crowd.

"He was a great orc! He was a wise orc! He spoke of a time that would come when orcs would once more take their rightful place. He spoke of prophecy and a Dark Lord Rising. A Dark Lord who would lead his nation to the greatness that is their destiny."

Morden let the words sink in. He had their attention now.

"He spoke the truth. I am that Dark Lord, and I will set you free as he asked me to. You will fulfil your destiny."

Morden paused for dramatic effect, and for a split second thought perhaps he had not been heard. But then a cheer exploded from the mass of orcs that sent pulses of excitement through him. He was taken by the strongest of compulsions and he reached into his robe, clutched the Handbook, and held it aloft like a trophy.

"It starts here! It starts now!"

The sheer power of his voice silenced the orcs—not that they would have been heard above him. His words were like a summer storm.

"Orcs, throw aside your shackles and join me, Morden the Dark Lord, and you will reclaim the pride that was taken from you. Sharpen your weapons, and sharpen your teeth, for tonight, Bostokov burns!"

The orcs went into a frenzy. They shouted and jumped as one solid mass of furious muscle and teeth. Until now he had been intoxicated by what he thought was power, but now he had a taste of what real power was, and he wanted more. This was a few thousand slum orcs who were more a rabble than an army. He couldn't imagine what it must feel like to stand in front of a host with the world at their mercy. Just thinking about it made his flesh burn in anticipation.

For now, though, there was a city to sack.

He got off the crate and cut a path through the mob.

"How did I do?" he asked Stonearm, who was close to his right elbow, ever alert for danger.

"Not bad, Boss," said the orc. "A bit short, but not too shabby for your first monologue."

Morden looked sideways at Stonearm, who returned the look and winked.

*****

Gaining entrance to the city was straightforward. Word had been sent to the host of orcs who worked as servants and menials in the posh houses inside the walls. They had slipped out at the appropriate time, overpowered the half-asleep gate guard, and greeted their fellows with broad smiles.

Morden strode through the gate at the head of his rabble and past the row of pikes bearing the first trophies of the night. The guards had been hung by their undergarments while still wearing them. The wedgie, as the orcs called it, was apparently not only deeply humiliating but painful. By the contorted face of the guard captain, it indeed seemed a less than pleasant way to be suspended.

From there the orcs spread through the city on a burning and looting spree. The fact that Bostokov was largely built from stone helped them be particular and prevented the city becoming one big fire pit.

Morden, in the meantime, headed with a hand-chosen band to the Hall of Justice. The lofty hall was adorned with humorous gargoyles and stained glass depicting rich people dispensing largess. At one end, on a raised dais, was a mahogany throne used by the Head Justice in pronouncing his rulings. Morden found it comfortable with good back support.

It took little time for the orcs to round up the city's finest. They had been rather rudely turned from their feather beds and now stood shivering (in fear; it was quite a warm night, what with all the fires) in their night shifts. If their indignant expressions were anything to go by, they were wondering what the hell was going on.

"I expect you're wondering what is going on," said Morden once the last few had been brought in and feeling the need to voice their thoughts.

Grunts of consternation came from the assembled gentry. Chuckles came from the surrounding orcs. Some beat nasty looking clubs into ham-sized fists.

A man with a bushy white moustache, and wearing a finely embroidered night shift, stepped forward. "Now look here, what's the meaning of all this? I demand you tell us who you are and what is going on. What gives you the right?"

Morden stood. "The right?" He laughed. The sound echoed around the hall and within it was amusement tinged with menace. He drew himself up and took a step forward. The man took a step back. "I am Morden." The man's hair noticeably raised an inch off his scalp. "That is what gives me the right. Your city has what I need and so I am taking it. If you want to live I suggest you are both civil and accommodating."

There was a commotion and a scuffle from the back of the group. A woman was pushing her way forward, shaking free the clinging arms that tried to restrain her.

"Let me go!" she commanded, thrusting an elbow to loosen the last restraining hand. She stepped forward of the group and glowered at Morden. The woman was young, little more than a girl. Morden guessed she was barely a few years older than himself. She was dressed in fine silks that hinted at delights that lay beneath. "Do you know who I am?" she demanded. Morden couldn't help but notice the little dimples in her cheeks that twitched with fury. She was without doubt the most beautiful thing he had ever seen. "I'm Rosemary Cathcart and I demand you release us."

He was about to say something charming when he caught himself. He was a Dark Lord pillaging a city. Now was not the time to let his attentions wander to other pleasures.

"Stonearm." He motioned the orc forward. "Take her. I'll deal with her later. Personally." He laughed in a way he hoped would suggest that whatever he had in mind involved sharp, and possibly red-hot, implements of torture.

The big orc advanced on the girl who looked at Morden with disbelief. "You can't. You're meant to ask me who I am. Well, I'm important. My father will hear of this. You wait. Get off me, you brute."

As Stonearm got close, the girl began to thrash and scream. The noise was piercing and set Morden's teeth on edge.

"For gods' sake, shut her up," said Morden, trying hard not to cover his ears; after all, it would not be Dark Lord-like to do so.

Stonearm cuffed the girl and she collapsed in a heap. Morden hoped the orc hadn't broken anything; he didn't seem to realise how strong he was. Stonearm picked the girl up and threw her over his shoulder like she was nothing and stomped off. The assembled nobility watched in horror.

"If you wish to avoid her fate," said Morden, "I suggest you stop wailing and complaining, and start cooperating. Now, who is the city treasurer? I'd like to open an account and make a withdrawal."

The old man with the bushy moustache stepped forward. "I am the treasurer. I think you'll find we have the most agreeable rates, if it's a loan you want?"

Morden laughed. "Oh, I am sure they are, Mr. Treasurer. Now be a good man and show these orcs the treasury."

"And what about the rest of us?" piped up a voice. "What are you going to do to us?"

The orcs chuckled in a way that, for many of the cowering dignitaries, answered the question without the need for Morden to say a word.

"We're very rich, you know? Can't we come to some kind of arrangement?" said the same voice, and there were assenting mutters all around.

"Yes, rich."

"We can pay you anything."

"I have five daughters, and they're all quite orcish."

Morden raised a hand to silence them and, apart from the odd sob, it had the desired effect.

"Take them back to their houses."

A sigh of relief escaped the crowd.

"Wedgie them on their front gates and take everything of value."

The sigh turned to wails of despair. "You can't just kill us!" complained one voice as the orcs dragged them off.

Though being suspended on their gate posts by their undergarments was unlikely to prove fatal, Morden didn't feel the need to disabuse them of their dread thoughts and sat back down in the Seat of Justice. He was going to enjoy this Dark Lord business.

The hall had emptied and Morden settled for a few minutes of personal brooding time. It had been a while since he had had the opportunity to sit and think and the throne reminded him of Bindelburg. It seemed a long way away now, and an even longer time ago. He was a Dark Lord Rising and he had a host of orc minions out on the town. All around him a city was burning as an army of disenfranchised orcs emancipated themselves, or more accurately burned and pillaged. All in all, assassination attempts and the death of Grimtooth aside, life was not bad.

Morden took time to soak in his surroundings. The flickering light from the burning city cast eerie shadows through the stained glass windows. It combined well with the noise of the city being pillaged and the strong smell of smoke to create an apocalyptic atmosphere Morden found entrancing. He was so caught up in the dancing shapes he almost missed the large hardwood doors opening at the far end of the hall.

A man entered and strode purposefully towards Morden. Behind him trailed a man and woman who seemed to be tugged reluctantly along.

The confidence with which the man approached a throne upon which sat a black cowled figure while a city burned outside struck Morden as unusual. As the man got closer, the pendant at Morden's throat began to grow warm. Given its track record for alerting him to potential danger, Morden stood.

The man's boots beat on the stone floor. He was tall; a little taller than himself. His face was narrow, dark, and disturbingly draconian. Morden wasn't sure where the latter thought came from but it made his heart beat a bit faster.

"You must be Morden," said the man, coming to a stop, his two companions standing heads downcast behind him. "Let me take a good look at you."

Morden was curiously at a loss as what to say.

"Do you think you could pull that cowl back?" asked the man. He took a step onto the dais.

Morden pulled his hood back and met the eyes of this strange man, and as he did so he saw both darkness and fire.

"Do I know you?" asked Morden. The pendant was burning painfully and his skin was itching.

The man looked genuinely surprised. "You don't recognise me?"

"Should I?"

The man smiled to reveal a perfect row of white, razor-sharp teeth. He spread his arms. "Morden, I am your father."

As soon as he heard the words, without doubt he knew this was indeed his true father. Despite this, part of him recoiled in denial. "My father? You can't be. My father is Harold Thrumpty. How can you be?"

The man laughed. "Son. You honestly think poor old Harold could make you? A dragon *and* a Dark Lord? I am your father. Look at your heart. You know it's true."

Morden put a hand to his chest. He could feel hard scales under the robe where the pendant lay.

His father sat on the top step and patted the stair next to him. "Come sit. We have a lot of catching up to do."

Morden sank to the ground in a daze. "I can't believe this. So who am I? And who are they? What's your name?"

Morden's father laughed. It was painfully loud, sitting so close.

"You can call me dad. And we're Deathwings," said his father, wiping a tear from his eye. "That's Griselda, and that fellow is Kristoff. You may know him. He's from Little Wassop as well."

At the mention of his name, Kristoff looked up and Morden was shocked. It was indeed the same dreamy-eyed poet who had driven him to Bindelburg all those years ago, but time, and perhaps fate, had not been kind. He had aged and in his eyes there was pain; although on seeing Morden it seemed to wash away briefly. When he glanced back to Morden's father it returned and his head dropped once more.

Morden's mind was spinning with questions. Maybe at last he would know who or what he was. Why had his real father left him? Why was he here now? What did Kristoff have to do with it all?

"And what about her, then?" asked Morden.

"That's Griselda. She's very important and in some danger. I rescued her and brought her here for you to protect. Griselda, say hello to Morden."

Griselda's head rose, as though under some compulsion.

It had been a scarce few minutes since Morden thought he had seen the most beautiful girl in the world when he had met the feisty Rosemary Cathcart, but he had been hasty in his assessment of that title. Where Rosemary had girlish good looks, Griselda had beauty that not so much suggested but rather announced loudly that she was a woman. Though her clothes were ragged, and her face dirtied with soot, she was captivating. But more than anything, her eyes were somewhere he felt he could be lost forever.

"A pleasure to meet you, Griselda," was all Morden could manage without making an idiot of himself.

Morden watched for what seemed an eternity as Griselda's head turned so she looked him in the eye. Her full lips broke apart to make a reply. He ached with the thought of what pleasure he would feel if he were ever to taste the sweetness of those lips.

"Get fucked," she smiled.

Morden's father winced. "She has got a mouth on her."

Chapter 27   A Dark Lord Rises

The only good publicity is bad publicity.
The Dark Lord's Handbook

Penbury couldn't sleep. It wasn't the faint dawn sunlight that crept around the edges of the thick velvet curtains that kept sleep at bay, it was his mind that was awake and refusing sleep. Some may have been worried with the events unfolding in the world but Penbury didn't do worry. Worry was a short step away from being neurotic. While not every problem had a solution, and on occasion things would not always go as one desired, that was not a reason to worry. That was life. While worry was a stranger to him, thinking was not and it was his mind that was full of thoughts and permutations. He wished he could turn over and get another hour of cotton-padded comfort before Chidwick would knock and enter with his cup of tea to start another day of business, but any chance of that was gone.

Instead he threw the blankets back and let the crisp spring air invigorate his body to the wakefulness his mind enjoyed. He dressed quickly and decided to do something reckless. He needed some thinking time. He would go for a walk. Alone.

For a man such as himself, going anywhere alone was neither practical nor safe. If he had been the worrying type, the sheer number of enemies he had would have kept him imprisoned behind a regiment of guards, too scared to get out of bed. Though he did not live in fear like this, the regiment of guards was still present and under the watchful eye of Chidwick. Getting out would be tricky, but he had a plan.

The house he lived in used to belong to the well-known philanderer, the Duke of Firena. This had been his bedroom. His wife did not share his bed outside of their monthly appointment, which was necessary for appearance's sake and quite in keeping for the aristocracy of this region. It was widely known the duke made other arrangements for the rest of the month and, being a duke, discretion had been his watchword.

Penbury went to the corner of the room next to the extravagant bay window. What he was looking for was somewhere around here. He pushed at wood panels and tugged at the candle holders. At last a section of veneered wood gave way under his fingers and a lever was revealed. A swift tug and a section of the wall swung back. The young ladies the duke had entertained must have had to stoop to use it but there it was: the duke's love stair.

Penbury lit his night light and squeezed in. For someone as large as he, it was a tight fit. Beyond the secret door there was more room and he could straighten up. A narrow spiral stair led him down. His candlelight showed names carved into the stone. They were the names of women, and there were a lot of them. The duke had been a busy man and it looked like his lovers had left their mark as a record. By some of the remarks scratched in with the names, the duke was more than popular; one sketch suggested he was hung like a horse. Either that or he was an ass.

At the bottom of the stair there was another, more obvious lever to tug and a section of the outer wall, which turned out to be wood with a light stone coating, opened onto the flower bed below his window.

No one was in sight. A quick dash and Penbury made the safety of the shrubbery across the narrow lawn. Soon after he had made his way by paths that only he knew down onto the dunes below the estate. The sun was up now and warmed him as he started his walk. For the first mile he pushed the weighty matters that had been on his mind to one side and enjoyed the morning. He bent to examine the wild flowers in the grass dunes that were hard to grow in his gardens; they were both delicate and hardy.

It wasn't often he got to spend time like this, completely alone. Although he could see no one, he could not know with certainty that behind that sandy bank, or in that long grass, there weren't bodyguards recruited, trained and deployed by Chidwick. He thought he had made good his rebellious escape, but he could not be sure.

It was no matter, the illusion was for all intents and purposes a reality as he could neither hear nor see anyone and it left him to stroll gently along, taking in his surroundings. He turned his mind to other matters.

While the news from the Snort twins was good—the Hero and his sword had been located in an army being raised by Count Vladovitch, and Morden had been tracked to Bostokov—Penbury suspected his commissioning of them may have been a tactical mistake. Not that he would admit publicly to such a thing.

His conclusion had come from going back and studying the archives, and there seemed to be a pattern to historical events. It was as though they had a life of their own. He had never been one for gods, or fate, or any kind of predetermination, but there seemed to be a trend of inevitability about certain passages of history. If he were to hold fast to his beliefs and suppose there were no divine beings (the idea they had nothing better to do than have a chuckle at his and humanity's expense was ludicrous), then he could account for this inevitability in terms of a limited view of the cause and effect.

The world was a complex place, with a myriad of forces at work that most people were oblivious to, and even men of superior intellect, such as himself, could only glimpse part of the whole. The parts he saw happened to be large—mostly economic and social—but what of the others? He could only guess. Now, he surmised, just as there were inevitable consequences to the restriction of supply to price—and most of his enormous fortune was based on the simplest of economic principles such as this—then to an external observer could there not be an inevitable consequence to other things, like a Dark Lord Rising?

So far he had been mostly concerned with the consequences of this happening and had ignored completely the reason for it. His hiring of Snort and Snort was a reaction to this. If they were successful then all well and good, but if, as he suspected would be the case, they failed then the problem remained.

What he needed to do was understand why now, of all times, a Dark Lord was Rising and why this inevitably resulted in a Hero appearing as a counterbalance. It was clear from the histories that, in all likelihood, a series of reasonably predictable events was about to unfold, which would involve armies, destruction, stirring speeches, shiny armour, maidens, last ditch defences, volcanoes, attacks at dawn, and dragons.

Why volcanoes figured so frequently was a mystery, and one which Penbury was happy to leave for now, bar making a mental note to look up a map of all currently active volcanoes and to steer well clear.

What was of more interest was the last item: dragons. While there was no doubt dragons had existed, there had been little evidence of them since they had last been seen swooping over Zoon's great army. It was true that occasionally an addled peasant girl would attest to having been seduced by a dark lover that turned out to be a dragon, but they never lived long and so it was hard to corroborate.

The problem seemed to centre on the fact that dragons had two major things in their favour. The first was that, if the books were to be believed, they were highly magical and actually spent little time in their recognisable form (big wings, breathing fire), and instead appeared human. The second thing they had to their advantage, and this was reflected by the fact they tried to blend in most of the time, was they were also highly intelligent. This made sense. Though powerful, they could still be hunted down and killed, and there was plenty of evidence to suggest there were breeds of dragon that either refused to shape-shift, or could not, that were now extinct. There were records in the archives, dating back a thousand years, of payments to dragon slayers, and given the number of entries, there had been a lot of dragon slaying back then.

The conclusion Penbury came to in light of this evidence was that any dragons still around were both smart and dangerous. This was a matter of concern.

Penbury was so wrapped up in thought he'd lost track of where he was wandering. The irate calls of a pair of Suicide Gulls brought his attention to the fact he may have come a little too close to their nest. The birds were both large and persistent. They swooped and squawked and Penbury had to raise an arm to ward off their hooked bills.

As one came especially close he actually had to duck. As he did so he heard a squeal more than a squawk and a thud. Looking up, the gull lay a few yards away with a crossbow bolt in its chest. It was quite dead.

"A touch overzealous, wouldn't you say?" asked the chancellor, straightening and casting around to see if he could spot his protector. There was no sign. So much for having slipped his minders.

Penbury walked over to the bird and hefted it up by its legs. It weighed a couple of pounds, which was a lot for a seabird such as this. It would fill a crust that evening with ease. The dead gull's mate continued its protests as the chancellor walked away.

"And don't you dare shoot that one," he said loudly to no one in particular. He was a firm believer in only killing what you ate, and one gull would be more than enough.

Having settled supper in his mind, he went back to the world and its problems. The real issue, as he saw it, was the upsetting of a status quo which had kept the civilised world in relative peace for a few hundred years. With this peace had come great prosperity, at least for a minority of the population, and decent enough comfort for the rest. This Dark Lord business threatened to upset all of this. He also knew it wasn't so much an issue of right or wrong, good or evil—he knew himself to be as amoral as the next man—but rather self-interest. The foundation of much of his economic theories relied on the quintessential idea that the majority act in self-interest, whether at the individual or group level. Genuine philanthropy was rare.

Curiously, for one who was more enlightened and self-interested than most, Penbury had often found it ironic that he was most likely, far and away, the most philanthropic person in the known world. Personal wealth had long since stopped being a concern; he could have anything he wanted. What had replaced it was a desire for experience and pleasure, and these took many forms. It had come as some surprise to find that giving aroused a not unpleasant feeling.

The issue at hand, though, was what was to be done? He could raise an army and oppose the Dark Lord, but that seemed like something that could only worsen things.

He could back the Hero he had rumour of, but that was little better, and was barely more appealing as a winner than the Dark Lord. At least the Dark Lord was overtly self-interested, whereas Penbury's experience of most self-proclaimed good people was that they were outwardly righteous while hiding their self-interest.

Perhaps it was this self-interest he could accommodate. If he could find out what both parties really wanted, then in all likelihood he was in a position to arrange it. If the Dark Lord wanted a kingdom he was sure he could manage something, maybe even with a volcano.

So that was it. He needed to go and do what he did best, and negotiate a deal. With the vast resources he had to command, he was sure that with a little prudent jiggery-pokery, he could settle matters without the need for any battles, or volcanoes exploding, or dragons.

A rumble from his stomach reminded him he had not yet eaten that morning. He turned around to see he had come quite a way. He thought it would be another half an hour before he could enjoy breakfast when a smell came to him on the swirling breeze. It was unmistakably bacon. The chancellor turned to align his nose with the direction of the smell. Topping the next dune the source of the smell became clear; in a sheltered hollow between two dunes a table had been laid, and to one side a chef was preparing breakfast over an open fire. Chidwick was pouring coffee into a cup at the single seat at the table.

Penbury strolled down to the table and handed Chidwick the gull he was carrying. "I'll have that in a pie for supper, Chidwick," he said, taking the seat. "Did I miss anything while I was walking?"

"Just this, sir," said Chidwick, handing the chancellor a note.

Penbury read it and it confirmed his worst fears.

Snort had failed and Bostokov was burning. A Dark Lord was indeed Rising.

"Chidwick."

"Sir?"

"When we get back, start packing. After breakfast we're going on a trip."

Chapter 28   Enemies

The enemy of my enemy is also my enemy.
A Dark Lord has no friends.
The Dark Lord's Handbook

When Edwin woke he was lying on his back in a cot under canvas. Turning his head to the left and right, he could see other men lying on similar cots. They had blood-stained bandages around their heads, arms, legs and torsos. Had he been in a battle? He reached one hand up to his face and ran the other over his body. He had a bandage on his leg and it was sore to his touch. His brow was wet with sweat and he felt thick-headed, like he had a fever. He tried to sit up and immediately regretted it. He slumped back onto the hard pillow.

Edwin tried to think. He knew his own name but little else. How had he come to be here? Flashes of memory started to go off in his mind. He remembered being surrounded. He had lost something, something he had to get back, that he loved. Or was it someone? Yes. He was searching for someone who was in great danger and only he could save them. He remembered a moor, desolate and grey. He remembered cold, hunger and desperation before stumbling off the high ground and into a forest. He had been lost. Where had they taken her? That was it. He had lost *her*. Then it hit him.

Griselda!

The memories came flooding back. His sword, his love, his loss, the pain and anger. They had surrounded him and he had tried to fight them but they were too many. His hand went to his leg as he remembered being shot.

He had to get out of here. Raising his head barely off the pillow he looked around. There didn't seem to be any guards. A few men who seemed to have only minor injuries were playing cards around a table near the entrance to the tent. But he didn't have to leave that way; the bottom of the tent had a gap running along it. It would be tight but he could slide under that. He tried to move. The wound sent pain shooting up his leg as the muscle tensed, and his head throbbed. He felt like a rag doll. He was so weak.

He slumped back in despair. He was useless, and surely for every moment he lay here unspeakable acts were being committed on his love, Griselda. He could only imagine her despair as she called his name in desperate hope that he would rescue her. He hoped her love for him kept her strong; for love such as theirs could not be denied. There was destiny in them being together. Nothing could keep them apart as long as they were true to that love, and he was as sure of his love as he knew she was of hers.

His grief overwhelmed him and he fell into a half-waking dream where he struggled in vain to rescue her. In his dream he could see her, standing at the side of a dark-cowled figure. She had been bewitched and was draped over him like a harlot, dressed in the flimsiest of skirts and veils. The Dark Lord mocked him.

He tried to get to them so he could cut his tormentor down and break the spell on his love, but as he moved it was as though he were wading through mud. He fell and found he was drowning. He struggled for breath. Above him he could see the surface of the water shimmering with light. He reached out as he sank. His lungs burned and he thrashed around. He was going to die.

No!

Griselda could not be left to her fate. He would rescue her. Fighting against darkness that sought to swallow him, he headed for the glimmer of light that was left.

Then he was awake. His lungs were screaming with agony but he could not cry out or draw breath. There was a pillow over his face and a great weight holding it down. Someone was trying to smother him.

With all his might and fury, Edwin swung a fist round and felt it connect with a satisfying smack. Someone fell sideways and hit the ground with a thud. The pillow was released and Edwin gasped in a huge breath. He rolled to one side and savoured the taste of the cold night air. The burning in his lungs became an ache.

With painful slowness, his head thick and his leg still sore, Edwin leaned over the edge of the cot to see who his attacker had been, but there was no one there. The pillow lay by itself, scrunched up on either side where it had been held, an impression of Edwin's face visible in the low moonlight.

Around him the other men slept and snored, oblivious to what had happened. Someone had tried to kill him.

No. Not someone. Edwin knew who had tried to kill him, if not in person then by dispatching an assassin: the man in black from his dreams, who had summoned the foulest of creatures to steal away his love. He had done this. Edwin knew he could tarry no longer. He would bear the pain, for what was that next to the suffering of Griselda? It was nothing. A test of his love. It was pain he could bear.

He sat up.

He steadied himself and, grimacing with pain, he swung himself out of the cot and stood. At least his leg was good. It hurt but could bear his weight; the arrow had not shattered bone. He took a step. And then another. He stumbled, and as he did so he felt something brush his face. There was a thud from the tent post to his side. His hand went up to his face automatically. It came away wet, and then came the sting. Without thinking he rolled to the ground and there was another thud. The man on the cot he had fallen next to jerked. There was a sickening gurgle from the man and he twitched in death throes. Edwin rolled under the cot and tried to work out where the assassin was firing from, but he could not see much from where he was. He instinctively rolled sideways. A bolt hit the earth where he had been a second before. He was a dead man unless he did something. There was only one thing he could do.

He filled his lungs and roared. As he did so, he burst to his feet and turned over the next cot, tumbling the man onto the floor. Another bolt swished past him but his roar had woken people. Within seconds there was a general commotion as Edwin continued to bellow and everyone woke up.

Then the dead man was found, a bolt through his neck, and Edwin was seized.

"It wasn't me!" he bellowed. He was held by four men, and they were having a tough time of it. He struggled as hard as he could. "Let me go. Let me go!"

He wasn't going to break free struggling like this so he relaxed, going limp in their hands. He felt their grip loosen in response. He took a deep breath and exploded outwards with his arms and sent his captors flying in all directions.

Then there was a blow to the back of his head. He fell and the world went black.

This time when he woke and tried to move his arms, he couldn't. He was bound to the cot. Then the pain came flooding in. His head felt like the time when he had been running in the smithy as a boy and had slipped and smacked it on the anvil.

"He's awake," said a man's voice. It was an old voice that had a touch of weariness about it.

Edwin kept his eyes closed and tried to feign sleep. What was going on? It all made no sense. Why was he still alive? Who had tried to kill him and why was he being kept alive now? Did they mean to torture him further? Perhaps the Dark Lord wanted to gloat over him before he was dispatched.

"So he is. Edwin?"

The voice was a woman's. Not Griselda though. This voice was sibilant, but also hard. There was something in it that chilled his heart. Whoever they were, they obviously knew he was awake. He opened his eyes.

Peering down at him were an old man with a bearded and scarred face, and a woman who was both beautiful and terrible. It was her eyes. They were like ovals of fire as they burned into him. She had a slender face and high cheekbones. Her hair was black and straight. She reached for his forehead to rest the back of her hand against it. Her touch was like cold stone. She pinched his cheek; her nails were like talons.

"He's got a fever," she said. "But he'll live."

She whispered something in his ear and sleep rushed in on him.

When he woke it felt like he had slept for a week. He couldn't remember dreaming at all and it took a moment to remember where he was and what had happened. His head should be hurting, but it wasn't. He could feel where he had been shot but the wound itched like it had healed and caused no pain.

He was still bound, though, so he was a prisoner. Rage welled up and he fought to keep it down. He needed to save it for when he could make his escape and punish those who had done this.

Looking around, he found his surroundings had changed. He was in a much smaller tent and alone. There was a plain wooden table and chair. Clothes were draped over the chair and his sword was leant against it in its scabbard. On the table was a stoup and bowl. Through an open flap he could see two guards.

A head dipped in through the flap, a young woman with a plain but warm face. She smiled when she saw him look up at her and immediately disappeared.

Edwin heard the sound of leather heels snapping together and the flap was thrown back; the old man and woman swept in.

"Bring me two chairs," said the man over his shoulder.

The two looked at him impassively. He, in return, examined each in more detail.

The man was obviously military and, from his scars and attire, experienced. Edwin was not sure how he knew, but there were little things, like how he wore his dagger there, across his front rather than at his side, and how his attire was tied and strapped, that only came from seasons of campaigning and represented years of hard-won victory. Edwin couldn't help feeling respect for what this man represented. He may be his enemy but he gave every impression of being a solid, grim, determined foe who would neither give nor expect quarter. That was fine with Edwin, for mercy encouraged only weakness. Strength was what he respected, and this man was strong.

The woman was entirely different. Her clothes were not quite right, as though from a bygone era. She wore a mixture of leather and cloth that served to both show off a feminine figure and yet was subtly functional in a practical way. She could ride a horse or even fight with those clothes. Certainly she was no soft noblewoman, although there was an air of aristocracy about her. She held her nose slightly up, as though offended by the smell (which had to be said was a ripe mixture of horse, mud and men).

Her straight black hair framed a slender face with thin lips and oval eyes that still had fire in them. As he scrutinized her, she held his stare, cupped her chin and tapped her talon-like fingernails against her cheek.

"He's not all brawn then," she said. "Good."

Two soldiers with chairs for his captors appeared and were then dismissed. It seemed they didn't need guards, especially given he was bound.

"You are wondering who we are and why you are bound," said the woman. "I am required to be a woman of discretion so who I am must remain my secret, but you may call me Black Orchid. This is Count Vladovitch. Together, we represent a group that is most worried about certain things and we would like you to help us."

Edwin was puzzled. He wasn't sure what he had expected—he should be dead—but conspiratorial introductions was not what had sprung to mind.

"There is a darkness rising," continued Black Orchid, "that will bring ruin to the world and it must be stopped. The count here has been building an army to that end."

"The Dark Lord," said Edwin. So they knew of him, but he was their enemy? It made no sense. They were playing with him like some fool. This time he could not keep the fury down. From across the room he could hear his sword whispering. It wanted blood.

"You must forgive me, madam," he started quietly, "but what, in all that is sacred, is happening here?" His voice rose as he spoke, his anger getting the better of him. "Why am I bound? Where is Griselda? Where are you keeping HER?"

He strained against his bonds, but they were thick and well tied. His shout brought in the guards. The count, if that was indeed what he was, waved them away.

Black Orchid was shaking her head. "Edwin, Edwin. I'm so sorry. Of course, I should have said. Morden, the Dark Lord, has Griselda. Even as we speak he takes her east."

Edwin listened with disbelief.

"Bastards!" he spat at them.

Then the rage took him again. He shook and strained, managing to topple the cot. It took four men to set him straight. All the while, Black Orchid watched with amusement that made him angrier. He wanted to smash that smile from those lips. And yet, her beauty was terrible and roused him in ways that made him hate himself. He wanted to taste her lips, to feel that body.

He shook his head to force the images out and focussed on Griselda. She was his love and he hers. He would be with no other woman. This he'd sworn to himself and to her.

Black Orchid laughed and blew him a kiss. Could she read his mind?

Eventually he had no more energy. They had moved him to a chair and bound his legs to it so he could not kick, and hitched his arms behind him.

"You say you want my help and yet you bind me like an animal," said Edwin, glaring at them.

Black Orchid laughed again. "It's for your own good, my dear boy. We can't have you tearing this place up and getting hurt. What good would you be to Griselda if you did that? Or to us, for that matter? If you would calm down and listen, then perhaps you might realise we are here to help you."

Part of him wanted to believe, but there were so many things that told him not to. "So who tried to kill me?" asked Edwin.

"Morden's assassins," said Black Orchid. "Now, are you ready to listen? We have a lot to go through, and the count here is a busy man."

What she said made sense. If they had wanted him dead, he would be. And although he was bound, he did see that maybe it was for their safety. He had to admit that had he not been tied he would have hacked them into chunks and fed them to swine. Maybe they were telling the truth. If they were, and this Morden was taking Griselda to the east, he would need a new horse at the very least. If the count had an army he could use, that would be even better.

"I'm listening," he said.

"Good," said Black Orchid, smiling. "If you're willing to lend us that strapping sword-arm of yours, here's what we can do for you."

For the first time in weeks, Edwin felt his spirits rise. If it was his sword-arm they wanted, then he was sure he could oblige them.

"There's going to be a war, Edwin," continued Black Orchid. "Morden is a Dark Lord and he seeks dominion over the world. As I speak, he raises an army and heads east to his fortress. From there he will gather to him all the evil in the world before Coming Forth in an apocalyptic fashion. It's going to be messy."

She paused and Edwin let her words sink in. His dreams made sense now. Morden had his Griselda and meant to make her his Dark Queen. But that wasn't going to happen. He wouldn't let it happen. Every Dark Lord had a nemesis, and Edwin knew his love for Griselda and his sword were Morden's.

"The count here," said Black Orchid, indicating the grizzled veteran, "is raising and training an army that will oppose Morden and his host. It will be a small army, hopelessly outnumbered, but well trained."

"And well fed," said the count brightly. "We have the best chefs."

Black Orchid gave him a withering stare. "And well fed."

"I will lead your army," said Edwin. It was as he had dreamt. He would ride into battle, a glorious host of knights in his train, and they would break the Dark Host.

Black Orchid coughed. "Yes, well. In a figurative sense that will be excellent, but perhaps you ought to let the count do the tactical thinking, yes? We were hoping you would handle the inspirational side of things."

Edwin barely heard her. He was not concerned with the details. He was running over the things he'd need to rescue his Griselda. "Give me a horse, armour, and my sword. That's all I want. And a regiment of the bravest knights. Yes, that should do it. Now where can I find this Dark Lord?"

Chapter 29   Machinations

With great power comes
the greater responsibility to wield it.
The Dark Lord's Handbook

The Handbook was pleased. The vessel for its plans, that is to say, Morden, was following the advice he was reading from the book as though it were Canon Law. The sacking of Bostokov had been the first big test of Morden's Will to bring destruction to the world and he had passed; though if he was to be marked down it would have to be for the astonishingly low body count. The streets had not run red from the blood of Bostokov's residents but from the broken casks of red wine in the warehouses. (Apparently it had not been to the taste of Morden's orcs.)

But no matter. Morden had a fledgling army, a fleet, and was ready to set sail eastward where he could make his way to his spiritual home of the Great Fortress, gathering his army as he went. Once there, he could raise the fortress back to its formidable former glory and, soon after that, issue forth with his black army and lay waste the world.

Yes. All seemed well enough. Although there were a few strange things happening that the Handbook had not seen happen before, at least not to a Dark Lord. The sudden appearance of Morden's father was one. It was well known that paternal issues were in the demesne of the opposition, and often a device used by a Dark Lord to inflict crippling psychological scars. In Morden's case, however, there was little of great concern. In fact, Morden's father had quite conveniently educated Morden in several key areas, not least of which was this whole thing about him being a dragon and having unimagined magical powers. Being able to transform into a huge black dragon, breathe fire hot enough to vaporize stone, and fly, would almost certainly prove useful. It also impressed the minions.

What was more, Morden's father showed no interest at all in crashing his son's party, or becoming any kind of paternal burden by hanging around. On the contrary, after a few days bringing Morden up to speed on his heritage and abilities (and he did bang on a lot about how persuasive he could be when it came to humans, especially women), he was off. Had to be somewhere else rather urgently, which suited the Handbook just fine.

The other oddity the Handbook had not seen before was Morden's apparent infatuation with the Griselda woman. While Dark Lords often had involvements with women they tended to be non-consensual, or twisted and kinky, or both. Any emotions were always primal, mainly lust-driven, and easily understood. Dark Lords had needs much like the next man, except Zoon, who being More Dead didn't have a single lustful bone in his otherwise complete skeletal frame, and necrophilia had surprisingly not been his thing.

But Morden was behaving oddly. Instead of taking what he wanted and then discarding it once used, as any Dark Lord should, he was being charming. What was even more astonishing was that when Morden was rebuffed with scorn and foul language, the like of which Bostokov's orcish sailors would have been proud, instead of dominating her with his iron Will, or rendering her helpless with desire using his dragon powers, he instead sulked and moped around. Morden's father had been equally disgusted with his son's behaviour, saying a Deathwing never had to ask for anything, least of all the attentions of a woman.

But Morden was adamant. He would not take her against her will and violate her. It was a serious character flaw the Handbook would have to keep a close eye on.

Fortunately there were many other concerns that Morden had to keep him busy, and he consulted the book frequently to ensure he was getting them right. He'd plundered Bostokov, gathering an ample supply of hard currency and supplies for his modest orcish army. He'd established ranks, officers and the discipline necessary to manage such an army. The orcs had taken to it extremely well, especially when Morden had unveiled his Social Partnership. The Handbook was not completely clear what it meant but it had something to do with Morden being in charge and the orcs doing what he said, and in return he guaranteed them freedom from crappy jobs, decent living conditions, the right to sharp teeth, conquest and plundering. As far as the Handbook was concerned, Morden could dress up dictatorship anyway he liked as long as he was the absolute ruler and everyone did exactly as they were told.

Though there was still a long way to go, both figuratively and literally (the Great Fortress was a long way away), the Handbook was happy enough that Morden the Dark Lord was Rising and that, given time, he would indeed be the one who would finally realise the Handbook's vision of a world that had been laid waste by war and had every drop of hope wrung from it. Morden would sit on his Dark Throne in kingship over it all, and the Handbook would be in his hand.

Chapter 30   A New Order

Be wary of love's guile for it is merely
lust in romantic guise.
The Dark Lord's Handbook

The preparations were complete and Morden's fleet was ready to sail. All that remained was to make a dramatic exit. Morden gave Kurgen, the orc captain he was leaving in charge of Mordengrad (as Bostokov had been renamed), his final instructions and then proceeded to the docks where his fleet was waiting for the tide. He rode through the streets on a black stallion and exuded The Fear as his father had taught him. Mordengrad's population had been *encouraged* to line the streets to see him off, but any exuberance they managed was dampened as they were gripped with terror as he passed. Morden hoped when he was gone they would remember the feeling and pray it never returned. It would do so only if he had cause to come back, and he made it clear he would return if they did not embrace the New Order of things that Kurgen would be enacting.

The New Order was not particularly odious. The major change was that orcs would be running things and a tithe would be paid to Morden. The rich had been reclassified as well-off middle class and their wealth had been redistributed, principally into Morden's coffers. Morden had dismissed suggestions of creating a genuine proletariat state, as he was a firm believer in ambition and the use of incentives. In this case, he wanted everyone's ambition to be to stay alive and the incentive was that they do what he told them or suffer the consequences.

To reinforce this he had employed the orcs, and Stonearm in particular, in much the way he had used Billard in Bindelburg; he instituted a violent but brief reign of terror that left a battered and bruised populace in no doubt who was in charge but at the same time left them alive. Dead people didn't make money and Morden would be needing lots of money. And food. And weapons.

The logistics of being a Dark Lord were becoming clear. Even with the modest army of orcs he had it was a nightmare to feed them, keep them in beer, and pay them a token that suggested one day they may afford a few luxuries in life.

Down at the dock a crowd had been gathered to witness his leaving and to give him the opportunity for a few last words. A single skiff was tied up to take Morden and his newly commissioned Dark Guard out to the Black Ship—the fleet's flagship (a merchantman that had been painted black; a touch obvious but it seemed to work).

As he strode onto the platform, a row of trumpeters silenced the crowd with a harsh clarion call that made Morden wince. Still, it was all part of the show and therefore necessary.

Stonearm was standing at the back of the platform, resplendent in a newly crafted set of armour that must have weighed as much as the mammoth orc himself. Stonearm had continued to warrant Morden's every confidence and he was standing proudly, casting what Morden knew to be a totally fake menacing glare over the assembled people.

Next to him was Kristoff who, while looking a lot healthier, still had a despondent air about him. Beside Kristoff, and ignoring him, was Griselda. If Kristoff was in love with Griselda then Morden could fully understand his mood.

As for the look she gave Morden, it could have withered fruit on the vine. Her beauty, while great, was tempered by an unforgiving temperament and a caustic tongue. Despite this, Morden felt a knot in his stomach every time he saw her. It could not be love, for surely love should not hurt like this?

Morden was looking forward to the voyage if for no other reason than to show Griselda there was another side to him that was not a Dark Lord but a man. Part man, at least. Part dragon admittedly but, from what his father had to say, the Deathwing males made great lovers, which was something he hoped Griselda would come to appreciate.

He had been so busy with the sacking of Mordengrad, organising the fleet and its departure, that he had had little time to spend with either Griselda or Kristoff. There were many unanswered questions; his father had been little help, merely saying he had saved them from a worse peril, and Morden was the one person in the world who could make sure neither came to harm. Why Lord Deathwing should give half a thought for either was a mystery, as he showed scant regard for anything other than his libido.

Perhaps that was harsh. In the few days Morden had spent with his father they had grown close. Much of the time had been spent learning the extent of his powers as a Deathwing. It seemed to come down to the ability to appear human at will and exercise considerable mind powers over others. As a dragon he was apparently not only able to fly and breathe fire, but was astonishingly tough. Being a hybrid it was not clear whether he possessed the full range of magical abilities, or even more, and only time would tell.

Morden was happy enough to have some answers, and more than pleased to find out his natural powers of persuasion would only get stronger over the decades to come. That was one other fact he'd been left with: dragons lived a very, very long time. This put a whole new angle on the Dark Lord business. If he got it right then he could rule the world for hundreds, if not thousands, of years to come. In some ways, it made it even more important that he did not fail.

Not that he had any intention of doing so, but he did feel young as he mounted the podium, nodded at Stonearm, and turned to address the crowd. He'd been reading the Handbook all night and he judged now was the time to show them Morden Deathwing, the Dark Lord, in all his glory.

Morden exuded The Fear and the crowd was silenced and rooted in place.

Somewhere close by, a crow cawed.

"Citizens of Mordengrad."

Morden released The Fear and a weak cheer went up.

"Today the world changes. How fortunate you are to be here to witness these momentous events. You are now free men, no longer slaves to the rich."

With Stonearm leading, the thousand or so orcs present cheered. Morden was happy to see a few humans, mostly the poorer, joining in.

"No more will you be trodden underfoot and ignored, underpaid and uncared for. I have raised you up. Your destiny is now in your hands. All I ask is that you join me in this great liberation. Help me spread this revolution and set all people free from poverty."

This time the crowd cheered his name. There was even a faint hint of enthusiasm. Morden could feel the Handbook under his robe. He didn't know how, but he knew it was pleased. Which was a little strange. But no matter.

"Be clear, though, that this is no small thing we do. It will require hard work and sacrifice. There will be those who oppose us. They will seek to put us once more under their privileged boot and rub our faces in the dirt. But I won't let them. I, Morden, will oppose all those who seek to oppress the poor and the weak. I will raise you up, make you strong, and together we shall claim what is rightly ours. Together we will fulfil our destiny!"

This time the crowd exploded with shouts and cheers. Morden had no doubt they would follow him now. It wasn't so much what he'd said as how he had said it. Combining the power of Zoon's robe with a few tricks his father had shown him had worked. A wave of compulsion gripped the mass.

Morden turned and nodded at Stonearm. The orc barked an order and the platform cleared, leaving Morden by himself.

Now for the showstopper. Words and magic could do much, but so far all they had seen was Morden, a man in black.

Morden centred himself and willed the Change.

It was much like the first time, the difference being that he knew what was happening. He felt his body fill up with energy. His skin felt like it was going to explode and then, in an instant, he was no longer man-shaped but a dragon.

The crowd froze as one, paralysed with terror. Morden reared up on massive legs and spread his wings.

"I am Morden Deathwing."

Morden knew this was the critical moment. The mob had a choice. Either he was a terrible black dragon that was about to consume them and they had better get the hell away as fast as possible, or he was indeed their leader, the one to lead them into a future that promised much more than being a dragon snack. Morden was sure most people wanted to believe they were more than an appetiser. He was not wrong. The first to break were the orcs. They began to chant his name.

"Morden. Morden. Morden."

Morden took a deep breath and exhaled a blast of fire into the sky. The humans had joined the orcs and the chant grew louder. And now it was time for his exit.

Morden brought his wings down and leapt into the air. As he rose there was momentary doubt. He'd never flown before. For a dreadful second he seemed to hang there above the crowd. He was so big. How was it possible something so large could fly? It was impossible. He was going to belly flop to the ground and squash a bunch of people into dragon burger. Looking down, he could see similar thoughts pass rapidly through the crowd. Eyes widened and some started to push violently backwards.

He beat his wings hard and the down rush of air forced the front of the crowd to their knees.

But he rose.

He wasn't sure how it worked. He beat his wings slowly but powerfully and he stayed aloft. All heads were upturned to look at him. The panic had gone and the chant had died; the crowd stared in open amazement. Morden could only imagine what they were thinking. Their astonishment was evident. Who could blame them? Dragons were the stuff of myth and legend and yet here was one, hanging in the air above them. It had breathed fire, just like they were meant to.

But this one was also a man. Or had been a mere second beforehand. One who had been saying a lot about freedom, working rights, fighting together and stuff, and they had played along hoping he would go away if they did. But it was real. He wasn't kidding around. Maybe he was telling the truth. After all, it wasn't every day a city was sacked by a Deathwing dragon that promised to set them free.

As one the crowd broke from their paralysis and went wild. From the streets around, more people flooded in and stopped in awe before joining the call.

"Morden!"

Morden felt the ever-more-familiar tingle of power as once more his name was called. They were his to do his bidding. The death and destruction of the last few days was cast aside by his power over them. Their city had been burned, and in places was still smouldering, but all they could see was an amazing thing: a man, a dragon, one and the same with a message of liberation.

Morden turned and rose higher until the crowd was like maggots. Then, tucking his wings in, he dove. As he did he let The Fear come again. The crowd flattened themselves and the cheers turned to shrieks of terror. Morden released a blast of fire above them hot enough to singe eyebrows but not actually burn anyone. As he snapped into the air, he let The Fear go and hovered above them, beating his wings slowly to keep his place.

From below there was a palpable release of tension and applause; cheers rang out. It had only been a bit of fun, a demonstration, but one Morden knew would stick indelibly in their minds. The stuff of legend was real. They had the singed hair to prove it. There was a new power in the world and Morden Deathwing was it.

As planned, Morden could see a small flotilla of skiffs leaving the dock, orchestrated by Stonearm. They were the last of his Guard heading for his ship. In the boat with Stonearm, Morden could see Kristoff and Griselda. Kristoff was looking back and up at Morden. To Morden's disappointment, Griselda was sitting facing forward, her arms folded. The show had been as much for her as anyone, and it seemed she had ignored it all. A gut-wrenching pang gripped Morden. He tried hard not to sigh. That would not look good.

It was time to leave, join his fleet and sail east.

With a few strong beats of his wings, Morden was soon over his flagship. The speed with which he flew was at first a surprise—he could easily have outpaced a galloping horse—but, in consideration of his size, it was not that surprising. There was tremendous power in his dragon form.

He hovered over the ship and immediately spotted a problem. He had nowhere to land. The ship's rigging obscured the deck, and even if it had been one of the slave driven oar-ships from the east, he was far too big to land on it.

The orcs who were manning the ship were little help. They were standing on the deck cheering, oblivious to his predicament.

It was frustrating. It looked like he was going to have to land in the water, change back into a man and get fished out of the sea. Hardly befitting a Dark Lord.

Then he had an idea that would save him not only a soaking but also get Griselda's attention. The skiffs were about halfway out to the fleet and making good progress. The sea was calm and the orcs were pulling hard on their oars.

Morden flew back to hover over the skiff that held Griselda. He kept his wing beats to a minimum to hold position, but even so he could see the skiff was taking a buffeting and the sea was being chopped up. Everyone in the skiff was looking up at him. Fear was written on many of their faces, but it was fury written on Griselda's.

"What the hell are you doing?" she screamed.

Hoping he had got his aim correct, Morden came down as low as he dared without overturning the skiff and Changed. Fortunately his aim was good, but his height judgement was not. He was suddenly a man hanging fifteen feet in the air.

Gravity considered his predicament and acted accordingly.

Morden tensed as he fell. For a dreadful second it occurred to him he might even fall right through the bottom of the skiff and sink it. He needn't have worried.

"Gotcha," said Stonearm, as Morden thumped into the orc's massive arms. The skiff rocked but stayed afloat.

At the stern end, Kristoff was looking morose next to Griselda, who was now standing, hands on hips and glaring. Morden was suddenly aware he was being held in the arms of a giant orc much like a baby.

"You moron," said Griselda, her face screwed up with contempt. "You could have killed us all. Twat."

"You can put me down now," whispered Morden to Stonearm.

The orc let him go and Morden thumped to the bottom of the skiff. It was awash with a couple of inches of sea water.

Trying his hardest to salvage even a mote of credibility, Morden thought it best to ignore Griselda. She was obviously not in the mood to be impressed.

"Row!" commanded Morden, indicating the Black Ship as their destination.

The orcs at the oars looked at each other with confused expressions.

"You heard Lord Deathwing. Stroke, you miserable lot," ordered Stonearm, cuffing the nearest oarsmen.

Morden struck what he hoped was a suitably dramatic pose as the skiff ploughed towards his flagship. He dare not look to the stern where all he could hear were the continued curses from a pissed-off Griselda. So much for making an impression.

Soon they were at the fleet and he had no time to wallow in his depression. Orders were given, sails were set and signals were made. From the main mast a flag was unfurled—a black dragon on a white hand, resplendent on a field of red.

The flag lifted Morden's spirits. Stonearm must have been using his ever-increasing initiative, as it was a detail he had overlooked.

"Excellent flag, Stonearm," said Morden with some pride.

"The White Hand is an old orcish symbol," said Stonearm.

"It goes rather well," said Morden. He was aware of heraldry but he had no notion what much of it meant. "What does the hand represent? Strength?"

"Close. It means that whoever bears this flag is going to give you a good slapping," said the big orc.

"I like it," said Morden. "Good job, *General* Stonearm."

The emphasis was not lost on the big orc. "Thank you, my lord," said Stonearm, puffing his chest out.

Standing on the poop, the black canvas sails stiff in the wind and the fleet following, Morden felt calm come to his mind. Though Griselda was still a pain, and even now he could feel the tug at his loins, he was happy to savour the moment. They were on their way east. Who knew what lay ahead?

For Morden, it didn't matter. He had an army and destiny lay ahead of him. Conquest, riches and power beckoned. He would head east, gather an even bigger army as he went, and rally orcs to his banner. He would keep his promise to Grimtooth and give them back their pride. In return they would fight for him against all those who may oppose him, because Morden was aware that Penbury was still out there. What had happened at Bostokov—Mordengrad—could not have gone unmarked or be left unanswered. It would be interesting to see what the chancellor did. If it were him, Morden would use his exceptional resources to raise an army and squash Morden like a bug. That was why he had to keep moving. He wasn't ready yet to face that challenge. A few thousand orcs and himself was not enough to go up against the kind of army Penbury could raise.

He had to prepare. Taking Bostokov had been a gamble. He was still Rising and the Handbook warned him against premature battles. He needed to find Zoon's old fortress, rebuild it, gather his strength and rally all the orcs of the world to his banner, along with anyone else who would follow a Dark Lord. He was proof positive that creatures of myth were in fact real, so who knew what else from the old tales was still out there? Trolls, giants, ogres, demons, harpies, gryphons, vampires, zombies, mammoths, manticores, goblins, killer whales, sabre tooth cats, werewolves, witches, troglodytes.

Anything was possible.

Chapter 31   Intelligence

The best laid plans of mice and men fail,
therefore you must be neither mouse nor man.
The Dark Lord's Handbook

It had been twenty years since Penbury had been to Al-Frahzi to aggressively negotiate trade from the spice route that ran to the east of the city. The city was ancient and smelled of camels. Its streets were narrow and lined either side with mud brick buildings that were pleasantly cool in the midday sun.

These narrow streets were also notoriously not the place to be with the moon full in the sky, as it was now. They were home to the infamous kari-kari wielding street thieves of Al-Frahzi. The kari-kari was famous for being the knife most likely to be found in someone's back. Once it had been plunged in, it was ridiculously difficult to remove due to its curved shape and the razor teeth that lined the back edge. While more modern designs overcame this problem, the knife remained popular, particularly among the footpad population where it was seen as the traditional weapon that separated the proud Al-Frahzi thieves from common muggers. If you were to be robbed and murdered then it was their solemn duty to ensure they provided the most authentic cultural experience they could.

Twenty years ago, Penbury had been out in these streets on a night not dissimilar to this, celebrating his successful cornering of the peppercorn market. He had been young, and in hindsight careless, but fortunately for him he was already a keen duellist and his rapier had seen off the attempt made on his purse.

Hooded and moving from shadow to shadow to avoid the bright beams of moonlight that pierced the alleyways, Penbury was beginning to think that insisting he go alone to meet Snort and Snort was a mistake. His heart was beating far too fast and he was sure he had picked up a tail. It wasn't far now, though, so perhaps he had nothing to worry about.

Maybe it was Chidwick ignoring his orders.

He ducked into a doorway and stood still, looking back the way he had come. The contrast of dark and light the full moon created made it hard to see much. Instead he looked for movement. If he spotted something it was unlikely to be anything but trouble; Al-Frahzi was not known for stray cats since the Great Famine a century past when a taste for a wide range of foods had been developed. Their ingenuity when it came to what could be eaten was one of the reasons Penbury came to the city in pursuit of his gastronomic interests.

Relieved that he saw nothing, he carried his bulk as lightly as he could further down the alley. He had memorised the route in his mind and it was down to the end, a left, then first right, second door on the right.

Perhaps it was because he was going over the knocking sequence he would have to perform once he reached the door that he let slip an old saying in Al-Frahzi:

'One never knows what is around the next corner, but one should make sure it is not a kari-kari.'

(Some even went as far as to suggest the shape of the blade had been developed to make stabbing around corners easier.)

Moonlight glinting on metal saved Penbury as, at the very last moment, he skipped backwards away from the lunging blade. He may well have been carrying a few (well, a lot) of extra pounds these days, but he could still move when he needed to, and though his body may not have been quite what it was, his mind was still sharp. He sidestepped to avoid the kari-kari that was thrust at his back. He had been right about the tail, just not good enough to spot the street-trained thief. Penbury put his back to the wall to avoid any other stabbings from the rear. His two attackers didn't seem in too much of a hurry though. The first assailant slid around the corner as smoothly as an Al-Frahzi belly dancer across a dance floor.

"You missed," said the first. He had assumed a half-crouched position and was flicking his wicked kari-kari between his hands. He spoke a street dialect Penbury barely understood.

The second looked over to his partner. "So did you, goat fucker," he retorted.

"You are getting complacent when you miss a whale like this," continued the first. "My niece could have put her kari-kari in this one's back."

The second stood from his cat-like stance while his partner made playful lunges at Penbury. "Listen to who speaks. Like you could do a simple thing like stab him in the chest. My blind grandmother could have removed his heart with her knitting needles. You smoke too much weed, my friend."

Penbury hadn't come out unarmed and he surreptitiously slid a hand under his robe for the dirk he had there.

"Nuh-uh," said the first, flicking his kari-kari at Penbury.

Penbury withdrew his hand and showed a bare palm.

"I was just going to give you gentlemen my ..." Penbury scrabbled madly for the word, "small sack that holds round things?"

The footpads' laughter sounded like they had both been smoking too much weed.

Penbury took advantage of their situation to release his purse and dangle it in front of him. "Here, take my ... purse. Yes, purse."

The second had his hands on his knees and was dragging in lungs full of breath. "I am getting too old for this shit," he said, wheezing. "Kill him and let's go home."

The first became suddenly serious. The grip on his kari-kari changed. "I am sorry," he shrugged. "It's just business, you know."

If it hadn't been the dead of night in a city that boasted no free-running animals of any kind, the footpads may have missed the two soft thumps. But they did hear, and they also saw Penbury's eyes move to look at something behind them. It could have been the oldest scam in the book, but the look they gave each other was one of 'oh shit' rather than 'oh really?'

Their eyes widened a notch when a Nichi-on blade appeared in their chests. They couldn't scream because they were already dead. The blades slid out easily as the corpses toppled forward.

"Ah, gentlemen," said Penbury, straightening.

Snort and Snort nodded. "This way," said one of them. Penbury couldn't be sure whether it was Franz or Josef.

The rest of the short trip through the streets passed uneventfully. Even if there had been other thieves around, Penbury was sure they would have witnessed what had happened and were unlikely to mess with the Snort brothers. Doing over fat tourists was one thing, but assassins were best left alone.

The chancellor was glad for the cup of water they provided once they were safe in the meeting house. The combination of fear and heat had made his throat dry. At least the room was cool, if a little basic in its comforts. The decoration consisted of a plain table with benches down either side and a brass oil lamp in the middle, a wall rug depicting a camel, and a parrot in a cage that looked at best asleep and at worst dead.

"And now to business," said Penbury, setting the cup aside. "I understand there were difficulties with the original commission?"

"Yes, Chancellor," said one of the Snort brothers.

"I'm sorry, you are?" enquired Penbury. Though they had taken off their headgear and were sitting next to each other, they were no easier to tell apart.

"Franz."

"So both estates remain un-executed?"

"Yes, sir," said Franz.

The chancellor nodded. He knew this, of course, but it was always best to be completely clear when it came to management.

"Well, let's put that behind us."

The Snort brothers exchanged a glance.

"If you'll permit us to be so bold, we would like another opportunity to carry out the contract," said Josef.

"We've never failed," said Franz.

"Professional pride, if you will," said Josef.

"Yes, yes, I understand, but things have changed and I will be exploring alternative avenues to settle this matter," said Penbury. He could see momentary disappointment flicker across the brothers' faces. "But I attach no blame. You did a fine job."

"But we failed," said Franz with a hint of annoyance.

"In detail, perhaps," said Penbury, "but consider this. You are among the best in the world in what you do. Correct?"

The brothers nodded.

"And, as you say, you never fail. And these were relatively straightforward estates to execute?"

The brothers exchanged looks again. They were hard to read but

Penbury was finally tuning in to their body language, and if he was right they were asking themselves when he was going to get to the point.

"The point is, gentlemen, that these two men are not fated—and I do hate to use that word—to die at your hands."

This time there was open puzzlement.

"We thought you were a man of reason," said Franz.

Penbury nodded vigorously. "Indeed, yes I am. I don't hold any truck by all that fatalism, or divine intervention or whatnot. But I also know there are times when there are forces at work which remain as yet undiscovered that, if known, would completely explain why dispensing with Edwin and Morden is, for all intents and purposes, a practical impossibility."

Penbury could see there remained some convincing to be done. "It has nothing to do with your skills. You know both of these men should be, by any rights, dead. Yet they are not. I myself was taken aback by this, but there is precedent. Gentlemen, I think we are living in interesting times. I suspect Morden is a Dark Lord Rising and Edwin is the Hero to oppose him."

The brothers sat, eyes locked on Penbury, inscrutable.

"That would explain matters," said Josef at last.

"Indeed," said Penbury. "So like I said, let's set the past aside and move on to new matters. I have other work for you."

"We shall not fail this time," said Franz. "And we appreciate your consideration of the last task."

"Yes, yes," said Penbury. "Now, given that these two cannot simply be done away with, the next best thing is to find out all we can about both parties and try to negotiate a settlement between the two. Or failing that, ensure they do away with each other."

"And how may we help, Chancellor? Whose estate stands in your way?"

Penbury shook his head. "You misunderstand. I want you to go, one to each camp, and gather this information and relay it back to me."

"You want us to spy for you?" asked Josef.

The disdain with which the question was asked had Penbury hurrying for a better tack to take. He had obviously offended their professional standing. "Not so much spy, in a spying sense, but more a due diligence."

"So you want us to act in our legal guise?" said Franz.

"In a manner of speaking, but should you need to employ other skills to help you in the delivery of this work then that would be acceptable," said Penbury. When it came to matters of pride it was his experience that it was normally sufficient to give a face-saving way out to resolve such issues.

"Very well," said Josef. "What is it you wish to know?"

The chancellor was inwardly relieved. "Excellent. Right. What I need to know is everything. I need to know their habits. Whom do they trust? What do they want and what do they like? Do they sleep alone or in company, and if the latter what company is it? Who, how many, what species, and so on."

"Shouldn't be a problem," said Franz. "It's often what we do before executing the more difficult estates."

"Good, good," said Penbury. "Then I also need to know about everyone around them. Same as before. Also, the particulars of their armies, their dispositions and arrangements, and so forth." He was a firm believer that although a little knowledge could go a long way, a lot of knowledge tended to go a lot further. "And I'm going to give you access to my personal service to relay all this information. You will be able to reach me by pigeon from anywhere in the world—from any major city— in a matter of days."

While some raced homing pigeons, he had immediately seen the potential for long distance communications. It was one of the little-known ways he kept tabs on what was going on all over the known world. He had contacts in every city with pigeons that could be used to send him information he needed to act on quickly, whether it be business or politics. The pamphlets were acceptable enough for general information, but they were too slow if he had to quickly corner a market, or arrange a political succession at short notice when some prince had gone over a cliff on a skiing holiday.

His enthusiasm for the service did not seem to be matched by the Snort brothers.

"If you don't mind," said Franz.

"We'd like to instead offer our own system," said Josef.

"We reserve this for our most important clients," said Franz, producing a scroll case and a needle. From the case he produced a rolled sheaf of papers. "If we ever have need for urgent communication we can manage it instantaneously over any distance."

Franz flattened out the papers on the table so they formed a pad.

Penbury thought he must have misheard. Had he just said instantaneous from anywhere in the world?

"We like to call it trans visio," said Josef.

"From anywhere? Instantly?" asked Penbury. "How?"

The brothers exchanged glances. "This is possibly the most valuable thing we possess and it is extraordinarily hard to make, but perhaps a demonstration is in order," said Josef.

The brother took two pieces of paper from the pad and gave one to his sibling. "This is a one-time pad," said Josef. "That is to say, each pair of pages is linked and can only be used once. We therefore write with a needle so we can get the greatest amount of information on a single piece."

Franz came around the side of the table and sat next to Penbury. He flattened the paper in front of the chancellor. "Observe," he said.

Josef bent over his sheet and started to scratch with the needle.

"Look carefully," said Franz, pointing at the top left of the paper in front of Penbury.

Sure enough, as he could hear the scratching of the needle from Josef, tiny spidery writing appeared on his sheet of paper.

"Please read," said Franz, producing a magnifying glass and holding it over the text.

"Greetings to all and sundry," read Penbury.

"I'll hold the paper here if you'd like to take this and go round and read what my brother has written," said Franz, giving the lens to Penbury.

Penbury took the glass and went round to read what Josef had written, but only to buy himself seconds to get over the astonishment of what he was seeing. Sure enough, the text on Josef's paper was exactly as he had read on the paper still held by Franz.

Penbury sat back down and took a moment. The brothers sat patiently, their inscrutable expressions back in place. Though very similar in appearance, Penbury was starting to notice differences. Franz's hair had a tighter curl and Josef had narrower eyebrows.

"I don't suppose this is any kind of sleight of hand trick, is it?" said

Penbury, as much to himself as to the two Snorts. "Incredible. Might I ask where you get this?"

"You might, and we might even tell you," said Franz.

"But then we'd have to execute your estate," said Josef.

Neither brother smiled. Penbury decided he was perhaps better off not knowing.

"Some lawyer humour," said Franz.

"Hilarious," said Penbury.

"We will give you two pieces of paper for each of us," said Franz. "I shall write my name on the top left of these two, and my brother's on these two, then you can tell who is reporting. We also have this." Franz produced a small notebook. "It is a list of common abbreviations we use to save space. I will make a copy and have it sent to you in the next week."

Penbury nodded. "I must say, gentlemen, you have exceeded yourselves. All that remains is to discuss your payment."

Again, the two brothers looked at each other. Penbury could read nothing in their blank expressions; the two seemed to share sibling telepathy.

"We would like to retire," said Josef.

"Comfortably," said Franz.

"Agreed," said Penbury. Given the enormity of the events that were unfolding, it was a small price, especially for a man of his means. "I think we are concluded for this evening. Thank you, gentlemen. It's been most illuminating."

The two brothers gave curt nods in unison. "We shall ensure your safe return," said Josef.

"That would be generous," said Penbury. The next time Chidwick tried to insist on an escort he would listen to his secretary.

Penbury enjoyed his stroll back through the moonlit alleyways of Al-Frahzi with nothing but the odd strangled scream of a thief to break his thoughts. At the forefront of these was what he should do next. Now that his intelligence was sorted out he needed to make plans for all eventualities. He would try to ensure there was no war. It would be such an inconvenience if there was, but if it couldn't be avoided then he needed to be sure whoever won would quickly come under his control; and this was where the Snort brothers' intelligence would come in doubly handy. If he could establish their dependency on him, then they were his to command.

Chapter 32   A Hero's Treachery

If your opponent has a cause to die for,
this is a good thing.
The Dark Lord's Handbook

When word arrived of the burning of Bostokov, it caused a degree of consternation in the kingdoms of the Western Reaches. There were calls for action. As a result, after two months of recruiting, training and fine eating, Count Vladovitch announced it was time for the army to move.

The count was pleased because Sir Edwin—he had been forced to knight the blacksmith's son to give him a rank—had been driving him crazy with his constant diatribes against the evil that was abroad with the woman he loved.

Also, he needed the exercise a field campaign would afford. His waistline had grown uncomfortably large thanks to Baron Fanfaron's chefs. The count's initial scepticism about the baron had long been dispelled and the two had become good friends. As his letter of introduction had said, the baron was an excellent raconteur and the count enjoyed the baron's stories enormously, not only because they were genuinely interesting and funny, but because they also kept his wife silent as she listened.

It had been ten years, possibly more, since he had been on campaign. Below on the parade grounds the army was standing arrayed in its splendour—rank upon rank of stout pikemen, keen-eyed archers and blood-crazed knights. The count enjoyed such moments. After all, it was downhill from here as far as looks went. The practicalities of being in the field would muddy those jerkins soon enough and take the shine off that plate.

Except the plate on Sir Edwin's back, who maintained a zealous attention to his own armour. Even now, the count could see him on the field, riding up and down the line of mounted knights who would be the count's hammer in battles to come. If there was one element of his army the count had no reservations about it was Edwin's men. In a few short months, he had formed them into the most formidable, and frankly terrifying, group of killers the count had seen under a banner. Though there was much talk of might and right, pride and the rescuing of flowered maidens (and the count suspected de-flowering shortly after), underneath the shine and the glamour there was a ruthless efficiency. He was glad he would not have to face them.

"Have you got a clean handkerchief, dear?"

If there was one thing he missed when he was away, it was his wife. He couldn't abide her fussing and her tears, but he knew it was because she still loved him. He was a lucky man. Many a noblemen had ridden off to campaign and glory leaving behind a beautiful young wife only to return to find her with child and the summing of the months not right. More than a few of his friends had sons who looked more like the gardener than the man of the castle.

But not he. She had remained faithful, and he to her. They'd had two sons, both tragically lost—one in battle, the other in a freak fishing accident (even now he did not know how the pole managed to get where it had)—who had been as like to him as his reflection.

He had thought this time it would be different, that he would be glad to get away from the gentle scolding and nagging, but he was mistaken. That one harmless question pulled hard on his heart and he questioned if he was doing the right thing. He probably wasn't, but what choice did he have? His earlier enthusiasm for battle had long since gone and now he was embroiled in a venture he could only see ending badly.

Black Orchid, however, left him little choice. As much as he loved his wife and would rather see out his days spoiled rotten by her, he would not see her a pauper, and that was the fact of it. They were broke. Then there was the abject fear he had of Black Orchid herself. His imagination was not sufficient when it came to thinking about what she may do to him, and more importantly his wife, should he let her down.

No, he had little choice, and so he had to make the best of it.

"Right here," said the count, producing the kerchief she had given him just yesterday, his monogram on one corner.

He could see her eyes were full and ready to burst. He felt a sharp tug inside and he had to affect a cough to prevent tears of his own. That would never do, especially not with his guard drawn up and ready to leave with him.

"I'd best be off," he said. "I should not keep the men waiting."

Leaning forward, he pecked his wife on the check.

"I love you," she whispered, so only he would hear.

He drew back an inch so she could see him and what his eyes were saying before kissing her again, this time full on the mouth.

"I'll be back before you know it," he said softly.

He turned to address his men. Eyes snapped to the front as he did so, but not fast enough for him to miss a fullness in the eye among his older and most loyal guards.

"Can't a man kiss his wife without you horrible lot staring?" bellowed the count.

It was his good-natured bellow they all knew, and more than a few were smirking.

"Three cheers for the count," commanded his guard captain.

"Huzzah! Huzzah! HUZZAH!" cheered the guard.

As he rode down the hill from the castle, the count tried hard not to look back; he never had in the past, believing if you went anywhere with regret then your heart was not ready for battle. But this time, he turned to look at his wife; she was at the gate, watching them leave. She must have seen him look as she raised her scarf. He raised his arm in reply and swore to himself he would be back to retrieve the lady's favour.

Taking a deep breath, he brought himself back to the matter in hand. He had a campaign to run, a battle to fight, and a city to save. There was no room for sentiment when his and his men's lives were on the line.

"At the trot!" he ordered, and spurred his horse on down to the waiting troops.

Baron Fanfaron and Sir Edwin were mounted and waiting.

"Good morning, gentlemen," said the count.

The baron inclined his head.

"All present and ready for inspection," barked Sir Edwin.

The lad was keen, but an inspection was the last thing the count needed. "They look magnificent, Sir Edwin. But let's not tarry, shall we?"

"Sir, yes, sir," said Edwin.

The young knight had become quite the horseman in a short time, and turned his mount on a shilling to face the men. Sir Edwin drew his sword and held it high.

"To Bostokov!" shouted Edwin. "And to glory!"

A ragged cheer went up from the men.

It took two hours to get the army moving. Apart from the fighting men, there were the supplies and camp followers, all of whom needed to move off down the rutted road. Baron Fanfaron's men brought up the rear, close to their much-loved cooking utensils and supplies, doubling as a rear guard on the march.

The count was glad for the early onset of spring as it promised fairer weather, though the rain may muddy the roads. If he was to sleep in a field tent for the next months, at least it would be temperate. He was definitely of the Old School that believed the campaign season should be spring to late summer, that autumn should see armies heading home, and winter should be spent next to a roaring fire with hounds at one's side.

*****

It took three weeks to march to within a day of Bostokov, which was where the count called a halt. The army had swollen, especially as they drew closer to Bostokov and the provincial nobles contributed handfuls of men. The halt gave the count an opportunity to call a council of war where he would weigh up whom he could rely on should the going get tough.

There was a familiar buzz of excitement in the tent when the count and Baron Fanfaron entered—there hadn't been a major engagement, of the military kind, for years. It was an opportunity for the Western Marches' nobility to send their sons off to learn a man's work, and for a few to dust off their own gear and meet up with old friends.

Count Vladovitch was relieved to see grizzled veterans among the youthful faces that could barely manage a single beard between them. There was Baron Haldoron, stern looking, battle-scarred and still a gleam in his grey eyes. Next to him was Sir Romquist, a keen tactician and a master of siege warfare (handy given Bostokov's walls). There were others who nodded respectfully as his gaze passed over the assembly. There were also many pansy-eyed fops barely out of baby linen, but they could be given menial jobs.

"Gentlemen," said the count, his voice clear and commanding above the general babble.

A mock-up of the area had been constructed on a large table. It was impressively detailed, with miniature woods, streams and even sheep and cows. Little men stood on the wall that surrounded Bostokov and in its narrow streets with their slate roofs and chimneys. There were tufts of grey cotton for smoke. Outside the walls, beyond the carefully crafted slum area, with what looked like real mud, was arrayed an army that was equally detailed. Little figurines carried pikes and bows, and even the flags were accurately painted with the heraldry of those present.

The count took in all the details, not so much the little men and women who had been placed in the town square, but the terrain, the walls and the slum that skirted them, the availability of fresh water and wood. There was a small hill a mile from the edge of the slums that commanded a good view.

"I'll establish my headquarters here," said the count, stabbing at the hill with a handy stick that had been provided for him. "Sir Romquist, your thoughts?"

Sir Romquist nodded at the acknowledgement and coughed. "We'll have to clear this," he said, waving at the slums. "It will get in the way of the siege engines. We can establish road blocks here, and here, and here, and screen the areas between. There seems to be no good sally point so I don't anticipate a problem there."

"How long?" asked the count.

Sir Romquist twitched his nose and stroked his short beard. "Well, we can't starve them out, they have the sea and we have no fleet. So it will have to be assault. Say, three weeks to clear and build the machinery, a week for probes and feints to determine weakness. I'd say, in a month we could be in."

The count couldn't help but notice Sir Edwin pump his fist at this. It seemed bloody assault was right up Sir Edwin's alley. Though siege by starvation would cost fewer men and would have been the count's preference, regrettably he had to agree with Sir Romquist's assessment.

"Very well. It all seems straightforward enough. I'll put together a parley to give them the opportunity to surrender ..." the count paused for polite guffaws that greeted this notion. "... and then we can start the clearance and siege. Shall we say, day after tomorrow?"

There seemed to be a general assent, except for one person.

Sir Edwin.

Though his lips were tight shut, the count could see the muscles in his neck were taut with anger and there was a rising flush. Then what little control he had evaporated:

"This is NOT what we should be doing," exploded Edwin, banging his fist down on the table. "We should go immediately to the gates." With a sweep of his hand he brushed away the carefully crafted slum houses and sprayed them across the room. "We break them down," he continued, jabbing a finger at the finely detailed gates, pushing them in and a good section of the wall. "Defeat this so-called Dark Lord Morden and his foul creatures, and rescue Griselda. We don't need any siege, and certainly no parley. Anyone left alive in there is obviously a traitor, as it would be better to kill yourself than live under scum like this Morden." He pounded the city, where a miniature figure in a black robe stood in the middle of the city square, flattening it. "This is what I think of this Dark Lord." Sir Edwin picked up the squashed figure and ripped its head off. "So let's not have any of this namby pamby parleys and siege and niceness. Let's get in there, kill these evil orcs, and be done with it. Who's with me?"

In his time, Count Vladovitch had seen many outbursts by zealous or pissed off commanders, and this was right up there with the best of them. Among his assembled officers and nobles there was open-mouthed amazement. Sir Romquist even went as far as rubbing his eyes, perhaps in disbelief at what he had just witnessed. Sir Reginald Pother, a young lad with a bookish air, was close to tears at the sight of his carefully created model beaten to a pulp. The count knew he had been up all night working on it and now it was just so much smashed board and lead.

The count himself was at a loss for words. Sir Edwin was standing there, fists planted on the table, glaring, defying anyone present to better his military judgement. Though the plan was total excrement with obvious flaws, the count was not inclined to be so blunt. After Black Orchid, Sir Edwin and his cursed sword were the two things he feared most.

"An interesting alternative, Sir Edwin," said the count. "It's been a long march, so shall we adjourn for now, and you and I can go over the details of this idea? In the meantime, as a precaution, Sir Romquist, could you look into the siege engine situation? Good. Right, I think that's all for now. Gentlemen, if you'll excuse us."

The nobility filed out, muttering as they went. Several references to Edwin's humble birth rose above the general grumbles. Fortunately, Edwin did not seem to hear. He was standing as he had been, staring at the smashed city and fuming. The count could see Edwin's neck pulse with anger.

The tent was empty before Sir Edwin let rip again. "They are all fools. Every second we delay is a second longer Griselda spends in suffering. What do they know of war? Have they stood on the Desolate Plains and faced the innumerable armies of evil? Have they plunged their swords into the hearts of dragons, or wrested victory from many-tentacled Bog Lords of Crenzo? We should act now."

Count Vladovitch was at a loss for a reply. It was a strange thing to say for the son of a blacksmith barely into adulthood who, until a few months ago, had never gone further than the local provincial town. The hairs on his neck told him something dangerous was at work here. As if to confirm it, the flap to the tent was swept aside as a familiar figure made an entrance.

Black Orchid had been quiet in the last few weeks, coming and going as she pleased and happy to let the count and Edwin do their thing. The count was pleased she at least had faith in his military prowess. He hated meddlers who thought they knew everything because they held the purse strings or, as in Black Orchid's case, had him by the nuts.

"Ah, my two favourite men," said Black Orchid. She walked to the table to stand between them. She ran a long fingernail under Edwin's chin. "And how are you, my sweet? You seem agitated."

The count could see Edwin blushing. Black Orchid did have a terrible beauty about her. Or was it anger rising once more? Either way, the lad was dumbstruck, as he often was in her presence.

"We were going over the military alternatives, my lady," said the count. "Edwin here was proposing a direct approach, while the more seasoned among us were inclined to give them a chance to surrender with little loss of life."

The count wasn't sure Black Orchid had heard him, as her attention was still completely on Edwin. "You want to kill those evil kidnappers, don't you? Poor Griselda must be suffering so terribly."

Edwin's eyes were burning into Black Orchid and the count felt like he might as well not be there.

"I don't think you should worry so much about how many people get killed, count," said Black Orchid, all the while caressing Edwin's face with her nails. "We are at war, after all."

"Well," said the count, "strictly speaking, we aren't at war yet."

"We aren't?" said Black Orchid. "Well, if that's the case, I suggest we remedy that immediately. Arrange a meeting for tomorrow morning with whoever is in charge in Bostokov, and let's see what they have to say for themselves. And take Edwin."

The count was relieved. There was always hope if he could convince them to hand over the city. Having Edwin on hand may even expedite matters when they saw him and realised they were deadly serious.

"Very good, my lady," said the count.

"And be sure to negotiate aggressively, won't you, Edwin?" said Black Orchid. She was staring, unblinking, into Edwin's eyes.

"Certainly," said Edwin, breaking his silence and holding Black Orchid's gaze. "I will ensure we get what we want."

Suddenly the count was less than sure this was a good idea after all. The gleam in Edwin's eye was disconcerting.

"I'll leave you boys to it then," said Black Orchid, and with a swish of her black silk dress, she was gone.

"I'd better prepare my men," said Edwin. He followed her out with a definite spring in his step.

Count Vladovitch found himself alone in the tent. He picked up one of the figurines from the tabletop. It was a pikeman and his pike was bent over where Edwin had smashed it. The little man's comrades lay spread over the table, mixed in with the broken remains of the city. He wasn't sure what was going to happen tomorrow but he was certain it wouldn't be pleasant. A guilty part of him hoped it would be every bit as swift and bloody as he feared, and then at least he would be home with the wife before the harvest festival.

He laid the broken pikeman back on the table. In the following weeks he would be putting real men into the earth. That was the price of war, and one that in years past he had happily paid. Perhaps it was because he had always imagined he would fight hard and die young. Having avoided that fate and seeing the bright young men that made up his army, he hoped they too would enjoy his luck and see out their days.

It was a naïve thought and he gave himself a mental slap. War was never pretty, never clean and nice, like many imagined, and always had a price to be paid. He had better get over this melancholy and get his head clear. The lives of his men depended upon it.

*****

The morning after the pathetic council of war, Edwin was clear in his mind what he must do. The count was weak and did not have the will to face evil on its own terms. It was his age. Edwin was sure Count Vladovitch had been a great leader in his time, but now he was old and obviously would have preferred to be at home with his twittering wife.

Though he was still unclear where Black Orchid fitted into things, it was more than clear she was the one who was really in command, and that she appreciated Edwin in ways the count never could. You could not pander to evil. You had to be strong and have the will to do what was necessary. The only negotiation that would be had today would be at lance tip and sword point.

The meeting was to take place at a crossroads a mile from the slum that skirted the city walls. A single tree marked the crossing so, in theory, there was no opportunity for hiding troops for ambush. It had been well chosen, but fortune had smiled upon Edwin and he had been able to make the needed arrangements for his men. The thickening mist would serve him well.

The delegation from Bostokov was waiting for them at the crossroads. A large orc sat astride what looked like a work horse. Behind him was a small guard standing twenty yards back; they were all orcs, unmounted, and armed with an array of pikes and vicious-looking bill hooks. The weapons were intended as defence against knights, and Edwin wondered if he had been betrayed. If he had, he would deal with the betrayer after the orcs had been cut down.

As they drew near the orcs opened their mouths in a rictus of sharpened teeth. Edwin had done his research in training and knew those lines of teeth for what they were, a challenge. There was no peace to be had here today. All this parley was pretence, a sham to justify the notion of war conducted by rules. Edwin laughed inside. He knew there was only total war, with no quarter asked or given. There were no civilians or rules or niceties. War was conducted for one purpose alone, and that was victory. Any army that fought otherwise had lost already. But if the count wanted to play his games then Edwin would let him. He, however, would not be fooled by polite chit-chat.

Edwin nudged his horse forward to a few paces behind Count Vladovitch. The orc was waiting patiently on his mount. Close up, he looked older than Edwin had first presumed. He had thick, ugly features that suggested a lifetime of hard labour outdoors. The silver ring in his ear marked him as a dock worker. His uniform, if that's what it was, was an assortment of chain and leather, with a curved blade hung at his side.

"Good morning, Count Vladovitch. I am Kurgen," said the orc. "I am Lord Morden's representative in Mordengrad."

Edwin was taken aback by the gall of the orc. "That would be Bostokov," snorted Edwin.

He was about to pronounce the orc to be a number of other reprehensible things, but the count's raised gauntlet cut him short. Although he thought the count weak and unable to do what was necessary, he was still in charge and his rank deserved respect. He had also knighted Edwin, which was no small thing in itself.

"Kurgen," said the count, his Eastern provinces accent coming to the fore in pronouncing the orc's name. "We should try to keep this civil and so I must apologise for Sir Edwin; he is young and unschooled in diplomacy."

Edwin had to clench his jaw tight to prevent the retort that naturally came with the observation that Kurgen was hardly schooled himself. He was at best a dock foreman, not a prince.

Kurgen inclined his head in acknowledgement. "What can I do for you gentlemen?"

"I require that you surrender Bostokov to me, Count Vladovitch, as representative of the legal rulers of the city, and in return we will listen to the grievances that forced this unfortunate state of affairs. We also require Morden, so he can be held to account for his actions. If you comply you will be spared your lives. This I guarantee."

It was the weak-kneed offer Edwin had expected. Why they should pander to these menials in their rebellion, and worse, their aligning with a person as evil as Morden, was beyond him. But Edwin was not completely without mercy, as it was a recognised virtue, so he would have offered them a swift death should they surrender immediately or face agony should they not.

"I don't think so," said Kurgen. "For centuries we have been an oppressed people. We would rather die than go back to the slavery that was our lives. And I would not assume you will run over us with your army. You will find we are made of stern stuff."

"We want no bloodshed if it can be avoided," said the count. "But you have broken the rule of law, and you must answer for that."

"Your laws, not ours," said Kurgen.

Edwin could barely contain himself, but it was not quite time. He needed a few minutes more.

"Perhaps, but they are the only laws we have," said the count.

"We have Lord Morden Deathwing's law now," said Kurgen.

"Deathwing?" said the count.

The tone of the count's question made Edwin look over to him. Was that fear he heard? The count certainly looked like blood was draining from his face.

"I see you know the name," said Kurgen. "And so you should, for all the world will know it. Morden Deathwing, a black dragon and man of legend, has come and set the orc nation free. And there's nothing you can do about it!"

From behind Kurgen, the orcs raised their weapons and began to shout:

"Morden! Morden! Morden!"

Edwin was both surprised and pleased. So Morden was the dragon he had seen; the dragon who had snatched away his minion and Griselda. Anger swelled up inside him, and a familiar fury. If only Morden were here now. But he was not. He would have to make do with what was on hand. The orcs' reaction to Morden's name would work perfectly for him. This could not have worked out better. "Treachery!" he shouted, turning his horse to the honour guard and drawing his sword. "Treachery!"

It was the signal he had given his men in the escort, and swords sang from scabbards. "Treachery!" they shouted, joining Edwin in his accusation. Though dampened by the fog, an answering cry came from off to the left.

"We have been betrayed," shouted Edwin. "Treachery!"

To Edwin's right, the count had drawn his sword and was swinging his mount around in a tight circle, looking for the source of the threat.

Strangely, Kurgen seemed completely unsurprised. With a yank of the reins he turned his huge horse around and was inside a ring of steel before Edwin could reach him to cut him down.

Edwin's allies in the escort jumped forward on their mounts and formed up either side. From the mist came the sound of thundering hooves as the rest of Edwin's men came galloping in. Just as they had trained for, they formed a wedge designed to break lines such as the orcs had formed. Their mounts had steel plates across their fronts that would turn a blade, and the sheer power of the formation alone would smash pikes apart.

Edwin deftly kicked his horse up to speed and swung it in behind the wedge. The knights hit the orcs full on and broke them. Not for hundreds of years had orcs met such a charge and, despite their set position and long weapons, their front rank was swept away. Steel flashed and orc blood sprayed the ground.

Edwin cut and sliced to either side. He knocked away spear points and hooks that sought to grab him. He reared his horse to bring its hooves down on the skull of an orc and crushed it like a soft fruit.

In seconds, Kurgen was left with a small group of orcs who had reformed and were holding the knights at bay. They had learnt quickly and poked at the horses' legs; the chest and heads were too well armoured.

It was clear what Edwin had to do. He spurred his horse and put some distance between himself and the knot of orcs.

"To me!" he ordered, and the knights followed.

Ahead of him was the count. Edwin drew up his horse as the other knights arranged themselves around him.

"Sir Edwin!" bellowed the count. "What in all the hells do you think you're doing?"

"Killing the enemy," said Edwin. "We were betrayed." The lie came easily. Let the count rant at him. He would butcher these orcs, take the head of their leader, Kurgen, and be proclaimed a Hero. There was nothing the count could do.

The count's face was a picture of rage. He seemed to be trying to raise a retort but was left speechless. "Do your worst," he managed at last. "But I'll have no part of it." The count kicked his spurs and disappeared into the mist.

Edwin was pleased to see him go. He turned his attention back to the matter at hand. The knights had reformed their wedge. A hundred yards away, barely visible, Edwin could see the orcs in a tight knot. A few of the wounded had been pulled to their knees and thickened the clump. Kurgen sat impassively on his horse.

It was strange they were not retreating. He had expected them to break and run as he rallied his men. He had hoped his short withdrawal might tempt them into fleeing so they could give pursuit and cut them down with ease. But there they were, unmoved. They must be resigned to their fate.

Edwin was about to order his men forward in a gallop that would annihilate the remaining orcs when, to Edwin's left, a horse spooked. Then another. Then there was a dampened sound from the surrounding mist, but growing quickly louder.

It was the sound of feet and armour. Lots of feet.

"Hold!" ordered Edwin. Though the sword in his hand was hungry for more blood, something whispered caution.

Out of the mist to either side of Kurgen emerged ranks of mailed orcs. The front ranks held spear, and behind Edwin could see bowmen. They came to a halt but the sound of feet did not stop. With a dreadful realization, Edwin looked left and right. The mist had played tricks with sound and ranks of orc appeared to either side. Edwin's knights were having difficulties controlling their horses, as though they could sense the growing panic even Edwin could feel rising among the men. Edwin twisted in his saddle to confirm what he already knew. They were surrounded.

"I would ask you to surrender," bellowed Kurgen from his position, surprisingly clear given the distance. "But you're not going to, so why bother?"

He raised an arm and the rear ranks raised their bows.

A sick feeling grabbed Edwin's stomach. They had been undone. They only had one chance.

"Charge!" ordered Edwin, and he spurred his horse forward and veered it to the left. There was no way out ahead, but maybe they could burst through to the side. Edwin had drilled his men well, and as one they sprang forward with him, immediately understanding the plan.

There was a sudden hiss from all around as bows were released. Edwin didn't have to look to know a cloud of death was about to rain upon them. He hunched forward and kicked his horse again.

Around him, arrows thudded into horse flesh and pierced armour. Man and beast fell screaming but miraculously, Edwin and his mount remained unscathed.

Their number had been halved in that volley and many who remained mounted were wounded. They had no choice though. They had to keep riding. They were close to the orcs now, who were bracing themselves for impact. A wall of spears was ahead of them and Edwin felt his anger rise. He could not die like this. Not today. Griselda needed him. He had to rescue her from foul clutches. Such an ignominious death could not be his. He raised his sword, kicked once more, and pulled on the reins to send his mount into a leap.

"Val elohinir!" he cried as he sailed into the wall of spears. They were words that came unbidden but they had power. Edwin could feel the energy flow in him.

The orcs also felt it. Where a mere second before they had been resolute, they suddenly collapsed. Spears dropped and orcs cowered. While to either side the remaining knights were caught on a wall of steel, Edwin crashed through. He swung his sword. It sang in the air as it separated an orc head from its shoulders. Another leap and he was beyond the back rank and clear. Arrows flew past as he fled into the mist and was lost to the archers' sight.

As Edwin rode back to the army, he went over the events that had just occurred. His plan had been faultless. As he thought more, he came to the only conclusion he could that made sense. There was a traitor in their ranks. The grim truth made him grind his teeth in anger. Betrayed. Good men lay dead because of this betrayal. Men loyal to him and his cause. He hoped they found peace in death, because he would find none until he had found whoever it was who had done this. He would find them and they would know his righteous wrath. He would grind their bones to dust and scatter it to the wind. He would have vengeance.

Chapter 33   Temptation

Keep your friends close and your enemies dead.
The Dark Lord's Handbook

Nighttime was an opportunity for Morden to be alone. If he had been in a dark fortress with private quarters he could have found more time for solitary brooding but on a ship, even with his own cabin, there was little respite. Being a Dark Lord was hard work. Having everyone bound to your Will was exactly what the Handbook said you wanted but it also meant you ended up having to make all the decisions.

He was going to have to delegate more effectively. So far, when he had tried there were precious few willing to step forward and risk the penalty of failure. On consulting the Handbook he had discovered asking for volunteers was not the Dark Lord's way. He had to thrust responsibility on minions and let them be forged by experience. If they failed then they were retired.

It was a warm night as spring gave way to summer; a little too warm for Morden's taste. The black robe was light, and let in some air, but it still covered him from head to foot. He wished sometimes he could wear more suitable clothes, but that was out of the question. Even though there was only the night watch on deck he had to be the Dark Lord. It was a full time job. He couldn't just set his robe and the role aside each night if he was tired or didn't feel like it. Back in Bindelburg it had been a game. Now, with a series of port cities sacked and burned in the fleet's wake, it was as serious as it got. But that was all right. He was going to rule the world and if that meant discomfort then that was a small price to pay.

One good thing about being so busy was that he had little time to concern himself with Griselda. If he didn't see her he was fine. She made it easier for him by staying in her cabin where, by all accounts, she spent most of the time writing or talking to Kristoff. Morden couldn't work out their relationship. He had been initially jealous, but that had been allayed when it was apparent the only thing Kristoff was dipping his quill into was an ink well. It seemed their closeness was based on a common love of the written word, and in particular poetry.

Morden reached into his robe and pulled out a cinnabar cigar. He had never been a smoker until he had tried these cigars. They had a relaxing effect without loss of faculties. After a stressful day sacking a city they had proven a good way to unwind.

He held the cigar by one end and lit it with a controlled breath of fire. He'd been discovering many things about what he was and what he could do, and it turned out that although he might look like a man, he was a dragon inside and that included a set of fire glands.

It was a tricky skill. Dragon breath tended to be an all-or-nothing thing used to incinerate large areas. Breathing a reed of fire that danced over the end of a cigar long enough for it to catch required a good deal of concentration. It was one example of the many things Morden had learnt about himself. Landing on a ship when he was a big dragon had been solved rather elegantly; he became a small dragon. In fact, he seemed to be able to control his relative size while a dragon by quite a bit. He could also alter his appearance in human form—skin, teeth, eyes, and so on—while his general features remained the same. He was stuck at being a little over six feet tall and skinny, but he could have black skin that no blade could pierce, eyes that could devour a man's soul, and two rows of white, razor-sharp teeth capable of dealing with the toughest cut of meat the ship's cook could put before him. He could breathe fire while in either form, bend most men and orcs to his Will with a glance, and make suggestions so powerful few could resist.

He smoked the last of the cigar and thought about sleep but he was still not tired. Not the gentle roll of the ship nor the lap of waves on the hull could lull him. Looking out over the ocean, his fleet spread in every direction. From its humble beginnings it had assumed armada-sized proportions. While crewed mostly by orcs, he had been joined by men as well, and even a giant (who sailed his own dinghy which was the size of most ships). They also had pirates, which was useful when it came to knowing where they could stop for fresh water or to sack a city for provisions.

They were still heading east, but not for much longer. Soon they would make landfall on the Great Land. They had left the civilised western nations behind a week ago and would soon be on the shores of a land where everything was Great, the people were strange, and few had ever travelled. From the Great Shore they would make their way across the Great Jungle and the Great Desert to the Great Mountains where Zoon had built his legendary Great Fortress.

He would raise up that fortress and gather his forces. When the time was right he would then Come Forth and finish what he had begun, setting the orc nation free in a river of fire that would burn across the known world.

That was what was to come, but for now he was at a loss. He was not at all tired. Perhaps a flight would tire him. He could scout ahead and be the first to look upon the Great Land.

From behind him Morden heard the slightest of sounds. Someone was coming up the ladder to the deck. He thought it might be a patrolling deckhand. To his surprise, it was Griselda. She was wearing a dark night shift and had her blonde hair tied back, exposing her long, pale neck. When she saw him he expected her to immediately go back the way she had come, but she did not. She walked confidently across the deck barefooted to stand next to him. Of all the men and orcs Morden knew, she was one of the few who was not afraid of him. Stonearm wasn't either, but then he was as hard as nails. Griselda was also hard, though not physically. She came to stand next to him and looked out over the sea as if he were not there at all.

As ever, Morden was at a loss for words. All manner of observations, greetings, quips, jokes, compliments, rhetorical questions (a beautiful night, isn't it?), rebuffs, threats, pleas and animal grunts presented themselves as means of acknowledging her, but none were forthcoming.

He was about to stalk off in a Dark Lord kind of way when she spoke:

"Why haven't you tried to sleep with me?"

If he had been confused before, now he was in total disarray. What kind of question was that? Presumptuous? Not really. Every man and most of the orcs had tried one way or the other to share her bed. Haughty stares, vitriolic put-downs and a few black eyes had seen off all comers; when she walked the decks she was given a wide berth.

Rather than answer directly he saw an opportunity to clarify what he suspected.

"I respect Kristoff. He is an old friend and, although I am in a position to have anything I desire, I would not see him hurt." Even as he spoke he groaned inside at the blunder.

"So you do desire me?" There was a note of triumph in her voice. "I thought as much. You men are all the same. All you see is this body and you're not interested in anything else." Her hands went to her breasts and she hoisted them up. "Never mind that underneath these beats a heart with feelings."

Mesmerised as he was with her demonstration of how ample her breasts were, Morden's pedantic nature came to the fore. "Dark Lord. I'm not a man, I'm a Dark Lord."

"Don't be stupid," said Griselda. "Unless you're telling me you not a man under that robe?"

Morden almost choked. The implication was clear. "That's not what I meant," he said. "Physically I am every inch a man."

"And dragon, if we're being pedantic, and I know you are."

"Half dragon, yes. But what I am physically and what I am to you and everyone else is entirely different, and you'd best remember that. I am a Dark Lord and not to be trifled with."

"Or what?" She had turned to face him square on and she stuck her chin out. Her hands rested on her hips. "You're a boy in a black robe from where I'm standing."

He knew she was goading him and she was succeeding. He could feel anger rising to replace the embarrassment. "I am a Dark Lord."

A smile was playing across her lips. "If you were a Dark Lord you'd take whatever you desired. You said it yourself. You wouldn't care for what anyone thought. But you're not, are you? You're a scared little boy playing games in a black robe."

"You don't know what I'm capable of," he said, trying hard not to rise to her goads.

"Maybe. But from a woman's view it's pretty clear what you're incapable of being."

"Really?"

"Yes, really."

"And what's that?"

"Being a man."

Every part of him was on fire. His desire for her was barely in check. He could hear his father's voice urging him to take her and be done with it. And why shouldn't he? She was right, wasn't she? Was he a Dark Lord or was he a boy playing games? If he was to rule the world and be feared across continents, how could he let this woman talk to him like this?

He took a step towards her. He grabbed her arm and he could feel her tremble under his grip. All he had to do was tear the flimsy shift and she would be his. She took a step back but he held her arm firmly. She could back away all she wanted; there was nowhere she could go. Was that fear in her eyes? Now who's scared? Now who's the little girl playing at being a woman?

Something inside gave way. He threw her back against the bulwark.

"Please don't," she whimpered.

"I was never going to," he said and he leaped into the air. As he did, he changed into his dragon form in a single fluid movement. A beat of his wings and he rose and let himself grow. He roared and flame burst from inside him, lighting up the night.

He didn't look down but rather up. With powerful strokes he rose and circled until he could see the whole fleet below him. He circled twice, sent another shot of fire into the sky, and then headed east to see what destiny awaited him there. Let Griselda play her games. He may want her, but he didn't need her. There were far more important things than her seductive charms.

It was good to be airborne. The rush of cold wind was exhilarating. He headed east and climbed until he hit a current of air that swept him along even faster. Soon the fleet was out of sight, even to his keen dragon vision. It was hard to judge being so high, but he seemed to be moving fast. After an hour or so the touch of dawn came to the far horizon. The sunrise that followed revealed just how big the Great Land was.

He was still over the ocean, but the sun was coming up behind distant peaks. They cast a long shadow across a desert that looked as big as the Western Reaches. On the near side of the desert was another mountain range, albeit smaller than the far range.

Off to the south there were vast glistening swamps, and closer to him, on the shore he was fast approaching, was a jungle. He could see areas of it had been cleared and cultivated, and thin ribbons wound their way through it between what were, he realised, huge cities. There were several rivers, but one was far wider than the rest and gathered up the others as it made its way to the ocean.

Closer now, he could see boats on the ocean close to the land—strange looking vessels with angular sails that bobbed in the swell. They were operating in small fleets. Morden decided to take a closer look and began to lose height. The sun had risen enough to clear the far mountains and the clouds over them brought a pink light.

The boats had slowed in their progress and, now that he was lower, Morden could see nets being thrown over the sides. It was a fishing fleet. Morden had never seen anything like it, at least not on this scale. In the west a few boats may sail together, but this spoke of much more organisation. There must be thirty boats in this one fleet. When he had been higher he had seen other fleets up and down the coast.

That many boats must be catching a lot of fish, and a lot of fish meant a lot of mouths to feed. Morden had imagined they would be landing in a sparsely populated land that was still wild and yet, although the jungle was dense, it was clear there was a major civilisation down there; one that was organised enough to have cleared jungle, built roads, cultivated land and organised fishing fleets.

Morden decided to get a closer look at the boats and their occupants. There was low cloud he used to mask his approach—not that he thought they would be looking skyward. He dove down through the cloud and skimmed across the sea, letting his wing tips splash on the wave tops. He was travelling fast and coming up on the boats. The fishermen were busy about their work, though, and had not seen him. At the last moment he pulled up and soared over the first one, a few feet above the sails. His wing beats buffeted the boat and it rocked heavily. The fisherman looked up at him. He hung in the air above them, hardly able to believe what he was seeing.

They were orcs.

Not quite the same orcs he knew, but there was no doubt. They had yellowish skin instead of green-tinged, and their eyes were thinner and slanted, but they had the same fat, rugged features and he was low enough to see their teeth. Unlike his orcs, they were so long they overhung the lips and when they shouted and pointed he could see they had both an upper and lower set of sharp canines.

Suddenly from below there was an explosion and a second later he felt a sharp pain in his side.

A bolt was lodged in his side, ballista-sized and with rope dangling from it. There was a shout from the ship and the rope went taught. His side flared in pain and he was tugged downwards. He clawed at the rope but missed. He could see a group of orc fishermen had the rope in hand and it had been tied off next to a strange-looking weapon on the prow of the ship. One of the orcs shouted and brought his arm down. The others pulled hard on the rope and Morden was drawn closer to them.

Another orc was doing something to the weapon. There was a second bolt in it and it was being pointed up at him. There was another crack and the bolt came shooting up at him.

In an instant, Morden breathed.

A great gout of flame shot out and met the oncoming bolt, incinerating it. The flame shot down the length of the rope attached to the bolt in his side, burning it and the orcs on the end of it. The flame flattened as it hit the boat and engulfed it. A moment later the boat was an inferno. Burning orcs made hissing sounds as their bodies hit the water.

Morden beat his wings and rose to gain height. Other boats in the fleet were coming towards him from the windward side and there was a puff from the first one. He easily dodged the bolt. Having seen what he had just done to the boat below, he had to admit they were a fearless lot.

He could roast more of the boats, but he didn't want to risk getting hit again. Every beat of his wings was agony as the muscle twisted around the bolt. He climbed higher, leaving the boats behind. Looking at his side, he could see he was bleeding badly. If he tried to fly back to his fleet he might pass out, and if he was over water when that happened it would not be good. His only choice was to make land and try to get the bolt out and take it from there.

As he flew towards land, he could see some of the boats were bobbing around the burning wreck while others had abandoned their fishing and were headed back to land. They would have a fine story to tell once they made port.

Morden pushed on towards land. He could feel himself weakening and he sank lower in the air. Ahead waves crashed on a clear beach with no sign of habitation in either direction. That would have to do. He couldn't go any farther.

He barely made land before he passed out. The sole comfort he had was in the last thing he heard: somewhere above him, a crow cawed.

Chapter 34   The Council

Attachment is the cause of suffering.
So are red hot pokers.   ·
The Dark Lord's Handbook

The news from the Snort brothers was not good. Count Vladovitch and a growing ensemble of nobility were laying siege to Bostokov, or Mordengrad as the new rulers insisted upon calling it, and getting nowhere. Meanwhile, the self-styled Lord Morden Deathwing had sailed east, dipping onto the coast to sack cities at will. Both the name Deathwing and his orcish army had sent a wave of terror across the western civilised world. The pamphlets were full of it, proclaiming Morden as the first serious Dark Lord in over five hundred years.

The economic effects had been varied. The loss of the cities had hit hard, but there had been a rush on gold and arms, both of which were profitable markets. While peace and economic stability were certainly the preferred state of affairs, there was an old chancellor's saying: no one went broke in war. Certainly no chancellor.

Nevertheless, these were concerning times and Chancellor Penbury had succumbed to pressure and called together the council. While seemingly a rich man's club with a common interest in the best food and wine the world had to offer, they were in fact the eight most powerful men in the world sat in committee with the chancellor as the chair. They met infrequently but events had overtaken them and nerves needed to be calmed.

Penbury's own nerves needed calming, but not for any of these reasons. His concern was that the chef who would be laying on the dinner was as competent as he claimed. When it came to these matters, Penbury took a hands-on approach and his initial impressions of the man were good. He seemed to understand the nineteen ways to cook a steak and the secret of good custard. Precious knowledge indeed, but now that the first guests were coming down from their rooms to gather and enjoy an aperitif the chancellor was having his first qualms. The hors d'oeuvres were as they should be, like the wink of a young temptress that promised pleasures to come, and the menu looked like it would deliver those promises. But still, the chancellor was suffering anticipatory anxiety he hoped would be mollified well before the end of the fish course.

If there was one thing the chancellor had no worries about it was the smooth running of the evening itself. Chidwick was orchestrating affairs with his customary efficiency while remaining practically invisible. The guests were seated and nibbling on fresh bread rolls without being able to remember quite how they had got there, so adept was Chidwick's ushering.

For the first few courses, talk was confined to appreciative comments regarding the food and wine. As well as being obscenely rich and powerful, seven of the eight of them shared a common interest in gastronomic affairs. It was only Karoof who ate modestly regardless of the fare, and drank equally sparingly. It was as though his legendary thrift in waste management and associated systems extended to every part of his life. Penbury thought there may be more to it than that and, in fact, the man had no sense of taste after all these years. How anyone could put his nose to a glass of Riola wine and not pass out with the heady pleasure it brought was beyond the chancellor, unless that person was without a sense of smell.

With the main course served, gravy having been suitably drizzled and glasses refilled, Penbury decided now was the time to address the reason they had gathered.

"You are all probably wondering why I called this meeting," he said, addressing the table in general.

Jesper Konovova poked at the innards of a roast potato and, finding it fluffy under its crisp exterior, smiled. "Not at all, Chancellor. We're not fools, you know."

Penbury slapped himself mentally. It was indeed a failing he had in assuming all but himself, and probably Chidwick, were not that quick on the uptake. Still, he had face to save. "Forgive me, gentlemen. Of course, you are right. For are we none of us fools to find ourselves in this position?"

"Touché," said Jesper, raising his glass.

Murmurs of concern and harrumphs rolled around the table.

"In short, gentlemen," said Penbury, "we have a situation. One that demands our attention and I thought it prudent we as a group came to a consensus on the matter."

Furrowed brows and grunts of agreement made it clear Penbury's summation was accurate.

"Should we not clarify exactly the issue on hand?" suggested Hans Birkenfeldt from the other end of the table. Penbury knew him as a precise man in all matters, from the perfect angle of the kerchief in his top pocket to the cut of his hair, and the legendary legalese of his business contracts. If he had a touch more imagination he may well have been chancellor after Penbury, as he was still relatively young.

"Very well," said Penbury. "On one hand we have one Morden Deathwing declaring himself a Dark Lord and saviour to the orc nation, and on the other we have a suddenly energised aristocracy that seems intent upon stopping him. Now, we all know the Deathwing name and the implication that has, and we have all seen the pamphlets with firsthand accounts of this Morden becoming a dragon and doing dragon-like things, breathing fire and so on and so forth; so I think we can safely take it as a point of fact that, although he may not as yet be a Dark Lord, he is certainly well on his way. And that can't be good."

A silence followed as those present digested what the chancellor had said. It was broken by Pierre Hautville:

"Wars have never concerned us particularly?"

"Indeed not," conceded Penbury, "when those wars have been limited and executed according to well-known rules. But I fear in this case it may not be the same."

"Do enlighten us, dear Chancellor," said Pierre, leaning back in his chair with an insouciant smile.

"Very well," said Penbury. He took a sip of wine and let it wash around his mouth while he gathered his thoughts. "As I am sure you know, war has been traditionally fought between the ruling classes, with the working classes as their implements of war, and the merchant classes as their suppliers, whether it be food, weapons, or what have you. It is a system that works well, at least for two of the three parties concerned." Penbury paused for effect and was rewarded with polite guffaws. "The other common element of war, as we have known it for centuries, has been that it has been waged over things, like national boundaries, lines of succession, and marital infidelities. In other words, nothing a good battle couldn't settle. But Morden is different. His war is one of conquest, and more disturbingly, one of ideas."

Penbury paused again to let his last point sink in. The mood at the table had gone quite sober as his guests digested what they had heard and their dinners.

"You make a good point," said Hautville. "I had not considered this thing about ideas. It explains much."

"Indeed," said Sven Trondheim, a bullish man with extravagant facial hair. "This thing with the orcs is most disturbing. My human workers have started talking in the same way."

"Forgive me, Sven," said Birkenfeldt, "I am a man of numbers, not workers, what is it you talk about?"

"You know," said Sven, waving his fork, "this talk of workers' rights and conditions."

"Old hat," said Pierre, sniffing.

"Yes, yes," said Sven, "We have all heard this when it is localised to a mine or a mill, but now they are talking in wider circles. They are organising."

"Bah," said Pierre. "We have had guilds for centuries."

"True again, my friend," said Sven. Penbury could see the big man was trying to contain his temper by the way his beard was positively bristling. "But these are not guilds. These are not a loose collection of tradesmen but workers: loggers, miners, herders, dockers, even foot soldiers. They are getting together and talking about withholding labour. Strikes, they call it. They demand better pay, better conditions, and holidays."

"Again," said Pierre, "this is not new. Send in your boys and break some bones and it will go away. It always does. Or sack them and get someone else. There are a hundred people ready to do any man's work."

"I thought that too," said Sven. "But things have changed. They are organised and they fight back. They blockade my wood mills and they have this thing called scabs."

"A pox?" asked Pierre, screwing his face up.

"No. They use shame and big sticks to stop the men I get to replace them working. They call those who would break the strike scabs. An effective taunt, as it turns out. Soon my mills stop and I am forced to talk to them. It's not right. And this Morden is to blame. His orcs started it all and it's catching on, I tell you."

Everything Sven said confirmed to Penbury what he had been reading in the Snort reports. What was worrying was that it was spreading beyond the cities Morden had sacked.

"And where is Morden now?" asked Paolo de Luca, the olive oil baron whose interests included most of the shipping they all used to move goods. "He has much of my fleet and I would like it back."

"He has sailed east," said Penbury. "Beyond the Great Sea."

A ripple of surprised grunts ran around the table.

"But this is good news, is it not?" said Sven. "If he has sailed that far then surely that is the last of him?"

Penbury wished that were so. "I am afraid not, Sven. If only he were a common pirate, but he is not. He is a Deathwing, and worse: a Dark Lord Rising. He heads east to gather his power. If I am right, he is going to the Great Fortress of Zoon the Reviled."

"Fairy tales!" said Pierre. "If that is the case then he will be gone forever and we are rid of him."

"Zoon the Reviled was no fairy tale," said Penbury. "He is clearly described in the archives."

Though available only to the chancellor, the existence of the archives and the reliability of them was well known among those present. The chancellor's words caused great consternation.

"If you are correct, Chancellor," said Birkenfeldt once the muttering had subsided, "and you expect Morden to return in full power and with a host that befits a Dark Lord, the question before us is, what should we do?"

"It seems to me," said Karoof, entering the conversation, "there are two sides and it is a matter of choosing the winning side. With the resources we have, surely whomever we back will win?"

"Do these nobles have a chance even with our backing?" asked Pierre. "They are full of huff and puff but let's be honest, with the odd exception, there is hardly a brain between them."

Penbury let the laughter die down before replying. The discussion was going as he had expected, but he had one more tidbit to throw into the mix. "They have a Hero."

That silenced them all.

"A Hero? Like Uther?" Trondheim's voice cracked as he mentioned the name.

The only one who seemed unaffected was Birkenfeldt. "You have me at a disadvantage, gentlemen. Who is this Uther?"

"Let's just say," said Penbury, "if there is one thing worse than a Dark Lord, it's a Hero."

"Forgive me," said Birkenfeldt, "but isn't having a Hero to oppose the Dark Lord a good thing?"

Penbury felt a warm glow inside, partly due to the slight heartburn he had developed but mostly as a reaction to young Birkenfeldt's comment. It was good to see that even among a group such as themselves, driven by profit and power, such naivety was still present, even if it was confined to the youngest.

"I suggest you go and read the histories," said Penbury as gently as he could manage. "While it is true that Uther defeated Zoon and thus saved the world from an Undead Lord who would have laid jealous ruin across the world, what he replaced it with was barely any better; forty years of righteousness and inquisition the like of which the world had never seen. Many more died in those terrible years, denounced as heretics and blasphemers, as had been killed in the war itself. It was only thanks to the secular revolution of Chancellor Huffenhoff that religion was finally put in its place. So far we have been lucky and this current Hero, Edwin, has not yet played the religion card, but you can bet he will."

Penbury sat back and steepled his fingers. Waiters nipped in to clear the main course and to refill glasses. A mood of quiet contemplation descended as the group considered what had been said. In Penbury's mind it was a conundrum. Ideally he didn't want to have to pick either side in what seemed to be an inevitable conflict. As far as he was concerned, they were both as bad as each other and would seriously upset the stability that he, as chancellor, managed. While he was aware of those who despised and feared him, and he did on occasion have to employ rather radical practices, it was all for the best. Not necessarily the good, but the best.

His mind wandered back to his recent cornering of the drug market, and in particular Headfucker, as it was so charmingly known on the street. He could have left it in the hands of organised crime and let them continue to make huge profits, which could only be bad for business if they used that money to acquire power. Penbury was a practical man. He recognised there would always be drug takers, and if that was the case then it was better he did the supplying. At least he was happy with the market as it was and would not seek to expand it into unsavoury areas.

There seemed to be strong parallels with the current situation. It wasn't a question of morals or ethics but more of practical expediency.

Sven was the first to break the meditation. "Have we tried lawyers yet?" he asked.

"If by that," said Penbury, "you mean, have attempts been made to shorten their lives, then yes, with the obvious lack of success."

"Not so easy to kill a Hero, I suppose?" asked Pierre.

"Indeed not," said Penbury. "They have the most incredible good fortune."

"And Morden is equally impervious?" asked Karoof.

Penbury nodded and there was a collective sigh from the group.

"Is there anyone close to them we can use as leverage?" asked Birkenfeldt.

"A fine idea," said Pierre. "Everyone has a weakness. Chancellor?"

In instructing the Snort brothers he had asked them to find out all they could about Morden and Edwin and there had been mention of a girl. "The only thing that springs to mind is a girl. Apparently Edwin's love, Griselda, was stolen from him by Morden and he has sworn to save her. He couldn't give a pig's nipple about anything else, or so I hear."

"There we have it," said Paolo, slapping the table. "The girl is the key."

"Maybe," said Penbury. "But I fear there are other forces at work here. How is it that Morden, an odd but unremarkable child from a monastery of brewers, turns out to be a black dragon and a Dark Lord Rising? And Edwin. Yes, he is an orphan raised by a blacksmith, and we all know what that means, but there are thousands of blacksmiths' sons with barely a heroic hair between them. How is it he has become such a Hero? Besides, kidnapping the girl isn't going to solve our problem, merely attract unwanted attention from both parties."

"There is one thing I have noticed that I find curious," said Birkenfeldt. "As you know, I am probably the biggest banker here, the chancellor excepted. Borrowing over the last decade is up, but of late it has increased dramatically; mainly among the aristocrats."

"Is that not to fund their war games?" asked Pierre.

"I thought so too, until I tied it into other areas. While spending on armour, weapons and the supplies of war has increased, it does not match the amount being borrowed. What has gone up is the price of gold. This is normal in uncertain times, but the movements cannot be attributed purely to speculators and worried savers. Somebody, somewhere, is stockpiling."

This was the first bit of news Penbury did not already know himself, and it was both interesting and disturbing. With everything that had been going on it was also a reminder that he needed to maintain a close eye on his own businesses and the markets. As had just been shown, movements of goods and hard currency often gave away preparations for war and other, less visible activities.

"Very good, Birkenfeldt," said Penbury. "A most interesting observation. Clearly we need to look into matters more closely. If, as I am beginning to suspect, Morden and Edwin are mere puppets, then we need to know who is pulling the strings."

As the other seven murmured their assent, the doors at the far end of the hall swung open and a procession of waiters entered each with a covered platter held aloft.

"Ah, dessert," said Penbury.

While chatter at the table turned to the quality of the sponge, the use of vanilla and various thickening agents in custard, and the sweetness of dessert wine, Penbury's mind was going over the discussion so far. It was, as he had thought, a tricky situation and one that could not be solved by a hostile takeover or a well-targeted slanderous pamphlet campaign.

Once dessert had been given due diligence and the eight were once more left alone, cigars in hand, port glasses full, and cheeseboard arrayed appropriately, Penbury guided discussion away from how long soft yak cheese should be left and back to weightier matters.

"Gentlemen," said Penbury, tapping his glass. "Let's wrap up this Dark Lord issue before we retire."

The seven other richest, most powerful men in the western world made sure their glasses were full, their cigars lit, and waistbands adjusted.

"We find ourselves in a situation that has not been faced for centuries. A Dark Lord is Rising and a Hero has appeared, leaving a trail of blood behind him. These are indeed worrying events. I shall continue in my intelligence gathering and keep you all appraised. The goal is to find a resolution that will cause the least disruption to our affairs so the world, and most particularly ourselves, may continue to prosper. We must also accept, however, that the world as we know it may well be laid waste."

There were grunts of consternation at this frank observation but Penbury had always believed in not dressing things up or avoiding hard truths. That kind of head-in-the-sand thinking led to companies overextending and losing far too much money long after they should have been wrapped up.

"Gentlemen," said Penbury, calming them with a raised hand. "Let us also not forget one of the immutable truths: you can't beat economics. Whatever transpires in the world, people will still need feeding and Paolo will ship their food. They will need houses and Sven will build them. There will still be money to be lent and Birkenfeldt will lend it. While ideally we would like things to continue as they are, and I pledge I will do everything in my power to ensure this is the case, if the worst does happen and there is a Dark Lord holding dominion over us all, he'll still need us. Because it is us, gentlemen, who make things work; for where there is a profit to be made, we will be there."

It was the insight the first chancellor had written down and had passed on to every chancellor that had followed. Kings and queens, despots and dictators, came and went; people were richer and poorer, but there was always, always, always a profit to be made.

Chapter 35   Foreign Lands

Pain is a great motivator.
The Dark Lord's Handbook

Morden wasn't sure how long he had been unconscious. The last thing he remembered was collapsing onto the beach and hearing a crow. He opened one eye. There was a fly on the end of his nose. It sat there for a second and then took off. Around him there was a buzzing sound consistent with a pile of dung and a hot summer's day. Opening his other eye, but still lacking the strength to move, Morden could see a cloud of flies dipping and buzzing over the sand next to him. His first thought was that the way his luck had been going something had wandered along and crapped on him.

Well, whatever had happened while he had been out cold, he couldn't lie there forever. The sun was blazing down and his mouth felt drier than the hot sand he was lying on. Bracing himself for the anticipated pain, he lifted himself onto one elbow, sending flies into an annoyed cloud. But the pain didn't come. He did feel stiff around the middle, but there was no sharp pain as he would have expected having been impaled.

The harpoon lay on the sand next to him on a large patch of dark sand, which Morden quickly realised was blood-soaked. It was the blood that had attracted the flies. By the look of it he had lost a lot of blood. No wonder he felt strange. He was lucky to be alive. He sat up and reached one hand to his side to feel the wound. There was a tear in the robe with congealed blood around it. Exploring with his fingers, Morden could feel a sizeable gash that was still open but not bleeding. It felt sticky to touch.

He thought about looking to see how bad it was but, feeling as he did, he thought it best not to. The last thing he needed was to be sick and provide the flies with pudding.

Morden got slowly to his feet, which further agitated the flies. The blood he'd lost had spread under him and, judging from the dark stain of the sand, he couldn't have much left.

First things first, though, he needed to get out of this sun and find water. Looking up and down the beach he could see no signs of civilisation. That left the jungle. At the edge, where it met the beach, it was thin, like a fringe, but became dense a few yards in. It wasn't as though he had much choice. If he stuck to the fringe he would have shade.

Gingerly at first, and then with confidence as he felt no pain, he made his way to the edge of the jungle. The canopy provided by the broad green leaves of strange-looking trees was welcome indeed. The trees were not like any he had seen before, with banded trunks and no lower branches at all. They grew fairly straight, with a slight bend, before spreading their rubbery leaves. Clustered at the top, where the leaves branched, were clusters of what looked like giant nuts. Looking around, he could see where some of these had fallen and split open. Most of what had been inside had been scavenged by beast or insect, but there were traces of white juicy flesh.

To get at these fruits a normal man would have to hope to shake them loose, or maybe get the harpoon and knock them loose, or even use the thick bands to climb up and pull them off, but he was Morden Deathwing. All he had to do was turn into a dragon and fly up. He could crack them with a talon, and cook them should they need it. All he had to do was apply his Will and Change.

Nothing happened.

He tried again as he had taught himself. All he had to do was will it so and … nothing. He could feel it, the power, but there was something else. Maybe it was his weakness from the injury. He concentrated harder and gave it another go. Again, nothing. There was something horribly wrong. It wasn't a lack of strength. He didn't actually feel that bad. As he had learnt to recognise the dragon power he had inside himself, so now he could sense there something else there, something new.

Whatever it was, it was stopping him Changing.

What else had it affected? Morden tried to breathe fire but all he got was a splutter of smoke. It was as though his throat was empty of fire. Had his glands dried up?

Then a dreadful thought struck him. If he couldn't fly, then he couldn't get back to the fleet and they had no idea where he was. He was stranded.

That was not good. Not good at all.

As his predicament began to sink in he could feel panic start to rise. What was he going to do? Damn it. Damn those orcs and their harpoon they had fired at him. Damn Penbury for having ruined his safe empire, and damn Grimtooth for having found him with his stupid book. He was going to die on a beach in the middle of nowhere and all they would find would be a black robe.

He punched the tree in frustration.

A second later something hard hit him on the head. There was a crack as whatever it was fell to the ground. It was one of the nuts and it had a split in the side, out of which white milk was leaking. Quickly, Morden scooped it up and drank. It didn't seem to taste of much—not much did these days, with all the fire breathing—but he could feel the cool fluid running down his throat and it felt good.

When the milk had run dry, he smacked the nut against a rock in the sand to try and break it open. It proved to be an extremely hard nut to crack, but he got there in the end. As he thought, there was hard flesh on the inside.

He sat on the rock and considered the other nuts. There were plenty of them. It might not prove to be a varied diet, but now he was sure he wasn't going to starve. They were hard buggers though.

And with that thought, he put his hand to his head. The nut falling on his head should have knocked him out cold, at the very least hurt a lot. Feeling his skull, there wasn't even a lump. In fact, thinking about it, he had hardly felt the nut hit him.

Morden didn't have time to consider this further as an arrow whistled past his nose and thumped into the trunk of the tree.

"Gruk ng kasz!"

The order came from Morden's right and he spun to see who had shot at him. There was an orc. His skin had a yellow tinge to it over the normal green, and his eyes were slanted, but he was unmistakably an orc. He was holding a bow, rather shakily it had to be said, and perhaps that is why he had missed.

"Gruk ng kasz!" said the orc again, and this time Morden's brain kicked in.

"It's all right. I have no intention of moving," said Morden in what he thought were soothing tones, but he startled even himself as he spoke. His speech had dropped an octave and his voice sounded like the older men in the pub who had smoked pipes all their lives. Morden cleared his throat and a disgusting sound came out. The orc took a step backwards.

"Gruk ng kasz!" insisted the orc.

"Look!" said Morden. "I'm not moving, you stupid orc. Now put that bow down before you hurt somebody, and in particular, me."

The orc took another step backwards and his hands were shaking so much Morden was worried he would loose his arrow. Not that he could have hit anything the way his aim was wavering.

Morden spread his arms to show he was unarmed and was no threat. The orc's response was not quite what Morden expected. The orc, obviously scared, now looked terrified and with a yelp threw his bow in the air, collapsed on the ground in a quivering heap and started muttering something over and over that Morden couldn't quite make out.

"Where do you live?" asked Morden, realising his concerns about survival, being shot aside, were now gone. But the orc lay there shaking and muttering. Morden asked again, slipping effortlessly into the orc's own tongue this time. "Gkar mpu fegz?"

When Morden had first discovered his gift of tongues he had found it disconcerting. Now it was just useful. The orc seemed startled to hear his own language. With some effort, he brought himself under control and assumed a kneeling position in front of Morden. The muttering assumed a chant like quality. The orc's face was pretty much in the sand so it was hard to make out but it sounded like,

"Zoon. Dark Master. Zoon. Lord of All. Zoon," over and over.

While Morden had got used to how he was viewed by orcs in the west, he was used to being addressed as Morden. He was taken aback by being called Zoon. Shrugging inwardly, and assuming it was the robe that did it, he had more pressing matters to deal with.

"Get up," he commanded, and the orc sprang to his feet as though a puppet. "Show me where you live."

The orc scurried off and led Morden through the jungle along a path he wouldn't have known was there from just looking. The jungle was dense; branches and vines hung over the path and snagged at his robe. It became feverishly hot and the orc had to pause and wait for Morden to catch up on several occasions. Morden wished he could fly. Then he could have sailed above this mess. He tried to Change; he could not. It was worrying. As before, he could feel the power there, but there was something else now that was getting in the way. It wasn't exactly foreign, rather something different—much like when he had first looked inward and seen the dragon power. Unlike that power, this new thing made Morden's hackles rise. There was a deeply disturbing quality to whatever it was. Though he had grown used to being called a Dark Lord, he had not until now felt dark. This thing inside him, that he could feel growing, was truly dark.

After what must have been another thirty minutes or so, but felt like several weeks, they popped suddenly into a clearing of huts. It was a small village, maybe twenty dwellings, one bigger than the rest, made from the stuff of the jungle, with green thatching. There were more orcs here, all about their business: tending pigs, fixing a roof, playing with children, scratching their arses.

Morden took in the scene unnoticed. It was one of lively peace. Though the conditions would be considered meagre by the standards of Bindelburg, unlike the orcs in the slums around the cities in the west, it was obvious these orcs had no master but themselves and were happy. As Morden cast his eye around, evidence that they shared some common heritage with their western cousins became more apparent. At one end of the village was a fire pit, and behind it were a number of stakes with heads impaled upon them. The male orcs were all armed with crude clubs and knives. One had a bow slung across his shoulders. When they laughed, long sharp teeth were much in evidence. These orcs had not had their tusk-like canines filed flat.

"Hey! Shitheads!" Morden found himself translating the guide's insult without thinking.

His guide was mostly ignored, but some looked over. In seconds, a transformation occurred. Women scooped up children, men drew weapons, and before Morden had even a chance to say hello he was surrounded by a bristling group of orcs, all of them with bared teeth, guttural growls, and snarls in abundance. Spears poked forward but didn't make contact.

"What the fuck is going on?" came a loud voice from the back of the pack and a huge orc muscled his way through.

When he saw Morden, he stopped and frowned. He glanced sideways at the orc who had led Morden to the village and then turned his back on them.

"Kill him," he said over his shoulder and strode off.

The thicket of spears closed behind the orc as he left.

Morden's hand went instinctively to his chest where the dragon pendant lay under his robe. It had always been his talisman. He didn't understand how, even after his father had tried to explain the technicalities, but it always protected him. Expecting it to be roasting hot in the face of an imminent skewering, it was in fact quite cool to his touch.

The orcs seemed to gain confidence from his inaction. One let rip a shout and sprang forward and stabbed at Morden. Though he didn't feel pain, it was with amazement Morden looked down and saw the spear sticking into his midriff.

Then another orc stabbed him, and the orc with the bow shot him. The arrow twisted his shoulder backwards as it hit; again, he felt impact but no pain. The orcs let go of their spears and jumped backwards. They looked confused. Morden himself was not entirely clear what was happening—beyond he was getting pissed off with being shot and speared.

He supposed at this point he should be writhing around on the ground in death throes, but frankly he was far too annoyed to play along. He was a Dark Lord and he had important Dark Lord business to be getting on with, if he could find a way to get back to his fleet and army. Being abused and poked at was not the way he should be treated. Didn't they know who he was?

The orcs looked perplexed as well. Another orc jumped forward and stabbed his spear into Morden's belly and jumped back, as if it was a matter of enough spears to do the trick. All it left was a third spear dangling ineffectually.

"ENOUGH!" bellowed Morden.

The orcs shrank back. The one who had led him to the village fell to his belly and started his chanting again; the others looked at him with open amusement. Morden realised he'd probably been rescued by the village idiot.

Bracing himself for pain that so far had not come, Morden tugged the arrow free from his shoulder and tossed it aside. He gripped one of the spears close to his body and pulled hard. It came free with a horrible slurp and a few gobbets of flesh came out as well. In short order, Morden removed the other two spears. Looking at his robe, he should have been drenched in blood but, apart from rather disgusting wounds, there was none.

Instead there was a gurgling sound and Morden's stomach heaved. It took him by surprise. The last time he'd felt like this was when he had inadvisedly eaten the cook's lamb special at his Bindelburg school (special in that it was plainly raw). He retched and couldn't keep back the bile. He bent over and a stream of white sick spewed onto the ground. The surrounding orcs leapt even further back to avoid the splash with cries of disgust.

And it kept coming until Morden was forced to his knees, his stomach knotting itself trying to empty its contents. At last all he could manage was dry retching.

That about did it for Morden. He'd had enough of being shot at, stabbed, puking, being laughed at, and generally not taken seriously.

He forced himself up and straightened.

"I said enough!" roared Morden.

It was as if his voice was a blast of wind. It blew out from him and knocked the orcs off their feet. They screamed as they fell, many grabbing at their faces. The bushes blew backwards, blackened and shrivelled. The huts bent and creaked; bits of wood and roof flew off into the jungle.

Morden had, to some extent, got used to the strange and gratifyingly powerful things he had been able to do, but this was different.

He strode forward to see what had happened to the orcs as they were still writhing in pain and screaming. He was angry but he didn't mean to hurt them. He liked orcs. As he walked something caught his eye, and looking down he saw that where his feet fell the ground blackened and what greenery there was withered into black ash in seconds. As he got to within a yard or so of the nearest orc, the screams grew and it scrambled away from him as best it could. Morden could see its face and it was as though it had been pickled.

The one orc that seemed unaffected was the one who had first found him. He was knelt as he had always been and was now staring at Morden with a look of adoration. He looked completely unaffected by Morden's powers.

The entire village was gathered now around the big orc, who Morden surmised must be the chief. There seemed to be a heated debate going on.

Morden wasn't inclined to wait and see what decision they came to regarding him. There was a single track that ran through the village which, given the direction they had come from, ran parallel to the coast. Morden decided to go left.

The orcs parted like a flock of sheep at the approach of a rabid dog.

As Morden headed north the jungle withered. From the village behind him, drums started beating. A short while later, they were answered by drums that seemed a good distance ahead of him. So they knew he was coming. That was good. Let them know and let them be afraid.

Somewhere above him a bird called and a parrot fell dead at his feet.

Chapter 36   A New Hope

Power corrupts. But isn't that the point?
The Dark Lord's Handbook

From his command tent on the hill a mile from the city, Count
Vladovitch had a clear view of the army spread around the walls. It had
been a month since the Betrayal at Bostokov, as Edwin had named it,
and this great injustice had rallied even more to the banner. Edwin's lost
knights had been replaced, this time with fewer romantics and more
grizzled veterans and zealots. Trebuchets had been built, ladders made,
armour and swords forged, countryside raped and men exhorted until,
this day, all was ready.

Knowing as he did what had actually happened, it left a bitter taste
in the count's mouth to watch Edwin riding the length of the centre,
sword raised, spewing some nonsense about death and glory. There was
going to be plenty of the former and precious little of the latter today.
The orcs would make a good fight of it, but there was little hope for
them against such numbers. The war had captured the imagination of the
Western Reaches and men had flocked in to see the evil overthrown.
And Sir Edwin, Knight Resplendent, was their Hero. He was the sole
survivor (overlooking the count himself) of the dark treachery of the
loathsome green skins.

"We may as well get this over with," said the count to no one in
particular. "Make the signal for the attack to begin."

The mood was grim among the generals gathered there. They all
knew the count, and most shared his dislike for the way events had
turned out. Nevertheless, word was passed and the signaller raised his
flag and waved it in the still air. It was greeted by a roar from the
assembled army as the tension of waiting was released. It was something
the count knew well. There had been a time when he too had been eager
for the fray, but it had taken only a battle or two, seeing men cut like
meat at the butcher, to understand there was nothing to be eager about,

nor glory in the work he performed.

From below, the trebuchets groaned into action, hurling their rocks in graceful arcs. Where they hit the wall there was an explosion of rock and dust. Where they sailed over the wall the count didn't have to imagine what it would do to a house it hit. He had seen it. It would be matchwood.

After the second salvo, the front line started forward; the sound of thousands of hobnailed feet drowned out the creaks from the trebuchets as they were wound back. A few answering rocks came from behind the city walls, but were largely ineffectual. The count had the best artillery men in the Western Marches; the orc defenders were rather newer to the art.

The city walls proved to be next to no obstacle; they had been built mainly to keep slum dwellers out, not well-formed armies. There hadn't been an army like this for hundreds of years.

When there was a clear breach, Edwin led his knights forward. Though cavalry was not normally suited to city assaults, it was clear there would be little resistance and the count felt sorry for anyone, man or orc, those knights came across. Their steel shone brightly even in the dim sunlight of the day, pennants snapping as they galloped the last hundred yards to the city. Edwin himself was at their head, standing in his stirrups, his sword raised. In an age long past, the count may have found the scene uplifting, but now it just scared him. What had he unleashed?

By the time the army had advanced into the city, and the first plumes of smoke were rising from the burning and looting, there was a stack of unused ladders at the breaches the artillery had made.

"If you wouldn't mind, would you go and make sure he doesn't get too carried away," said the count to Baron Fanfaron on his left. The baron had proven his worth in culinary matters and become a close friend. He too seemed to share the count's distaste with affairs, but was always willing in his duties.

"Of course," said the baron, nodding, and he called for his mount.

"Sir Romquist," said the count, turning to his siege commander, "secure the artillery. Good work."

Sir Romquist bowed and headed down to the trebuchets and ballistae (which had not been needed). Surveying the field for the last time, and seeing no need to remain present a moment longer, the count addressed the remainder of the staff and generals standing around. "Gentlemen, I think I shall retire for lunch. Call me when he is done."

To mutters of congratulations, and shaking the hands of his senior staff, the count made his way to his tent. He needed a drink to get the bitter taste from his mouth. He waved away his aide and ducked into his tent. It was dark and cool, and the heavy sides dampened the sound from outside so it was quiet. A pitcher of wine sat next to his mug on his writing desk. He filled the mug and emptied it, filled it again and collapsed onto his field cot.

His thoughts turned to his wife. It would be months before he could return to her. Even after Bostokov had been captured, there were the other cities Morden had taken along the seaboard that needed to be reclaimed. They would be lucky if they were done before winter set in. He had hoped that if all went well, and it certainly looked as if it would, he could be released and the mopping up be left to Edwin, but Black Orchid had been clear that she expected him to be there to the end, and she was not to be argued with. She still made him terrified to the core of his being when she was around.

A polite cough from behind him interrupted his thoughts.

"Don't get up," said a voice with calm assurance. Recognising it would be extraordinarily unwise to move, the count froze in position.

"We are going to have a conversation, but you are not going to see who I am. All you need to know is who I represent, and that is Chancellor Penbury, and what he wants me to communicate to you. Do you understand?"

"Are you a lawyer?" asked the count.

"I see you do understand. Excellent. You should also understand that I am not here to execute any estates. My client would like to enter into negotiations, the end result of which would be the cessation of hostilities by all parties."

The count had to let what he was hearing sink in. It was everything he could possibly have hoped for; almost too good to be true.

"You'll have my full cooperation," said the count. "I wish for nothing other than the end to this madness."

"A good start," observed the voice. "Very well. So what are the barriers to this, as you see them? What is it you want?"

"Personally? Nothing. I'd like nothing more than to go home."

There was a scratching sound from behind the count before the voice spoke again. "If you want nothing then why do you lead this army in this war? My client seems somewhat confused."

It was the count's turn to be at a loss for words. Where to start?

"How long do you have?" he asked.

"Time enough," said the voice. "Though brevity is a virtue."

Conciseness and accuracy were two qualities the count admired in commanders and strove for in everything he did. It took little time, therefore, for the count to explain how the entire charade was the work of Black Orchid. She was none other than a Deathwing, and her plan was to reclaim the rightful position of aristocracy, freeing themselves from the merchant middle classes, by allowing Morden to lay ruin across the world and to step in and save everyone.

When described so succinctly, the count could hardly believe he ever signed up to such insanity. While he wanted nothing but the best for his wife, and hated the idea that they should be paupers, the deaths of thousands to pay for his later life comforts did, in hindsight, seem like an unreasonable price.

There was another pause as the count finished, the scratching being the only noise bar the distant sound of battle.

"My client asks if all it would take to put an end to this would be a large cash injection into the upper classes to provide fiscal relief?"

"Yes," said the count, but then a thought struck. "And no. My greatest fear is that we have unleashed a terror on the world."

"Edwin?"

"Yes, Edwin. He will not rest until Morden is dead and he has recovered from him the love of his life."

"And that would be Griselda?"

This voice is well informed, thought the count. "Yes, Griselda. And I think after today there will be many more who will have acquired a taste for blood. I'm not sure we could stop it, even if we wanted to."

"I see," said the voice. There was some more scratching. "Thank you, count. You have been most helpful. We'll be in touch."

The count lay still and listened for any sound, but there was none. After what he judged was a safe period of time, the count sat up to look at where the voice had come from. It was no surprise to see no one there.

Chapter 37   Reclamation

Dead last is better than dead first.
The Dark Lord's Handbook

Morden walked all day, and into the night. He didn't know quite where he was going, only that he needed to find something bigger than the villages that straddled his path northwards. He swept through them like a Dark Lord, which was good as that was what he was supposed to be. The orcs who were around to see what was happening fell by the side as his aura hit them. The jungle itself shrivelled as he painted a dark line through it.

As the sun dipped in the west and the moon rose over the jungle, it occurred to Morden that he should feel tired, or hungry, but he was neither. In fact, after being sick in the first village, he felt fantastic. He tried Changing again but could not. It was the same each time. He could sense the power to change within himself, but there seemed to be something else preventing him assuming his dragon form.

At the pace he was going, he was not too concerned. It couldn't be long before he came across somewhere substantial and from there could get back to his fleet. He hoped Stonearm continued on course eastward. The lumbering orc had proven to have brain as well as brawn so it wasn't too much to hope for. What was more worrying was what effect his absence would have on the fleet itself. He was, after all, the one thing that kept it together. It was his dark vision, and more specifically his dark presence, to which his minions were drawn.

The path he had been on was now a road, which Morden took as a good sign. Roads meant civilisation, even if in this case the road was a wider path with deeper ruts. The half moon was high in the sky when Morden crested a rise and was met by the sight of a river across his path. It wasn't particularly wide but there was no bridge in evidence. Swimming was out of the question, so he had to consider the alternatives.

Looking west to where the river met the ocean, Morden could see a glow in the sky. It must be a city. With renewed urgency, Morden headed west along the road that hugged the river on a raised bank.

It was not long before he came across an orc. He was asleep under a tree surrounded by clutter: a pack, what looked like fishing spears, and a net with dead fish in it. The orc was snoring loudly.

Tethered to a log was the orc's canoe. It had been hewn from a single trunk and a paddle lay in the back. It took a mere moment of consideration before Morden got in the canoe, tugged the tether loose, and pushed off with the paddle. Though he couldn't swim, so if he was tipped over he would be in trouble, the obvious advantage of boating down the river as opposed to walking far outweighed the risk. Besides, how hard could it be? He was going with the current so barely had to paddle. It was more a question of steering.

Morden left the snoring orc in his wake.

It proved to be so easy Morden thought he may as well take a nap and let the canoe take him down river. He lay back and shut his eyes. By rights, he should have been exhausted, but strangely he wasn't tired at all. All the same, he lay full length, closed his eyes, and relaxed. He let the sounds of the river and the jungle fill him. The splashes of fish, animal cries and bird calls was at first a cacophony but after a while blended into a discordant masterpiece.

He lost track of time as he began to think of matters other than being stranded in a strange land. He wasn't too concerned about his fleet and plans for conquest. He would get back to civilisation and find his army. It would be hard to miss, after all. Maybe he should use the time to read the Handbook? He still had a lot to learn, but lying there being drifted downriver in a canoe was a rare opportunity to care less. There would be plenty of time to be a Dark Lord when he reached the sea and found his men.

She would be there as well. Griselda. She did things to him he found disturbing. He was a Dark Lord; well, almost a Dark Lord. He was going to lay waste the world and hold it under his dominion. So why was it that this woman was able to control him so easily? He let her get to him and he shouldn't. What did her opinion count for, anyway? He knew who and what he was and she ought to be more grateful for his mercy. If it wasn't for Kristoff he would have discarded her. There were many other alluring women. She was nothing special.

He sighed to himself. When he got back he would have to first talk to Kristoff and then to her. She would be his, and if she wasn't interested then they would have to go. He couldn't have her around distracting him when he had important things to do.

Not that he doubted she would want him. Who wouldn't? He was young, tall, apparently good looking if the serving maids back in Bindelburg were anything to go by (they teased him tirelessly), and was going to be ruler of the world. Who wouldn't go for a man like that? He was quite familiar with playing hard to get. If she didn't like him, then why had she come up on deck to speak to him? She could have stayed below and avoided him altogether.

The more he thought about it, the more he was convinced she liked him every bit as much as he had to admit he liked her. And that was good. She could be his queen. She was well suited. She had a wicked tongue on her. She would be stern, commanding, and beautiful, as befits a Dark Lord's spouse.

Settling on this image he dozed. Light on his eyelids told him that dawn had come, but the day could wait. He wouldn't have time to daydream in the days to come, so he may as well get as much as he could in now.

The drums had stopped a while back but now they had started again, though something was different. Whereas before they had beaten a complex rhythm that sounded like a language, now they beat a steady rhythm that drowned out the sound of the jungle. Morden could feel the boat had slowed as well. He ought to sit up and see where he was but it was so comfortable lying there and brooding that one more minute wouldn't hurt.

Another sound joined the drums. It was unmistakably orcs. He'd heard enough of their dulcet tones over the months to know an orc chant when he heard one; though the tone and accent of this one was different. Now he was straining hard to listen and as he did he picked up other sounds. Was that the sound of paddles? Then it occurred to him they probably couldn't see him. Lying flat as he was, all they could likely see was an empty canoe floating down the river. If he lay still he might just float past. Much as he loved them, he was in no mood to have to deal with any Dark Lord business.

The chant was becoming more distinct. It was in the same language the orcs in the village had spoken, but less provincial.

"Zoon, Zoooon, Zoooooon."

The chant was low and throaty. And it was getting louder.

Without doubt he could hear paddles in the water now, and he had a sense there was more than one other canoe on the river with him. There seemed nothing for it. He had to see what was going on. Making sure his hood was up over his head, Morden sat up.

It was a lot to take in at once. The river had widened considerably and slowed down. Canoes of all sizes surrounded him. Orcs, wearing little more than the odd rag over their taut muscles, paddled along in single-man canoes, crudely hewn from single logs. Among them were what looked like war canoes. These had a crew of eight, or more, burly orcs stroking slowly, dressed in armour made from wood, reeds, and plates of dull metal. The larger canoes had been crafted with jagged patterns and faces of orcs baring their teeth.

All of them were at least ten yards away. Looking behind him, Morden could see why; there was a trail of dead fish in his wake. Fascinated, he looked ahead. Dead fish popped to the surface at the bow of his canoe.

At his appearance the chant became an almost continuous 'Zoon'.

Morden decided to risk standing up so he could see better. The river was so placid there was little risk of tipping over, if he was careful. All the same, he rose slowly to avoid any sudden shifts in weight.

The chant became louder.

But it faded into the background now that he could clearly see what was ahead. The river was widening into a lake, in the middle of which was a large island. A city rose off the island in a mixture of chaos and order. The wooden buildings were arrayed chaotically around a number of stepped pyramids that were precise in their symmetry. But what really caught his attention was the statue that towered over the whole city from the top of the biggest ziggurat. It was unmistakably him: a cowled figure standing over the city, its arms spread to either side with, unless Morden was mistaken, a book in its right hand.

It was too hot for a chill to run down his spine, but he was sure the intent was there. It was spooky to say the least.

A thunk from the front of his canoe distracted him from the statue.

An arrow was lodged in the front of the boat. Morden was about to get very angry he was being shot at again when he noticed there was cord attached to it. The cord tightened, snapped out of the water, and his canoe jerked forward. One of the war canoes began to tow him towards a jetty.

Part of him was uneasy with what was happening, but given that he seemed to have lost his ability to fly there was little he could do short of taking a plunge in the lake. He thought about sitting down but decided striking a lordly pose served him better.

They made swift progress towards the jetty now that a canoe full of burly orcs was stroking hard to get them there. A reception committee was hurriedly arranging itself on the jetty as he approached. A line of large orcs in plated wood and metal armour formed a line along the jetty's length. They held an assortment of wicked-looking polearms with jagged blades and spikes. In front of them, a gang of smaller orcs huddled together. They wore black robes adorned in skulls, bones and zig-zag patterns. As Morden got closer, their level of agitation increased.

With a last deft bit of manoeuvring and a tug on the tow rope, Morden's canoe was released and glided perfectly to the landing stage where the robed orcs pushed forward one of their number. As the canoe bumped gently into the jetty, the orc managed to gather some composure, stand up straight, and pull his shoulders back.

Morden stepped onto the wooden pier and surveyed the orcs with a brooding stare. As his gaze swept over them, Morden was pleased to see their heads ducked and his gaze was avoided. If they were not yet bent to his Will, it was clear they were bending.

"My Lord Zoon," said the orc, bowing. "Welcome to Deathcropolis, City of Death. I hope you will find everything ready and to your liking."

It took a second for the words to sink in. Lord Zoon? City of Death? Ready for him?

"You were expecting me?" asked Morden.

The orc raised his head from its bowed position, surprise very much evident.

"But of course, my Lord Zoon. We have been expecting you for centuries."

"Really?"

"Yes, my lord. Though we thought you would arrive on the back of a dragon and not in a canoe."

Morden shrugged inwardly. He was happy to play along for now. They could believe what they wanted until he had had a good meal and a proper lie down. Once rested, he was sure he'd be able to assume his dragon form as before. And then everything would be fine.

"My apologies if I kept you waiting," said Morden. "Lead on."

The orc's eyes widened even further and he managed a nervous laugh. "My lord's humour truly is as the histories say. If you'll follow me, Archpriest Lopang is readying your residence."

Morden allowed himself to be led. His honour guard, if that was what it was, formed up ahead and behind. The robed orcs, who Morden now assumed were some kind of cult leadership, tagged behind. He couldn't help but notice they all kept a good few feet from him. When he quickened his pace, the orcs in front jerked forward as he closed with them. As he slowed, the ones behind backed off. It kept him briefly amused to make sudden changes in pace and see them skip forward and back.

The route they took was direct, but still gave Morden time to drink in the details of the city around him. It was nothing like anything he had seen before. The roads were cobbled and, contrary to the chaotic architectural style of the buildings, laid out in a regular grid. The city itself was a strange mix of uncontrolled growth, as plants and trees filled every free nook and cranny, and carefully laid avenues. Underneath the chaos of the plants and buildings was a precisely laid out city. The buildings were a blend of stone, bamboo and slatted wood with precise angles and a simple but functional feel to them. The heavily rain-worn stone made Morden wonder how long the city had been here.

The other immediately obvious thing he noticed was the number of orcs. It was a complete reversal of cities he was used to in the west. This was an orc city, with the occasional human looking out of place as they went about their business. The orcs had full teeth they showed off with rings that slotted over the needle tips and chains that hung down over their chins between the teeth.

Morden drew a lot of attention as he passed, and word spread faster than they walked. Soon the streets were lined with onlookers. His passing seemed to have a varied effect from open amazement, through shy curiosity, to what might have been fear, or equally hostility.

(Morden still had difficulty with orcish expressions when it came to teeth.)

At last they arrived at the foot of the ziggurat, at the top of which towered the statue that so closely resembled himself. It was even bigger than it had looked out on the water. Morden hoped they did not have to climb it.

Somewhere overhead a crow cawed. Morden looked around, somewhat surprised that even here the damn birds found him, but all he could see were parrots.

Fortunately, they didn't have to do any climbing. At the base of the ziggurat was an arch, beyond which a tunnel was drilled into the base of the monument. His escort lined up on either side and he was led in.

The morning sunlight was soon lost and torches in brackets lit the way. The air was hot and damp. The walls were etched with carvings of intricate geometric shapes, and graphic depictions of death and sacrifice. A thin film of moisture covered them and there was a constant background drip. If anyone lived in here, it could not have been pleasant.

The corridor opened into a large chamber whose roof mirrored the stepped sides of the outside of the ziggurat. At one end there was a plinth and throne that came straight out of Morden's dreams. Not only was it ridiculously large, but it was covered in bones and skulls, with jewels in the skull eyes, and gold braziers to each side that lit the room with their fires.

At the foot of the plinth, a massive orc stood in black-plated armour holding the biggest sword Morden had ever seen. Its blade must have been five feet long and it curved wickedly along its length.

"Tell Archpriest Lopang that Lord Zoon has arrived," said one of his escorts.

The massive orc swivelled and disappeared into a side chamber.

Minutes passed. Then a few more. Whoever this archpriest was, he was taking his time. Morden surveyed the room once more. It was a touch on the bare side for his liking, and although he had to admire the craftsmanship, he would be making changes. Wall hangings would help.

And still there was no archpriest. He was about to complain about being kept waiting when he felt something. It came from the room the big orc had disappeared into. The orcs behind him seemed to have felt it as well; they first shrank back, and then fled as fast as they could.

Morden was left alone. A sense of dread grew that felt like something was reaching inside him and slowly squeezing. Then the smell came. It was the same smell that had sometimes drifted over the school in Bindelburg if the wind switched from its normal westerly to the south; it was the smell of the abattoir. It was the smell of death, of open corpses and stale blood.

Fear gripped him as a figure drifted into the room, with the big orc and his sword a few yards behind. A wooden mask covered the figure's face. It was a grotesque caricature of an orc's face painted bone white. The figure wore a floor-length black shift covered in the symmetric glyphs and patterns of the room, with the odd skull thrown in for good measure.

Two holes were drilled into the eyes of the mask, and through them Morden could just make out a burning, hate-filled stare. Morden struggled to stay on his feet. It was as if the eyes were pressing him to the floor.

Now that the figure was close, the smell was overwhelming. Every part of Morden wanted to turn and flee the room, but something told him that if he tried the big orc would cut him in half before he had taken five steps.

"Who … are … you?" The voice was strangled, like it had to be forced out between locked teeth.

Morden's mind raced. If he got this wrong, it could well be the last thing he did.

"I am Lord Zoon," he answered, trying hard to sound commanding. "I have come to claim my kingdom and my throne."

At first Morden thought the creature standing before him had a sudden nasty cough, but soon realised it was laughing. It was a derisive laugh, one that shredded and demeaned, a laugh that could tear away any sense of self-worth or being. It was the laugh of a Dark Lord. Even as the figure raised what was clearly a fleshless hand to its mask, Morden knew —with dead certainty—who was behind it.

"How can you be Lord Zoon the Reviled?" asked the figure. The mask came free with a disgusting tear to reveal a decomposed skull. "When I am Lord Zoon the Reviled? Now give me back my robe and book."

Chapter 38   A Righteous Knight

Having the biggest army doesn't mean
you will definitely win, but it helps.
The Dark Lord's Handbook

The few remaining orcs in the city were making their last stand at the docks. They were buying time for the ships with the orcish women and children to make an escape. Griselda might also be on those boats. Edwin couldn't let them get away.

"On me! My Righteous Knights! On me!" he cried and held his sword aloft to show the rally point. He had lost his horse a while back. The streets of Bostokov were no place for cavalry. While their glorious charge into the city would live forever in song, the practical disadvantages of being mounted in narrow streets became quickly apparent, especially with a cowardly foe that cut at the legs of the mounts.

Ahead was a hastily assembled barricade. Now and then, an arrow arched towards them from behind it. Twenty of Edwin's knights gathered around him, trying their hardest to ignore the arrows as they clattered around them.

"Form up," commanded Edwin, and they made a wall of steel with sword and shield. "Forward!"

Edwin's tight phalanx of knights moved inexorably down the street, gathering pace for the last twenty yards, and smashed into the flimsy barricade, which disintegrated.

Edwin's sword rose and hacked into the wrinkly orc in front of him. Though it was disappointing his foe was so old, it was one less orc in the world, and that was a good thing. Edwin's sword, tasting blood, began to sing. As his weapon rose and fell, Edwin half imagined he was somewhere else, on the dry plains from his dreams, cutting his way through a dark host to the lord who commanded them. He could feel strength flow into him every time the sword took another life. It filled him with a thirst for more, to taste the power that could only be fed with the souls of the fallen. He set about his work with furious abandon and none could stand before him.

Soon the street was awash with orcish blood and the knights tore a frenzied swathe towards the docks. But they were too late. Edwin howled with fury at the sight of the last ships pulling rapidly away from the dock, their sails full. Only a handful of orcs remained on the dock itself, a last desperate rearguard. At their front was an orc Edwin recognised: Kurgen.

Edwin's men gathered around him, forty yards from the orcs that still lived. When Edwin saw the orc leader say something over his shoulder, and the orcs dropped their weapons, he thought they were going to surrender. But they didn't. Instead they turned, bent over, and bared their backsides.

"Kill them! Kill them all!" raged Edwin, and he sprang forward to attack.

The orcs hastily grabbed their swords and shields, and prepared for the assault as best they could.

"For Morden!" shouted Kurgen.

The orcs surged forward to meet the knights. Though they fought bravely enough, none could stand Edwin's onslaught. No shield, nor armour, could withstand his sword as it cleaved into bone and flesh.

The last orc fell and Edwin was left feeling the glory of battle, but also empty as he watched the ships sail away.

"Griselda!" he called after them. "Griselda! I will come for you."

From behind him came a gurgling sound Edwin realised was a laugh. Rage welled up as he spun around to see who it was. The orc, Kurgen, had pulled himself against a crate and was coughing blood as he laughed even more.

"Griselda?" wheezed the orc. "She's your girl, is she?"

The orc winced in pain. He was badly cut and blood covered him.

Edwin fought the urge to separate the orc's head from its shoulders. What did this orc know of his love? Had he seen her? Edwin knelt at the orc's side and pushed his face close. He poked two fingers into an open wound and the orc roared in pain. "Speak swiftly, orc, and let me send you on your way. What do you know of Griselda?"

Kurgen gasped for breath and blood oozed from his mouth. Edwin was suddenly worried he had gone too far and the orc was going to die before he had told him what he wanted to know. He pulled his fingers free.

"Water," he shouted at a clump of knights who were standing watching. "Quickly." He waved his free hand urgently as the knights floundered around looking for a water skin.

One was finally looted from a dead orc. Edwin propped Kurgen's head and dribbled water between the orc's lips.

"Tell me," said Edwin softly, trying hard to gain some calm. "What do you know of Griselda?"

With some effort the orc drew breath and looked Edwin in the eye.

"She's got quite a tongue on her," said Kurgen. The orc laughed again, spluttered and coughed, spraying blood all over Edwin.

Edwin stood. This was useless. He was being taunted. He put both hands to the hilt of his sword and held it high. Time to serve up justice. Kurgen looked up at him and smiled. The orc's teeth were sharp. Edwin tensed to strike and the orc spoke his last words:

"She loves Morden."

Rage filled Edwin.

Suddenly he was not on a dockside in Bostokov, but on a dark stair. Griselda was cowering in front of him. Behind her was the fallen body of her dark lover, Morden. She raised a hand as if she could ward off the sword that plunged down to take off her head.

The orc's head rolled from its body and hit the wooden pier with a thunk. The mouth was still grinning. Edwin kicked at it and it rolled into the water.

*****

That night Edwin had trouble sleeping. Not only was Rosemary Cathcart a vocal and vociferous hater of Morden (or so she said), but she also snored loudly in her sleep. He should have been able to fall dead asleep after their energetic lovemaking, like she had; after all, it had been a long day killing orcs. But he could not.

At least she wasn't a chatterer like some girls he had known; they would lie there and ask stupid questions like *do you love me?* There was only one woman he loved, and that was Griselda. That he had to sate his manly needs with these young temptresses instead of his love was bad enough without having to engage in bolster talk afterwards.

He felt nothing for Rosemary, and could even forgive her when she'd called out Morden's name at the height of passion, for it was not her Edwin had on his mind. Barely a moment went by, except perhaps in the midst of battle, when Griselda was not foremost in his thoughts. He strained every sinew to get her back but she was getting further away from him.

Armies were too slow, too cumbersome. They would be another month in marching, and another in fighting to take the next city, while Morden would have fled even further, coward that he was, taking his Griselda with him. It made his stomach knot itself into a ball of frustration thinking about it.

It was no good. Sleep would not be coming that night.

He slid out from under Rosemary's quilt, made himself decent as was necessary before gathering up the rest of his gear and slipping out of the room, leaving Rosemary snuffling like a pig.

Making good the rest of his attire, Edwin decided to walk the city. It was quiet, with only the odd patrol on the streets. Martial law had been declared, and a curfew, so only the criminal would be abroad. Not that Edwin expected to see anyone after the demonstration of his will when the city had been taken. The few collaborators that had been identified had been dealt with swiftly. Edwin himself executed the sentences, declaring that if he could not deliver the necessary justice then how could he ask another man?

There was one head he wanted to take above all others. Thinking of the day Morden's lifeless body would lie at his feet was the one thing, besides the tender caresses from Griselda, that kept him going.

But when? There were a thousand things to do in this city alone before they would march in pursuit. It was all too slow.

He was so lost in thought he did not hear the first challenge. It was the sound of drawn steel that alerted him.

"I said halt and declare yourself!"

Edwin had walked a wide circle through the city and was back at the barracks he had commandeered for his remaining knights. It was good to see they were awake.

"Stay your weapon, sergeant. It is Sir Edwin."

The sergeant snapped to attention as Edwin passed him.

The barracks and stable were quiet. If only he could share the well-earned, deep sleep his men were enjoying. There was a brazier in one corner of the yard and Edwin went to warm himself. Staring into the sky, he wondered if Griselda was looking at the same stars.

A shooting star streaked high above out of the west. It was like an arrow into the east, where the first hint of dawn was lightening the sky. If only he could be that star, he would be with her in a heartbeat.

With a jolt, he realised that was it. He had to be that star. He had to streak towards her. He didn't need an army. All he needed was his armour, his sword and his determination. He would leave this very minute. Let the count play his war games. He had a Dark Lord to face and a love to rescue.

"I'm coming, my love," he whispered to the star as it blinked out of existence on the horizon. "I'm coming."

Chapter 39   Dark Lords

Fairness and hope are the bedfellows
of disappointment and despondency.
The Dark Lord's Handbook

Zoon's words rolled around inside Morden's head. The game was up. He had been found out. He could feel the strength of Zoon's compulsion and it took every bit of his Will not to immediately toss off the robe, get naked, and relinquish the Handbook.

"No," said Morden. "I am Morden. This is my robe and my book. You had your chance and you blew it."

If it were possible, Morden would have sworn Zoon's lidless eye sockets widened.

"You dare challenge me, boy?" said Zoon, stepping forward.

The stench was terrible and Morden could feel waves of compulsion beat against him, a cascading whispering in his head telling him to submit and bow before his master. But he would not. He had come this far and it was his destiny to rule.

Morden took a deep breath, took a step forward, and drew on his own considerable Will. "I am the only Dark Lord here."

They were eye-to-eye now, and Morden had to fight hard not to gag from the putrescent smell that came off Zoon. This close, Morden could see Zoon's flesh was alive with maggots and insects that crawled and slid over the damp skin and bone.

"I am the Dark Lord," hissed Zoon.

"Says who?" rebuked Morden. He could feel his own strength build and the two wills pushed against each other. The air crackled around them and they stared eye-to-eye socket.

"Give me the book," said Zoon.

Morden was unsure, but it looked like Zoon was beginning to strain. Given Zoon's lipless mouth it was hard to tell if he was gritting his teeth or not.

"Take it from me," whispered Morden. "If you want to lose your other hand."

This time Zoon's grin definitely widened. He raised his left arm and clicked his bony fingers. Orcs appeared from alcoves and passageways around the vault. They were not like the ones outside. These were like the one standing behind Zoon: big, well-armed and, on close inspection, suspiciously dead looking. It did make some sense, a lich having an undead retinue.

"Take him," said Zoon.

Morden took a step back. "Stop!" But they kept shuffling towards him. He had no power over these orcs. He was doomed. "Now, Zoon, let's be reasonable. I'm sure I can find a place for you in my organisation. A lich of your talents would be a great asset. Can't we work something out?"

A gurgling laugh came from Zoon. "I do like it when they beg. But you grow tiresome. Silence him."

Morden took another step back. The undead orcs and their vicious two-handed swords were a few paces away. This was it.

"Wait. You can't kill me," said Morden. "I'm a Dark Lord."

Zoon's laugh grew louder and echoed around the chamber. "Kill you? Who said anything about killing? Besides, you are mostly dead already."

The ring of zombie orcs was tightening. Some raised their arms to grab him. He slapped away dead flesh and bits fell off.

"Stop!" ordered Morden. "Hang on a second."

Zoon clicked his fingers and the orcs stopped.

"*Mostly* dead? What's that supposed to mean?"

The lich was silent for a moment, as though considering the question.

"The greater part? Not quite completely? You'll work it out, I'm sure," Zoon shrugged and clicked his fingers again.

Clammy hands grabbed Morden and, though he struggled, he knew it was useless. He had never been that strong despite his size. He wasn't going to fight his way out of this one so, after token resistance, he went limp.

The orcs raised him above their heads and fell in behind Zoon as he stalked from the chamber. The passage they went into was dark and wet.

Stuff that wasn't water, and smelled gross, dripped from the ceiling onto his upturned face. They were going down, and soon they were in what seemed to be a labyrinth of tunnels. Morden recognised the design from the Handbook. A hero could get lost for an age in tunnels such as these. The wet walls made them hard to mark, and the subtle turns and dips made it impossible to tell what level you were on or what direction you were facing. In no time, Morden had lost all sense of where they were and, even if he could have struggled free, he had no idea which way was out.

Eventually he heard a heavy grating sound as a door was pulled open. He was unceremoniously dumped onto the floor which, like everything else, was cold, slime-covered, and hard. Soon after he was naked except for a loin cloth and the pendant round his neck. The latter surprised him. Surely they would have taken that as well? But when fingers had grasped it they had recoiled and left it hanging. Morden hoped Zoon wasn't watching, but it seemed the lich had left his minions to do the stripping.

When they left and dragged the door shut, he was left alone in total darkness. There was no sound except the dripping from the ceiling. After what seemed an age, but was more likely a minute or so, faint specks on the ceiling provided the dimmest of light. All that did was confirm to him the dire situation he was in: trapped in an admittedly spacious cell, one devoid of furniture or company, in a maze under a temple that was meant to be his, usurped by a Dark Lich he had assumed was dead and buried centuries ago. Well, buried; Zoon was clearly dead in a weird way.

And yet he was still here. Zoon could have had him ripped limb from limb. It was the only comfort he could hang onto as all else lay in ruin in his mind. His dreams of conquest, domination and getting the girl were nothing now. No one knew where he was, and even if they did it wasn't as though they would be straining to come and rescue him. Maybe Stonearm, but no one else. Certainly not Griselda.

How could it all have gone wrong so fast? The Handbook had promised he was going to be a Dark Lord. He was going to build a fortress, raise an army and lay ruin the world. He would have dominion over everything and bend all to his Will, and yet here he was, naked in a dungeon.

Then he had a thought, one he recognised immediately as ridiculous. Of the many things he had learnt from the Handbook, one was that nothing was fair. Indeed, the sense of fairness was one to be avoided and exploited. A sense of fairness made people do the stupidest things. The mistake he had made was believing everything he had read. He'd obviously been taken as a sap by the Handbook and was the means to get it back to Zoon.

But that didn't make sense either. If the Handbook had wanted to find Zoon, then why hadn't Grimtooth come here? He could have delivered the lich his robe at the same time. And his hand, for that matter. It was far too convoluted a road to take.

Luckily Zoon was making mistakes, too. Leaving him alive was the biggest. It was grim now, but while he was alive there was possibility. Though he could feel the word 'hope' practically begging to be used, as a Dark Lord he knew that hope, like fairness, was a crutch for the weak-minded. Faith and hope wouldn't get him out of this.

Then another odd thought struck him. Zoon had been a Dark Lord. He had read the Handbook and presumably learnt something from it. One lesson came to mind that would explain Zoon's curious behaviour. What if he thought Morden was a Hero?

Morden's laugh echoed off the walls.

Him, a Hero? Now that was funny. It did make some sense though. Zoon would know, much as Morden did, that killing a Hero was nigh impossible. Could it be that Zoon didn't even want to try, in case he incurred some unbelievable consequence? There may have been an earthquake, or something, and Morden could have escaped in the chaos. Rather, wouldn't it be better to make sure he was alive and well, and safe somewhere? Like a dungeon cell in a labyrinth?

Except Zoon didn't seem to think he was alive and well. Mostly dead, he had said. It was a curious thing to say. Thinking back, had the strain he had seen in Zoon been him trying to fight the urge to monologue? The Handbook had warned about waxing lyrical and giving everything away. If Zoon thought he had a Hero in front of him, the urge to monologue must have been tremendous. But he had let slip this one thing. What did it mean?

If only he hadn't flown off from the fleet, then none of this would have happened. He wouldn't have got shot, stranded, and ended up here.

Was that it? If he hadn't got shot. Morden's hand drifted to his side where the bolt had hit him. It had healed, but was still tender. The scar was more a welt and quite raw and sore. He had lost a lot of blood lying on that beach. When he had come round the sand had been soaked. A normal man may have bled to death.

Then there was the way everything seemed to shrivel and die around him when he walked through the jungle. And the fish. And the birds, for that matter. And the orcs kept a good distance as well. In fact, the only things that had got close to him without obvious ill effects were Zoon and his minions, and they were already dead, or undead, or more dead, or whatever it was they were.

So he was undead? Or more dead?

That couldn't be it. Zoon had said mostly dead. There must be something left alive inside him. He didn't feel like a zombie. He had no urge to stagger around, arms outstretched, searching for warm brains to eat. But what if part of him *had* died? What did that leave? What if it was the dragon in him that had died? That would explain why he couldn't change any longer. But then, the amulet still seemed to have some power in it. His hand went to his amulet; it felt cool. He'd had it all his life and had never taken it off. The only time it had been removed had been by that captain at the ambush, when he had discovered he was more than a man. He was also a dragon. He was a Deathwing. Surely a single bolt could not kill a dragon?

It was all very confusing. Whatever had happened, he was stuck here in a dungeon with a Dark Lord upstairs pretending to be him, which was somewhat ironic as Morden had to admit to himself he had been pretending to be Zoon.

Morden felt suddenly tired. He hadn't slept for several days. The hard, goo-covered floor wasn't appealing but there was no other choice for a bed. He scraped clear an area of stones, as best he could, and lay down. Perhaps if he slept, he would wake up back on his ship and all this would have been a bad dream. As the thought occurred, he gave himself a mental slap. He had to banish such weak thinking. It was stupid hope trying to disguise harsh reality. He slid into an uncomfortable sleep knowing that when he woke it would not be in a cabin, but in a dungeon. That was all right, though; he was still Morden Deathwing, Dark Lord.

Chapter 40   Boxes of Stuff

Just remember: they are all morons.
The Dark Lord's Handbook

Chancellor Penbury's study was normally a place of meticulous order. The chancellor liked to think it was a reflection of his own mind. The centrepiece was a vast polished mahogany desk with an inkwell and pen holder to one side, and one of the very latest and most accurate time pieces on the other. The walls were laden with books ordered by subject and author according to his own classification system; most were Only Editions, being the work of the world's greatest minds. Several he had penned himself, principally on economic power and political systems, covering such topics as 'Interest Rates and their use in Regime Change' and 'The Price of Bananas? Who would have Thought it?'

Today though, the chancellor surveyed a desk and floor strewn with boxes. The boxes (some were closer to being small trunks) were mostly still closed and secured with padlocks. Each had a slit in the top through which papers could be pushed and a small notebook attached by a thin chain to the lid. They looked like ballot boxes that were emerging in some of the newer democracies.

(Democracy: a brilliant invention, that Penbury wished he had thought of, whereby citizens could voice their political will on pieces of paper, which actually gave them little or no choice, that were then deposited in a sealed box which, when opened elsewhere, were emptied onto the nearest fire and ignored while the politicians brokered real power between themselves. Genius.)

On each box, written on a slate embedded into the lid, was written a big number. In the general population most could count as far as their digits, or the sheep in their flock. Penbury only knew a handful of people who knew the correct word for the size of the values written here, and they were all bankers and council members.

Several of the boxes had been opened; one on the desk in front of the chancellor, the others to either side of his chair. The keys had been lost and so the padlocks lay broken, having succumbed to Penbury's efforts with the crowbar he normally used to open cases of wine.

On the other side of the desk was an unusually fidgety Birkenfeldt. He had arrived, along with his boxes, an hour ago. A matter of urgency, he had said. That Birkenfeldt thought anything was urgent was odd. Birkenfeldt was a fastidious banker who never got flustered, not even by Penbury.

Penbury reached out and thumbed through the notebook attached to the box on the desk in front of him. It was filled with accounting, though not with the precise and clear columns Penbury had learnt in his youth; these were barely understandable. Shorthand had run wild; corrections were rampant, and many figures were unintelligible.

"So let me be clear," said Penbury, fixing Birkenfeldt with his eyes. The banker pushed himself even deeper into the soft leather of the visitor's chair. "All these boxes are full of loan papers?"

"Uhm, no."

"They aren't?" Penbury arched an eyebrow quite consciously, to emphasise his surprise. "I thought you just said they were?"

"Well, yes, in as much that they represent a transfer of funds and/or equivalent assets, from one party to another, with some form of repayment schedule and securities; sometimes assurances, sometimes insurances, often with capital assets held against such vehicles, though often case with other parties having already assured, insured, or otherwise made good, as best as they can ascertain, all that is contained within the schedule, note, bond or mortgage."

"So really," said Penbury, in as measured a tone as he could manage, "you have no idea what is in these boxes?"

Birkenfeldt scrunched his nose. Penbury had only seen him do that once before, at the man's wedding when he had been asked if he would take his bride, forsaking all others. Cutting one's options was something a money man did not like to do. It could have been nerves as well, and given the current situation, it seemed the more likely.

"No," admitted Birkenfeldt weakly.

Penbury leaned back in his chair and let the scale of what he was being told sink in.

"Allow me to recap, so I am clear. After our little get-together, when it came to light there had been a massive increase in lending, mainly to aristocrats and royals, you thought you would dig a little deeper and this is what you found: the most bizarre financial process ever practised at an all-encompassing, even institutionalised level, that until now you were unaware of taking place?"

Birkenfeldt took a second to reply. Penbury knew the man always counted to at least three before answering any loaded question, to give his rapier intellect an eternity to consider all possible options.

"Yes."

"Incredible."

"Indeed," said Birkenfeldt, "but also quite ingenious."

It had been a while since the chancellor had lowered himself to the level of having to perform actual financial transactions; he worked more at the strategic level. He thought he had been aware of every financial practice, both legal and otherwise, known to man. Until Birkenfeldt had turned up with his boxes.

"Go on," said Penbury, by way of encouragement. Any explanation, no matter how weird, was welcome.

Birkenfeldt cleared his throat. "As you know, the vast majority of finance works on confidence."

Penbury nodded. There were men he would lend to and require nothing but a handshake, whereas there were others who would have to offer up their firstborn as hostage, and even then they were likely to welch.

"It seems that about ten years ago, someone, it's not clear who, came up with an idea of how to bring forward profits from loans and mortgages that relied almost entirely on confidence. What he seems to have done is take a loan from party A and sell it to party B at a discount. Party B is quite happy because he has effectively bought a repayment amount for less than its value, so over time he will register a profit."

Birkenfeldt paused for breath, sufficient time for Penbury to interject a question. "But what about the person who gave the loan? Surely they are squeezing their margin?"

Birkenfeldt nodded. "Indeed. But here is the clever bit. Rather than wait ten years for the loan to be repaid—he got less than the full amount by selling it on—he got it now. And that meant two things. He could make an accounting entry showing a big fat profit, make his bosses happy, get a bonus. And he could use the money to invest in ways that gave a better return than the loan would have."

Penbury picked up one of the papers in front of him. It was a loan for a considerable amount to Baron Romney of Kirkland and secured against the baron's castle. Penbury had known the baron personally. He had hunted with him on his estates, and had been saddened to hear of the squabble the baron had got into with a neighbour that not only resulted in the poor baron's death, but reduced the castle to rubble. Not only was the loan never going to be repaid, but the castle it was held against was now distributed across a dozen different villages in the form of swanky new cottages.

While Penbury could appreciate the cunning of what Birkenfeldt had described, he could also see potential issues. Now that he understood the underlying mechanism it didn't take him long to make the leap to what was in front of him now.

Birkenfeldt opened his mouth to continue, but the chancellor raised a finger to silence him.

"Let me," said Penbury. "This seemingly simple idea worked fantastically well at the start and a few got very rich."

Birkenfeldt nodded.

"But then, as with all good things, more stupid people, who never really understood the underlying ideas, got involved and cocked it up?"

"Indeed," said Birkenfeldt.

"It rapidly got out of hand. This system of holding these traded securities was invented and soon a meta market in box trading evolved, whereby people traded boxes, that notionally represented who knows what, for enormous sums of money. Only it didn't matter."

Penbury's mind galloped to the conclusion and he was horrified.

"It didn't matter, because as long as no one opened a box, and merely went by what was on the box, and they had confidence in what was in those boxes, everything was fine. Fine until …" Even to Penbury, the enormity of what had happened was staggering. He could barely utter the words. "… until someone opened a box to see what was in it."

It all made sense now.

"And that was you, wasn't it, Birkenfeldt? Because you are a man of details. You couldn't trust in what some book said was in the box and a number scribbled on a slate. You had to see for yourself."

Birkenfeldt looked stricken. All blood had drained from him. "I'm sorry, Chancellor. Truly I am."

For a moment, Penbury thought the most powerful banker in the world, and probably the second most powerful man after himself, was about to cry.

"It's not your fault, Birkenfeldt," said Penbury. "It was a disaster waiting to happen."

And it was. As soon as one box was opened and the real value of what was inside could be seen, thcn that was it. Penbury had no idea how much of what was contained was recoverable, but he suspected it was not a lot. Even if there were good loans in there, confidence would now be shattered. The box market would collapse. No one would want to trade them. They'd be forced to look at what they held and account for it. Penbury shuddered at the losses some would make. As a major stakeholder in about every major business institution known, it would hurt him as well.

Birkenfeldt coughed.

"How many people know about this?" asked Penbury. It was going to take a huge amount of effort to limit the damage. With the recent surge in borrowing from the ruling classes there must be a lot of bad debt out there.

"Just you," said Birkenfeldt. "And myself, of course."

"Say again?" Penbury had heard correctly, but couldn't quite believe it.

"The only ones who know are yourself and me," said Birkenfeldt.

Penbury didn't believe in miracles. He thought the only thing that was divine was good food and drink. He also did not believe in luck. It was a commodity conjured in the minds of irrational and weak people, or the falsely modest.

So the news Birkenfeldt had given, that the greatest economic disaster the world would ever suffer was privy only to himself and his banker friend, was no miracle or good fortune, it was an opportunity. Quite what that opportunity was he was not completely clear on, but he would work it out.

"Not a word," said Penbury.

"I'm sorry?"

"You are to tell no one what you have found out."

Birkenfeldt looked stunned. "But what happens if someone else opens a box? They are bound to sooner or later. This can't go on forever."

"You're right, it can't. But it will have to until I can work out how to fix it."

Penbury could feel the relief flowing from Birkenfeldt. Understandably. He'd been let off the hook. It wasn't his problem any more.

"Leave these with me. I assume they are yours?"

Birkenfeldt nodded. "They are a few of the boxes from our warehouse."

"Warehouse?"

"Yes," said Birkenfeldt. "We have a warehouse full of them."

"And presumably, other banks have similar?"

"Actually, no. The box system was centralised, for convenience, so the actual boxes didn't have to move. While there are several warehouses spread around an estate, to save on costs, the banks and insurers maintain a shared box marketplace."

"Box marketplace?"

"The warehouses where boxes are traded. Seemed to make sense."

"Of course it did."

Penbury started to think. It had been a long while since he'd been faced with such a challenge. Even this business with the Dark Lord Morden was a mere light entertainment compared to the true disaster that had been placed before him. It was going to take all his wits to sort this mess out.

After some time, Penbury realised Birkenfeldt was still sitting there, hands on his lap, waiting patiently.

"I'm sorry, Birkenfeldt," said Penbury. "You can go now. And remember, not a word. And don't dump your boxes in the market. It may cause a panic. Sit tight."

"Of course, Chancellor," said Birkenfeldt, standing. The banker clicked his heels and left.

After Birkenfeldt had left, Chidwick came in to see if there was anything to be done. Penbury had him tidy the boxes. He ordered a beef and radish sandwich and a cup of tea. A glass of wine would have been nice to go with the beef, but he had thinking to do.

Two hours later he was no nearer a solution and it was time to check the Snort reports. He took the pads out of a locked desk drawer with a minute to spare and laid them on the desk. He polished his magnifying glass and bent over the paper. He reread the previous report to bring himself back up to speed and awaited news. To the second, writing started to appear on both pads. It was spooky how they did that, but then the Snort brothers were spooks of the spookiest kind.

News from the west was brief. Bostokov had been secured. The army was marching east to the next city. Count Vladovitch was still having secret meetings with a conspiring woman who went by the name Black Orchid and was, in fact, Lady Deathwing. These dragons certainly seemed to be coming out of the closet. Was she Morden's mother? It would make some sense, but then why would she be supporting the count and Edwin against Morden?

And Sir Edwin had disappeared. It was thought he had a falling out with the count and had either gone home or was headed east after Morden and his love, Griselda. Penbury thought the latter more likely, given Edwin was almost certainly a Hero. It would take him a while to reach Morden, but it would be a meeting that would be more than interesting.

Penbury scribbled instructions regarding the count. He was glad to see the first contact had been so well received. Given the fiasco Birkenfeldt had revealed, Penbury needed to know how the count and his army fitted into all of it. He assumed much of the borrowing was to finance such a big army, but there had to be more. He suspected Black Orchid had more to do with this.

News from the east was curious. Morden had been seen flying off and had not returned. In the meantime, the fleet had continued and been picked up by a smaller orcish fleet. They were apparently eastern orcs from a little-known empire.

Penbury, of course, knew of them. They were the source of many interesting herbs, spices, and culinary dishes, as well as traders in rarer things like exploding black powder.

The two fleets of orcs had greeted each other like long-lost cousins and were currently anchored off an orcish city. They would be going ashore shortly. An orc, Stonearm, had assumed control and was to meet the city's leader.

Penbury stopped and rubbed his eye. He must have misread. He brought the glass back over the paper and read again.

They were going ashore to meet the city's leader, Zoon the Reviled.

Now this changed everything. Was it the Zoon of legend? If it was, then the fence sitting would have to stop and, whether he liked it or not, he would have to back the count and Edwin. Or was this Zoon merely Morden role playing? He had no way of knowing.

One of the qualities Penbury attributed to himself was a keen sense of timing. It was as though he could see the whole world turning and the pieces upon it. Now and then he would reach down and make his presence felt, but mostly he worked from above.

Now, he felt, was one of those times. He needed to get moving, and fast. Events were speeding and it was not a time for lackeys.

Chapter 41   Dungeon

Tyranny is government for the weak.
The Dark Lord's Handbook

Morden had lost track of time. It was impossible to judge how long he slept or how long he was awake. Time passed. Slime dripped. Guards came to deliver food Morden ate mechanically. It seemed being mostly dead meant he had no appetite. Apart from that, he was no nearer understanding his condition. As for his situation, desperate was the only thing that came to mind. He could see no reason he wouldn't be stuck in his cell until mostly dead became completely dead. He'd known depressed people in his life but had never counted himself in their company. Now, however, he sensed a cloud in his mind, lurking, that was growing slowly, but growing nonetheless.

The bolts on the door grated and Morden turned, expecting to see orcs dumping a plate of slop onto the floor. Instead, Zoon strode in. Morden hadn't seen his rival since he'd been left in the cell. The cloud in Morden's mind shrank, burned away by anger at seeing Zoon in the robe Morden had claimed as his own.

"You disappoint me, Morden," said Zoon, staring first at Morden and then casting an eye socket around the room.

"And you stink," said Morden. It wasn't a classy retort, but it was all he had. If he'd still been able to breathe fire he would have burned the walking corpse in front of him in an instant.

Zoon made a rasping, wheezing sound that could have been a laugh or an attempt to cough up something disgusting.

"What's so funny?" asked Morden.

Zoon continued to wheeze. "The irony," managed the Dark Lord, regaining his composure. "You'll be glad to know your fleet has arrived. I thank you for raising such a fine army. It will make my conquests so much easier."

"My fleet is here?" Morden said.

Zoon cleared his throat and spat. A cockroach scurried off from where it landed.

"Technically, it's now my fleet," said Zoon. The lich coughed again; it was a gurgling, phlegm-ridden cough that sounded like his lungs, if he had any, would shortly be on the floor with the rest of the slime. "Anyway, enough of that. I've brought you company. I'll say goodbye and leave you to get reacquainted.

"Not staying for a gloat?" asked Morden.

Zoon stopped at the door.

"You know, I'd love to hear all your plans," continued Morden.

"I know what you're trying to do," said Zoon, without bothering to turn around.

"What? Can't one Dark Lord take an interest in another?"

"I've read the book, young Morden. It was my book, after all."

"So you have been reading it after all?"

Zoon's left hand went to where Morden knew the book would be under the robe, but instead of answering, Zoon left. There were noises outside. A woman's raised voice, a thump, and the door was thrown open.

Stonearm was immediately recognisable. He came through the door horizontally, about three feet off the ground. He landed on the slime-covered floor and slid. He came to a stop, face down, at Morden's feet.

He was closely followed by a woman, her arms and legs flailing as a large undead orc hauled her in by her waist. A man was pushed in behind her. He stumbled but kept his feet. It was Kristoff. That meant the woman was ...

"Griselda?"

The orc dumped her into the muck and left. The door crashed shut and the bolts slid home.

"Lord Morden!" said Stonearm from Morden's feet.

Griselda ignored Morden and assaulted the door.

"You undead piece of shit!" she screamed, pounding the door. "You're going to pay for this."

"Griselda!" said Morden. He couldn't believe she was here.

"Lord Morden," said Stonearm, getting to his feet. He brushed off goo and wrapped his huge arms around Morden. "It's good to see you, Boss."

"Zoon, you lich bastard. Let me out now!" railed Griselda.

"Griselda, language," said Kristoff.

Stonearm had Morden in a tight bear hug.

"You're breaking my ribs," gasped Morden. Stonearm let him go. "Good to see you too, Stonearm." His ribs were thankfully intact but it was clear that whatever had happened, Stonearm had lost none of his strength.

"I'm going to rip your lungs out, you corpse fucker!" screamed Griselda through the small grill in the door.

"Morden?" Kristoff had given up on Griselda as she smashed the door with her tiny fists.

"*Lord* Morden," Stonearm reminded Kristoff.

"It's all right, Stonearm," said Morden. "Morden is fine. Yes, Kristoff, it's me. Good to see you, old friend. Please, come and sit."

In his time in the cell, Morden had scraped away a section of the floor where slime didn't drip and used it as the place he could sit and sleep. He ushered Kristoff and Stonearm over.

They settled themselves, leaving Griselda pounding on the door. She had a lot of energy but her efforts seemed to be weakening.

Stonearm was first to speak, bringing Morden up to date with the fleet and what had happened since he had flown off. No one had suspected anything was wrong until Griselda had got close to Zoon.

"You thought Zoon was me?" asked Morden. "That's a little surprising."

Stonearm shrugged. "Tall, black robe. Was hard to tell."

"What about the speech? The, you know, looks? The smell?"

Stonearm shrugged. "Who knows what Dark Lords get up to? Sure, there were changes but you, I mean he, did explain it, sort of."

"Oh, really?"

"He said he had walked dark paths, faced death and overcome it, and with him at our head we would spread across the world, lay waste the living and bring ruin to all."

"And you didn't find that strange?"

"You'll forgive me, Lord Morden, if I say it's standard stuff for a Dark Lord. We orcs have listened to that talk for hundreds of years. Anyway, he said he wanted to be called Lord Zoon and we should prepare ourselves for conquest."

"But you didn't believe him, did you?" said Morden. "And he couldn't allow you to say anything so he threw you in here before you could gather the boys together and rescue me." Morden placed his hand on Stonearm's shoulder. "You are a faithful servant, Stonearm, and you shall be first among orcs when I rule."

There was a loud snort from behind Morden. "Bah. That dumb ox believed every word," said Griselda, throwing herself down.

Stonearm coughed and had the decency to look embarrassed. "Sorry, Boss."

Feeling put out or angry was the last thing on Morden's mind. Griselda was here and looking as amazing as ever, even in a ripped, slime-covered shift. If anything, it gave her that rough look he often fantasized about, with her wild hair and hot passion.

Morden became aware he was staring. So did Griselda.

"What are you gawping at?"

Her breasts were what came to mind. "Nothing," said Morden, averting his eyes. "So, Kristoff, tell me what happened."

Kristoff's mouth opened but it was Griselda who spoke.

"I was the one who spotted that Zoon wasn't you."

Morden was both surprised and happy. She had noticed?

"He didn't behave like a puppy dog around me," continued Griselda. "It was obvious."

Puppy dog? "Don't flatter yourself," said Morden.

"Woof," said Griselda.

"I was merely being polite," said Morden. "Out of deference to Kristoff."

Morden looked at Kristoff for support but he merely raised his hands as though to say *leave me out of this.*

"Woof. Woof," said Griselda.

"Don't be ridiculous," said Morden. "I'm a Dark Lord. Don't fool with me, woman."

Griselda sighed. "Cut the crap and admit it."

This was getting out of hand. Morden looked to Stonearm for help but the big orc was staring assiduously at the ceiling.

"So it was obvious Zoon wasn't you. Besides, he smelt better." Griselda smiled and stuck her tongue out.

Then it struck him. And he was amazed. She was pleased to see him.

More than pleased. It was true. She had known Zoon wasn't him, but not for the reasons she gave. How stupid he had been.

"What are you grinning at?"

"You like me," said Morden.

"Fuck off."

Morden laughed.

"Griselda," said Kristoff. "Stop tormenting him. She does this, you know."

Griselda slapped Kristoff's arm. "Shut it."

"She never stops talking about you," continued Kristoff, pulling his arm away from Griselda's assault. "Morden this. Morden that."

"Will you SHUT up!" screamed Griselda.

Morden didn't know what to say. He was astonished, pleased, scared, happy, and wanting to jump up and down and scream some more. But he was a Dark Lord. He'd make do with merely enjoying the truth of his feelings and the fact that Griselda, in her own slightly warped way, seemed to feel the same.

"It's true," said Stonearm, the ceiling apparently having lost his interest. "She said Zoon wasn't you and insisted I confront him."

Griselda folded her arms and hunched up, trying hard not to look at Morden, but he could see her glancing his way.

"How did you do that?" asked Morden, making a point of ignoring the fuming Griselda. "Did you ask him about something only you and I would know? Like when you rescued me and we jumped over that fence? Remember? That was funny. Well, at the time it wasn't. But looking back."

"I asked him if I could ravish Griselda," said Stonearm.

"You what?" Morden was shocked.

"It was her idea," said the orc. "She's not my type at all. Look at her. She's not even an orc. Anyway, Zoon said yes, so I knew she was right."

Morden was stuck on the idea of Stonearm ravishing Griselda when the rest of what Stonearm had said sank in. "You did? How? I could have said yes as well."

"If you say so, my lord," said the orc.

"I could. I'm a Dark Lord."

"I wish you two would get over each other," said Kristoff. "It would make it a whole lot easier for the rest of us."

"It would at that," agreed Stonearm.

"There's nothing to get over," said Morden.

"Exactly," agreed Griselda.

Stonearm and Kristoff exchanged glances and shrugged.

"Now, how are you going to get us out of here?" asked Griselda, rounding on Morden. "In fact, why are you stuck in here at all, Mr. 'I'm a dragon' Dark Lord? You lost your puff?"

The three of them were looking at him expectantly. For all her taunts, Griselda was right. Would a Dark Lord really be stuck in a dungeon like this? Probably not. But there was no way he was going to give her the satisfaction.

"Don't you worry your pretty little head," said Morden. He gave them what he hoped was a deep, brooding, significant look, one from the depths of his Dark Lord soul. "I have everything under control."

Chapter 42   A Pact

**Misery acquaints a man with strange bedfellows,
and often it's a king size bed.**
The Dark Lord's Handbook

It was a dark and gusty night, with far-off lightning promising to make it stormy. Edwin sat huddled over the meagre fire he had managed to make. As he had headed east, the land had turned from wooded hills and lowlands to vast open steppes. He was burning the last of the wood he had gathered when he had noted the change. After this it would be cold at night, with little to no cover.

Somewhere nearby a bird called out. Further west he would have said it was a crow, but out here he imagined it was some other scavenger, perhaps waiting for him to die out in this wilderness.

Another gust brought the first licks of rain and Edwin gathered his cloak around him. If it rained he would have no fire. It was discomfort he could bear though. All he had to do was imagine the intolerable agonies his love must be suffering, and the trials he underwent seemed nothing in comparison.

A movement out in the flickering dark caught Edwin's eye and he reached for a stone. There were dog-like beasts out here, not dissimilar to wolves, that had started to tag along behind him. But instead of a dog, a man stepped into the light. Edwin dropped the stone and reached for his sword.

"You'll have no need for that," said the man. "I merely wish to share your fire, if I may."

The man had stopped at the limit of the small camp. He was dressed in black leathers, but seemed unarmed. There may be a dirk hidden in his boot or belt, but that would not trouble Edwin. Under his cloak he still wore his armour.

"Of course," said Edwin, indicating a spot next to the fire. "Never let it be said that Sir Edwin would refuse comfort on a night such as this."

The man bowed slightly and sat opposite Edwin. "You are most gracious."

Edwin could see his guest more clearly now. He had sharp features: a pointed nose, high cheeks, straight dark hair, and the fire, such as it was, reflected off eyes that were as dark as the storm that hurried towards them.

Neither said a word and a sense of wrongness began to niggle in Edwin's mind. The man made no chatter, but nor did he warm himself on the fire, or ask for food, or even move. He sat quite still, staring at Edwin, unblinking.

"I am at a disadvantage, sir," said Edwin. "You have not introduced yourself."

The man's lips twitched into a half smile. His answer was not immediate as he continued to study Edwin.

"You must excuse my manners, Sir Edwin. I am Lord Deathwing."

Edwin's hand stretched out to grasp his sword. His foe was here! He had to fight to remain calm. No sudden moves. He was confident he could slay his enemy, but he had to choose his moment to strike.

"Your fire is ailing somewhat," said Deathwing. He pursed his lips and a jet of liquid fire spat out, hitting the embers, and setting it roaring. "That could have been you, Edwin. So why don't you let go of that sword and we can talk."

Edwin leapt to his feet in a fluid movement and brought his sword up into guard. It sang in the shimmering air.

"You monster. Prepare to die," spat Edwin.

Rather than transform into the dragon Edwin now knew his guest to be, Deathwing instead laughed.

"I do like your style, Edwin. Really, I do. Now calm down. I came here to help you get Griselda back. Harm me, and you'll never see her again."

"Griselda?"

"Yes, Griselda. Now drop the sword."

"I could kill you here and still rescue her," insisted Edwin. The sword was starting to whisper to him. It wanted blood, and so did he.

"I doubt that," said Deathwing. "If you wish to be reunited with your true love, you will drop the sword and listen to what I have to say."

"Why don't you tell me something that convinces me I shouldn't kill you instead?" countered Edwin.

"Touché," said Deathwing. "How about I want Morden dead as much as you do?"

Of all the things the demon dragon could have said, this was not what he'd expected. It didn't make sense. It had to be a trick. He raised the tip of his sword. "Explain yourself, and it had better be good, dragon."

Deathwing looked nonplussed by the threat. "Very well. Morden is an unfortunate accident that has grown to embarrass me and he needs to be dealt with. For centuries we have lived unnoticed and unmolested; he has come along with his Dark Lord pretensions and ruined it all. He has Griselda. I want him dead. They are both a long way away and I can take you to where he is before he gets too powerful even for you and your sword. I will deliver you and you can do the rest. Morden will be dead. You will have Griselda back, and the Deathwings will once more recede into legend."

"An unfortunate accident?" asked Edwin. "I'm sure Mrs. Deathwing may not agree."

"*Lady* Deathwing is not pleased he is my bastard by a serving wench, and that is part of the reason I want him dead. It would smooth over things at home."

"Ah, so he is a bastard. Even so, you would have your own son dead?"

"Is that a problem?"

Edwin was horrified by the idea. What kind of person would kill their own offspring? And talk about it so coldly? A black-hearted dragon is who would do exactly that. Not so much a person as a thing. The foulest, most evil spawn from the darkest reaches of the world. He knew he could never trust such a person. There must be more to what was being offered. He would likely try to kill Edwin once the deed was done.

"Why don't you kill him yourself?"

Deathwing sighed. "If only I could. But it would be no sure thing. He is young and I am older than I look. Already he has grown powerful and it may be me who ends up dead if we fought. Whereas you, with that sword in particular, will have no problem. You will be Griselda's Hero and rescue her. What can stand in the way of love?"

"You're a coward," said Edwin.

"If you like," said Deathwing.

Though the sword still wanted blood, the dragon's plan had merit. He had no idea where Morden was, and if this thing could take him there faster, the sooner he and Griselda would be reunited.

"Where is Morden?" asked Edwin.

"Across the sea, in the orc city of Deathcropolis."

"Never heard of it."

"You come from a hovel in the Western Reaches, why am I not surprised?"

"Across the sea?"

"Well, ocean if you are being picky."

That was a blow. Even if he killed Deathwing now and continued on his way, if Morden was that far away it would take him an age to reach him. Of course, it could all still be part of a ruse. But he couldn't see how that made sense.

"You would fly me there?" asked Edwin.

"That would seem best," conceded the man-come-dragon. "You have heard the scorpion parable?"

"Of course."

"Well, you'll not be riding my back with your stinger. I shall carry you in my claws with your arms pinned."

"And what stops you dropping me from a great height? I'm not stupid, you know."

"If I wanted you dead, Edwin, I would have dropped a rock on you while you slept."

The dragon had a point. Even so, he didn't like the idea of being grasped helplessly while he was flown to Morden. "What if you dump me at his feet?"

"That's exactly what I am going to do."

"You what?"

"Well, not literally at his feet. Somewhere close by from where you can approach him, and then you are going to take that sword of yours and remove his head from his shoulders."

It was a simple plan, but Edwin couldn't find fault. It was direct and to the point. In fact, very much his kind of plan.

"All right, Dragon. You have a deal."

Chapter 43   Party Planning

Money not only talks, but it speaks all languages.
The Dark Lord's Handbook

Count Vladovitch was not sleeping well. The army had come to a halt. The public reason was to allow the logistics to catch up, but in reality it had been due to another night visit from the chancellor's man in the camp asking if they may stop. The count was only too happy to oblige. He was in no hurry to get to the next city and the battle that would ensue. With Edwin gone life was a lot quieter. The mood had assumed one of a summer campaign with the unpleasantness of actual fighting being kept to a minimum.

While the count was happy to drag his feet, Lady Deathwing was not. As soon as they had stopped she made an appearance, demanding they push faster and catch up with Sir Edwin. The count recognised a plan unravelling into ruin when he saw one, and Sir Edwin hotfooting it after his strumpet was not in Lady Deathwing's plan at all. The count had had to use all his powers of persuasion to convince her that the delay was necessary. But she was not happy.

The light from under the tent flap told him dawn was here. There was no point lounging in his field cot. Besides, Baron Fanfaron would doubtless be presenting breakfast shortly. It had become one of their things. They both shared the common notion that a good breakfast made you ready for the day. What each thought constituted a good breakfast varied, the count preferring his black pudding and eggs, whereas the baron cooked these sweet crescent-shaped butter pastries that he dunked in coffee.

The count had just cleared a space on the fold-away table he kept in his tent when the flap opened and the baron ducked in. Any other man would have received a roasting for such impertinence, but the baron had become a firm friend.

"Good morning, Sergei. And how are you this fine day?"

Pierre was always insufferably cheerful in the morning. The count merely grunted his reply. He took a folded chair and opened it up, placing it opposite his own chair. He indicated Pierre should sit.

With both men in place, a procession of the baron's chefs appeared bearing plates of croissant, a pot of coffee, plates of meats and eggs, fresh bread and butter, condiments, and serviettes. It was all a little too much fuss for the count, but he was happy enough to indulge Pierre's need to do things just so (as he liked to say).

"You have not slept again?" asked Pierre, once all was in place and the two had been left alone.

The count shook his head. "My visitor made another appearance." The baron was the only one of the count's staff who knew of his contact with Chancellor Penbury's spy in the camp. He was the only one he could trust, which was fortunate given what he had been told last night about what was soon to happen.

The baron slurped heavily on his coffee but didn't say anything. The count appreciated how Pierre understood when to keep his council and wait for him to talk.

"Penbury will be here tomorrow," said the count.

"The chancellor? Merde."

"Merde, indeed," agreed the count. "And he wants you to cook for him."

"Me?" The baron looked perplexed. "But how does he even know I am ... ah, but he is the chancellor. He has ways of knowing. But, of course, it would be an honour." The baron put a finger to his pursed lips. He looked excited. "But what to cook?! We have nothing. Nothing, I tell you. Sergei! What shall I do? The greatest gourmet in the world is coming here to eat my food and we have nothing but rations! I am undone."

The count pushed a slip of paper across the table to his friend. "My visitor left this. It is the menu. The guest list is at the bottom."

The baron took the list and ran his eye down it. After sniffing dismissively, he tossed it on the table. "Impossible," he said, waving the list away. "These things cannot be found unless ..."

"Unless you are the chancellor," said the count. "He will be sending the harder-to-find things in advance of his arrival. They should be here today."

Pierre snatched the list back. The count had never seen him so absorbed. As his friend read he started to mutter to himself.

"Yes, yes. We could do that, but then even if I started now, it will be close, but perhaps, yes, I can do this."

The count went back to his breakfast. The eggs were especially good. Pierre had taught him to appreciate food in a way he had never done before.

The muttering had stopped. The count looked up to see Pierre watching him eat.

"And what is the meaning of this?" asked his friend. The baron slid the paper back over to the count and jabbed first at one spot, and then another further down. "I am not an assassin, you know."

The count had been waiting for him to get to this part. "The spriggle?"

"Yes, the spriggle! And this, this, this, *woman* who is coming as well. You think I don't know what is going on here?"

"Neither you, nor I, are assassins," said the count. "But am I not correct in thinking that the chancellor has, in fact, eaten spriggle and lived? Perhaps it is only for him."

"It says two portions," said Pierre. "Two!"

While Pierre had become a close confidant, there were some things the count had not told him, and revealing the truth behind the mysterious Black Orchid was one of them. While he was not sure what Penbury was up to, he had no doubts Lady Deathwing could look after herself.

"What can we do, my friend?" asked the count. "I am too old for plots and talk of assassins. I do what I am asked and hope I will see my wife again. It's a meal."

"A dinner."

"A dinner. It's a dinner for two special guests. I assume they are meeting to settle certain issues, of which I do not know nor wish to, and that we will be their gracious hosts. That is all. We will not be assassinating anyone."

Though he did not look completely happy, Pierre did look mollified.

"Very well. But you must excuse me. There are preparations to be made. There is barely enough time as it is." Pierre dabbed his mouth on his serviette, got to his feet, and bowed. "Count."

"Thank you, Pierre. You are a good friend."

The baron left, leaving the count to contemplate black pudding and wondering what would kill him first: the pudding, or the dinner he was to host between an ancient evil dragon queen and the most powerful man in the world.

Chapter 44   Rock Bottom

There are good reasons a Dark Lord often stays single.
The Dark Lord's Handbook

Morden had preferred it when he was alone in captivity. At least then he didn't have to suffer the incessant nagging along with the deprivations and humiliation of being held by his rival Dark Lord. It wasn't made easier by the lack of privacy. There were certain things none of them was happy doing with others present, except Stonearm, who seemed devoid of shame.

Morden had tried to use the time to learn more about Griselda from Kristoff, while she played Stonearm at a simple board game they had etched onto the slime-covered floor. But Kristoff had not been forthcoming. He was left knowing only that Kristoff and Griselda were not together in anything other than a platonic sense (and Kristoff physically shuddered when Morden had suggested otherwise) based on shared interests. Equally, he had little to say about her ex-boyfriend, Edwin, and why he was stalking them halfway across the Western Marches. It was all muddy waters. So they ate, argued, played a stupid game invented by an orc, and slept as best they could.

The sonorous drone from Griselda told him she was still asleep. He wished he could enjoy sleep as he remembered it, in that it brought welcome relief from consciousness, whereas now the sleep he enjoyed was more a thoughtful doze. He lay there on his patch of cell floor, listening to Griselda's breath rise, like a bellows sucking air, and fall, like a bear clearing its throat. He was amazed the other two could sleep at all.

His thoughts turned to Zoon, who had not reappeared, even to gloat, and what he was up to. The only source of news was Stonearm, as he had managed to strike up chat with the orcs who brought them food (the undead variety made good guards; they were not so good at tasks which required more tactile skill, like carrying plates of slop).

From all accounts, the city was alive, and undead, with activity. Preparations were being made for some big event, though Zoon had not yet announced what it was to be. Morden could guess. If the Handbook was anything to go by, Zoon would hold a huge rally prior to setting out to conquer the world. He would hold it at night so he could use massed flaming torches to best effect. The flickering light would make the shadows dance and lend an ominous tone to the proceedings. There would be drums and chanting, and a procession of rank upon rank of elite, death-dealing orc zombies. He would work them up into a frenzy of bloodlust, exhorting them to go forth and claim what was rightfully theirs (which technically it wasn't but that wouldn't fit the rhetoric).

It was what Morden would do, if he were the Dark Lord preparing to Come Forth before Laying Waste the world. All the time he had spent reading the Handbook had not been wasted. The problem was that he was in a cell and Zoon was upstairs with his army, and he was no closer to making an escape, as Griselda liked to point out continually.

For now, Morden had nothing better to do than lie there and listen to the avalanche-like snores from Griselda. They were so loud he almost missed the scratching sound. It was probably a rat. A brave one at that, seeing as Stonearm had decimated the population in short order. If Stonearm woke he'd soon be joining his brothers as an orcish dietary supplement.

Morden raised his head to see if he could spot the little bugger. It was a rat, but rather than chewing on some cell detritus, it was chewing on his foot.

"Aaaaaaarh!" Morden screamed and kicked out.

Griselda jerked awake and sat up just in time to get a rat in her lap.

"Aaaaaaaaaaaaaaaaaaaaaaah!" she screamed, grabbing the rat and throwing it.

Stonearm sat up and the rat hit him in the face. It tried to scurry away but the orc was too fast and he grabbed it. "Breakfast!" said the big orc, grinning.

"What the hell was that?" shrieked Griselda, looking at Morden.

Inwardly he sighed. If anything was upsetting, uncomfortable, smelly, itchy, unfair or inconvenient, it was his fault.

"Eh?" said Kristoff, sitting up. Of them all, he was the heaviest sleeper by far. "What's going on?"

"Nice bit of rat, this," said Stonearm, proffering the rodent to the others.

Given that most small birds and mammals that came anywhere near Morden seemed to die in short order, Morden imagined it was a rather tough rat.

"Disgusting," said Griselda, turning her nose up.

It was both an infuriating and cute habit she had. Though he could happily watch Griselda all day, the state of his toes was of more concern. It couldn't be that bad, as he'd felt nothing, but he'd better check. Sitting up, he pulled his foot up onto his thigh so he could examine it.

Two toes were missing gobbets of flesh. He could even see the bone with little teeth marks on the big toe. Strangely, there was no blood. Given the damage done, he should be bleeding profusely. But he wasn't. He should also be in pain, but he couldn't feel a thing.

"Ow," he said experimentally. Maybe he was in shock and had to acknowledge the injury before he could feel the pain.

"What's the matter?" asked Griselda. "Ratty bite your toe? Wuss."

Kristoff came over to have a look. If his expression was anything to go by, the wounds were as disgusting to him as they were to Morden. "That must hurt," he said.

"Actually, no," replied Morden. "In fact, I can't feel a thing."

Griselda's curiosity got the better of her and she came over to have a look as well.

"That's disgusting," she pronounced.

"Yes it is," said Morden. "Thank you."

Stonearm had made short work of the offender and, tossing the remains into a corner, came to complete the group gathered around Morden's foot.

"You'll want to put something on that," he said helpfully. "Those bites could go bad."

"Oh really?" said Morden. "Maybe if I ask nicely they'll let me see an apothecary."

Morden prodded at the wounds and the surrounding toes. Nothing. The flesh looked pale and felt rubbery. For that matter, the rest of his foot looked the same. He jabbed himself and still nothing. The same up his leg. He couldn't feel anything anywhere.

He lifted up the rags he was wearing to look at the wound in his left side where the spear, or whatever it was, had hit him in the ribs. The wound, though closed, was still livid on the flesh.

"What's that?" asked Griselda.

Was that genuine concern in her voice? thought Morden. "I was shot," he said, probing the wound gently. It should still hurt, but didn't. Then Zoon's words came crashing down on him and his hand recoiled from the wound.

"Mostly dead," said Morden. "He said I was mostly dead."

"Mostly dead?" said Kristoff. "Who said?"

"Zoon. He told me I was mostly dead."

"I've been saying that for ages," suggested Griselda, and she laughed at her own joke.

"What's that mean?" asked Stonearm. "Mostly? Nearly dead, I get. Dead, I get. Not dead is fairly obvious. What's mostly dead?"

Morden poked his leg. "This. This is dead. I'm a walking corpse."

The thought was horrifying, but made so much sense. It explained everything and yet, if he was mostly dead, how was he not completely dead? Or undead, for that matter? Had he actually died on that beach, or was he still dying?

"You can't feel anything?" asked Griselda, and this time the concern was clear. "Anything at all?" Her eyes darted to his nether region.

It was true. He'd spent the last few days near the woman who used to boil his blood, but now there was nothing. He'd caught more glimpses of womanly flesh in the last few days, both unintentional and completely intentional, to satisfy his wildest imaginations, but thinking about it, while mentally he had been excited, physically it had produced no reaction. His sword had lost its steel. That was not good. How could he answer? Griselda couldn't possibly be with someone who was incapable of satisfying her physical needs. It was a disaster.

Left floundering for something to say, Morden was saved by the grate on the cell door being pushed open. Something that wasn't food was pushed through and slapped onto the ground. With palpable collective relief that here was something to distract them, the four rushed over to see what it was.

Stonearm got there first and picked up a sheet of vellum with something written on it. Stonearm held it in one hand while running a thick finger along the words and mouthing to himself.

"What does it say, you big oaf?" demanded Griselda.

Stonearm was frowning, as though he were having some difficulty with what he was reading, but when he looked up at Griselda he smiled (a good smile, not one of those 'I'm going to kill you' smiles).

"Congratulations," said the orc.

"Congratulations?" asked Morden, Griselda, and Kristoff as one.

"This is an invitation," said Stonearm, waving the vellum at Griselda. "To her wedding."

"What?"

"Wedding?"

"Here, give that to me," said Morden, putting a hand out. He scanned it once and then read out loud as though he had to hear it to believe it.

'To Prisoners it may concern, You are cordially invited to the Ziggurat of Death on the happy occasion of the wedding of Lord Zoon and Griselda at midnight of the full moon, at which time you will be sacrificed. RSVP. (Formal attire.)'

Morden flipped the vellum to see if there was anything else but all it had was an address, 'Lord Zoon, The Ziggurat of Death, Deathcropolis.'

The grate on the door opened again and several packages were thrust through. Each was a bound bundle with a tag.

Kristoff picked up one and tossed it to Stonearm. "That's yours."

There was one for each of them.

"He's a funny man," said Stonearm, ripping his package open. Inside was a black shift. The orc put it on quickly. It was floor-length and plain. He did a little spin. "Least it fits."

Morden held his package and tried to work out how he could turn this to his advantage. While he was initially shocked by the invitation, he quickly realised this was the opportunity they needed. They couldn't possibly escape from the cell, but maybe they could escape getting sacrificed and stop Zoon at his wedding. He wasn't sure quite how he might do it, but he was sure something would come to him.

Meanwhile, Griselda had opened her package and held up a dress. It was beautiful. Unsurprisingly, it was black, covered in jet stones and embroidered with roses and skulls in a silk thread. Low cut, it would without doubt contrast well with Griselda's pale skin. Morden's first thought was that he couldn't wait to see her in it, but then he remembered the reason she was expected to wear it and was not so keen.

"Well, I'm not marrying anyone," said Griselda. She threw the dress on the ground and glared at Morden. "So what are you going to do about it, Mr. 'I've got everything under control'?"

"I don't particularly want to be sacrificed, either," said Kristoff. "Anyone know when the full moon is?"

"In about 16 hours," said Stonearm with certainty.

"How do you know that?" said Morden.

"Just do," shrugged Stonearm. "It's an orc thing."

"Well?" demanded Griselda.

"This isn't as bad as it looks," said Morden.

Griselda's eyebrows raised as though to say 'oh really?'. "Well, I'd like to be fucking told when it's going to get worse than marrying a fucking lich," she screamed.

Kristoff and Stonearm winced.

"Calm down," said Morden. "Everything will be fine."

"Fine? Fine? I'll give you fucking fine," Griselda shouted.

Then something snapped inside Morden. He'd had about enough of this. "Well, it's not you who's going to be sacrificed, you selfish bitch," he shouted back. "At least you'll still be alive."

He expected her to recoil at his outburst, but it seemed to have the opposite effect.

"Alive? What, to have little undead babies? You fucking moron, I'd rather be dead."

"I wish you were," shouted Morden, and then clamped his mouth shut.

Griselda quivered in front of him.

"You bastard," she whispered. She stooped and grabbed the package. "You fucking bastard." She went to the far side of the cell and hunched down. Her shoulders started to shake and Morden was sure she was crying.

"I'll talk to her," said Kristoff, putting a hand on Morden's arm.

"You'll think of something," said Stonearm.

"I will?" asked Morden.

"Of course," said Stonearm. "You're Dark Lord Morden Deathwing."

Chapter 45   Gastronomy

Pain is the seasoning of life.
The Dark Lord's Handbook

It had been a number of years since Chancellor Penbury had seen
such a large and well-organised army. It was pitched in rolling
fields that had been commandeered from local farmers. Lines of
tents made neat ranks. On a rough parade square, soldiers drilled. It
spoke volumes of its leader, Count Sergei Vladovitch, who was
standing with an honour guard ready to welcome their guest.
Penbury had travelled light, with only Chidwick and a handful of
men, making the best speed they could. Their only stop had been
for some special ingredients for the banquet planned for that
evening.

As Penbury got out of his carriage, an order was barked and the
honour guard snapped to attention. An elderly man in a general's finery
was standing with some officers. The man's gaze was steady and rested
comfortably on the chancellor. There was an intelligence and steel in the
man's eyes.

"Count Vladovitch," said Penbury, offering a handshake. "Good to
meet you at last." The count's grip was firm and Penbury could feel the
man assessing him in the shake, both with grip and eye. Penbury turned
to the slightly nervous-looking man to the count's right. "Baron
Fanfaron, a pleasure after all these years. I am so looking forward to this
evening."

"Msr. Chancellor," replied the baron, nodding in acknowledgement.
"The honour is mine to cook for a palate such as yours."

"I take it you received all the items I sent ahead?" asked the
chancellor. The last thing he needed now was to find that his special
ingredients had gone astray. So much depended on them.

"They arrived safely last night," the count assured him. "You must
be tired. If you would follow me, I will show you to your quarters."

"If you will excuse me," said the baron, "but I have many preparations to make."

The baron scurried off in the direction of a set of tents which were a hive of activity. Open-sided, they contained benches and stoves around which a small battalion of chefs manoeuvred. It looked like they were cooking to feed an army (which the chancellor realised they probably were) rather than just for two.

The count led him through the camp. As they passed by men, without fail, gave a salute. It was clear the count commanded a deal of genuine respect from his men. The count stopped occasionally for a word with an officer, or an NCO, to deal with matters as minor as a correctly fastened tent to receiving a scout report. The army seemed to be run in a way Penbury himself would have been proud.

Penbury kept his eyes peeled but he did not spot his man, Snort. But then, he would have been disappointed if he had. Though he had faith in Chidwick who trailed behind, there was comfort in Snort's singular skills being on hand, which he was sure they were.

When not dealing with the odd military matter they came across, the count was not one for small talk.

"Has our guest arrived?" asked Penbury, to break the silence.

"Not as far as I know," replied the count. "But then, you can never tell with her."

For the first time, the chancellor detected a hint of nervousness. It wasn't surprising.

"Here we are," said the count, stopping outside a tent set aside from the rest and large enough that you didn't have to duck to enter it. "We've tried to make it comfortable."

"I'm sure it will be fine," said the chancellor. "What time is dinner?"

"Eight o'clock," said the count. "I'll leave you to it. I have an army to look after, you understand."

The tent proved to be more comfortable than the chancellor had anticipated. Not that it mattered. While he was a creature of comforts, there were more pressing matters than the surprising presence of a chaise longue (probably borrowed from Fanfaron) and a teak desk (the count's, no doubt).

Chidwick set about organising the things they had brought with them. Toiletries aside, the thing that concerned Penbury most was a small wooden case. Chidwick placed it carefully on the table and Penbury produced his key for the lock.

Inside was a collection of seven small containers: several vials, two small sealed jars and a tiny silk purse. They contained the antidotes he would need to take if he was going to survive the entrée. He didn't have much time. Each had to be taken in particular order and at a precise time between each. The process also had to be completed a specific amount of time prior to the course, and not too soon, in order that otherwise lethal doses would be countered by what he was going to eat.

It was no wonder he was one of a select few who had ever tasted spriggle and survived. There were millions of permutations required to find the precise mix of ingredients, not to mention the harder-to-find elements, such as the deadly, but rare, miniature crab spider (to be eaten fresh and so was kept in the silk purse). The combination had come after centuries of research by a dedicated group of gastronomes, Les Bons Vivants. When close to death, they would try the latest theoretical permutation, seeing as they had nothing to lose. It was only the members of this select group, of whom Penbury was head, who knew the secret, and only Penbury himself who had both the stomach and palate to rise to the challenge.

"Dinner at eight, and so the entrée should be served by nine at the latest," said Penbury.

"Very good, sir," said Chidwick. "I'll confirm with the baron."

While Chidwick did so, Penbury started on the breathing and relaxation exercises required. Being near death was also an important part of the process, probably because the body's actions were all slowed down. It would take thirty minutes or so for him to be ready. Chidwick was back in twenty. Ten minutes after that he helped Penbury eat, drink and sniff each of the components.

It was another thirty minutes before Penbury was able to stand.

Then he wrote his last instructions as chancellor, should things not go well. He had a will Chidwick would execute, but that was personal. Every chancellor was responsible for handing on the office, and that was normally done at a gracious retirement dinner. On odd occasions through history the current chancellor's end had come more suddenly, and after one unfortunate incident there resulted a nasty bout of economic warfare that had seen thousands of companies go to the wall before a new chancellor had established himself. To avert such a happenstance again, all chancellors now made succession clear.

Penbury sealed the letter, made his mark on it, and handed it to Chidwick. "Just in case," he said.

"I'm sure everything will be fine, sir," said Chidwick, pocketing the letter. "Will you be dressing for dinner?"

"I think so, Chidwick. I think so."

Chapter 46   To the Rescue

Might makes Right, and often Wrong as well.
The Dark Lord's Handbook

Edwin had to fight every instinct he had not to draw his sword and plunge it into the chest of the black dragon before him. The sword was screaming in his mind. It burned in his heart. He wanted to bellow with rage and indignation at the bargain he had entered into with this creature. It was an affront to everything he held to be good and true; that he should sully himself thusly was only made bearable by the knowledge that some good would come of it when he saved his love, Griselda, from the clutches of an even greater evil.

"Are you ready?" asked Lord Deathwing.

Edwin nodded.

The dragon unfurled and beat his wings. Impossibly, the beast rose and hovered over Edwin. A wave of primal terror assaulted him and he had to stand strong against the urge to cower. The talon that reached out and grasped him could have opened him up like a butcher would a pig carcass, but it merely pinned his arms so he was held helplessly.

"Right then," said the dragon. "We'd better get going. I don't think we have long."

A few strong beats later, and they were soaring high above the ground. Everything below rapidly shrank in size, not that there was much to see in this wilderness. They approached low cloud and Edwin assumed they would stop climbing, but they kept going. For a minute they were lost in a fog before breaking out into brilliant sunshine. A white folded carpet lay beneath them. Edwin noticed it was getting colder. And still they climbed. The wind rushed around him in a gale. Edwin could feel the first pangs of panic.

"What are you doing?" he shouted.

The dragon stooped his head to look at him. "Going as fast as I can without killing you, if that's all right? Now stop wriggling. I wouldn't want to drop you. It's a long way down."

The implication was clear, and Edwin decided he was at the dragon's mercy. If the dragon was going to kill him, he was going about it in a convoluted manner. Edwin was better off saving his energy and concentrating on the one thing that mattered, and that was the rescue of Griselda.

Though it made no sense, Edwin had imagined they would not be flying for that long, but hours passed. Through gaps in the cloud he could see land and sea pass beneath. He had no idea how far they had come or had to go. Tiredness won against the cold and he drifted into an uneasy sleep that was troubled by the familiar dream of the Dark Lord on the stair with Edwin's love at his side.

He woke shouting her name.

"You'd better keep quiet," suggested his dragon transport. "We're nearly there."

It was night now, but the moon was full. It reflected off the ocean far below. Ahead there was a dark line across the horizon that must be land. Growing rapidly bigger was what had to be a city. It was bright against the black of night. Curiously, though the night was clear, over the city itself there was a disc of cloud that twisted and roiled like angry smoke.

They began to drop and the air got warmer. Approaching the city, Edwin could see it was on an island in the mouth of the widest river he had ever seen, which wasn't hard given that until recently he hadn't strayed more than a few miles from home. Nevertheless, it was on a scale he struggled to fit into his mind. The city was a confusion of light, given order by towering buildings that rose jaggedly above the flat roofs. The light breeze brought the first strains of drums and a smell of orc. The smell made Edwin flare inside. A city of orcs ready to be purged.

"Damned moon," said the dragon, dipping to within a few feet of the water. "I'll land you on that spur and then you're on your own."

"So your courage fails you," said Edwin as a matter of fact.

"If I drop you now, you'll sink like a stone and drown, so less of the jibing and listen. You'll need something to cover that armour and sword. Though there are humans in the city, you will stick out looking like you do. You'll want to find out what you can from any humans you do meet; they will mostly be slaves or pirates. I'd suggest heading for the Temple of Zoon. That seems the most likely place you'll find Morden."

Edwin couldn't find it in himself to thank the dragon, so merely grunted his understanding. When all was done, it would be the dragon's turn to feel his justice. He could not countenance the thought of something so evil free in the world. He would hunt it down and kill it. The world would be a better place.

"I would wish you luck," said the dragon, as the island reared ahead. "But I suspect that won't be necessary."

The drop-off was done at speed and high enough it hurt when Edwin landed. He suspected it wasn't entirely necessary. He came to rest against a tree with a banded trunk. A second later, something hard hit him on the head. It was a huge hairy nut-shaped thing. This was a strange land, without doubt.

From the assortment of hung nets and jetties, the spur of land had to be used by fishermen. Where the spur widened to meet the main island there were crude huts. All was quiet on the spur; the drums and noise were coming from inland. Edwin crept as quietly as he could to the nearest huts. Fortune smiled on him; there was a line outside hung with what passed as clothing. It was threadbare and ill-made but ideal for Edwin's purpose. In short order he was wrapped in fishy-smelling rags and hobbling down the street; the affected stagger would make him look more like a beggar.

He headed towards the part of the city that sounded awake. The moon was bright enough to light his way. There were main streets that formed a large grid and were cobbled; alleys criss-crossed between them. This was as much order as he could make out in the dark. Whereas places like Bindelburg had obvious districts based on wealth or purpose, this city was a confusion of huts, hovels, stone buildings hung with vines, small shrines covered in offerings, tethered goats, and misshapen trees from whose branches hung parasitic plants and the odd man with a placard around his neck.

He neared a central square where avenues converged. The drumming got louder and the smell of orc even stronger. The road he was on emptied into a wide area thronged with revelling orcs, with what looked like drunken pirates mixed in. Orcs danced around a pyre that lit up the night. Edwin didn't think there was a sober orc (or man) present. He wondered what they were celebrating, and then a dreadful thought occurred. What if he was too late?

"This is mad, isn't it?" said a voice to Edwin's right. It was a man wearing a tricorn hat, a filthy ruffed shirt under a knee-length frock coat, and sea boots. "I've seen a few things in my life, but nothing like this," continued the man.

"Garr," replied Edwin, unsure what the correct response was. All he wanted to do was cut a swath of blood and destruction through the teeming crowd.

"Here," said the man, thrusting a bottle at Edwin and fishing a replacement from a pocket. Edwin's new friend prized the cork out with his teeth, spat it to one side and took a swig, dribbling dark liquid down his chin. He raised the bottle to Edwin. "To Morden!"

At the sound of Morden's name it took all of Edwin's will not to cut the man in half and spread his innards on the street. Instead he gritted his teeth, clinked bottles and made the toast, "Garrr!"

"Or should I say, to Zoon!" said the man, making a second toast. "Can't keep up with these Dark Lords and their name changes."

Confused, Edwin merely took another drink. Sweet fire ran down the back of his throat. He coughed and felt tears in his eyes.

"Good stuff, eh?" said his new friend.

"Garrr," gasped Edwin.

The man slapped him on the shoulder. "I've got some dancin' and collapsin' to do, so you go ahead and enjoy yourself. Maybe I'll see you after the wedding tomorrow night." The man, true to his word, skipped a few paces in time with the drumbeats and then fell flat on his face, shattering the bottle he was holding.

Wedding? thought Edwin. Then it all fell into place. His dreams became clear. The army arrayed beneath the stairs were orcs like these. On the far side of the square a huge ziggurat rose, and at the top was a massive statue that could only be a Dark Lord. He wasn't late at all. That must be the Temple of Zoon the dragon had mentioned. Tomorrow there would be a wedding, but when it came to the bit about anyone objecting, he would be doing so, with steel.

Edwin tossed his own evil brew aside and staggered down the side of the square. He would find a spot where he could wait and when the time came, strike and rescue Griselda. In the confusion that followed, the Dark Lord cut down, they could make their escape.

Chapter 47   Reluctant Bride

For forms of government let fools contest,
for without doubt, the Dark Lord is best.
The Dark Lord's Handbook (A. Pope edition)

"Our only chance is to play along and grab an opportunity to escape when it appears," insisted Morden for the thousandth time.

"And I'm telling you, I'm not wearing this dress or marrying a skeleton," riposted Griselda.

"He'll only drug you if you don't," said Morden. "Or bend you to his Will. Dark Lords do that."

"Let him try," said Griselda. "It never worked for you."

Stonearm and Kristoff had long given up trying to help Morden. They agreed with him and were wearing their sacrificial shifts, like Morden himself. The last thing he wanted was for them to be taken by force or be drugged. They needed their wits about them if they were going to make a break for it. It sounded like a less-than-detailed plan, and one that didn't seem to offer much, if any, chance of success, but it was the best they had. Morden knew Zoon wouldn't be able to resist making a spectacle of it. In the brief time observing Zoon and how he operated, it was obvious that although he may well own the Handbook, it was not at all clear he either understood or followed some of the basic and important lessons contained within it. No wonder he had screwed up all those centuries ago. This made Morden certain the lich would cock it up again.

"Black is slimming," suggested Morden.

"Is that why you wear it all the time, fat boy?"

This was going nowhere. They'd been at it for hours and time was running out. Any second Morden expected them to be dragged off for the evening wedding and sacrifice special Zoon had planned for his army. It was not a bad plan. Everyone loved a wedding, and by assuming Morden's persona, while throwing in adoption of a name that resonated back to the glory days of the orc nation, Zoon was showing he had a few moves politically. Eliminating loose ends in a crowd-pleasing blood sacrifice was an evil touch that was bound to go down well.

"I give up," said Morden sighing. "Have it your way."

He turned his back on Griselda and stalked over to his fellow sacrifices-to-be.

"She's impossible," he proclaimed.

"There's a good heart in there," said Kristoff. "She takes after her mother. Very stubborn."

It was the first mention Morden had heard Kristoff make of Griselda's past, or his, for that matter.

"She's naked," said Stonearm, looking past Morden.

As a matter of reflex, Morden spun round. Griselda was pulling up the black dress over her shoulders.

"Bit skinny," said the orc.

"Hey!" said Griselda, noticing the attention she was getting, at least from Morden and Stonearm. Kristoff had averted his eyes. "Stare at something else, will you?"

She did look fantastic in the dress. It was full length but tightly fitting. Stonearm's observation was true, she had lost even more weight and was slim in the dress. Morden reluctantly averted his eyes. He had to slap Stonearm to do the same.

"Didn't think humans were your type."

"True, but when there's nothing else, you make do with what there is," said the orc.

Morden glowered. If anyone had staring rights around here, it was him.

"You're right," said Stonearm. "She's not my type."

"You knew her mother?" Morden asked Kristoff. The ageing poet seemed to have descended into one of his bouts of melancholy. "Kristoff? Her mother?"

"What? Oh, yes. I used to go out Wellow way. Beautiful lake there. Good for inspiration. Poems and all that. You know. Met her one day when she was swimming in the lake. A summer's day that made you glad you were young," Kristoff sighed. "Griselda has her mother's looks as well as her temper."

This was all very interesting. Kristoff had known Griselda's mother.

Morden couldn't help but wonder how well. Given all the facts on hand, it would seem very well indeed. Morden opened his mouth to confirm this, but just as he was about to ask Stonearm elbowed him in the ribs. While it didn't hurt it did knock him off balance.

"What was that for?" asked Morden, rubbing his side more from habit than anything.

"Someone's coming," said Stonearm. "Orcs. Dead ones. Shall we jump them when they take us?"

It was more of a plan than Morden had, but something told him the time was not right. "No. We'll play along and wait for a better opportunity. If we jump them now we'll only spend hours wandering around down here."

When the door was slammed open and twenty undead orcs stomped in, the suggested plan became moot. There was no way they could have overwhelmed that many, especially given Stonearm was the only one with any real martial prowess. With much grumbling from Griselda, the four of them were hemmed in on all sides and marched out.

Morden tried to keep track of the route they took but it was impossible; there were far too many turns, rises and dips. After a while they reached a stair that spiralled up. The steps were worn and slippery. Griselda nearly lost her footing and Morden grabbed her to stop her falling. She shrugged off his hand.

The stair proved to be long and soon Griselda and Kristoff were both panting. Stonearm seemed fine, and Morden didn't feel out of breath. In fact, he didn't feel much at all. *Hardly surprising*, he thought, *seeing as I am mostly dead.*

At last they came into a small chamber with a bench carved into one wall. The sides of the room were sloped and from that, and the noise Morden could hear from outside, they had to be near the top of Zoon's temple.

The zombie orcs forced them onto the stone bench. Morden didn't have long to wonder what was going to happen next, because he felt Zoon approaching. The lich came up the same stair they had used. The smell of death preceded him. He was wearing Morden's robe. The single tear where he had been shot by the fisherman's spear had been sewn up, but was visible. In his one good hand, Zoon clutched the Handbook. The zombies parted to allow him to stand in front of the four.

"Excellent," said the lich with what Morden thought was a rather smug tone for a lich who had difficulties speaking clearly.

"You'd better let us go," said Morden.

Zoon's now-familiar wheezing laugh greeted Morden's warning. "Don't worry, boy. You won't have to endure much longer. Soon you and your friends will have joined my ranks of undead slaves, except for Griselda here. She will be my obedient wife. A Dark Queen at my side."

"Don't say I didn't warn you," said Morden. He wasn't sure what he was doing, but any bluff was better than none at all. Anything that could buy them time. Not that he was sure more time helped, but something nagged at him. Whatever was happening to him was finally coming to an end. Something inside was starting to burn. It was so small, but it was there. It was like the feeling he had when he could assume his dragon form, but it was different.

Zoon raised the Handbook. "You seem to forget, young Morden Deathwing, we have read the same book. Your bravado can't fool me."

"And you must have a head full of maggots if you think I'm going to marry you," said Griselda, standing.

"Actually I do," said Zoon. "On both counts. Now sit."

Griselda's mouth opened as though to say something, but it seemed she couldn't. Morden could see her struggling against some invisible force that pressed her back down onto the stone.

"That's better," said Zoon. "Now, this is how it's going to be. I'm going to go up there and work my army of orcs up to the cusp of a slavering climax. Then I'm going to bring you lot up, marry Griselda, and seal it with an old school sacrifice. Don't worry, Morden, it's not that bad. Soon you'll stop being mostly dead and instead join the ranks of my undead as a slave. I shall Lay Waste the world and you shall be there to witness it, and eat brains along the way. Not quite how you imagined it, but then life, or death, is not fair. You, of all people, know that."

Chapter 48   Repartee

If you do indulge a last meal,
make it a single course only.
The Dark Lord's Handbook

The table was immaculately laid. Penbury could have been at home rather than in the field with a ten-thousand-strong army arrayed around in tented lines. All the other preparations had been made; Baron Fanfaron had assumed the position of head chef to ensure everything was perfection. Chidwick had exerted his customary attention to detail and was standing attentively on hand to serve the table.

Penbury swilled the pale golden kotch and composed himself. It had been decades since he had felt anything approaching nerves when it came to a business dinner.

At five to eight their guest for the evening was led in by Count Vladovitch. The count looked as though he had aged several years in a few hours. There was a harrowed look about the veteran. Perhaps it was because their guest had dispensed with any subterfuge regarding who she was, as made evident by her appearance.

"Lady Deathwing," said the count, "may I present to you Chancellor Penbury."

Lady Deathwing was tall, slim, and elegantly dressed in a dark burgundy dress that hugged her figure. A pale bosom heaving in a low-cut neckline would have been in keeping, but her skin was as dark as night and had a serpentine sheen to it. (The bosom was ample enough—though Penbury rarely concerned himself with such things, he was still a man.) A ferocious red flame licked in her eyes. When she smiled to greet him and offer her hand, her teeth were needle sharp and white, and her nails were curved talons.

"Chancellor," said Lady Deathwing.

"Lady Deathwing," said Penbury, kissing her hand. It was smooth to his touch, but hot on his lips.

Chidwick had slid behind Lady Deathwing and pulled back a chair for her.

"I'll leave you to it," said the count, hovering.

"Thank you, Count," said Penbury, and his host made a rapid exit. "A good man," observed Penbury.

"If you like that kind of thing," said Lady Deathwing. Her hand went to a wine glass and Chidwick filled it. It was a hundred-year-old red he had brought from his own cellar.

"A Bellagrino red," said Penbury.

A flicker of amusement crossed Lady Deathwing's face before she tasted the wine. "A seventy-four," she said, arching an eyebrow as though to challenge Penbury to tell her she was wrong.

She wasn't, and he nodded his appreciation of her palate. It was a shame she was a dragon intent on ripping civilisation apart, as otherwise he was sure they shared many tastes and would have got on famously. Chidwick assisted Penbury in seating himself opposite Lady Deathwing and then went to fetch a taper to light the candles on the table, but a thin jet of flame from Lady Deathwing took care of the matter. It was a point well taken by the chancellor.

"I think we'll take the first course, Chidwick," said Penbury.

While they waited, Penbury snapped off a breadstick and drank more of the wine. Lady Deathwing seemed happy to sit and wait. Small talk, or the lack of need for it, seemed to be something else they had in common.

In short order, Chidwick appeared with a terrine of eels and asparagus, accompanied by salted wholemeal snaps. Cutting slices for both, Chidwick served first Lady Deathwing and then Penbury. The chancellor hoped his message was clear. They would be eating off the same plate. His instructions for serving were that everything was to be brought in and served from the same dish.

"I'm hungrier than I thought," said Lady Deathwing, not waiting for the chancellor. She took a sliver of the terrine on the snap and took a bite. An appreciative grunt followed swiftly. "I shall have to borrow your chef. Quite exquisite."

Penbury had to agree. It was indeed delicious. The contrasting texture of eel, asparagus and snap was perfect, while the asparagus also lent a solid back note to the subtle eel flavouring.

"So how do you want to do this?" asked Lady Deathwing between mouthfuls. "We could joust around for a while, or we could get right to the point."

"I was never one for jousting," said Penbury. In fact, nothing annoyed him more than a meeting where those present were ill-prepared and discussion quickly spiralled into a repetition of the same points.

"I didn't think you were," said Lady Deathwing. "So what is troubling you, Chancellor?"

"Aside from a Dark Lord rising and this army running amok across the land?"

"Yes, apart from that."

"It seems to me this whole situation is littered with a slew of odd coincidences and contradictions that suggest what we are seeing is not a natural course of affairs."

Lady Deathwing popped the last part of her terrine in her mouth and pushed her plate aside. Chidwick swept in and whisked it away. The fish course would be a few minutes, so they could talk uninterrupted.

"Go on," said the dragon.

"It is odd," continued Penbury, "that Morden *Deathwing* is that Dark Lord, and yet I find Lady *Deathwing* is the person behind this army that opposes him, and is in fact directly responsible for finding and arming a Hero."

"Ah, I see," said Lady Deathwing. She held up her wine glass for Chidwick to refill. "Odd perhaps, but perfectly understandable. You see, this Morden is a bastard mistake. He is not a pureblood but an error of judgement made by my randy husband. Lord Deathwing may be a dragon, but he has a man's appetite when it comes to women."

Penbury couldn't help but smile. While it put light on the situation, there was obviously more. "So you are a wounded spouse trying to set things right and do the world a public service at the same time? I'm touched, Lady Deathwing."

Lady Deathwing laughed. It was high-pitched and could have cracked crystal, and would have done if Penbury had been willing to bring his rather than make do with the cheaper glass they were drinking from.

"Indeed not, Chancellor. My fool of a husband merely played into my hands. This Morden is nothing. A boy playing in a game he is unaware of. Even if he were, he is out of his depth."

"And yet he is useful," said Penbury. It was a genuine pleasure to have her as an adversary worthy of the title. "As is Edwin."

"Ah, Edwin," said Lady Deathwing. "A lovely boy, if a little headstrong."

"Headstrong? Blood-crazed maniac, no?"

"But he's in love," said Lady Deathwing. "Don't you find that sweet? No? Nor do I. But again, it makes life easier."

"Until he runs off?"

At last Penbury seemed to have hit a nerve and a brief look of annoyance was evident.

Lady Deathwing shrugged it off with another laugh. "It seems we are jousting after all."

For the first time there was an air of tension, but luckily it was relieved by the arrival of the fish course. A full salmon was laid on a bed of fresh green leaves. It had been poached and been given the lightest of dressings so it remained the star of the course. Chidwick served them both and melted away into the background.

For the next minute Penbury was happy to enjoy the fish and gather his thoughts. So far everything was going as planned. As long as he could survive as far as dessert, all would be well. Letting salmon melt in his mouth not only bought him more time, but was an exquisite pleasure. It was obviously as fresh as the dew that had been on the ground that morning.

"I don't think I have had fish as good as this," pronounced Lady Deathwing.

"Agreed," said Penbury.

"So where were we?"

"Edwin?" suggested the chancellor. "I can only assume you know how dangerous a Hero can be for us all. So I am puzzled why you would unleash one."

"I was there when Uther cut down Zoon. Of course I know about Heroes. How do you suppose I got the sword? It is Uther's, the damned thing. Edwin is necessary. People need a Hero."

"And you need a diversion."

Lady Deathwing took another mouthful from her plate and stared at Penbury. He could feel her will lightly touching his mind. *What do you know?*

"This play-acting at war is not what this is all about, is it?"

"On the contrary," said Lady Deathwing, "I want war. I want the world to burn. I want a clean slate. And I shall have it. You can't stop a good war."

"Interesting choice of adjective," observed Penbury. "Good."

Lady Deathwing was obviously finding this all very amusing, as she laughed once more. That suited Penbury. As long as she assumed she was here in a position of power, they may have a chance.

"Let's not do the whole 'good and evil' thing, Chancellor," said Lady Deathwing. "We both know better than that. It's our interests, and Edwin's, and Morden's, that count."

The fish was done and Chidwick serviced the plates away, leaving a folded note with the chancellor as he did so. Penbury recognised the paper; it was from a Snort pad. Trying to maintain a level of composure while his heart pounded in his chest, Penbury flipped the note open in one hand, fished out his reading glasses with his other, and read:

Gathering clouds, outlook stormy. Advise: Severe weather imminent.

The serendipity of events in two places coming to a climax at the same time was not lost on the chancellor. But rather than good fortune, accident, or luck, he preferred the notion of good planning.

"Not bad news, I hope," said Lady Deathwing.

"Bad weather," said Penbury smoothly. "It's touch and go at this time of year with the Tempranillo grape."

"Of course it is," said Lady Deathwing.

Penbury took the second sheet that backed the message and scratched a reply. He hoped he was not too late.

Offer every assistance to avoid disaster.

Chidwick, ever efficient, wheeled in a large silver-covered platter on a trolley. Chidwick positioned the trolley mid-table and removed the hood with a flourish. On the platter was a cage fashioned from pork ribs dripping with a velouté sauce.

Inside, flopping around in a sea of purée, were two spriggles. Penbury's gourmet eye could tell immediately they were the highest quality. Not quite adult, their eye stalks not too full of length which would make their eating easier, because to eat spriggle properly they had to be swallowed whole. If they were too young, however, they would not have developed the slightly crusty skin across their back which not only gave textural contrast to their scallop-like flesh but, through some extraordinary contrivance of nature, added a seasoned, crispy bacon flavouring. It was this skin that also was one of the eight deadly elements of the little critter. It was commonly thought there were only seven ways to die eating a spriggle, but that was not so. The chef had to lightly brush the back with a perfectly balanced sauce that neutralised the burning acid no antidote could counter while leaving the base flavours intact.

"Ah, spriggle," said the chancellor. "A particular favourite of mine. Have you ever had the pleasure?"

"Live food," said Lady Deathwing. "How interesting." Lady Deathwing fixed Penbury with her eyes and smiled to reveal her full set of razor teeth. "You wouldn't be trying to poison me now, would you, Chancellor?"

Chapter 49   Wedding

It's a nice day for a Dark Lord's wedding.
The Dark Lord's Handbook (Idol edition.)

Edwin was woken by someone stepping on him where he lay. It was night again, though bright with a full moon. He had only lain down for a minute to gather his strength, but he must have slept all day. How he had fallen asleep with the riotous party going on around him was a mystery. The square around the base of the temple was heaving with revelling orcs, with a smattering of humans (mostly pirates) mixed in. There was a heavy driving beat of drums that had the mass moving as one in a rhythmic bounce.

Edwin got up slowly. He was sore and stiff from sleeping in his armour. He must have been exhausted. At least he would be well rested for the butchery that was soon to follow. Under his rough shawl he could feel the comforting presence of his sword. Already he could sense its anticipation and excitement. It would drink heavily this night.

Edwin looked around to regain his bearings. He had found cover under bushes close to the bottom of the ziggurat stairs. Columns of torches lit either side of the stair. Massive orcs, bare to the waist and muscled like cart horses, beat huge drums positioned on either side at the bottom.

The throng had been allowed part way up the ziggurat. On the stair above them stood a line of bigger orcs. Apart from the armour they wore, and the large axes in hand, there was something else that set them apart from the partygoers. They barely moved and, in the flickering flame, what little skin was exposed seemed to glisten as though oiled. They also seemed to exert a repulsion over the revellers below because instead of being pushed against the line of guards, the partying orcs maintained a distance of several yards.

There was no sign of Morden at the top of the ziggurat. Preparations were being made, centred on a stone altar that ran sideways across the head of the stair. At this distance it was hard to see clearly, so Edwin started forward. It would take a while to press through the crowd.

At first, Edwin tried to slip between the bodies thrashing around to the music, falling over drunk, and singing strangled orc ballads, but it was taking too long. The moon was creeping higher and Edwin had a strong sense that something was going to happen soon. He barged his way through, throwing friendly punches to knock belligerent orcs to the ground as he went. His armour helped him force his way through faster.

He was nearing the line of hulking orcs when Morden appeared from the back of the platform at the top and raised his arms. A wave of silence swept across the square and suddenly everyone was still and staring up at the robed figure. It took Edwin every ounce of will to force his legs into moving again. He had no time to lose.

He put his head down and started to push upward. He had taken only a few steps when there was a roar from around him that stopped him in his tracks and he looked up.

Morden stood, his left arm outstretched and holding the hand of a woman.

"I present to you my Dread Queen, Griselda!"

The words came from the grave, laden with death and decay. They shrivelled Edwin's heart. It was his love as he had seen her a thousand times in his dreams. She was terrifying and beautiful, her body stiff, her smile a rictus.

"Griselda!" he shouted and pushed forward.

His cry was taken up by those around him and soon there were thousands of voices calling her name. He pushed through the last revellers but hesitated at the line of armoured orcs. They were much bigger up close. Four of them were arrayed across the width of the stair, blocking it. They were more than twice the size of a normal orc and had heavy plated armour. Dead eyes stared out from their helms. There was no mistaking the work of the Dark Lord. There was no other choice but to fight his way through. Edwin reached for his sword.

It was halfway out of its sheath when a blur swept across the stair behind the orc guard. There was a flash of silver from behind each and a thin line appeared across the thick necks just below the helmet line and above the pauldrons. The first orc toppled slowly forward, its head parting company with its body as it did so; the others followed in a macabre line. Edwin had to sidestep the heads and bodies as they clattered past him and into the orcs behind. An avalanche of orcs rolled down the steep ziggurat and swept into the crowd, flattening all before it.

Edwin looked up the stair. This was his chance. Pulling his sword free, he bounded up. He almost didn't see the figure in black, a sword in each hand, flipping nimbly over the stone balustrade.

He took the stairs two at a time. He was ablaze with energy and fury. At first, it seemed his assault would go unanswered—but then from either side of Morden, orcs poured forward and down. They were not brutish guards in plate but were wearing vestments adorned in skulls and strange sigils. They waved wickedly curved knives in slashing arcs. He cut through them. Their corpses rained down the ziggurat as he hacked a bloody path up.

He could hear a woman's laughter. Sparing a glance from the slaughter he could see Griselda laughing hysterically. Next to her, Morden's cowled figure had let her hand drop and was moving to meet him.

Edwin brushed aside the last of the orcs and raised his sword into a guard. The Dark Lord was a mere few paces away.

"Griselda!" shouted Edwin.

Then the Dark Lord spoke. It was as though Edwin had been physically hit. Darkness and fear filled Edwin's mind. Despair gripped him. Griselda was pointing at him and laughing. He was covered in blood and the stench of death surrounded him. He was too late. She was lost. The Dark Lord had his queen and her hatred and derision washed over him, mixed in with the contempt of his rival's words:

"You are too late. She is mine."

Chapter 50   Poison

It's not a question of Good and Evil.
It's a matter of self-interest.
The Dark Lord's Handbook

If there was one thing spriggle did not taste like, it was chicken. It didn't taste like anything else for that matter. It was spriggle. It was an exquisite ensemble of texture and flavours so powerful it needed a host of ways to kill you to avoid total extinction; for surely once tasted no man could do anything else other than go out and hunt spriggle until there were no more.

To prevent it struggling too much, Penbury liked to wrap his in a thin pancake. Many could not stomach the notion of eating a spriggle alive. To Penbury it was no different than eating an oyster. In fact, eating anything alive was to him the ultimate test of any gastronome. If you could not eat a creature alive then you may as well just eat vegetables. The only reason he did not eat more things alive was because it was often too inconvenient and did not taste nearly as good as having been sealed, slow roasted, and served with greens.

It had been a while since he had had spriggle, but as soon as he popped the little critter in his mouth and crunched into it he was transported on a wave of gastronomic pleasure to the first time he had risked the treat. Now, as then, a complex series of high and low notes created a symphony of flavour that played out in his mouth. And just as he thought it was over and had swallowed, the inevitable belch as spriggle hit his stomach was a welcome encore.

When Lady Deathwing belched she set fire to the tablecloth and Chidwick had to hurriedly beat the flames out.

"Delicious," said Lady Deathwing. "I can see what all the fuss is about now. Quite extraordinary."

"Indeed," said Penbury, trying to ladle as much disappointment into his voice as possible without being melodramatic. Penbury hadn't expected the spriggle to prove fatal to the dragon. If it had, that would have been a bonus. "I'm so glad you enjoyed it."

Lady Deathwing smiled again. "Any more? I seem to have quite the stomach for it."

"Regrettably not," said Penbury.

He reached for one of the ribs that had caged the spriggles. The savoury ribs with their sticky sweet sauce were just the ticket after such a complex taste experience. Lady Deathwing took a rib and picked her teeth with it.

"So where were we?" she asked.

"We were talking about war," said Penbury. "You must know that a war is of no consequence to me and those I represent."

"There's profit in war," said Lady Deathwing.

"Indeed," said Penbury. "But there is more profit in peace. We prefer the latter, but if a war cannot be avoided then we do not meddle. Can this be avoided?"

Lady Deathwing looked thoughtful.

"I think not," she said at last. "Now, don't look so disappointed. I shall have my war, the world will be ruined, and then I shall save it."

"But only after it has burned and we, and by that I mean me in particular, have been ruined with it?"

"Collateral damage," said Lady Deathwing. "Is there dessert?"

"Chidwick!" said Penbury. "We'll take dessert now."

The chancellor could feel the smugness that emanated from the other end of the table. That was good. He hoped his silence while Chidwick brought in cream-filled meringues, strawberries (out of season to all but himself) and cream, with crystallised basil twills, would reinforce her triumphant air. She had come to gloat. His pathetic attempt to poison her had failed and there was nothing he could do.

Chidwick served them both and filled their glasses with a syrupy dessert wine before retiring.

"To war and all that it brings," said Lady Deathwing, raising her glass in a toast.

"I hope you'll forgive me if I lack your enthusiasm," said Penbury.

"Suit yourself. These meringues look delicious. I must say, Chancellor, your reputation after this meal can only be enhanced."

Chapter 51   A Dark Lord Dies – Again

Bad guys finish first.
The Dark Lord's Handbook

If they were going to escape, time was running out. Zoon had been true to his word and they were on the top of the temple ziggurat. The statue of Zoon towered above them and straddled the ceremonial altar. There were chains, grooves in the stone that waited for their blood, priests with wickedly sharp knives, smoking oil lamps, and more priests with more knives.

"This doesn't look good, Boss," said Stonearm.

Morden could barely hear his faithful minion above the noise of the crowd and drums; it was a party he wished he hadn't been invited to. Kristoff had become a gibbering wreck and Griselda seemed to have become a kind of living dead that had her mechanically moving at Zoon's behest with a terrible fixed grin. Whatever Zoon had done to her, the real Griselda was still in there. Morden could see it in her eyes. They were screaming at him to do something, but he was powerless. There were far too many orcs to fight their way out. Stonearm could probably have taken a few before they were skewered, but Morden's own talents were more at the strategic level. He tried exerting his Will but it seemed to slide off the orc priests. Zoon's power held them in thrall.

The three of them were held by priests while Zoon led Griselda to the head of steep steps that went down the front of the ziggurat. He held her hand high and presented her to his minions:

"I present to you my Dread Queen, Griselda!"

There was pandemonium. Thousands of voices were suddenly calling her name. Zoon was revelling in the moment.

But then something below Zoon caught his attention. He took a step back and the priests that surrounded Morden, Kristoff and Stonearm leapt forward. Griselda started to laugh hysterically and point at something. Gouts of blood and body parts flew into the air.

"That's fighting," said Stonearm.

Morden could see the orc tense, but there were still priests around them. Now was not the time. Then from the stair rose an armoured figure with a sword that had blue fire running its length. The man was covered in blood and gore and was screaming his lungs out.

"Griselda!" shouted the knight.

Morden could sense Zoon's power building, and then he spoke:

"You are too late. She is mine."

The knight staggered back as though struck. Morden didn't know what to make of it. He held a hand out to restrain Stonearm. "Wait. Let's see what happens."

"You sad, pathetic fool," said Zoon, taking a step towards the man. "All this for love? She doesn't love you."

The knight sank to his knees. He was shaking and had to rest on his sword to stop himself falling over. Morden could feel the waves of hatred and loathing sweep out from Zoon. When Morden had bent others to his Will, it was but a fraction of the power Zoon exerted.

"Grovel, you worm," said Zoon, towering over the knight.

Zoon's acolytes now circled the knight in a tight ring. There was no escape. It was going to be another demonstration of Zoon's power as a true Dark Lord.

"Kill him," said Zoon dismissively, and turned his back on the stricken knight.

Morden's heart leapt. Now! It was unbelievable that Zoon would make such a basic error. Could he not see who he had in front of him? It was one of the Golden Rules from the Handbook: Never turn your back on a Hero.

Morden watched in delighted fascination as the knight rose, roaring his defiance and hatred, swinging his sword in a wide arc as he did. The circle of priests toppled backwards, blood geysering, as they were split in two across the middle.

Zoon turned when he heard the screams, but all that did was allow the knight to plunge his sword into the Lich Lord's chest. There was an eruption of blue flame that jetted out from Zoon's sleeves and cowl. It transfixed the Dark Lord in a shuddering pillar of flame. The knight was wide-eyed and screaming as he struggled to hold the sword in Zoon's chest. Zoon thrashed and burned from within and dropped the

Handbook, which looked singed but intact.

Then Zoon collapsed, the robe falling in a heap. There was a detonation, like the biggest firework Morden had ever seen. Those near Zoon were knocked back so that only the knight and his sword were left standing.

Morden expected the undead orcs to recover and rush the knight, but he should have known better. Zoon's power was gone. The undead orcs in their armour collapsed into heaps of rapidly decaying flesh.

The knight stopped screaming. He rushed over to where Griselda had collapsed in a black heap. There was a small pool of blood around her head. The knight threw his sword to the floor and knelt.

"Griselda?" said the knight, taking a pale hand in his own. "Griselda?"

There was growing despair in the knight's voice. He sank back on his haunches and let his head hang back.

"GRISELDA!" bellowed the knight.

Was she dead? That wasn't possible, was it? Not now. Not after everything that had happened. He stepped forward.

"Griselda?" Morden said quietly, kneeling at her side, but there was no answer, no sign of life.

Anger burned inside Morden. And hatred. This knight had killed the one person he had ever loved. With the thought of her gone, something inside died, leaving coldness in its place. Without her, there was only one thing left for him.

He went over and picked up the robe. Whatever Zoon had been, he was no more. There was nothing left. Not even ash or goo. As the robe slid over his head he could feel it moulding to him like it had before.

Somewhere close by a crow cawed. It sounded pleased. Which was odd.

Kristoff seemed to have pulled himself together enough to come over to where Griselda lay. He knelt at her side and stroked her hair. Tears streamed down his face. He took her hand and buried his head in her neck.

The knight was a catatonic wreck and could be safely ignored. Morden stretched over and took the Handbook from where it lay. An electric jolt went up his arm and a familiar voice was back in his head.

Something stirred inside Morden.

Make them pay, it said. *Make them all pay.*

His hand went to the dragon pendant. It was cool under his touch. He ripped it loose and threw it on the floor. He didn't need that any more. His death was complete. He was reborn a Dark Lord.

Chapter 52   Hubris

There is no such thing as a mercy killing.
The Dark Lord's Handbook

Lady Deathwing sampled the meringues and washed them down with the dessert wine. She looked very pleased with herself.

"Shouldn't I be?" asked Lady Deathwing.

"So you can see my thoughts," said Penbury.

Lady Deathwing laughed. "You silly man, of course I can. You are quite transparent to me."

"I had suspected as much," said Penbury. *Was the borrowing your idea?* he thought.

"It was indeed. But please. I do prefer talking. Besides, you can't read my mind, now can you?"

"So not content with seeing the world thrown into a war, of which you fanned the flames, you saw fit to bankrupt everyone at the same time," said Penbury.

"Well, not everyone," said Lady Deathwing. "What did you think this was all about, anyway? You of all people should appreciate how detestable poverty is."

"But that's not all, is it?"

Lady Deathwing sat forward, emptied her glass, and helped herself to more from the bottle. "This is good wine," she remarked. "No, that was not all. Being poor was bad enough, but being in penury to those horrid bankers ..." she shuddered. "They had to be ruined, and you had to be brought down with them. How could I tolerate one as powerful as you? Me—Lady Deathwing? I was there when we had proper wars, you know? With proper Dark Lords, not this, this, Morden. A boy. How ridiculous. Now Zoon—he was a *Dark Lord*. He knew how to do things right." Lady Deathwing giggled. "Zoon, do things right. How drôle. What I should say was that he knew how to do things wrong in the right way, if you get what I mean." She stopped talking and seemed to be going over what she was trying to say in her head. "Yes, I'm right. He was good at being bad. There. Now where were we?"

"You were rambling," suggested Penbury.

Lady Deathwing looked surprised. "I was, wasn't I?" She took another sip of wine to wash down the meringue she was nibbling at. "Did I say how good these meringues were? They are very nice. Very nice indeed. Who made them? I'm going to have to borrow your chef."

"Baron Fanfaron has been chef this evening. I think he's the best in the world."

Lady Deathwing's eyes widened. "Baron Fanfaron and his battalions of chefs? I am honoured. To the chef!" She raised her glass and drained it.

Penbury did not join her in the toast. It wasn't the fact that he found the toast undeserved, nor that the dessert wine itself was anything but spectacularly good, but more that the wine was heavily laden with Headfucker. Cornering that market had been good for one thing, and that was ensuring access to the highest quality product; no mixing it with baking powder. It was pure, concentrated Headfucker of the best quality known to man.

It had been hard work playing the part he had, the one of frustrated would-be spriggle poisoner, when in fact he had no doubt Lady Deathwing would make short work of the delicacy with little or no side effects. He had counted on it, as it made the actual poisoning so much easier. Her guard would be down. All he had to do was keep from his mind that she had been slipped enough Headfucker in her dessert wine to addle the brains of several elephants.

"You what?" said Lady Deathwing, looking at her glass.

"I'm afraid so," said Chancellor Penbury. "No, don't get up. Oh dear."

Lady Deathwing collapsed back into her chair. The glass fell to the floor; its spilled contents burned a hole in the fine rug the count had laid in the tent. Such a waste.

"You poisoned me? You can't poison me, it's impossible." Lady Deathwing tried to lift an arm at Penbury to emphasise the point, but it seemed too much effort. Instead, something on the ceiling became interesting. "What's that?" she asked, and giggled. There was a small spider crawling its way across the roof of the tent. "It's an itsy bitsy spider!"

Chidwick had appeared and picked up the glass.

"Would you like some more wine?" asked Penbury.

Chidwick reset the glass in reach of the dragon.

"Oh yes! This is good. More."

Chidwick filled the glass as instructed. "Will there be anything else?" he asked Penbury.

"No thank you, Chidwick. I can take it from here."

His secretary left and Penbury helped himself to a meringue while he gathered his thoughts. It was perfect; a crisp shell full of sweet, gooey, slightly chewy goodness. He took a moment to savour not only the fine dessert but the success of the meal overall. It had not only been cuisine of the highest standard, but it had been produced in difficult conditions and to a ferocious timetable. And he had bagged himself a dragon.

Chapter 53   Morden

Never be cruel to be kind.
Being cruel is what you do.
The Dark Lord's Handbook

Morden looked down the ziggurat to the sea of orcs filling the square below. All celebrations and drumming had stopped. There was an air of puzzlement. None of them seemed to be sure what had happened. They had seen Zoon attacked and explode. They had been knocked off their feet by the blast and yet here he was, his attacker a blubbering wreck at his feet. The remaining priests at the top of the ziggurat were cowering to one side. The queen lay at his feet, being tended by a man. Was she dead?

It was time to take control. Morden raised his arms. There was a hush.

"I am Morden Deathwing. I am your Lord and Master."

It took a second for the words to sink in, and then from behind him came the start of a chant. Morden recognised Stonearm's dulcet tones.

"Morden. Morden. Morden!"

The surviving priests took up the chant and it spread like fire down the temple and into the crowd. Soon there was a single orcish voice chanting his name.

"MORDEN!"

Morden let it wash over and into him. Zoon had been right. He had been a boy, but that was behind him now. Until he had seen Zoon he had not realised what it had meant to assume his destiny and truly embrace what he was. He was a Dark Lord. There was no room for niceness or consideration. There was no room for weak sentiments like love. There was only pain and suffering in the world, and you were either on the receiving end, as he had been, or you were dishing it out, like he would be in the days to come.

"Morden."

The voice was quiet, but it cut through the noise and struck him like the bolt that had shot him out of the sky.

"Morden," said Griselda insistently. "Don't just stand there. Help me up, you idiot."

She was alive. Kristoff was helping her stand, but she was obviously still shaky. Her dress was torn and there was blood coming from her ears. But she was alive. He helped Kristoff by taking her other arm and she stood, grabbing his arm so hard he could feel her nails digging in through the robe.

"Are you all right?" he asked.

"Eh?" she said.

"Are you all right?"

She let go of Kristoff and put a hand to her ear and came away with blood. "Oh crap."

"ARE YOU DEAF?" shouted Morden, without thinking.

Griselda looked at him like he was a moron. "No need to shout. Of course I'm not deaf, you fat head. You think I can't hear that lot?"

It was true. The orc chant hadn't let up, and the drums had joined in. Looking down, there was one big party on the go. They must have thought the show was over with the big bang and Morden's proclamation. Probably a good thing they had no idea what had really happened.

"I'm glad you're not dead," said Morden.

"So am I," said Griselda. She let go of him and steadied herself.

"Thanks," said Morden. So she really did care. "I thought I was going to be sacrificed for sure."

"I meant me, idiot," said Griselda. "I'm glad I'm not dead."

Morden looked to Kristoff for sympathy, but all he could manage was a shrug.

"Griselda?"

It was the knight who had been blubbering at their feet. He was struggling to his feet, using the hilt of his sword as a crutch.

Griselda looked at him with astonishment. "Edwin?! What are you doing here?"

But the knight ignored her. He was standing now, and glowering at Morden. "Stand away from her," said the knight, raising his sword.

"You know this man?" asked Morden.

The knight had raised his sword high over his head, ready to strike.

"Prepare to meet your doom, foul creature," said Edwin. "Stand clear, Griselda."

"Foul creature?" said Morden. The notion he was a foul creature made him laugh. It was a deep laugh that made the ground shake. The surrounding orcs covered their ears and cowered; even Stonearm took a step back and winced.

The knight roared as Morden laughed.

The sword swung in an arc. Morden was paralysed by its beauty as it cut through the air. To his right, there was a blur of movement as someone jumped in front of him.

"Edwin! Stop!" said Griselda.

There was a scream as the sword cut the air. Blue fire licked along its length. Griselda stood her ground and the sword came to a halt a fraction of an inch above her head.

"He has bewitched you, Griselda," said Edwin. "Step aside." The knight raised the sword one-handed and made to grab her, but she stepped back to stand so close in front of Morden he could smell her.

"I don't love you," said Griselda.

The knight froze. His rage was clear. The sword began to keen as the knight took a single step back and resumed his executioner's stance. "You are bewitched," said Edwin. "You will die with your master, witch."

This time the sword had not begun its arc before someone jumped in front of Griselda.

"Edwin! Stop!" commanded Kristoff.

Morden was not the only one to be taken completely by surprise in a day of many surprises. It wasn't often people queued up to save him.

Edwin hesitated.

"Do I know you? Stand aside or die." Edwin's guard tightened but it was clear he was struggling with something. "We have met. I am sure."

"I was at the bridge with the bandits, when you cut them down and then the dragon snatched us," offered Kristoff.

"Yes," said Edwin slowly, "I remember now. You are the one who kidnapped Griselda. You shall die first."

It occurred to Morden he ought to do something, but he seemed unable to move. It was as though the insane drama playing itself out had him rooted in place. For a second time the sword cut down. Griselda screamed. Morden watched in helpless fascination as the sword once more transfixed him.

"Edwin, stop!" shouted Kristoff. "I'm your father!"

The sword quivered in the air and a trickle of blood oozed out from where it had touched Kristoff's skull.

Isn't that my line? thought Morden. This was getting stranger by the second.

"You're what?" demanded Edwin.

"I'm your father," insisted Kristoff.

Edwin seemed to consider what he was being told. "Impossible," he declared, drawing his sword back.

"Wait! I can prove it," said Kristoff. "Please."

Edwin frowned. The sword was balanced high in the air and it looked as if Edwin was having to use some considerable force to keep it from slicing Kristoff in two. "Go on."

"You like poetry," declared Kristoff.

Edwin's frown deepened. "Poetry is for weak-minded fools."

"You know that's not true," said Kristoff. "There is still poetry in you. I can sense it. Do you not see the setting sun and unbidden similes come to mind? Do you not see a swan and it not stir something deep inside? Or a beggar in rags? Or a beautiful woman? The lake at Wellow ..."

Edwin blinked sharply. Turmoil was clear in his face. "... is mercurial," he whispered.

Morden was flabbergasted. He hadn't seen this coming at all. He had imagined a showdown with him and a Hero, but not for a long while. Maybe after he had conquered half the world. And even then, it should have been between him and the Hero. This was all about face. Wasn't he meant to be the one racked with deep psychological wounds of family and abandonment? It was quite annoying all in all. Who was the Dark Lord around here, anyway?

"Excuse me," said Morden, "but what is going on here?"

"Shut it," said Griselda, elbowing him hard in the ribs.

Kristoff took a step forward. "Edwin, Edwin, Edwin. I am so sorry. I have not been the father I should have been."

Edwin was poised, the sword still hovering in a high guard, ready to strike. "It's a lie. You cannot be my father. My mother was a virgin. Everyone said so."

The surprises keep coming, thought Morden.

"Prepare to die," said Edwin, and he tensed.

"No!" shouted Kristoff, raising his hands to ward the blow. "She said that to protect me. I was young and scared. I couldn't be a father to you. I was an artist ..."

If Morden didn't have the heart of a Dark Lord, he may have been touched by such heartfelt pain. As it was, he thought it rather pathetic. But it suited him. He couldn't have done a better job of scrambling Edwin's brain if he had tried.

"Very well, Father," said Edwin. "If that is who you are, step aside. I have work to do. There is a witch and her master to lay to rest."

"Griselda is your sister," said Kristoff, so quietly that at first Morden thought he had misheard.

"I'm his *what*?!" shouted Griselda, grabbing Kristoff's arm and spinning him around. Kristoff stumbled backwards, half-turned to face Griselda and Edwin, now side-by-side.

"NOOOOOOO," screamed Edwin.

"Kristoff!" said Morden, with open admiration. "You dirty old dog."

"This can't be," said Griselda. "We were ... We ... We ..."

It took a second for Morden to work out what Griselda was trying to say.

"You slept with him?" said Morden, realising the truth. "But if he's your brother ..."

"Shut the FUCK up," shouted Griselda. "Stay out of this."

"You lie," said Edwin.

"Edwin, my son," said Kristoff. "What was it that brought you and Griselda together? Poetry runs deep in my family. My father was a poet, I am a poet, Griselda loves poetry, and there is a poet in you. Look, and you will see it."

Edwin's entire frame seemed to be struggling with what he was hearing. To Morden it looked like he was having to fight to hold the sword in place. It was as though the sword was trying its hardest to chop everything within range into small pieces.

Seeing the three standing close together, Morden had to admit there was more than a passing resemblance between them. Even allowing for the kind of likenesses that were often present in small villages where everyone was related to everyone else, the similarities were striking: the same high cheekbones, intense eyes, feminine lips and straggled blonde hair (though Kristoff was short in this department). Now it had been made plain, it was obvious this was indeed a family reunion. The weirdness of the situation had almost made him forget what Griselda had said, but it came flashing back to mind.

"Wait a second. If you love poetry so much, how come you ran off with Kristoff?" said Morden, reaching out to touch Griselda's arm.

But she didn't hear him, or ignored what he said. She stepped up to Edwin, who was now visibly shaking, to bring her hand to his cheek. The sword quivered above her.

"Brother," she said, "I will always love you ... as your sister."

When Edwin screamed it was a howl of pain Morden had hoped he would only hear from his worst enemies. It was a howl rich with agony. Not the shriek of a stubbed toe, or even a hacked limb, but pain that came from the inner being—the kind of desolate, hopeless, alone, terrified, angst-ridden, existentialist howl that comes when the world is empty of joy or meaning. It was the scream from a mind unhinged. There was madness in its denial.

Edwin threw the sword to one side. It traced a graceful arc and took the arm off an onlooking orc. The orc's scream was a silent shout against the noise Edwin was making as he began to run, brushing aside Griselda and Kristoff. He ran past Morden and down the stairs of the ziggurat. The orcs on the stair parted to let him through. It was as though some primal instinct told them that to get in his way would be the last thing they did.

Morden watched his progress across the square, the anguish still clearly audible. He was dimly aware of figures coming to stand at his side and behind him.

Somewhere close by a crow cawed.

He glanced to one side. Griselda was standing next to him, and beyond her on a balustrade at the head of the stair perched a huge crow. Griselda was ignoring him, her attention entirely on her fleeing brother.

"He has gone mad," she said.

The crow cawed again and hopped down toward the floor. As it did so, it changed in a fluid movement. By the time its feet touched the ground, a man was standing in the crow's place. He was tall, thin, and his skin was blacker than slate. Fire burned in his eyes.

"Morden," said the man, smiling.

Although Morden, unlike Edwin, knew exactly who his father was, he was still surprised to see him there. He hadn't exactly been the hands-on parent. But memories flashed through his mind of all the times, ever since he could remember, when a crow had cawed nearby. Many of those times he had been in deep trouble, and all the while that crow had been his father and he had done nothing.

"Father," said Morden. "You bastard."

"What?" said his father. "What did I do?"

"Nothing. Absolutely nothing. What are you here for?"

"Why, for the wedding," said Lord Deathwing.

"You missed it," said Morden. "And Zoon is dead."

"Oh, I know," said Lord Deathwing. "I was watching. I meant your wedding."

At the mention of wedding, Griselda's head snapped around.

"You," she said, laying eyes on Morden's father. "What are you doing here?"

"To see you marry my son, of course."

"I've been married once today and it's not happening again," said Griselda. "I'd rather die."

"Will you stop that," said Morden.

"You don't believe me?" said Griselda. "If you were the last man in the world I wouldn't marry you, you half-dead freak."

"You can stop now," said Morden. "It's over. It's all right to fall in love with me."

"Are you deaf? Hello? You disgust me."

Morden looked over to his father. He didn't have to be a mind reader to see what he thought of the situation, and he was right. Who was she to treat him like this? He was the Dark Lord here. If he wanted a Dread Queen to stand at his side, that is what he was going to get. She couldn't speak to him like that, not in front of Stonearm and the other orcs. She needed to see who was boss here. An example had to be made. It was time to be a Dark Lord.

"Silence," said Morden, exerting his Will.

Griselda froze. He could see the anger in her eyes but she was unable to move, let alone continue her insults.

"Come here," he said, holding out his hand. Griselda seemed to struggle for a second, but then stepped forward.

"What are you doing?" asked Kristoff. "Morden? Stop."

With a wave of his hand, Morden rooted Kristoff in place. He wouldn't harm his old friend, but nor would he let him get in the way.

"Son," said Lord Deathwing, "I'm so proud."

As Morden turned to face the army of orcs arrayed beneath him, his new queen at his side, Morden's father leapt into the air and, with more grace than Morden had ever managed, transformed into his dragon form. His father beat his wings once and rose to hover above them. Morden raised his arms, the Handbook in one hand, Griselda's hand in the other.

"Your Queen lives," said Morden.

Morden could hear whispers in his head. They spoke of conquest.

Chapter 54   Epilogue

A Dark Lord's work is never done.
The Dark Lord's Handbook

The trouble with spriggle was that it took a while for the digestion to get back to normal. Although Chancellor Penbury was otherwise well, in as much as the spriggle had not killed him, his stomach was feeling delicate. As a consequence the breakfast Chidwick was serving consisted of the blandest food: dry toast, tea, poached egg with no hint of Benedict about it, and junket.

"Ah, the pamphlets," said Penbury, as Chidwick set a pile down on the table. "Anything interesting?"

"You might like to start with this one, sir," said Chidwick.

Penbury picked up the indicated pamphlet. He read the front page and grunted. "It's a knob joke, Chidwick. About the King of Phrenia admittedly, but still a knob joke."

"The other side, sir," said Chidwick.

Penbury flipped the pamphlet over. "A chicken with two heads?"

"Below that, sir," said Chidwick. He cleared away a plate with eggy remains on it.

"Ah, I see. The fire."

A warehouse had burned down, which in itself was not too unusual, but it had spread and about a quarter of Klopt had burned down. Not quite the collateral damage Penbury had imagined when he'd ordered the warehouses and the boxes of debt burned to the ground.

With Lady Deathwing spending her days off her trolley and waiting for her next dose of Headfucker, all that had remained was to deal with the financial mess she had left behind. Foreclosure was not an option. To do so would have meant opening all the boxes and Penbury suspected the fledgling financial system he had overseen for the last decades would come crashing down. It had been Lady Deathwing's plan after all, and it had been a good one. How better to defeat the richest man in the world than by reducing him to poverty?

No, it was better instead to take an accounting hit across the board and pretend it never happened. The world would never know. In fact, only himself and Birkenfeldt would ever know how close to the brink they had come. A good chunk of the aristocracy would also be more than happy to be told their loans were wiped clean and their estates safe. While the bankers would be outraged, Penbury was confident it would only be a short-term loss. Royalty could always be relied upon to be profligate.

Chidwick had finished his clear-up and was hovering.

Penbury put a finger to his lips. Breakfast had been fair enough but he wanted something more. Something to pep things up a touch. "Coffee, Chidwick."

"Are you sure, sir?"

His personal private secretary's worry was touching. He knew this soon after spriggle coffee was not wise, but life would be dull if there wasn't risk.

"Yes, Chidwick. Coffee. Strong. Black."

Penbury read more pamphlets. After the fuss of Morden's foray across the land, Count Vladovitch had concluded a successful summer campaign, returning the cities to their rightful rulers. He was being hailed as the greatest living commander whom any army would follow, to which he had apparently replied that an army marches on its stomach and any army would follow a good field kitchen.

As for Morden.

Penbury picked up the latest report from the Snort brothers. They were together again and with Morden's army. They had agreed to postpone their retirement for now and follow in Morden's retinue. Morden had announced he would leave Deathcropolis with his orcs and head east, across the Great Desert, the Great Plain, the Great Swamp, and into the Great Mountains. It was there that Zoon's old fortress lay, or what remained of it, and Morden intended to rebuild it for himself. From the spidery writing, it was clear Morden was going to be quite the busy Dark Lord.

Chidwick returned with the coffee and poured his master a cup.

"Will that be all, sir?" asked Chidwick.

The Snort brothers had served him well. He would have to bring them home. His pad was there at his side. He could write the order while he enjoyed his coffee.

"For now, Chidwick. For now."

About the author

Paul Dale lives in Bath, England. After the insanity of the late 90's dot com boom, he has since replaced internet technology with writing. He took a Master's degree in Creative Writing at Bath Spa University to go with his Physics degree from Bath University. His passion for writing is only matched by his love of film and cycling. He can be frequently found within fifty miles of Bath in the company of Bath CC and friends, enjoying the beautiful countryside.

Visit the author's website at www.pauladdale.co.uk

CPSIA information can be obtained
at www.ICGtesting.com
Printed in the USA
BVOW11s1429170416

444539BV00031B/712/P